WHEN DARKNESS HUNTS THE DAWN

DRAGONS OF ROKAHN • BOOK ONE

M. H. WOODSCOURT

Edited by Sarah B.

Map by CartographyBird Maps

Cover design by MiblArt

Published by True North Press

www.mhwoodscourt.com

Paperback ISBN: 978-1-959619-14-7

Hardback ISBN: 978-1-959619-13-0

Contents

Dedication

To all those who thought I couldn't.
For all those who knew I would.

And for my kitty, Lady Elsa de Wynter,
who makes certain I take plenty of breaks
in order to worship her properly.

PAE'TAL
LIRSHON
THE FLAME
FOREST
ELENTH
ANDY
MOUNT
DRAGON KING'S
WAR CAMP
SIMYNSHIN
G
H
ROKAHN
VORSAH
TO DISTANT SOUTHERN SEAS

TO UNCHARTED NORTHERN WATERS
THE FAE LANDS
SERIELIAS
TESHRELLE
THE ISLES OF KWILAJ
DRAJIN
BLIGHTED LANDS
THE SPIRE
THE PILLAR
CIMIN
CRESTFEL
OCEANA
RELVIN PROVINCE
BONE COVE
NAUTTIA
LINTHA
HOLORE
ISLES OF TEN GOLD
THE MANY LANDS OF
SIRINHIGHA
MAPPED
IN THE PRESENT AGE

Pronunciation Guide

People

Akonn – uh-KAHN
Athonen d'Ereth – uh-THAWN-en d-AIR-eth
Atlanse Chenta – AT-lanse CHEN-tuh
Cal – Kal
Cisharri - kish-ARR-ee
Crind – krind
Denroch – den-ROCK
Drayve – dray-v
Hess – hess
Hilker – HILL-ker
Jensirin – jen-SEER-inn
Jonatten – JAHN-uh-ten
Katanni – kat-TAN-aye
Kevva – KEV-uh
Latta Chenta – LOT-uh CHEN-tuh
Larkynven – LARR-kin-ven
Larta – LARR-tuh
Ligg – lig
Maya – MAY-uh
Mikoneh – mee-KO-nay
Minno – MIN-no
Mivena – min-VEN-uh
Nilo – n-AYE-low
Owenekiras Rokahn – oh-WEN-uh-KEE-*ras* (roll the R) RO-kawn
Penn – pen
Reteris – ret-TARE-iss
Reven – REV-en

Sathe – SAY-th
Seranni – SARE-un-NYE
Suld – SOO-ld
Tem – tem
Ter N'Avea – tare NAH-vay
Torel – tor-ELL
Trinn – trinn
Vlest – veh-LEST

PLACES

Andyan Mountains – ANN-dee-ehn
Cimin – KIM-inn
Crestfel – crest-fell
Elemeer Plains – Ell-eh-MEER
Elenth – ELL-en-th
Hyanython — HYE-uh-NYE-thon
Holore – hol-ORE
Kagon – KAG-on
Kenooshin – ken-OO-shin
Kwilaj – kwee-LAJJ
Lintha – LIN-th-uh
Mithrinn – MITH-rinn
Nauttia – NAW-tee-uh
Oceana – oh-shee-ON-uh
Pae'Tal – pay-TAL
Relvin Province – REL-vin
Rokahn – RO-kawn
Serielias – seer-ee-EL-lass
Simynshin – SIM-in-shin
Sirinhigha – seer-in-HYE-uh
TeshRelle – tesh-rell
Vorsah – VOR-suh

TERMS

Complété – kom-PLAY-TAY
Dayonryse – day-ON-RYE-s
Firia Leaves – FEE-ree-uh
Korta – KOR-tuh
Tiassana – TEE-uh-SAWN-uh

RACES

Ephe'ahn – eh-FAY-on
Nijaal – nee-TSAWL
Undrik – un-drik

WHEN DARKNESS HUNTS THE DAWN

CHAPTER 1

JUSTICE HAD LOST

*"Once, all Mages used light magic.
That was before they succumbed to avarice."*

- From Athonen d'Ereth's *The Fall of Mages in the Age of Dragons*

"You have been found guilty of treason. You are hereby sentenced to death by beheading at dawn tomorrow."

The booming voice of the high judge filled the grand chamber, ringing from the rafters where trident pennants limply hung. A murmuring buzz answered the pronouncement, the spectators—local gentry mostly—hungry at the prospect of bloodshed. The rows of jurors loomed in their perch before the prisoner's box, two lines of grim old noblemen who looked predisposed to deliver a guilty verdict simply for suffering from their gout.

That was it then: death. Mikoneh's fingers clenched the hem of his gray prisoner's tunic, more responsive to the verdict than his mind or heart. He'd expected this. There was no other outcome in Lord Drayve's court, especially not for a rebel.

I failed.

Beside him in the prisoner's box, Maya stood as tall and proud as he did, showing none of the fear she must be feeling. He uncurled his fingers and reached out. She answered, sliding her fingers between his, though her defiant gaze never left Lord Drayve's narrow, pinched face. She didn't need to glance at him. As Mikoneh's twin, she always knew when he reached for her, as he always did when she needed him.

Drayve, Earl of Relvin Province, glowered down at the prisoners from the high bench where he oversaw the proceedings of his court. He took a long drink from a bronze goblet, then dabbed wine from his thin lips before he waved at the guards flanking the twins, his rings sparkling in the light of a hundred candles. "Take them away."

A firm, gauntleted hand fell against Mikoneh's shoulder. He released Maya's fingers and followed his guard as the armored man tugged him from the box. Maya stayed on his heels, her own guard guiding her steps like she might bolt at any moment. Considering all the trouble Drayve's knights had taken to catch the twins, Mikoneh didn't blame them for being cautious.

Striding between the tiered rows of seated spectators, he kept his chin high and his shoulders back, the way Fa had taught him to. Eyes tracked him, so many of them, starved for blood.

Yet you wonder why we defied you?

A wry smile caught his lips, threatening to bloom. He wrestled it down. If Drayve glimpsed it, he might assume Mikoneh was plotting something—and while Mikoneh could face death with grace, he preferred to avoid further torture. A week of starvation, random beatings from the warden, and the filth of the straw bed in the dungeon cell had been enough already.

As Mikoneh approached the back of the courtroom, a dark figure shifted in the shadowed south corner. Mikoneh glanced toward the movement, and chills nibbled at his bones.

The man within the shadows was unnaturally tall and slender, cloaked in charcoal gray, with a deep hood—and through that hood, eyes peered out, glinting in the candle glow like two burning coals. Yet the man gave off a wintry chill. Mikoneh could almost see the figure's breath in a wisp of vapor. Something ravenous lurked in those eyes—different from the bloodlust of the gathered gentry. Something somehow darker.

The guard jerked Mikoneh forward using the rope lead tied to his wrists, breaking the spell. He hadn't known he'd halted. He trailed the armored man, trying to purge the cloaked figure from his thoughts. He couldn't waste time on a stranger—not now, with only a few full sandglass turns left before their execution at dawn.

"Bring forth the accused: Penn, son of Drayve." As the high judge's booming voice thundered across the courtroom, the chamber doors swung apart.

Mikoneh and his twin sister were forced aside while Penn entered the courtroom, flanked by a handful of guards. He was two years older than the twins' twenty years, with long honey-blond hair, and a tall build beneath his prisoner's garb. He glanced toward Mikoneh and their eyes locked. Penn offered up a smile that could dazzle the sun, his brown eyes warm like melted chocolate. Reluctant to offer false hope to his friend, Mikoneh answered with a grim nod. Penn would face the execution block, same as any other rebel who'd been captured. Even if he was the son of their enemy.

There were so few left. Most dissenters had been massacred in the forest among their meager belongings, betrayed by one of their own. A dozen had tucked their tails between their legs and returned to their farms to continue pouring outrageous taxes into Drayve's private coffers. The coins would never reach King Nilo in faraway Nauttia, capital of Oceana.

I shouldn't blame them for running back home. They have families.

Penn's guards shoved him forward, and he stumbled under a drizzle of laughter from the seated gentry. If that bothered Penn, he would never show it. Strange that Drayve's own heir, once popular with the people, would now face beheading—simply because he *cared.*

The world is upside-down. That's nothing new.

Mikoneh's guard jerked on his rope, leading him from the chamber. Maya and her guard followed.

Once, Mikoneh had believed right would win out, no matter what.

Now though, he strode toward the dungeons, sister at his side, while the kindest man he knew faced the same rigged trial upheld by judges in Drayve's pay.

Right had withered, justice had lost, kindness had died.

Mikoneh clenched his fists. Despite knowing how pointless it all was, he wouldn't have done anything different—except for putting his trust in a traitor.

THE DUNGEON REEKED OF URINE, mold, and rat droppings. The combined odors nearly knocked Mikoneh off his feet before the guards shoved him and Maya, one by one, into their shared cell. Mikoneh caught his balance on one knee and his dominant hand. Maya landed with a grunt nearby, her gray skirts deflating around her.

The wooden door slammed shut with a screech of rusty

hinges, then the key shrieked in the lock. The guards' boots scraped against grit, striding away, leaving the twins in the silence of the dreary underground prison.

Clenching his teeth, Mikoneh stood up, ignoring the sting of his grazed palm and a bruise across the pad of one bare foot. Threads of meager light painted the stone floor through the bars of a tiny window in the door. In his comings and goings throughout the trial, he'd noticed a single torch set in a bracket outside their door —a last mockery provided by Drayve's men. Light, but no warmth in the odorous, filthy confines of their tiny square cell.

He turned to find Maya still kneeling with her back to the door. He stooped close and looped a lock of her long blue-black hair around his finger, then gently tugged. "Maya, you with me?"

She inhaled a trembling breath. "Hard to believe, isn't it?"

"That we're gonna die tomorrow?" He uncoiled her hair and tucked it behind her pointed ear.

Her eyes pinched shut. "Yes...exactly. Twenty years seems too few—and barely that much. I thought I'd be married one day, at least."

Mikoneh fluted out a breath and flopped back, catching himself with both palms. "It didn't end like we planned, huh?" He lifted his eyes to a dark smear in the corner of the cell, above a slab of stone covered in decaying straw that served as their one bed. He strongly suspected the smear was black mold.

Maya shifted to sit facing him. She stretched out her bare feet. Her toes met his in the beam of light. Their connection was a comfort Mikoneh suspected those without a twin could never understand. His sister screwed up her face in an approximation of a smile. "At least we'll die together. That's something the battlefield never promised."

"There she is." Mikoneh grinned. "There's my optimistic half."

She rolled her eyes, but a laugh slipped loose. "Drat you, Mikoneh. You just won't let a girl sulk if she chooses."

"Never. Not if she's you. We can't both be pessimistic. This sorry world needs balance."

Her second eyeroll was more exaggerated than the first. "Good point. Heaven spare us two such cynics." She dragged her thigh-length hair over her shoulder and braided it.

"Better than two optimists locked up together," he said. "The dungeon might collapse under the burden of all that cheer and crush us." The scratch of rodents came from the corner behind him. He resisted an urge to glance toward the rats chewing strands of straw. "Not that either makes much difference now." He grimaced and pushed back to his feet, batting his long blue-black hair aside as he started to pace. "I wonder if Penn will join us at the execution block tomorrow or..." He trailed off, imagining what Drayve might do to his son to make an example of him.

It was one thing to betray one's country. It was quite another to betray one's illustrious family.

"If he must die, I hope it will be with us," Maya said. "I didn't get the chance to say goodbye."

Mikoneh glanced over his shoulder at her. She had a fondness for Penn that bordered on something deeper. "I think he'll understand, considering everything."

A smile twitched at one corner of her mouth. "Thanks for your sympathy, dear leader."

He shrugged. "Best accept what you can get. I'm all you have." His heart panged. Their once-tight circle of friends—so nearly family—were all gone. All but them and Penn, along with a few stragglers awaiting trial in some other corner of the dungeon—and *Kevva*.

His mind skittered away from thoughts of the traitor. It hardly mattered now.

Tomorrow, the fight would be over. He sighed and sat back down, letting his shoulders slump.

Maya tucked her feet behind her, then crawled to his side. She pressed her arm against his, then set her head on his shoulder. "Do you think we'll see Fa and Mama after we die?"

Mikoneh slid his eyes shut, chest tightening. "I don't know. I'm not sure there's anything *afterward*."

"I think there is," she whispered. "We're brighter than our frames, you know. Deeper. It doesn't just end."

He wanted her to be right, but he didn't dare seize the idea. He couldn't. Not after...everything. Fa and Mama had been reticent on the matter of faith, encouraging their children to discover what they believed for themselves. Once, Mikoneh had chosen to trust in a higher power, but lately...he wasn't sure he believed in much.

"Guess we'll find out soon." He wrapped an arm around his sister's shoulders. "Get some rest."

"No." She nestled her head closer, and her hot tears dampened his sleeve. "Not tonight. If these are our last turns together, I won't waste them."

He squeezed her shoulders tighter, fending off a swell of emotions. "Fair enough."

They didn't speak as time crept by. They didn't have to. Words were their second language.

CHAPTER 2

STORM OF MEMORY

"Before avarice, it was first curiosity that weakened them. Mages crave knowledge most of all, and knowledge has the power to blind as much as enlighten."

- From Athonen d'Ereth's *The Fall of Mages in the Age of Dragons*

Two guards hauled the twins through the dungeon, along a dozen passageways, and eventually outside. Daylight cuffed Mikoneh's eyes. The humming of voices grew on the wind. He blinked until he could see again. He stood in a courtyard where tiered rows of spectator seats had been erected around a stone platform.

Every seat was filled with feather-capped men and brocade-silk-gowned women. A bitter breeze swept through the autumn leaves of tall oaks bordering the walled yard. On the stone platform, a hooded man clutching an axe leaned against the blood-stained block. A basket sat ready to cradle its first head.

At Mikoneh's side, Maya choked back a sound. He glanced at his twin. Her cheeks had lost their natural rosy hue, but she wore no expression at all. Her gold eyes flashed in a strand of sunlight, but he couldn't call that fear.

He reached for her hand, but his guard shoved him forward. He staggered a few steps along the flagstone path before catching himself and straightening up amid gales of laughter from the onlookers. Ignoring them, he leveled his shoulders and tugged his tunic straight. Pebbles along the path bit into his feet until he reached the platform where the executioner waited. No priest of the Nijaal was on hand—likely one of Drayve's ideas. After all, what use were prayers for the damned?

At the bottom of the few wooden steps, Mikoneh scanned the crowd again until his eyes landed on Drayve seated in an audience box above his sycophants. He wore a gaudy, jeweled feather-cap that bobbed in a frigid wind picking up as clouds gathered overhead.

Maya stumbled up to Mikoneh's side, wincing as she shook pebbles from one bare foot. He caught her hand. She squeezed his fingers back. They stood in silence, awaiting Drayve's last words, while the crowd let out an appreciative cheer. The earl sat in serene silence, a chain of sapphires winking against his chest. After several moments, he rose from his plush chair and lifted a hand bedecked in rings. The crowd settled down until only the rustling leaves dared to defy him.

"Good people of Relvin, today we finally purge the rabble from our province and return these fair lands to peace and quiet. Indeed, though we're but a humble region in the great kingdom of Oceana, we can boast that we prevented Jonatten's rebel miscreants from marching against our beloved king and spreading terror across the land. I'm confident King Nilo will be pleased—very pleased. He may even reward us, though we sought none." Amid a smattering of cheers, Drayve dropped his beady gaze to the prisoners.

Mikoneh's spine tightened, disgust screaming at him to slay the tyrant—but he had no weapon, no path, and no chance. Months of scheming, of training, of dreaming, all for nothing.

Drayve carried on. "It's only fitting that we end this scourge with the deaths of these—let's not call them children. They're of age now. Besides, Jonatten and Seranni didn't raise children, they raised demons. Don't let their youthful features fool you. These are the same souls who burned down our church and our fields and ransacked our storehouse."

The crowd's ovations shifted to jeers. In truth, Drayve's knights had set fire to the church dedicated to the fabled Nijaal. The fields, though...that *had* been caused by the rebels, but it had only been one field, already harvested. As for the store-house, well, Mikoneh had needed to feed his forces somehow.

A frown dusted his lips, but he remained still, letting the earl have his say. This crowd of nobility and gentry was past caring about justice. They'd turned a blind eye to Drayve's abuse of the common folk for years, probably gaining from his high taxes, his demands for hard labor, and his unquenchable taste for young women. Mikoneh didn't know whether to thank the fabled Nijaal or a single thread of good fortune for Drayve's disinterest in Maya.

"Today," the earl continued, "Jonatten's unholy offspring will perish, burying his legacy—and that of his foul wife—forever more. It was one year ago that they met their end. We thought ourselves rid of the rebel filth after that; but alas, these vile, insufferable creatures took up their banner and subjected Relvin to unspeakable horrors."

Mikoneh had forgotten how much the earl liked his own voice. He shifted where he stood, shaking off a stray pebble gouging his bare foot with a clatter no one else heard.

"Usually, traitors are beheaded—and rest assured, you'll see heads roll this day; among them, my own misguided son and heir. But I've thought of a better end for these unholy twins. A most fitting one to commemorate the fate of their treacherous parents, who served the cause of the legendary Dragon King!"

Mikoneh scoffed. Was the earl really using the Dragon King's reputation in Oceana—a brutal warlord akin to demon spawn—to justify executing them? Sure, Mikoneh's parents had served that man, but Owenekiras Rokahn was a brilliant strategist and a capable swordsman, not a demon from hell. Unfortunately, Oceaneans didn't like to relinquish legend for truth, no matter how many times Fa and Mama had tried to correct the hearth stories.

Drayve's mouth split in a grin that showed crooked teeth. "Death by *fire*!"

The words ripped through Mikoneh like a gale, stripping him down to his core. Memories roared across his mind. Flames. Snow. The laughter of the knights. Maya's screams.

Chains across the cottage door and shuttered windows.

He nearly folded under the storm of memory. His breath hitched, and his vision glazed. His chest tightened until his heart stuttered. But he steeled himself.

I won't buckle.

Surrounding him, the murmur of the crowd rose. Bright, ravening eyes speared him.

"Bring forth the kindling!" Drayve's command was answered by a handful of servants scurrying from the shadows beneath the earl's elevated box. Bundles of wood were brought to the executioner's block, where a tall stake rose. It was seldom used by a court who favored rolling heads. Another servant raced across the courtyard clutching a torch. Mikoneh was shoved up the steps. The hooded executioner set aside his axe and accepted the torch with great solemnity.

Death by fire. The taste of smoke tinged Mikoneh's tongue as he was shoved past the hooded man and brought to the stake behind the bloodstained block and the empty basket.

"Bring forth the prisoner Penn!" shouted Drayve. "He will witness this display before his own end."

Cruel to the last breath. As a guard shoved him back against the stake, Mikoneh glared at the earl. The guard wrenched his hands behind him. Ropes wrapped around his wrists, biting deep.

This is it. Nothing left to do but embrace my fate.

Fear mingled with a strange, bitter sort of relief in his chest. A lump lodged in his throat. He turned his gaze toward Maya. Her golden eyes shone bright with fear but no tears. Good. He'd told her not to waste any on Drayve's sycophants. They'd only relish them like a trophy.

The servants slithered away, leaving Mikoneh a clear view of Drayve in his grand box.

"Any last words, demon spawn?" asked the earl. "Choose wisely now."

Mikoneh hefted his chin, letting his panic bleed away until he felt only satisfaction. He'd done all he could. This was enough. *It must be.* He drew a breath. "Long live King Nilo! Down with the tyrant of Relvin!"

Howls rose from the stands. Drayve's eyes widened. Had he really been foolish enough to think Mikoneh would beg for his own life? Fool, fool, three times the fool. Jonatten and Seranni—Fa and Mama—had taught Mikoneh better than to beg for scraps from a despot's table.

The earl rolled his hands into fists. His pointed chin worked while he sought a reply. "So, you would spew treason to the last. Light the flames. Let us purge these lands of a demon in mortal coils."

The executioner tipped the torch to the kindling. Flames sparked and caught with a single breath of chill wind. Mikoneh tensed, and his head butted against the stake at his back, but he refused to cower. He would endure this like his parents had. He lifted his eyes, determined to stare Drayve down until the fire blocked his view.

His heart stopped. In the audience box just behind Drayve, bold as gold, *she* stood. Kevva had shed her common tatters for an elegant gown of turquoise, and her rich auburn hair was coiffed around a silver circlet.

Wrath surged through Mikoneh, and the floodgates of his hatred burst open. As though in answer, the flames around his legs leapt up, staining his vision. He lurched back, slamming against the stake, wrists twisting against his bonds. The crowd cheered. Maya screamed his name.

Smoke curled around his face. Flames licked his skin, strangely cool. He squeezed his eyes shut, focusing on his fury rather than the fire consuming his body. Somehow, it didn't hurt. Over the past year, he'd imagined his parents' suffering, trapped in their cottage while violet flames tore down its walls. All that had remained of them afterward were two husks of bone and ash, huddled together against the remnants of the back wall. Beside Fa's remains, the man's sword lay across the stone floor—used in a last desperate bid to escape. Nothing else remained of them except an heirloom: a small, Ashwood box, untouched by the blaze. Impossible to open.

Drayve had stolen *everything* from Mikoneh. He'd even lost Maya for a time in her heartbreak.

I'll never forgive him, alive or dead. I'll haunt him forever.

His wrath coiled around him, numbing him to glutting

death. He longed to reach out, to harness the fire and hurl it at Drayve—at *her*—at all of them.

The crowd's cheers changed pitch. Mikoneh lifted his eyelids, expecting a wall of flame. Instead, he found his arms free—hands lifted—flames twining across his open palms. Reflex kicked in, seizing his motions. He strode across the platform, flames curling around his body, not burning. Drayve stared at him from his box, while Kevva huddled behind the pale earl, clutching at the man's fur-lined cloak, her green eyes wide.

'Release us,' the flames seemed to whisper. *'We'll devour them all.'*

Mikoneh set his teeth. His body shook under the will of fire. This was madness. He'd lost his mind. Tendrils of flame brushed his cheek. He stared down at a creature within the flame; it wore an almost-human shape. Then it burst into embers and floated away.

"Drayve." Mikoneh's voice cracked across the air. "You will release my twin, along with your son, and any remnant of my army. If you don't, I'll unleash this fire and tear your castle apart."

It was a bluff. He had next to no control over the fire wreathing his body. It might turn against him at any moment—might crisp him to a crust.

This is madness.

Screams erupted across the stands as people comprehended the fire dancing across Mikoneh's fingers and up his arms—not scorching him. Someone burst into tears, while another shouted "Demon!" At that pronouncement, pandemonium exploded. The crowd fought to escape the confines of the stands, trampling each other.

The earl came to himself, stumbling forward a step. His face was ashen. "Y-you *are* a demon! Begone! Leave this province. Take your fellow spirits with you." His hand shook as he gestured toward the west gate leading from the courtyard where several sycophants were fleeing. "Begone, I say!"

Mikoneh risked a glance toward his sister and her guard. "Release Maya."

The guard dropped his hands. Maya stared at Mikoneh, her gold eyes vivid and wide. "Mikoneh..."

Another wispy shape sparked up, and he flinched. He was as astonished as his twin, but they needed to get away while they had the chance. The creature settled on his shoulder, grounding him somehow. "Get Penn!"

Maya raced to where a handful of guards surrounded the disowned viscount. No one resisted as she squeezed between them, caught Penn's arm, and dragged him toward the platform. They vaulted onto it, avoiding the flames that spiraled around Mikoneh.

"All right, Drayve," Mikoneh said. "Now the rest of my soldiers."

"There's no one else." Drayve's voice quavered. "Your last few followers returned to their fields this morning after begging for their lives. Seems they didn't want to die for their cause." A sneer lifted his mouth. "If you don't believe me, check the dungeon."

Fury strengthened the flames around Mikoneh. It made sense. Drayve had spared the rebels who'd surrendered in the forest camp—not from some benevolent whim—but because he needed workers for his fields. Too many farmers had joined the twins' cause. The earl's coffers must be suffering the effects of untended fields over the past several years. And even if Drayve was lying, Mikoneh couldn't risk returning to the dungeons to check. He had no idea how long this fire would last. He needed to win free and take his twin and his friend with him.

"Maya, head for the gate."

She tugged Penn after her. Mikoneh turned, slowly, and followed them down the wooden steps from the platform, then across the courtyard. The flames remained with him. Stragglers veered out of their path. As they neared the open portcullis, the raised teeth of the gate gaping like a maw, Mikoneh's senses tingled.

Drayve's voice boomed across the courtyard. "Shoot them!"

Arrows whistled across the open air. Mikoneh pinched his eyes shut as he ran on—and flames roared in his ears. Shrieks followed.

He risked a glance back. The fire had expanded, curling over Drayve's box. The earl launched himself from it. Kevva jumped out behind him, her turquoise skirts billowing. The spectator stands were also ablaze, and the tiled roof of Drayve's castle billowed with smoke. Guards and servants dashed for the well in the courtyard.

Mikoneh whipped around and passed under the portcullis at Penn's heels. The young viscount's hands were bound behind his back, not with rope, but iron manacles.

They'll be tricky to remove.

"Make for the stables!" Mikoneh shouted.

They obeyed, Maya in the lead, her steps sure. They'd studied the lay of the castle and its grounds over and over, thanks to Penn's detailed drawings. Mikoneh caught up to the other two. Flames still cloaked his shoulders, warm yet comfortable. He didn't want to contemplate what it meant. He couldn't fathom anything that made sense.

He caught Penn's eye, and the viscount offered a strained smile, his brown eyes dancing across Mikoneh's flames. But he didn't accuse Mikoneh of being a demon, so at least the man still had his senses intact.

Unless I am one. Mikoneh cracked a dry smile.

They pounded across a narrow, arched bridge over a rushing stream. The stables were near the guard barracks and the training grounds.

"Where do we head?" asked Penn.

"Horses first. Then aim for the forest," Mikoneh said. "I need to grab something."

Maya threw open the stable doors and raced inside. The two men followed. The musky-sweet scent of horses and manure clung close and heavy.

A middle-aged stablehand turned from mucking a stall, clutching a shovel. "Oy, what's this?" His jaw dropped as he took in Mikoneh's wreathing flames. He flung himself aside, covering his face with both arms while his shovel thumped to the floor. "The Blessed Nijaal spare me!"

Mikoneh started for the earl's stall where Rook, a great black warhorse, stood serenely despite the fire circling the young man's head. Still, Mikoneh couldn't risk hurting the animal.

"This is problematic." He lifted his flaming hands. "How do I shut it off?"

"Try inhaling?" Maya guided a silver mare from another stall.

"Or picture darkness," Penn suggested, then clicked his tongue at his own horse: a chestnut mare he'd named Aspen. Mikoneh recognized the mare from the young lord's fond descriptions. Penn had hunted on her back a hundred times.

Turning back to Rook, Mikoneh shut his eyes and sucked in air. The tickling warmth of the fire died down, drawing inward, joining his anger in its private domain.

Right. My wrath's what caused it to grow.

He reached for calm, for quiet. The flames responded, shrinking, shrinking...then gone.

"It worked." Maya's voice was a breathless whisper. "Whatever you just did."

He cracked one eye open and peeked at his hand. No flame. He turned his palm over a few times, but the fire stayed quiescent. Exhaling with relief, he tucked away his questions, his skepticism, his fury. He could pull them out later, far away from here.

If he'd snuffed out these flames, had the castle fires died out, too?

"Hurry." He grabbed up a fine blanket and a saddle made of black leather and silver stitching. He slung them in turn over Rook's back, buckled the saddle with deft fingers, and snatched up the matching bit and reins.

Maya saddled Aspen with the same swiftness, then the twins readied the silver mare. Mikoneh let his twin finish with the bridle and hurried to the nearby wall where tools hung in organized rows. A quick scan revealed nothing strong enough to break Penn's manacles, and nothing slender enough to pick the locks. The stablehand remained in a corner of the nearby stall, unwilling to make a sound.

Sighing, Mikoneh caught up Aspen's reins and led the horse toward Rook. "We'll bring your horse, Penn, but you'll have to ride with Maya for now. She'll keep you upright. We can't waste more time."

He helped Penn onto the silver mare's back, then boosted Maya up behind the viscount. He then mounted Rook and led the way from the interior out into the open air. The wind had grown colder, and wisps of early snow fluttered from the gray heavens. The twins hadn't ridden horses in more than a year—not since Drayve had confiscated their farm and fields in retaliation for their parents' rebellion. Still, they knew how to handle horses.

His gaze skimmed the castle. Smoke and flame spread

across the roof, still raging. A grin stretched across his mouth, fleeting but gratified. He flicked his reins, nudged Rook's flanks, and galloped toward the earl's forest, leading Aspen. Maya and Penn stayed close at his back.

As they whipped past the wheelhouse where water churned and mist clung to the morning air, a set of eyes fell on him, sinister, hungry. Mikoneh hunched forward under the assault, but Rook flew on, and he tried to dismiss the feeling.

He must escape Relvin Province as quickly as possible. Nothing else mattered right now.

Chapter 3

Eyes of the Dead Man

"The Mage Queen was the first who changed altogether. She is the indisputable reason the rest fell into darkness."

- From Athonen d'Ereth's *The Fall of Mages in the Age of Dragons*

Frost crusted the bodies strewn across the snowy forest floor. Though it was midday, the canopy of brittle leaves shrouded the overcast sky, painting dusk across the broken camp. Maya held her reins and stayed seated in her saddle, unwilling to search the dead lying in the clearing surrounded by the quiet old trees. She couldn't imagine what her twin was seeking, but she knew he had a good reason for coming back here.

Mikoneh weaved his way through the corpses, halting now and then to stoop near a fallen soldier, searching the fresh snow. Each time he bent, his long hair slithered over his shoulder, and he caught up the strands without thought, holding them out of the way. As he rose, he tossed the tresses behind his back and moved closer to the shattered tent where he and Maya had made their home for the past year.

"Think he'll find any means to get me free?" asked Penn, his breath clouding before his lips. He craned his neck to glimpse Maya behind him on the saddle.

She sighed. "Doubt it. We'll probably have to locate a blacksmith."

"That's unfortunate. Most blacksmiths will be suspicious..."

She pursed her lips and nodded. Riding into any village or town with Penn clapped in irons would draw unwanted attention. Still, he couldn't stay like this. "We'll think of something."

"I don't doubt it." Penn's lips curved in a smile. "I just hope it's soon. My fingers are numb."

She dropped her gaze to the manacles pinning his hands against his spine. "I'm so sorry, Penn. Maybe Mikoneh's come up with something to help." She glanced toward her twin. He'd stooped again, catching his hair. He brushed his fingers against the snow, then knelt and dug around an armored body. Breaths later, he tugged a sword free. Maya's heart hitched. Not *a* sword. *Fa's sword.* The plain, scarred hilt was one she knew well. Mikoneh must've dropped it in his duel against one of Drayve's knights, just before they'd been captured.

She hated looking at the weapon. Hated the reminder of her parents' last moments before they'd succumbed to death.

Perhaps sensing her distress, Penn leaned back, gently bumping her. "Do you think any of our clothes are accessible? I'd love a cloak."

"Good thinking." She dismounted in a swift motion. As her bare feet met frozen ground, her toes flinched. "*Oh.* That's cold. I—I'll return soon."

Penn shivered atop the horse. "Hurry. My father's magician might easily divine our return to this place."

Maya hesitated. Penn had a strange inclination to believe in magic, though the rebels had often made fun of him for that. Even she and Mikoneh had gently teased him for his superstitions. But after today, after seeing Mikoneh control fire, Maya couldn't dismiss Penn's warning as mere fancy. Shelving that for later, she gathered her threadbare skirt up and dodged her way toward the twins' tent, where Mikoneh was now rummaging. Fa's sword was belted at his hip, and he'd found a leather tie to pull his hair into a tail. Her pace slowed as she neared, unwilling to examine the nearest bodies. Large snowflakes began to fall from the sky.

Mikoneh glanced up from a pile of frosty debris. "Looking for something?"

"Cloaks. Maybe some changes of clothing." She fingered her prisoner's garb. "Anything warm at all, really."

"Right." He turned back to the pile of broken bottles, smashed shelves, and splinters of wood. "A few of your herbs might be salvageable, too."

"Let me do that, then. You can look for the cloaks."

He stood up and brushed crusts of snow from his palms. "Sounds good. We need to hurry, though."

A biting breeze needled her flesh. "I agree wholeheartedly. Penn's worried we'll be discovered here."

"Agreed. Drayve's not stupid." Mikoneh picked his way around the torn canvas, toeing rubbish, moving methodically toward the back edge of the tent.

"Mikoneh?"

"Yeah?" He shoved aside a broken pole.

She chewed the inside of her mouth as she unburied bundles of dried herbs and tinctures. Most had been crushed or shattered. "That...that fire."

He sighed. "I don't know what to tell you, Maya. It didn't even burn me. When I saw Kevva, I just got so angry...and suddenly the fire responded." He threw back charred canvas and knelt at the tarnished but intact cedar chest where their belongings were kept. "I'm still not sure it really happened."

"It happened." She shuddered at the memory. "The fire shot up around you and ate the ropes binding your wrists—then it curled around you, and seemed to jump right into your hands. *You* were ablaze. I thought...I don't know what I thought. Nobody did. It was horrible, and wondrous, and..." Completely unbelievable, just like he'd said. Yet it *had* happened. She plucked up a vial of liquid meant to dull pain. "What does it mean, do you think?"

"You remember Penn's claims about Drayve's court magician?" he asked, opening the cedar chest.

"Yes. I thought of the same thing." When Penn had first joined the rebellion, he'd been determined to prove his worth and loyalty. Along with his castle sketches and guard rotation information, he'd also described Drayve's magician as someone who could perform real magic, specifically wielding flame.

She dug around for a pouch and soon found one among several ruined vials. Tucking what good herbs and powders she could find into the leather bag, she made a note to ask Penn more about the magician.

Mikoneh lifted out a crude pine box containing his strategy game of Fang and Claw. He set it carefully aside. After digging into the chest, he stood up and shook out a long, deep green cloak. "Here's yours. We had a spare or two, didn't we?"

"Yes." She stood up and moved to his side, then bent to rummage through their clothes. "Here's yours." She handed him a deep red cloak lined with black fur.

"A bit showy for our purposes."

"Still warm, though. You have a blue one, too, somewhere." She dug deeper and found a jerkin, shirt, pants, and woolen socks. "Here. Warm clothes. Change."

He accepted them and glanced around, then sighed. Vapor wafted before him. "No good place to change here. It's too blasted cold."

Maya switched the direction of her digging until her fingers brushed an empty satchel tucked into one side of the chest. "Put our things in this. We can find a place to change en route." She handed the satchel to her twin, meeting his gold eyes. "Where *are* we going? We can't stay in Relvin Province."

His mouth pinched sideways. "We can't stay in Oceana at all—not with Drayve's reach. We failed, Maya. *I* failed. I've cost us everything we aimed for. Even our country."

"You can't wear the burden of failure alone, Mikoneh. We all had a hand in what happened—and we did our best. Don't forget that. Fa and Mama would be proud, not disappointed."

He looked away, saying nothing.

Her fingers tightened around a spare jerkin. She shouldn't push the issue with him yet. Their defeat was too fresh. It was better to change tack and discuss their immediate future.

Oceana was the only home she'd ever known. Their parents' remains were buried here. But they didn't have another choice. She knew that. She inhaled a long breath. "Simynshin's near the Rokahn war, so we can't head that way. Were you thinking of Cimin?"

The idea of entering the northern kingdom terrified and fascinated her. Still, niggling doubts remained. Must they really leave Oceana's borders altogether? Had they really failed forever?

Mikoneh will rally and think of a new plan. He always does. We just need time.

He dragged a hand down his face. "We'll make our way to the southern coast first, hide in Bone Cove for a bit. No one would dare seek us there. We can choose our course once we're better hidden."

She bobbed a nod, fingering the stitching on the tunic. "We'll need food, and Penn needs to get out of those manacles." Shaking herself from her despair, she rolled up the jerkin and handed it to him. They packed in silence. A horse stamped its foot, nickering a protest against the cold.

Mikoneh crouched beside her and stuffed a plain, woolen dress into the satchel. "I don't know what to do about Penn. A smithy's out of the question."

Maya found the blue cloak. It was a tad thinner than the deep red one, and patched in two places, but Mikoneh had never been bothered much by the cold. "Here. Put this on, at least."

He obeyed, draping the cloak around him with a ripple of cold air. As he latched it at his throat, his eyes skimmed the cedar chest. "That'll do, right?"

Maya straightened to her full height. "I think so. We should look for some food."

"You do that." He handed over the satchel and red cloak. "Put this on Penn. There's one more thing I need to grab." He shut the cedar chest and moved toward the canvas covering what remained of his caved-in cot.

Maya almost lingered, curiosity tugging at her, but she shook herself and threw on her cloak. Then she moved toward the food pavilion. The canvas structure had been torn down and destroyed like every other tent. Drayve's knights hadn't spared anything, as brutal in their sport as they were in their manhunts. She moved as quickly as she could through the wreckage, finding little by way of salvageable food. Unburying a few intact jars of preserves, she tucked them into the satchel, along with some winter squashes and a few wrinkled apples. The bread was spotted with mold and frozen over. She uncovered a few wedges of cheese and packed them, then picked her way toward Penn.

An icy hand brushed up against her bare toes. Maya looked down against her will, freezing in place. She met the glassy eyes of a dead man she'd known well. His name was Crind. Tears misted in her vision, and she tried to move away, but somehow her feet had stuck to the ground.

So many, all dead. And she couldn't even bury them.

An arm wrapped around her shoulders. "Come on, Maya." Mikoneh's voice was a whisper. He pulled her away from the sight of poor Crind, toward the waiting horses.

"I hate to leave them like this," she murmured.

Mikoneh's soft sigh warmed her cheek. "Me, too. Here." He pressed something cold and stiff against the back of her hand. She nearly yelped, imagining a dead arm—but her eyes found the source of the sensation: leather boots. Hysterical laughter bubbled up her throat, but she swallowed it back down.

"Figured we'd want these." He pushed woolen socks into her other hand. "Found some that might work for Penn as well." He moved past her toward the horses, and she followed, determined not to look down. Her twin reached the three horses, and Mikoneh set down a second satchel he'd found somewhere, along with the boots. "We got a few things to warm you up, Penn."

The viscount offered a bright smile. "No complaints here."

Mikoneh helped him from the horse, led him to a jutting boulder near some brambles glittering with frozen berries, and helped tug socks and boots onto Penn's cold feet. Maya draped the red cloak over Penn's shoulders and latched it around his throat.

Through a shiver, Penn turned his radiant smile on her. "That's much better, thank you."

Maya blushed and turned her eyes away. He was always so kind to her—and to everyone else. She mustn't read anything deeper into it. After Mikoneh helped Penn up from the rock, Maya took her turn slipping her boots on, then she regathered her food and herbs, along with the satchel of clothes.

"There's a trapper's burrow due south," Mikoneh said, taking his turn on the rock to pull on socks and boots. "We can head there, get properly changed, then head on to Bone Cove."

Penn's winsome smile dropped like a wilted leaf. "Bone Cove?"

"Where else can we hide?" Mikoneh stood. "I'm open to suggestions."

Maya met Penn's rich brown eyes, reading the crease between his brows for what it was: fear. She couldn't blame him. While she'd not been raised on local superstitions like most of Oceana's natives, she'd nearly fainted from fright the one time Fa had taken her to that cold, wet, dreadful place. Her imagination had always been overactive in the wilds.

Still, Mikoneh knew what he was doing. She'd learned not to question him. Instead, she stepped to Penn's side and rested her palm against his arm through the thick cloak. "We'll be fine. There aren't really ghosts dwelling in the caves."

His mouth pinched in a flat line, while his eyes dimmed. He didn't believe her. That was fine. She didn't *quite* believe herself.

"Ready to go?" Mikoneh hitched his satchel onto his shoulder and eyed Maya and Penn with quiet expectation. He didn't say it, but he'd brook no argument.

"As much as I'll ever be," Penn offered. "I don't suppose that trapper's burrow will have anything to break these manacles?"

"Doubt it," Mikoneh said. "We'll get you free as soon as we can."

"I know." Penn grimaced. "It's just, I have a dreadful itch on my nose."

Maya nearly laughed, but the somber location—along with the growing chill and the pressing need to hide— stole the smile that twitched at her lips. Within a few heartbeats, the three had remounted their horses, and Mikoneh led the way south through the old forest, away from the remnants of their rebellion and their old lives.

Maya didn't look back. It would only hurt more.

CHAPTER 4

A FORGE WITHIN HIM

*"No one outside the innermost Mage circles suspected they'd
fallen from grace—not until the beautiful Fortress of TeshRelle
blackened."*

- From Athonen d'Ereth's *The Fall of Mages in the Age of Dragons*

The trapper's burrow had provided nothing beyond scant shelter to change into fresh clothes. Nothing within the dilapidated structure would help to get Penn's manacles off. Mikoneh wasn't surprised, but he'd hoped to be wrong.

Penn wore Mikoneh's trousers well enough, despite the lord's slightly taller frame. He was just as slim as Mikoneh, though he had two years on the young leader.

Former leader, Mikoneh corrected himself. He led nothing now; he'd failed to carry on his father's legacy, failed to bring justice to Relvin Province. All he'd managed to do was get good men and women—and even children—killed. He set his teeth as he guided Rook along the overgrown forest road leading toward the southern coast.

Stop it. He tightened his knuckles over the stallion's reins. *Nothing worthwhile comes of self-pity.* Hadn't Fa told him that more than once?

Wind whistled through the slumbering trees, rattling the dead leaves that hadn't fallen in the premature snow. Winter shouldn't set in for another month, yet snow crusted the boulders Mikoneh navigated past, and frost festooned the bark of the old, gnarled trees along the rutted path.

Despite Mikoneh's breath appearing before his face in the frigid air, or the shroud of night cloaking the world in a solemn stillness, or the crackle of puddles breaking under Rook's hooves—despite all that, Mikoneh didn't *feel* cold. Not his nose, not his fingers, not his pointed ears carefully hidden under his blue-black hair.

He didn't know what to make of anything that had happened since the morning execution. Somehow, he'd escaped Drayve's clutches—escaped death itself—by means of the very fires meant to kill him.

Why couldn't that have happened for my parents? The thought ripped through him like an arrow, sharp and true. He tried to shake it. To banish the thought. But his efforts only embedded it deeper. *Why now and not then?*

The snap of a twig caught his attention. He pulled Rook to a halt, straining his ears for the slightest noise in the growing gloom. A breeze swept past him, carrying the scent of a deer. He tracked the smell with his keen senses. There, twenty yards within the trees, he caught a glimpse of the animal's yellow-brown eyes reflecting at him. He relaxed and blew out a cloudy breath, then nudged Rook further along the path.

Moving at a steady pace, Mikoneh judged they'd reach the

cove in another full turn or so, which left him ample time to dwell on all the horrors of the past week. He tried to resist, but the thoughts crept in, bringing with them a sense of hopelessness, of fury, and a sense of loss he'd never heal from. Somehow, the massacre of his army, the knowledge that he, Maya, and Penn were all that remained beyond those who'd abandoned the cause—brought fresh grief, like he'd buried his parents all over again. But this time, he had nothing to throw himself into, to lessen the ache, to muffle his hatred for Drayve and Kevva.

No, this time, the fury was deeper and brighter, as though the fire he'd wielded against Drayve had turned into a forge within him, ceaselessly burning, numbing him to cold and to fear.

Hold on to it. Breathe through it. Let it give you purpose—but don't let it consume you.

He must find something to grasp, to keep him breathing. Maya needed him. He wouldn't abandon her. He wouldn't let her know what it felt like.

His chest throbbed, but he shoved those memories down with vehemence.

Think of something constructive.

Mikoneh ran over numbers. The leagues between the cove and Simynshin's nearest border in the west. Then between the cove and Lintha to the south. Then to Cimin up north. Even to the continent of Rokahn far away to the southwest. He didn't know the distance to the fabled fae lands further north, but he guessed, counting leagues in his mind. He pictured Fa's maps—lost treasures caught in the violet flames—but Mikoneh had pored over them countless times, fascinated with the larger world. The world Fa and Mama had traveled before settling in the more peaceful kingdom of Oceana to raise their children.

Peaceful. Scorn edged Mikoneh's mouth, pulling his thoughts back to his immediate troubles—but he slammed the mental door shut. *Fifty leagues to Lintha. Three hundred leagues to Simynshin. One hundred and fifty leagues to Cimin. Five hundred leagues to Rokahn.*

He kept the numbers going in his mind as fresh snow drifted down through the boughs, their faint crystalline *tink* sounding in his ears as the tiny flakes landed against his shoulders and cloak hood. The birds had fallen quiet, hiding from the coming storm. A distant chorus of wolf song fell into echoing stillness. The world was turning over in its bed early to sleep through a long, harsh winter. The cold air tasted fresh and fierce against Mikoneh's tongue, though it lacked its usual bite.

Ninety-five leagues to Nauttia. He'd considered visiting Oceana's capital and begging for an audience with King Nilo—to warn him of Drayve's treasonous plots—but now it was out of the question. Mikoneh had been tried and condemned. No agent of the king, or any royal member of the family, would heed his request. Not that they'd cared beforehand, even when Penn had gone to the king's court and hinted of trouble in Relvin. No one had let him speak with King Nilo.

The deepening dark and answering stillness stretched Mikoneh's nerves taut. He coiled the reins around his fingers, ready to bolt at the first sign of danger. Would Drayve consider this old road? Would he think to send knights to intercept them before they reached the cove?

An image of the cloaked man in the courtroom, the one with wintry eyes beneath a deep cowl, dashed across Mikoneh's mind like a falling star. He'd felt the same unnerving tension when he'd ridden past the wheelhouse.

Who was he? Mikoneh had a suspicion. It was the only one he could reach for. He slowed Rook's gait until he rode closer to Maya and Penn sharing the nameless silver mare. Aspen seemed content to remain at the back of the tiny company.

"Penn?" Mikoneh began.

"Yes?" asked the viscount.

"You used to speak of your father's court magician."

Penn shifted uneasily. That was surprising. The viscount used to relish the chance to discuss his father's court and offer up any insights. "What about him?"

"His fire," Maya piped up.

"Oh." Penn's eyes caught a glint of waning light as they widened. "You're right. He *does* wield fire like you did today." His gaze lowered as he seemed to weigh that. "But his flame was always a violet hue."

Mikoneh tensed, a memory skidding across his thoughts. Violet flames... *Later. Evaluate that later.* His fingers curled tighter around his reins. "What does he look like?"

Another pause. "Well...a bit like an albino snake, honestly. But dark, too." Penn blew out a cloudy breath. "His name is Sathe. He's terrifying. His skin is white as a corpse, but his eyes are like black tar. He—he feels like winter."

The fear behind Penn's words set Mikoneh's teeth on edge. His mind danced back to the cloaked figure in the courtroom again. "Was he at your trial?"

Penn flinched. "Yes. He testified against me."

"What could he possibly say against *you*?" asked Maya with no small degree of indignation.

Penn's frown cracked and lifted in a smile. "Plenty. Mostly about my betrayal of my blood and birthright. Of my mindless bewitching."

Mikoneh's eyebrow quirked up. "Were you doing the bewitching, or were you bewitched?"

"Both, I think. You two are very good at bewitching people —didn't you know?"

Maya chuckled, though Mikoneh couldn't bring himself to find anything funny just now.

Penn shrugged. "Sathe is maddeningly eloquent. He says a whole lot, none of it clear—but it sounds pretty."

"An eloquent court magician," Mikoneh grunted. "Exactly what Drayve needs. How long has he been at court?"

"Two years, I think." Penn's brows pinched together. "He appeared on the night of my father's birthday celebration, claiming he'd been hired to perform. Who hired him, I don't know. He's stayed on since. Flattery is my father's favorite form of currency, after all, and Sathe doled it out handsomely. I suspect he's spurred my father toward his lust for King Nilo's throne."

Mikoneh's mind returned to the eyes at the wheelhouse watching them flee. "I think he let us go."

Penn screwed up his face. "I don't recall Sathe at the execution."

"He wasn't there," Mikoneh said. "He was elsewhere. He watched us leave the stables."

"Surely not. Why would he stand by and watch us ride away?"

"Dunno." Mikoneh tracked a fat snowflake twirling toward the path before him. Rook crushed it under a hoof in passing. "I feel like..." *Like he wants something from us.* Mikoneh couldn't say the last part aloud. He didn't want to alarm anyone further.

"He was there," Maya whispered. "I felt him. A snake in a winter cloak."

Her words, spoken as soft as the falling snow, sent needling chills through Mikoneh—the first bite of cold he'd felt since the courtyard. They all fell quiet again, letting the snow play its muted symphony over the forest. What could they say? Mikoneh couldn't guess what Sathe wanted; too many possibilities existed. Was the magician a lecherous glutton like his lordly employer, eyeing Maya for himself? She was beautiful, with her raven-blue hair, molten eyes, and tall, willowy frame. Yet somehow Drayve hadn't seen it.

A suspicion darted across Mikoneh's mind. Court magician. Magic. Flames. Could a man like that have blinded Drayve to Maya's worth?

You're taking this too far. There's another explanation. Magic isn't real... No one in Oceana believed in actual magic. Dragons and fae folk were only hearthwives' stories. Only the devout worshipers of the Nijaal embraced any of that as truth, and they were followers of a dying faith.

Fa and Mama had never stated that magic was real either. Come to think of it, they'd never said anything one way or another, only sharing amused smiles at the local superstitions. That had been enough of an answer for Mikoneh, until now.

Is superstition the same as magic?

He couldn't ask them. His hand fell to his satchel and the swell there. All he had left of his parents was inside, and he couldn't open it to see what it contained.

Time passed at a turtle's pace, while snow built towers and bridges across the spanning boughs, dusting the world in pristine white. A lie, Mikoneh knew. Few things were pristine, least of all in the remote places of the world, where nature spread thorns, weeds, and vicious wildlife.

Eventually, Rook crested a slope, and Mikoneh reined the stallion in to study the snow-crusted beach and jagged cliffs beyond the forest's edge. Riddling holes gaped among the high-standing rocks, moaning in the wind that never ceased to buffet the crescent-shaped cove.

Maya's horse let out a snort and stamped one hoof. "Easy there." The woman stroked the horse's neck, cooing soft words, then she turned toward her twin. "Even the animals think this shore's haunted."

"Can't be helped." He patted Rook, glad the war horse seemed indifferent to the eerie cries of the cavernous cliffs. At a nudge, the stallion started down the overgrown path, leading the other two nervous animals with him. Fingers of wind tugged at Mikoneh's cloak and tossed handfuls of snow at his face. Ice clung to his dark lashes, rimming his view.

He hunched against the assault, though it didn't feel cold. Glancing back, he found Maya and Penn huddling against each other, their hoods pulled low over their chafed cheeks. He turned back to the path, urging Rook on a little faster. At last, the path leveled out. Drifts of snow smeared the road and billowed in blinding sheets, but Mikoneh knew the route to the largest cave in Bone Cove. He led the way, cutting through snow, risking backward glances now and then to be sure his twin and his friend followed close.

The cliffs curved near the beach, and Mikoneh broke from the trail to follow the crashing waves. Salt mingled with snow to tease his tongue. Wind flung ice crystals across his face with renewed ardor.

As he guided Rook near the frothing breakers, the cave loomed into view. He urged the stallion into a canter. They raced into the cave, the sound of Rook's hooves ringing across the high ceiling where stalactites glistened with water. More hooves answered. Mikoneh wheeled Rook around as Maya dragged her sopping hood from her face. Threads of hair clung to her red cheeks, and puffs of breath appeared before her lips. She met his golden gaze, then shifted to examine the old cave, while Penn did the same with chattering teeth.

"At least it's somewhat warmer." Penn spoke in low tones, but the words echoed in the wide cavern, and he winced.

"Don't worry," Mikoneh whispered. "The smaller tunnels

don't shout back at you." He jerked his head toward a back passage, then turned Rook around and led his companions into the darkness of the complicated network. His eyes adjusted fast, as they always did. He'd been surprised when he'd learned native Oceaneans couldn't see in the dark. Years ago, Fa had told Mikoneh and Maya not to reveal their night vision—or any of their heightened senses, including their keen, pointed ears—to anyone, and they'd vowed not to.

Navigating the passages was no issue for Mikoneh. His sense of direction was acute, and he led the other two to a small side cave he remembered from his times spent at the inlet fishing with his father. Despite the stories of Bone Cove, it held some of his favorite memories from happier days.

He swung from the black saddle and helped Maya and Penn down from their shared mount. Maya set to work unsaddling the horses, while Mikoneh helped Penn to sit down on a jutting rock nearby.

"Thanks," Penn murmured, shivering.

"I'll start a fire." Bringing his satchel with him, Mikoneh moved to a bundle of driftwood left over from the most recent fishing trip two years ago. As he picked through the termite-infested wood, a rat scurried away.

"Poor thing," said Maya. "We've invaded his home." She heaved Rook's saddle from his back and set it beside the other horses' accoutrements, then she dug inside one saddle pouch until she found a cloth and brush. While she dried and groomed the horses, Penn padded to Mikoneh's side.

"Can you summon fire again, do you think?"

"No idea." Mikoneh sprinkled kindling in the fire ring, positioned the logs, then rose and moved to the tiny airhole where the smoke could escape. Fa had chosen this cavern for that feature, along with its relative dryness. Mikoneh pinched one eye shut and looked up through the hole. It didn't look clogged, so he turned back to the fire and dug out the flint and steel he'd procured at the old encampment.

Kneeling, he struck them together. The first spark caught and burst into a full-sized flame without hesitation. He flinched back, though the fire didn't so much as warm the fine hairs on his wrists. In the blaze, a tiny figure danced into being, its form lithe and almost human, though its flowing hair lifted upward like a crown of flames, and its face had no distinctive features like eyes or mouth, just a suggestion of form.

"What are you?" he whispered.

The flames popped and crackled as though they acknowledged his question, and the tiny shape leaned out of the fire, reaching for him. He inched backward, panic hitching in his lungs.

"What's wrong?" asked Maya.

His panic mounted higher. Could his twin not see the— the *thing*? He tensed, unwilling to retreat further. Clenching his jaw, he tore his gaze from the flickering figure, finding Maya's eyes. "Do you see anything in the fire? Anything unusual?"

Her gaze shifted to the crackling flames eating away at the logs. She searched the licking tendrils of light, then shook her head. "No. What do *you* see?"

Just like her not to make him feel like a fool. He smiled crookedly as he conjured up the words to reassure her—but the *thing* in the flames twirled out of the fire ring and flickered toward him like a dancing candle without the wax stem.

A crackling, playful voice sounded from the tiny, wispy figure. '*You wish to know what we are? We can tell you. We are fire spirits.*'

Chapter 5

The Crack of Thin Ice

*"The Mage Queen used empty promises to reach her goals,
among them immortality for her underlings. Greed deafened
them to danger until it was far too late."*

- From Athonen d'Ereth's *The Fall of Mages in the Age of Dragons*

Mikoneh jumped to his feet, boots scuffing against the cavern grit. His heart pounded in his throat, while his mind hammered with one thought.

The fire just talked to me. It talked.

"What's wrong?" Maya snatched a long stick from the pile of driftwood and brandished it, scrutinizing the fire as though a mythical dragon might spring up from the logs. Penn tensed and looked around for an enemy, unable to do anything else, manacled as he was. Finding nothing, they both looked at Mikoneh askance.

"I—" The words still wouldn't form. Mikoneh gaped at the guttering fire spirit. "Why can I see you?" At least *that* came out.

'*You are a Fire Elementalist. 'Tis your gift*' was the simple reply.

"I don't..." Lightheadedness crept into Mikoneh's skull. *Don't let the panic take over. Breathe.* In childhood, he'd had panic attacks often, but he'd conquered them over the years for the most part. Staring at this tiny creature—what might be a hallucination—made him feel ten years old again and, frankly, ready to faint. The ground seemed to tip under him, and he swayed.

Maya caught his arm. "What do you see?"

"The, uh, fire is, eh...talking to me." Heat crept over his face. It sounded so ridiculous.

"It's talking?" Penn took a step closer, riveted by the flames.

A breath of winter blew in, cold enough to rake ice over Mikoneh's soul. He shuddered, despite the warmth of the fire. Instinct screamed a warning, and he whirled toward the cavern opening.

A cloaked figure stood in the entrance, hood drawn back to reveal the snakelike face Penn's description had painted. Needling fear pricked at Mikoneh's flesh, and he gripped his sword hilt.

"You must be Sathe."

Maya and Penn inched closer to Mikoneh, the former still clutching her long stick.

The man settled coal-like eyes on Mikoneh. His skin, stretched as tight as a corpse, looked papery and translucent, almost ready to tear away to reveal bone beneath. His cheekbones were high and pronounced, while dark shadows rimmed his otherworldly eyes. His thin lips had a blue tinge, like he didn't breathe enough air. Those lips twitched up in a smile that conjured fresh chills. "I am indeed Sathe."

His voice was like the crack of thin ice. Mikoneh's mind tripped over the inhuman sound.

He balled his hands into fists, determined not to back down, not to show his fear. "Come to take us back to your master?"

The wintry smile deepened. "Ah, no. Not that master." He drifted into the cavern chamber, wraithlike, not even casting a shadow. "Drayve's desire to end your lives was short-sighted. I have a great use for you." The coal eyes brightened like an inner flame had been kindled, but even that felt cold. "Indeed, Firebrand, you and I shall do unimaginable things together."

Mikoneh stumbled back, every muscle demanding he run —but he couldn't. The madman blocked their only exit. Mikoneh had been a fool to bring them into this cavern. He'd relied too much on the superstitious nature of humans, not considering that he'd left the realm of quantifiable understanding the moment he'd controlled fire.

"Your fear is reasonable." Sathe took a step closer. "Your instincts are finely honed, as they ought to be. Jonatten and Seranni did commendable work, always." He fell still, and his gaze slid toward Maya. "I've had my suspicions about the two of you for a while. I'd hoped to prove them the day your guardians met their end—but alas, you didn't respond in the way I'd expected."

"You were there?" Mikoneh growled.

Sathe turned back to him, smile turning smug. "Of course I was, Firebrand. Who do you think conjured up that otherworldly fire?"

Maya made a choked noise. Penn drew close to her, glowering at Sathe.

Mikoneh's fury caved to memory.

Violet flames, curling high into the dark, snowy sky. The gathered crowds watching in reticence. The silence of the cottage. Mikoneh squeezed his eyes shut, trying to banish the memories. Wrath licked at the flames of his heart. His eyes shot open. "So, you're the man I need to kill." He drew his sword.

A laugh scraped over Sathe's lips like rusty hinges rediscovering their use. "Ah, I *knew* you'd be strong enough. How long I've sought you, you've no idea. Your sister will have her uses as well. You should thank me for sparing her from Drayve until now." His eyes flicked to Penn, then away. "Perhaps even your noble friend will come in handy."

"Don't count on it," replied Penn, his eyes blazing with fury, stance tall and stately despite his imprisoned hands.

Maya stepped forward, coming into line with Mikoneh. "Whatever you want," she said, "you'll not find it here. I suggest you leave before this turns into a fight."

The eerie light in the man's eyes flared higher. "Is the woman as strong as her brother, I wonder?" He canted his head like a curious child examining an insect. "We shall see, I suppose." He scanned the room. "You were clever to choose Bone Cove. The rock foundation did make things more difficult for me—but I can be resourceful. Come, my children. Let us leave this snowy place behind and traverse the warmer delvings below." He pulled a scroll from within his cloak and unrolled it, revealing a complicated drawing of runes in a circle. He tossed the scroll to the floor.

Mikoneh lifted his hand, hoping fire would answer. Flames leapt across the air—but Sathe lifted his eyes, and violet flames shot out, striking at the tiny fire spirit. On contact, they burst asunder, plunging the room into pitch blackness.

A ring of violet light opened across the floor. The cavern walls moaned and rumbled.

"You'll crush us!" Penn cried out.

Mikoneh reached for Maya. The horses whinnied in fear. The ground gave a resounding *crack*, and Mikoneh's stomach slammed into his throat. His feet met open air. His twin let out a scream. He groped for her hand—but hard-packed earth struck him with immense force, blasting oxygen from his lungs. Stars burst before his eyes, and he lay on his back, wrestling to breathe.

Musty, earthy odors curled through his nostrils. A dim violet flame flickered above his head, hovering before the shadows of his blurry vision.

He coughed, then grimaced, digging his nails into the hard ground. Where was Fa's sword? Each breath burned through his lungs. He willed himself to sit up. Peering into the semi-darkness, his night vision engaged, adjusting to the violet flame hovering inches above Sathe's open palm. The man watched Mikoneh with hungry eyes, his lips split to reveal teeth in a grin that could freeze a sunbeam.

Maya lay on her stomach nearby, unmoving, long hair sprawled around her. Above, the gaping hole revealed the distant cavern ceiling. They'd fallen thirty feet or more into a wide tunnel, old and packed. Mikoneh dropped his eyes. Nowhere in the stillness could he find any horses or his weapon. There was Penn, laying on Maya's far side and coming to with a groan.

Relief slivered through Mikoneh, and he turned to glower at Sathe. "Now what?"

The man's grin stretched inhumanly wide. "Now, you're my prisoners." He gestured, and a strange whispering sound filled the stagnant air behind Mikoneh.

He shifted to his knees and craned his neck. Gooseflesh crawled up his arms.

They came from the darkness; slender, tall, pale things;

skeletons draped in tattered robes, their eye sockets flickering with violet light.

Mikoneh caught his sister's arm and dragged her upright, pinching through her sleeve to alert her. Her head jerked back, smacking his jaw. She groaned, then looked around with a grimace. She landed on the horrific line of grinning skulls perched atop flowing robes and shuddered.

"Mikoneh…"

"I know. I see them." He wrapped his arm around her shoulders, drawing her close. She dug her nails into his jerkin.

"I wish you didn't," Maya whispered. "Then I could dismiss this as a concussive hallucination." She pried one hand loose to rub a swelling lump on her forehead.

Motion snagged Mikoneh's eye. Penn had risen to his knees, arms still bound behind his back, expression grim rather than panicked. Drayve's disowned son was no coward.

The skeletons halted three yards away, their leering grins frightful in the flame's glow. Sathe veered around the three companions to take a stand before his contingent of horrors. He faced Mikoneh, the billowing of his cloak like a statement of authority.

"Welcome to the Underrealm of the Mages. It's wonderful to have you here at last. We hope you feel welcome." Sathe's tones dripped with sarcasm, laced with frost.

Mikoneh snorted. "Sure. It's so cozy and hospitable."

Sathe's chuckle was colder than the high frosts of Northern Simynshin. "Such bravado, little Firebrand. I look forward to breaking that indomitable spirit." He motioned with his slender fingers, and a half dozen skeletons marched forward, impossibly silent.

"Come quietly," Sathe said. "I'd hate for something to happen to the spare." His dark eyes glittered as he regarded Penn.

The skeleton in the fore of the contingent stooped, then straightened, clutching Fa's sword. Mikoneh's lungs pinched. The sword gleamed in the eerie violet light. The skeleton moved to Sathe's side and handed it over, a sense of wicked pleasure emanating from its grinning skull. Bits of rotten flesh hung from one cheek and around the jaw.

"Ah, thank you, Captain Torel."

Mikoneh's mind searched for any kind of escape route. Surely, there was a way out of this. They couldn't have escaped Drayve merely to end up in a similar situation so soon.

Conjure fire. The urge was powerful, but he resisted, stamping down on the idea hard. Tossing flames at Sathe had done nothing last time, and besides—

Why did it have to be fire? Of all things...

His jaw clenched. His heart missed a beat. Bony fingers seized Maya, and he threw himself forward, slamming his knuckles into the grinning skull before registering how pointless the action was—and how dangerous for Penn. The skeleton staggered backward. Mikoneh pulled Maya away from the encroaching enemies.

Penn kicked out with one foot, his natural agility keeping him upright as he sent one skeleton into another, knocking them both over.

Sathe's eyes burned as Mikoneh's gaze collided with his. The man held up his hand, and more skeletons poured forth. They raised their mottled hands. Spears materialized from the air in bony fingers.

Mikoneh jerked back, taking Maya with him. His satchel thwacked his hip. Penn crashed into him from behind, and they stood back-to-back to challenge the undead legion.

"Now, now," said Sathe. "I think that's enough defiance for one evening." He stepped into view beyond the cluster of skeletons, and his pit-like eyes blazed with a fervor that scoured Mikoneh's soul. "I'm excited to play our own version of Fang and Claw, Firebrand. But I suggest you surrender for now, or I'll be forced to kill the dead weight." His eyes flicked to Penn, then back to Mikoneh. "Your choice."

CHAPTER 6

A PALE BLUE STONE

They'd surrendered. Against those odds, they didn't have a choice.

Sathe had brought the three companions to a small earthen chamber, not unlike Drayve's dungeon cell, though this space lacked rats and moldy straw. Instead, the packed clay walls smelled of rich dirt and mildew, and beetles scuttled across the floor, heading for some unknown source of food. Sitting in the semi-darkness, Maya shivered and dug out a handkerchief to blow her nose.

Close by, Mikoneh was attempting to pick the lock on Penn's iron manacles with Maya's herb knife. Penn's arm had been broken in the fall from the cavern chamber, and while he bore up under the pain without a word of complaint, Maya needed to set the bone soon.

Mikoneh's mouth quirked sideways. He twisted his head to see the keyhole better, and his tongue appeared at the corner of his lips. He dug the knife a little deeper, leaning to one side —and the blade snapped, sending him slumping to the ground with a grunt.

"Drat and blast," he muttered, sitting back up to examine the broken knife. "There goes that." He tossed the knife to the dirt floor and rubbed a smear of blood from his knuckles. "Sorry, Penn."

The viscount sighed and shifted to rest against the nearest wall. "Thank you for trying just the same." He shut his eyes, lines of pain drawn on his brow and around his mouth. "I don't suppose my arm will matter for much longer anyway, considering everything."

Mikoneh had been examining the cut on his knuckle, but he dropped his hand at Penn's last words. "Don't *you* say that. What happened to your sanguinity?"

Penn grimaced, keeping his eyes shut. "I guess I dropped it somewhere along that tunnel with all the skeleton tracks."

Maya watched the torrent of fear and frustration bubbling up in her twin. She leaned forward and caught his arm. "Don't pick a fight. It's not Penn's fault any more than it's yours or mine."

Mikoneh resisted, his muscles tight beneath her touch, then his shoulders hunched. "I know." He lowered his eyes to the new bead of blood on his knuckle.

"Here." She reached for it.

He pulled away. "Don't bother. It'll stop."

She couldn't blame him for his frustration. Her own helplessness threatened to choke her. With a sigh, she shifted her weight from one knee to the other, and her gaze fell on her twin's satchel. Sathe hadn't bothered to take it away. Maya's satchel had been left behind with the horses, though her herb pouch was still tied to her belt.

"What's in that?" she asked, seeking any kind of distraction.

"In what?"

"That. Your satchel."

Mikoneh's blood-smeared hand fell to the pouch still hanging from his shoulder. "Nothing useful." He sighed. "What we really need got left behind."

She pushed that cheerless thought away. She didn't want to focus on the horses left in the cave, along with their meager store of food. Shifting closer, she brushed a finger against the satchel's leather surface. "Let me see."

He grimaced, then slid the strap from his shoulder and pushed it across the gritty ground. "Be my guest."

Maya untied the flap and peeked inside. A lump swelled in her throat. "Oh." Her fingers hovered near the edges of the small Ashwood box. It was about six inches long, three inches wide, and two inches tall, and felt like it held nothing but air. She'd not laid eyes on the box in months. In fact, she'd assumed Mikoneh had destroyed it ages ago, back when she was ill. Pursing her lips, she set her fingertips against the polished wood and traced the delicate scrollwork. "I'd forgotten how beautiful it is."

He remained quiet, averting his gaze. Was he embarrassed?

She scooted closer and lifted the box from the satchel. The tiny lock was delicate, just like the hinges holding the lid together. She drew a breath. "What's inside?"

"Dunno." He fell silent, but she stared at his back until he finally lifted his eyes to meet hers. He plucked it from her hand and tugged against the lid. "It won't open. I've tried everything.

Everything. Picking the lock, breaking the hinges. I even took an axe to it, and once I threw it in a fire. It won't open. It won't even scar."

Her jaw slackened. "That makes no sense."

"Neither does conjuring fire or being imprisoned by skeletons." He shrugged. "Yet here we are."

"Good point." She inhaled through her nose and gagged on the mildewed air. "I thought you'd thrown it away."

"I meant to..." He sighed and dragged a hand down the side of his face. "In a way I did, I suppose. But I went back for it again. It's...all we have." His eyes fell to his hip. "Now anyway."

Maya's heart throbbed. Sathe had Fa's sword, and the rest of their belongings remained in Bone Cove. The skeletons had marched them along a series of tunnels for several long, dark turns since. What direction they walked, to what end, she didn't know. Despite her good internal compass, she couldn't keep her bearings so far underground.

Glancing at Penn, Maya found him watching the twins, wearing a sympathetic smile. He remained where he'd been sitting, giving them space. She'd told him about the box once, after she'd recovered from her illness, but she'd thought it was lost back then.

Mikoneh rested the box on his lap and ran his fingers across the keyhole, rubbing stray beads of his blood from the lid. "I know how you feel, Maya. I want to know what's in—"

A faint click sounded.

They all stared at the box.

Mikoneh used a trembling finger to lift the lid. It sprang open on a hidden mechanism, revealing a glowing object laying on red velvet lining. He wiped his hand on his tunic, then reached inside to finger the object. It was a pale blue stone the size of his fingernail, clear like crystal, smooth as a river pebble.

Its center pulsed with light. Beside it lay a delicate bronze key along with dozens of chains and leather cords bearing pendants overshadowed by the glowing stone.

Maya gaped. The box shouldn't be able to hold so many objects, yet it did. Mikoneh curled his finger around the chains and cords and pulled them from the box with a faint jangle.

Upon close inspection, Maya recognized a few of the symbols engraved upon the pendants. Two birds in flight, a majestic tree, a stag, a trident, a dragon with crossing swords, a bundle of wheat and a sickle, a high tower, a lion—and many others. Some were the crests of neighboring countries, some the crests of Great Houses within Oceana's provinces, and others were entirely unfamiliar. She stared, trying to comprehend how vast the world must be to bear so many types of heraldry.

The last item in the box was a folded slip of parchment. Maya's heart lurched as she read the familiar scrawl:

To my fair ones.

She glanced at Mikoneh who nodded once. Swallowing, she unfolded the letter, blinked back the mist that gathered in her eyes, and read aloud:

My dear Mikoneh and Maya: Since you're reading this note, Seranni and I must no longer be with you. It's a strange prospect—

Maya's voice broke.

—a strange prospect to be dead, even as I

pen this letter. Know that we love you and will be with you even beyond the grave.

Mikoneh squeezed her arm to steady her. She cleared her throat and pressed on.

The box you hold has been sealed by magic.

Maya glanced up at Mikoneh. Magic. Sealed by magic. Her twin frowned and nodded for her to continue.

Oceana's southeastern provinces have no proper concept of magic; only enough to fear it as an ill omen. Rest assured, magic does exist, good and evil alike. Other lands are rampant with it. As we are no longer with you, I urge you to go westward. Seek the Prince of Rokahn. He can answer all the questions you will find along your way.

Beware of Dark Mages. They will seek you for your blood, as well as to discover the Prince of Rokahn's location. I wish I could say more, but even sealed magic may be breached.

You'll not go the journey without aid. Within the box I've placed the tools necessary to survive the perils of your future paths. The pendants will grant you passage through any human country. The stone will likewise grant you access through any fae land which may not acknowledge finite symbols. And the key will open any lock—which you must realize bears consequences if used unwisely. Be brave, rely on one another, and take care to trust few along your way. Present yourselves to the Prince of Rokahn, and he will keep you safe.

Yours faithfully forever, Sir Jonatten, Thane of Marcress, General under the Dragon King.

P.S. Forgive your Fa his formality. He can't help but sign things this way. It's that big, foolish head of his. You'll always be my precious jewels. —Mama

Mist drifted across Maya's vision. Fa and Mama's voices rolled over her mind, whispering the letter's words over and over. Always be my precious jewels. Go westward. Seek the Prince of Rokahn—*the Dragon King.*

The twins had been raised on stories of Owenekiras Rokahn—not hearth stories—but real accounts of his battle strategies. Fa and Mama had revered the Prince of Rokahn as a war hero. They'd often used the Fang and Claw boardgame Fa had carved to demonstrate the man's brilliant tactics in combat.

She swiped at a tear and glanced up at Mikoneh. "What should we do?"

He inhaled, then blew out a slow, deliberating breath. His eyes fell to the box on his lap. "They never lied to us. Not ever. And after the day we've had, I'm willing to bet Fa's letter isn't a cypher. It's literal." He plucked up the bronze key. "Penn, turn around."

The viscount had already started shifting. Mikoneh fitted the key into the manacle lock. At a faint click, the manacles clattered to the earthen floor.

Mikoneh lifted the key. "Either I've lost my mind or we have a way to escape." He shifted aside. "Maya, better look at his break."

She was already moving to do just that, digging through her pouch. She drew out some *firia* leaves.

"Chew."

Penn grimaced, having already suffered a dose of a bitter tincture to dull the pain en route to their prison. Still, he obeyed, gagging. "This is worse than the concoction in that vial."

"Unfortunately, I don't have any more of that," she said.

As she examined Penn's broken humerus bone, Maya watched Mikoneh from the corner of her eye while he read over Fa's letter again. His lips moved silently, poring over every word and glancing between lines into the box.

"You know," Penn said through a wince as Maya probed his arm. "Life hasn't been lackluster since I met the two of you."

She chuckled. "That's certainly true. Brace yourself."

As Penn tensed, Maya adjusted her fingers, then she set the bone back where it belonged with a smooth, confident jerk. Penn cried out. She ripped the hem of her skirt and made a wrap and sling while Penn drew deep breaths.

"There. Better?" She leaned around him.

He managed a watery smile. "That didn't hurt as bad as the break did."

"Your bravery is commendable." She brushed her skirts straight and dug through her pouch. "Even so, the ache will last a while. Chew." She passed Penn a few more leaves.

"Thanks." He chewed with a profound pout.

Mikoneh looked up from the box. "Maya, we need—"

He tensed. A breath later she heard the thud of heavy boots beyond the stone door. Mikoneh gestured to the manacles, and Penn shoved them behind his back, while Mikoneh tucked the Ashwood box under Maya's skirts. A breath more and the door rolled to one side, revealing Sathe draped in deep purple robes lined with silver runes along the hems of his sleeves. Two hooded figures stood behind him.

"Settling in well?" asked the man in his crackling, wintry voice.

"Comfier and comfier," drawled Mikoneh. He stood up and folded his arms. "What do you want?"

Sathe lifted one slim hand and pointed a long finger at Mikoneh. "*You*, Firebrand. Come."

Mikoneh lifted one eyebrow. "And if I refuse?"

"Then I will slaughter your useless friend, drink his blood, and absorb his soul for my magic." Sathe tipped his head to one side. "Pick."

Setting his jaw, Mikoneh glanced at Penn, then nodded. "Lead on." As he neared Maya, he stooped and brushed his fingers against her arm. "I'll be back."

She swallowed hard. "We'll be waiting for you."

His fingers wiggled at his side to catch her attention. The flash of the bronze key made her blink, then he pocketed the slender object.

"Do not fret, young Windfall," Sathe said, eyeing Maya. "This is not farewell. Come, Firebrand."

Mikoneh reached the door, and the two hooded figures set bony fingers on each of his shoulders to draw him from the cell. At their touch, he flinched.

Sathe swept out after them, and the door rumbled shut. Maya blinked a few times until her eyes adjusted to the darkness, then she pulled the box out from under her skirts. She swung it open, and the blue glow of the polished stone within spread beams across the room.

"Do you think Sathe is what your Fa warned about in his letter? A Dark Mage?" Penn asked.

Maya frowned. "It's likely. He seems to want us just like the letter warns."

"It can't be for Mikoneh's fire, though. Sathe wields fire himself. Do you think it's more to do with this Prince of Rokahn?"

"Possibly. But if Mikoneh can conjure fire, what *else* can he do? Or me? What can I do?" She mulled over that, trying to imagine fire playing across her hands without burning her. "Everything is topsy-turvy now. I never believed in magic, though you seemed to."

Penn crooked a smile. "I just always wanted to believe, but I never quite did. Even with Sathe's performances at court. Not until I saw your brother terrify my father and his court with his flames—I'll cherish that memory forever." He chuckled.

Maya tried for a smile, but it didn't stick. Her thoughts weighed too much, especially picturing Mikoneh wielding flame. After losing their parents to fire, did it torment him? She suspected it would plague her.

Penn spoke again into the silence. "The Prince of Rokahn is the same person as the legendary Dragon King, right?" His brows pinched together. "I'd thought him only a legend, but if your father claims otherwise..."

"He's real. Fa told us stories about serving under him."

"But isn't the Dragon King a tyrant or a pirate or something?" Penn rested a hand against his broken arm. "He wants to steal his sister's throne, doesn't he?"

"That's just the legend. Fa and Mama always said that *she* stole the throne from her twin brothers, and Owenekiras

Rokahn is trying to win it back. I'm inclined to believe them over hearth stories."

"Fair enough." He rested his head against the wall behind him. "Do you think Sathe will try to pry the Dragon King's location from Mikoneh—that he thinks your parents told you both where to find him?"

"Maybe. Though they never did. They only said he was in his war camp, wherever that is." She reached into the box and stroked the cool, smooth stone. She and her twin had spoken often of their parents' former leader, and both suspected his war camp was hidden in Simynshin in the west. Fa, too, had said to go westward. That kingdom was where Prince Atlanse and his songbird daughter lived, and they were known allies of the rightful Rokahnian ruler. "Knowing Mikoneh, he won't say anything either way."

Penn chuckled. "True, that. No one is more stubborn than your brother. He won't break, don't worry about that."

"I'm not." She wasn't lying. No one alive was stronger than her twin—not even the Dragon King.

Chapter 7

Stormlight Blazing

"Upon reflection, perhaps there are two instances of tragedy worse than what befell the lesser Dark Mages. The first is that of a Revenant's creation."

- From Athonen d'Ereth's *The Fall of Mages in the Age of Dragons*

Go westward. That's all well and good, but how do we escape to do that, Fa?

With Sathe striding ahead, Mikoneh was led between his skeletal guards down several twisting earthen passages until they reached a heavy stone door. Sathe motioned, and the two guards shoved it aside to reveal a large chamber made of granite. Veins of silver sparkled under the influence of violet torches in sconces dispersed about the cavern. At the chamber's center stood a long slab of stone: an altar. It was to this that Sathe guided Mikoneh while the guards remained behind.

Mikoneh halted before the altar. Intricate runes were etched along its edges. He couldn't read them, yet they spread chills across his flesh.

"Lie down." Sathe's voice was a frigid whisper in his ear.

"Don't do it." The voice that spoke was a low, soft monotone.

Mikoneh started and turned, seeking out the source of the voice. His gaze landed on a boy donned in gray from head to boot, including his long, sleek hair and lightless eyes. Only his skin was a warm, fair color. He was chained against the wall, hands bound above his head. The prisoner couldn't be older than ten years.

"Are you still here?" Sathe looked annoyed—or was that fear flitting across his face? "I told the captain to lock you back up."

The boy blinked like an owl. "He forgot."

Sathe cursed under his breath. "One more nuisance." He turned to Mikoneh. "Ignore him. Lie down to protect your friend."

"You'll regret it if you do that." The boy's voice remained monotone.

Mikoneh hesitated. He had no desire to climb onto an altar. "What's this for?"

"The benefit of Sirinhigha," was Sathe's cool reply.

Mikoneh's brows quirked up. "The benefit of the whole world? No one can promise that."

"It's not a promise. It's fate." Sathe placed his palm on the slab of stone. "This age was foretold at the dawn—"

"Liar." The boy dragged the word out, adding emphasis despite his lack of inflection.

A scowl flickered over Sathe's papery face. "Be silent, Minno, or I'll—"

"You'll what? Feed me to your *pets*?" The last word

dipped low, adding ominous intonation. Minno's eyes drifted from Sathe to land on Mikoneh. His gaze carried a weight that pressed into Mikoneh, as if this child was far, far older than he appeared. "Don't believe anything Sathe says. He's a fraud like all Mages, but worse because he's one of their generals."

"Mage, huh?" Mikoneh glanced at Sathe, recalling Fa's warning in his letter about Dark Mages. "What's this child done to deserve being locked up? Talk you half to death?"

"Nearly," said Minno above Sathe's start of a reply.

With another scowl, Sathe turned his back on the gray-clad boy. "He's done far worse things than you could fathom. Get onto the altar, Firebrand, and this will go much easier for all of you."

"What about him?" Mikoneh jerked his head toward Minno. "Will you spare him if I cooperate?"

"That isn't necessary," said the boy in the same flat tones. "I'm fine hanging here. I can't feel my arms anymore, so it doesn't matter much."

Certainly, the boy wasn't right in the head. Mikoneh wouldn't let him suffer. He turned back to Sathe. "Deal?"

Sathe's eyes narrowed. "No. You'll obey me to protect what already belongs to you, Firebrand. What I can do to Lord Penn is far, far worse than a merciful death. Lie on the altar and prepare yourself." He drew a dagger from within his heavy robes.

Mikoneh stiffened. "You plan to kill me?"

"Hardly." Sathe moved to the head of the rectangular slab. "Rest your skull here."

Instinct screamed, but Mikoneh couldn't lose Maya and Penn. He couldn't let his failure extend that far. Besides, skeletal guards stood at the only exit, and Minno, dangling from chains, needed his help. Taking several deep breaths,

Mikoneh hefted himself onto the altar, trying to conceal his shaking hands by clenching them into fists.

Think of a solution. How do we get out of this?

Shifting onto his back, he spread out across the altar. Runes covered the stone ceiling above him, shimmering in the torchlight.

"I didn't expect you to be an idiot." Minno sighed. "That will make this more complicated."

Heat washed across Mikoneh's face. He ground his teeth together.

Minno's voice rolled over him, still low and soft and monotone, yet carrying. "I'll have to do this myself, won't I?"

Sathe's dagger glinted above Mikoneh's head, sharp and bright. "Don't interfere, Minno. This is *not* your affair. I've had enough of your cheek—and your pranks. Don't add to the pain I will inflict."

"Is that supposed to scare me?" asked Minno flatly.

How could the boy disrupt them? He was chained to the wall.

Sathe lowered the dagger toward Mikoneh's throat. Mikoneh tensed up, every muscle screaming, every thought clattering: run, run, run. He choked on saliva. The blade slipped between his jerkin laces and cut into the skin shielding his sternum. Pain bloomed across his chest.

Think, Mikoneh. Think!

Black and white swirling light exploded across the chamber. Sathe cried out, and the dagger blade retreated from its shallow cut. Mikoneh sat upright, searching for the source of the light—and he found Minno standing free of his chains, black lightning cutting across a white corona surrounding his body. His irises had turned a smoky white-gray, eddying with tiny tendrils of more black lightning.

"Release him, Sathe." Minno's voice maintained its level,

invariant tone. He wore no hint of fury beyond the stormlight blazing around him.

"You were bound! And—you're meant to be a neutral party." The Mage straightened from his slouch. "If you interfere—"

"I'll do what I please." A bolt of lightning exploded in Minno's large, pale eyes. "You would be a fool to stop me." His gaze flicked to Mikoneh. "Come here before he tries again to bind you."

"Don't move, Firebrand," Sathe hissed.

Mikoneh didn't hesitate. It didn't take a genius to read the room. He scooted from the altar and jogged to Minno's side, careful to avoid the lightning snapping across the air.

"Aim for the door," Minno said.

Mikoneh considered the two skeletal guards—then he obeyed, hoping that his decision to side with Minno wouldn't cause any harm to come to his sister and friend.

Whatever happens, isn't it better to fight? He'd always believed so, but recent weeks and Kevva's betrayal had cracked his convictions.

The skeletal guards turned their hollow eye sockets toward him. Their bony fingers clacked against their spear shafts as they raised them. He halted, eyeing the sharp, gleaming tips.

"*Sathe.*" Minno's voice held an edge now. "You can release us, or I can bring these tunnels crashing down. You know I can."

"And kill what you're trying to protect?" scoffed the Mage.

Mikoneh glanced over his shoulder, frowning. *Not to mention get himself killed.*

"Anything is better than what you have in mind," Minno replied. As though to punctuate his stance, the ground rumbled.

"Fine!" Sathe's gaze bled black, flooding the whites of his

eyes. "*Take him.*" He turned those fathomless depths on Mikoneh. "This is not ended, Firebrand. You will be mine."

Chills traced Mikoneh's veins. He turned away from Sathe and found the guards stepping aside to let him pass, both emitting disappointment. Mikoneh wrenched the door open and stepped out into the earthen passageway. Two breaths later, Minno joined him, his personal storm tamer than before but still sparking with lightning.

"Lead the way if you remember the route to your prison." Minno waggled his fingers down the passage.

Mikoneh didn't need to remember. He could follow his own scent: woodsmoke and amber. He ran as fast as he dared, bearing the younger boy's short legs in mind. They turned down several corridors, the mildewed air teasing Mikoneh's nose until he sneezed.

"Bless you," Minno said.

Mikoneh grimaced and raced on, careful to check his senses when he reached a crossroads. They turned left. Eventually, a flickering torch set into the wall revealed a familiar stone door. "That's it." He tugged out the bronze key.

Now or never.

Darting to the door, he held out the key and searched for a keyhole.

Minno reached his side. "Just tap the door. It's magical, not tangible."

Mikoneh stabbed the key end against the stone barrier. With a shudder, the door rolled away. "I'm surprised there aren't guards."

"They're nearby," Minno said, "but this horde is chained to Sathe's will. They'll stand down for now."

Mikoneh stepped inside the cell. "Maya, Penn. Time to go!"

"Mikoneh!" Maya slammed into his chest, her arms wrapping around him. "Thank all the Nijaal you're safe!"

"Did Sathe hurt you?" Penn demanded.

"Not really," he grunted. "Better find an exit before we lose our advantage."

"How right you are," murmured Minno. "My power is already shrinking." He wobbled. "When it does, you must choose to carry me or leave me behind. I'm not particular. Do what you feel is best."

"Who is this?" asked Penn.

Ignoring him, Mikoneh eyed the boy, concern for Minno mingling with alarm at his attitude. "I don't leave people behind."

Minno offered him that same slow owl blink. "That's very reckless of you."

A scowl caught Mikoneh's lips. "Let's just go. Any idea which path to take?" He glanced up and down the corridor.

"None." Minno sighed. His eyes fell on Maya's hands. "What's that?"

"A family heirloom," Mikoneh said, taking the box from his twin protectively. "Why?"

"It's singing." The boy tipped his head to one side. "Don't you hear it?"

The company fell silent. Mikoneh strained his ears, accustomed to hearing what no one besides his twin could. "Uh. No. I don't hear anything."

"Ah." Minno nodded. "You're not yet awake."

"Awa—" Mikoneh cut himself off. This wasn't the time for irrelevant questions. "What does the singing signify?"

Minno held out his hand. "May I?"

With supreme reluctance, Mikoneh passed the box to the strange gray child. Minno took it with reverence and nudged open the lid. His eyes widened by a modicum. "Ah." He reached in and plucked out the smooth blue stone. "This is precisely what we need."

"That's good," Penn said, leaning toward the stone. "What's your plan?"

"You'll see," Minno answered flatly.

Maya brushed her fingers against Mikoneh's sternum. "You're bleeding."

"Which is a problem but one we'll need to solve later." Minno scrutinized the stone closer. "Good color. You've not used it before."

"We barely got the box open before Sathe took me away," Mikoneh said.

The gray boy's eyes flicked to the carved container. "Blood lock. Clever." His gaze darted to Mikoneh, piercing him like a glaive. "You should stop spreading your blood around, though. It isn't smart or healthy."

Mikoneh bristled. Why did the boy insist on taking jabs at him? "Thanks for the advice."

"You're welcome." Minno rolled the stone around on his palm. "I need your permission to activate this. It's assigned to your bloodline."

A throb of grief ripped over Mikoneh's chest, and he glanced toward Maya as a flash of pain brightened her eyes. When she nodded, Mikoneh offered the same silent assent. Minno mimicked their nods, though his actions were more subdued. He closed his fingers over the stone, shut his eyes, and whispered in low, breathy tones. Mikoneh caught a few words. *Summon. Aid. Rokahn.*

The combination of words jolted him. Rokahn?

Find the Prince of Rokahn.

Mikoneh rubbed his sweaty palm against his trousers. Was Minno summoning that legendary man *here*? Would it work? Or had Mikoneh cracked his head open in that fall, and now he was merely hallucinating about magic keys and glowing stones and strange gray boys who could summon warlords?

Did he imagine the stone in Minno's palm flashing brighter, brighter, brighter still? Light swallowed the corridor, spilling into the cell, erasing the lines of every companion standing around Mikoneh. He pinched his eyelids closed, shielding his face with one hand while he caught Maya's sleeve with his free fingers. She snagged the hem of his jerkin and pulled closer. She probably had a firm grip on Penn, too, just in case.

The light faded, draining from Mikoneh's closed eyes until he risked peeking. The figure who stood before him was *not* Owenekiras Rokahn, the legendary Dragon King. It couldn't be.

Chapter 8

Like the Breath of Winter

"But to speak of a Revenant, so they say, is to invite its presence. Even this old man isn't immune to all superstitions, so I will write no more on that subject."

- From Athonen d'Ereth's *The Fall of Mages in the Age of Dragons*, footnote

Standing beside Minno was a second boy, younger and brighter than the blasé gray youth. And *stranger*. The newcomer had wavy yellow-blond hair, bright sky-blue eyes, and long pointed ears that twitched as he offered up a smile that could blind the sun. He was draped in woodland clothes of greens and browns, with a feathered cap and a quiver of arrows. Despite the stranger's youthful appearance, Mikoneh read something vast and old in the boy's eyes—like somehow the newcomer could read his soul.

"Ah, marvelous." One of the boy's long ears twitched

again. "I've been looking for you two." His eyes slid between the twins. He glanced at Penn, still smiling—then Minno, and his ears drooped. "Greetings, Minno."

The gray boy gave him a solemn nod. "Hello, Ter." He turned to the three companions and held out a palm toward the newcomer. "This is Ter N'Avea, perhaps Mithrinn's greatest troublemaker."

The blond youth chuckled. "That's a tad rude, you know, true or not."

Mikoneh's mind churned. Ter. Mithrinn. A magical stone that could transport a child in order for said child to somehow aid them. Mikoneh's mind caught on the last point, and he furiously scrubbed at his scalp. "Listen. Um. Minno summoned you to help us. We're in, well…"

"Mage tunnels, yes." Ter blinked his big blue eyes, peering around the gloom. "You're absolutely correct, my dear fellow. This is no place for conversation. We should leave promptly." He twisted to face Minno. "May I?"

Minno dropped the stone into Ter's hand. "It's Blood Bound."

Ter clicked his tongue. "So it is. Jonatten has ever been clever." He pinched the glowing stone in two fingers and lifted it toward Mikoneh. "There isn't much magic left in it, but it should suffice. You'll need to—"

"I give you permission," Mikoneh said in a rush. "Hurry." Ter knew Fa, and he was somehow affiliated with the Dragon King, judging by Minno's mumbled summons. Mikoneh knew his parents had traveled the world in their war campaigns, yet they'd never said anything to him and Maya that confirmed the existence of fae creatures and magic, not ever. They'd assumed the 'dragon' part of the warlord's title had been purely ornamental. Now, though…

Don't worry about any of that right now.

Ter dropped the stone into one small palm. The child didn't use words like Minno had; the stone merely flashed, once, blindingly bright, and the earthen walls fell away. The dank odors of the tunnel fled in the wake of fresh air ripe with the smell of green, growing things. Close by, the roar of a waterfall filled Mikoneh's sharp ears. His eyes adjusted to the brilliant daylight of an old forest where moss draped from thick, towering trees like unraveling shawls. Outcrops of slick rocks glistened and winked under pillars of sunlight punching through the dense canopy.

"Ah." Ter perched his hands on his hips and turned in a slow circle. "We did not make it quite as far as I might've hoped. This is Southern Simynshin somewhere near Lintha's borders."

"*Where* did you just say?" asked Penn, staring around the forest.

Mikoneh started. How had they traveled so far in a mere blink? No matter how quickly Sathe and his undead horrors had herded them through the tunnels, it would've taken more than a week, not mere turns of a sandglass, to come so far.

"There really wasn't much magic left, then," Minno commented. "How far away were you when I invoked that summons?"

"I was near the Blighted Lands, guiding a few intrepid adventurers along on their quest for answers." Ter's left ear twitched like a rabbit. "I left them with a good friend, and they should be well—if they are not reckless." The child's smile crooked. "A tall order for some, I think." His blue eyes pinned Mikoneh in place. "Are *you* the reckless sort, my good fellow?"

"Yes," Maya chimed in with a giggle. "More than most."

"Ah." Ter's ears fell, but his eyes twinkled. "Somehow, I am not the least surprised." His ears perked up. "Well. Shall we be underway?"

Mikoneh narrowed his eyes. "Where to?"

"Why, to the camp of Owenekiras Rokahn, of course." Ter motioned northwest. "We had best go before those Mages pop up from their underground dwellings. They are most stubborn once fixated, you know."

"What did they want with us?" asked Maya. "They never said, although…" She trailed off at a sharp look from Mikoneh. It was unwise to divulge the contents of Fa's letter to strangers until they'd proven trustworthy.

Ter's smile wilted a little. "As to that…best let the Dragon King explain." He started off, moving toward a deer trail.

"You know where the Dragon King's camp is?" asked Mikoneh, following fast on the strange child's booted heels. "Is it safe to take us there?" The rest of the company filed in after Mikoneh, with Minno in the rear, lagging a yard or so behind.

"If we go the right paths, yes," Ter said without looking back.

"Is he a dread lord like some say?" asked Penn, sounding more curious than worried.

"He is quite dreadful," said Ter, "but only to those who are unjust and wanton."

"Is it true he's the rightful heir to the throne of Rokahn?" Penn pressed. "Stories in Oceana always suggest he murdered his parents to take the throne, but he was banished by his sister, who's now the queen."

Ter's steps faltered. "That story has lost its nuance, I'm afraid." His ear twitched again. "The short version is that he fought against his parents' alliance with Dark Mages, and ultimately defied them. He was banished for *that*. He remains the rightful heir of Rokahn, but his sister consorts with Mages, just as her parents did. That is why she has the throne now."

"See?" Maya beamed at Penn. "I told you so."

"Royal succession often ends up rather messy," Penn mused.

"But surely," Maya said, "the people of Rokahn would want the rightful ruler on the throne. Wouldn't they?"

Mikoneh scoffed. "Why should they? *I* don't put much stock in titles."

"That's true," Penn said. "He really doesn't."

Ter's ears flitted but remained upright. "Yet many people crave order to such a degree that they will accept and uphold traditions simply to keep the balance. Besides that, there are times when blood does matter. Inheritances can make or break a kingdom. After all, it is through your blood that you inherited fire, Mikoneh—and that birthright has an impact both on you and on the world around you."

Memories of the cottage fire flooded Mikoneh's mind, and his step faltered, but he righted himself and pushed ahead. He was determined to stay near the strange, ethereal boy. "What exactly are you? How do you know so much about us?"

Ter glanced over his shoulder. "I am an Ephe'ahn. A woodelf of sorts. And I knew your Fa and Mama very well, long ago."

"But they didn't know I could conjure fire—did they?"

"They knew many things which they couldn't disclose," Ter said. "Nor am I at liberty to do so for the same reasons. Yet I'm glad to answer any separate pressing questions you may have."

Mikoneh mulled over that for a few steps. If Ter was keeping the same secrets as the twins' parents, Mikoneh would let it rest for the time being. Instead, he should focus on the main issues. But where to start? He fingered the hem of his jerkin, turning over the past two days' events. "Why are you taking us to the Dragon King?"

Ter's wide, graceful steps didn't falter. "Is that not where you wish to go?"

"It is," Maya said. "Very much. Our parents—"

"Maya," Mikoneh growled. Familiar with their parents or not, he didn't want to spill all their own secrets straight up.

She batted him off with one hand. "He saved our lives, you know. And he knew Fa and Mama. I think for now we should choose to trust him." She held up the folded parchment. "Our parents wished us to find the Prince of Rokahn if anything happened to them."

"Rightly so." Ter nodded without looking back at them. "They were comrades in many battles."

"We knew that," Mikoneh said. Despite his misgivings, something tickled the base of his neck. He'd heard tales of the Rokahnian prince all his life, and not just from Fa and Mama. The local hearthwives always tried to outdo each other in their so-called knowledge of the warlord. Each story contradicted the next—sometimes the rightful heir of Rokahn was the villain, sometimes he was the misunderstood hero—yet all had shared a common thread: Owenekiras Rokahn was larger than life. His exploits on land and sea were unbelievable, even when Fa had described them. Mikoneh had written most up as pure lore.

Yet knowing now that magic was real lent credibility to Fa's stories. The tales seemed less impossible, less outlandish. And Mikoneh already knew how fiercely loyal his parents had been to the Dragon King, which meant the twins could trust him.

"You said you knew our parents well," said Maya. "Were you friends?"

Ter's pace slowed. His shoulders slumped. "I did have that honor, yes. It's sad I am to have their passing confirmed. It grieves me to my center, just here." He turned and rested his fist against his chest. "Had I known of it sooner, I would have sought you out."

A cold, silent grief slithered through Mikoneh, but he shoved it down. He couldn't let irrational feelings guide him, not right now. He needed to focus on their present situation.

Mikoneh's fingers brushed the crusted stripe of blood on his neck. His pulse pounded against the pads of his fingers. Twice in two days, he'd nearly met his end—unless he could take Sathe at his word that he wouldn't kill Mikoneh. But that only implied something worse than death. Had he been a fool to obey Sathe's directives? Was there a better alternative?

What should I have done? What was the answer?

He hated not knowing. Until recent weeks, he'd been confident of finding the right answer to any puzzle, certain he would always settle on the just thing to do. Now, his resolve and his stance wavered. He'd failed.

I just need to find a way to pivot. Think, Mikoneh. Think.

A hand caught his arm. "Mikoneh?"

Maya. He glanced at her, walking just behind him, her fingers gripping his sleeve. "Yeah?"

"You're staggering. And you're pale."

The forest fell back into place around him, with its verdant fragrances and wild sounds teasing his senses. "I'm fine. Just lost in my thoughts." He gently pried her fingers loose and squeezed her hand before letting go.

As they trudged through the endless ocean of trees, her eyes bored into his back. No one spoke for a long while, soaking in the atmosphere and the vibrant greenery of Simynshin. Autumn had barely breathed across the foreign kingdom: only splashes of gold, red, and orange tinged the deciduous trees. A few aspens wore their fall crowns, their leaves clacking in the faintest draft.

"Hold a moment." Penn's voice broke the stillness.

Mikoneh turned in time to witness Minno collapse on the path face-first. Maya untied her herb pouch and darted to the gray boy's side. As she knelt, Minno lifted his head, eyes unfocused, complexion white. Dirt smudged the tip of his nose.

"I'm fine." His voice threaded off. He snapped his mouth closed, his eyes sliding shut. "It's merely that I've run out of energy."

Ter loped to the company gathered around Minno, one ear twitching as though it mused over a solution. He tapped a finger to his lips. "This won't do at all. Doubtless, we're being hunted, and the stone's magic is spent." His ear twitched again. "Perhaps..." He scanned the forest.

A shudder ran the length of Mikoneh's spine, and the slice on his chest burned with sharp icy pain, biting deep. He pressed his hand to the wound and sucked in a breath. Maya glanced up at him with a frown, but when he shook his head, she turned back to examine Minno.

The trees surrounding Mikoneh creaked and trembled.

Minno spoke. "I only need a few moments. My strength will come back shortly."

"Even so," Ter said, "I would feel better if we were closer to our goal. These woods are not free of Dark Mage tunnels."

The searing pain climbed Mikoneh's neck, stabbing into the back of his head like icicles. The wind was cold against his cheeks. He clenched his jaw and glanced upward, but he couldn't see the sky beyond the ceiling of leaves.

It's not a winter storm and you know it, he told himself.

Even so, his mind refused to settle on the most likely reason for his chills. He set his feet wider apart and tried to focus on Maya offering Minno a drink from Ter's waterskin.

Did the trees lean closer? Were they breathing?

He tugged against his shirt collar. Claws of panic raked over him, urging him to run—run away—run fast.

Don't give in. Hysteria pays nothing back.

He curled his hands into fists. The icicles stretched across his mind, darkening his vision.

Firebrand, where are you?

The words drifted across Mikoneh's mind, distant, barely audible, like the breath of winter—but his heart slammed against his ribs. He whirled, facing the looming, oppressive trees—seeking a face—a figure—anything to go along with the disembodied voice.

"What is it?" Penn shifted next to Mikoneh, cradling his broken arm in its makeshift sling.

Mikoneh searched every shadow in the forest. How could he explain? The voice couldn't be his imagination.

"It's all right, my boy." Ter came up on his other side. "Speak what you feel. Silence weaves a weighty chain."

Drawing a breath, Mikoneh let his mind ease back into a place of calm, of rationality. "I...heard a voice. In—in here." He tapped the side of his head.

"A stranger's voice?"

"...No." Mikoneh's muscles tautened. "Sathe's." He glanced at Ter, expecting concern or a knowing nod. His stomach clenched. He read alarm and a quiver of fear in those large blue eyes.

Ter whirled toward Minno. "Did Sathe get his blood?"

"Yes." Minno wiped a bead of water from the side of his mouth and lowered the waterskin. "Because that man"—he jabbed a finger at Mikoneh, offsetting his monotone—"is an idiot."

Mikoneh bristled, fists clenching tighter. "How, by all the blasted Nijaal, was I supposed to know that was a problem? I still don't understand."

Ter hopped closer. "May I see your eyes?"

Turning toward the strange child, Mikoneh held still,

letting the Ephe'ahn read his face, while panic mounted a new attack inside him, closing his throat.

"Hm." Ter's ears trembled. "You're still not awake yet. Not quite. That is something." The child let out a faint sigh, his ears perking up.

Mikoneh wrenched back. "What are you talking about? What *are* both of you? Why do the Mages want our blood?" He dragged a hand over his head, shoving back strands of his long, dark hair.

Don't panic. Stop panicking.

"All fair questions," Ter replied with a kind smile. "But they are not mine to answer. I'll not breech that confidence. Nor is this a wise place to speak. Let us seek shelter." He turned back to Mikoneh and something in that crystalline gaze soothed Mikoneh's rising anxiety like a salve over a burn. "Can you carry Minno upon your back? I think a fairy ring stands near."

Fairy rings. Mages. Elemental magic. Mikoneh might've truly gone mad.

He inhaled, bringing his mind back into a realm of logic where it balanced on a precarious peak. He moved to Minno's side, crouched, and stuck out his hands behind him. "Climb on."

"You jest."

Mikoneh scowled and glanced over his shoulder. "I don't often jest."

"That's true lately," Penn chimed in.

Ter spoke up in his mild, pleasant voice. "Please, Minno. We are a tad bit rushed."

Minno sighed with surprising vehemence. "Fine." He shifted, allowing Maya to help him climb onto Mikoneh's back and straddle his trunk.

Tucking his arms beneath Minno, Mikoneh rose and adjusted his balance against the boy's weight. "Okay. Let's go."

"This way." Ter's ears twitched, then he was off, discarding the forest trail for the denser foliage and darker shadows. He hopped over a broken branch whose leaves had curled and turned a brittle brown.

They walked in silence. The world closed back in around Mikoneh, needling at his nerves, whispering dreadful, voiceless warnings. The cut on his chest sharpened its bite, while his head dully throbbed.

Ignore it. Ignore it for now.

He lengthened his stride, hoping Ter would quicken his pace, but the woodelf slowed instead and halted before a circle of large spotted mushrooms. Did Mikoneh imagine they glowed a faint blue?

"Here we are." Ter turned to smile at the company. "We'll need permission—"

A tiny female figure popped into sight, about the height of Maya's hand from wrist to middle finger, with iridescent wings beating behind her. Mikoneh lurched back, his heart stuttering. She zipped toward him, and he retreated another step.

"Minno!" Her voice was tiny, clear, and high like a crystal chime. Long curls of blood-red hair twined down her shoulders, rippling as she hovered at Mikoneh's eye level. "Minno, you've returned!" She wore a filmy white gown layered like the petals of a flower. It sparkled with the tiniest gemstones Mikoneh had ever seen—not that he'd seen many back in Relvin Province.

The gray boy lifted his head, and his voice sounded more drained than flat. "Greetings, Cisharri."

"You look terrible, Minno." She tipped her head to one side. "Why do you always look so when you stumble back for a visit?"

Ter cleared his throat and widened his warm smile. "Sorry to interrupt, Lady Cisharri, but we need to enter your realm if that's possible. We're being hunted by Mages." His tones remained mild.

Cisharri turned toward him, her wings glimmering. "By all means, Master Ter. Forgive my rudeness." She waved her tiny hand, and the mushrooms glowed brighter. Then she zipped back to the circle and curtseyed. "Be welcome in the realm of the Moon Veil, travelers."

CHAPTER 9

WRESTLE WITH DRAGONS

"The second tragedy is that not all Mages turned Dark."

- From Athonen d'Ereth's *The Fall of Mages in the Age of Dragons*

As Ter stepped inside the fairy ring, the mushrooms grew brighter. Mikoneh followed, Maya staying close behind him. Glancing back, Mikoneh found Penn coming last, his eyes wide with wonder.

A thin veil of light rose around the company, engulfing them within a net of magic. As the veil closed above Mikoneh, a shiver tracked down his back and he whirled, glimpsing what might be a pair of human eyes within the forest. They glowed a vivid purple.

The veil of light flashed brighter, blinding Mikoneh, and he pinched his eyelids shut. The rush of the wind changed. The air's perfume filled with flowers. He pried his eyes open and stared into a brighter, moonlit version of the same forest—

though this realm was bursting with blossoms, like the world had slipped forward into springtime at night.

"It's so beautiful," Maya whispered.

"Put me down," Minno said. "I can stand."

Mikoneh crouched to let Minno slide from his back to the boy's feet, then Mikoneh rotated his spine, welcoming the relief of having his burden removed.

Cisharri flitted into view, cupping both hands to her mouth. "Minno has come, everyone! Minno is back!"

A breeze lifted, and a host of tiny, winged women in gauzy flower-petal gowns popped out of the air and fluttered forth to swarm Minno. Their hair varied from palest white to deepest black, with every color of the rainbow in-between amongst them. Even in the moonlight, every color was bright as though the sun shone upon it.

The sparkling beauties festooned Minno, fawning over him. Two fairies claimed his shoulders, and they nestled against his cheeks, kissing him over and over. Minno stood there, unruffled. Unperturbed. A portrait of non-reaction.

Odd child. Either way, Mikoneh was glad they weren't swarming *him*.

"Hello there," chimed a new voice, deeper than the other bell-like tones.

Mikoneh whirled to find a male fairy hovering close to Maya. He wore gauzy robes, and his hair was a fiery red-orange tone. The fairy bowed to Maya and lifted his lips in a winsome smile.

"Welcome to the Moon Veil, my lady."

Mikoneh caught his twin's wrist and tugged her away from the fairy.

Maya stumbled to his side with a startled laugh. "Relax," she whispered. "He won't woo me, even with that lovely hair. I prefer tall men." Her eyes flitted to Penn, then away before the viscount noticed. Not that he seemed to notice anything beyond the host of fairies, gaze riveted, jaw slack. It might have been comical, except that Mikoneh related all too well to his friend's reaction.

"This is madness," he muttered.

"It's wonderful, though," Maya said.

Leave it to her to find the silver lining.

Ter hopped away from Minno's admirers and turned to the male fairy. "Hail, Vlest. Pray, where is Denroch?"

The winsome smile died, and the fiery-haired fairy slouched his shoulders. "Alas, he was attacked by Mages in the North. Mivena brought him hither. We pray mightily to the spirits that he will recover. He received a Limaia's blessing, which has sustained him so far."

Mikoneh chewed on the strange words and titles, trying to ingest them, to understand them. He'd thought his parents had prepared him for the world, but this was too foreign and too much all at once.

"Oh, Mikoneh, *look*." Maya dug her nails into his arm.

He turned with her to find a river close by, shimmering like millions of gemstones lay at its bottom. An impulse overcame his caution, and he moved toward the flowing water, taking his willing twin with him. Together they reached the bank, and stared into the depths, where gemstones of every color *did* wink up at them. A peculiar sense of awe filled Mikoneh's chest. He'd never put much stock in wealth, but these gems were beautiful. Breathtaking. The ice in his blood and around the scratch on his neck thawed by several degrees.

He knelt beside the water, eager to grab up a handful. A strange, enthralling hunger filled him. His fingers slid through the cool, rushing current, plunging into the depths until he closed a fist over a cluster of gems. Maya leaned close. He pulled the precious stones free of the river, water spilling from his hand. He opened his palm and stared at the glittering treasure.

Maya sucked in a breath, reaching her fingers tentatively toward the gems. "They're..."

"Flawless." He nodded. How he knew that, how he appreciated each perfect cut, each facet and sparkle, he couldn't guess. Something like a whisper from his soul told him, and he trusted that instinct like he trusted all his parents had taught him. Implicitly...

A chorus of laughter brought Mikoneh's head around, his cheeks warming. A dozen or more fairies hovered at his back, murmuring among themselves, their wings casting prisms across the water in the bright moonlight. The backdrop of the forest sang with color, splashes of pinks, whites, yellows, and purples against vibrant greens.

"Does my lord like our treasure?" The tiny fairy who spoke broke into fresh peals of laughter.

His cheeks blazed hotter, and he started to tip his hand, intending to drop the gems into the river, but his body stalled. His hand wouldn't relinquish the sparkling beauties. Setting his teeth, he jerked his hand, and the gems spilled back into the river, sending droplets of water flying.

Maya squeaked and jolted toward the fallen treasure but stopped herself at the last breath. She shook her head as though to clear it. Turning, she touched her fingers to her temple and lifted her lips in a cautious smile. "I'm not sure what came over me."

"Or me," he grunted. "Is it cursed or something?"

"Oh, no," said Ter, stepping through the flock of fairies. "Master Penn here is unaffected because his blood is Oceanean. Yours is not."

Penn and Minno strode at his back, the viscount holding

his sling with a faint grimace, the gray boy adorned with fairies sitting on his head like a crown of flowers.

Maya stood up and brushed her skirts free of petals and dirt. "Our parents traveled a great deal when we were too small to remember. They never told us where they first hailed from. Was it Simynshin? We've always suspected that."

Mikoneh straightened up. "No, Maya. I think we're Rokahnian. How else would Fa and Mama have worked so closely with the Dragon King?"

Her gold eyes widened. "I'd never considered." She bit her lower lip. "Are we Rokahnian, Ter?"

The woodelf nodded. "Indeed, you are."

Somehow, that felt right, though Mikoneh hadn't considered the possibility before now. He'd always been fascinated by those living on the neighboring island kingdom. Fa had once pointed out that the southwestern country was shaped like a sleeping dragon, which most folk saw as a warning to any who considered invading. One didn't wrestle with dragons, mythical or not, metaphorical or not.

"Strange they never told us," Maya said, tapping a knuckle to her chin. "They were careful with their words but never secretive."

Threads of doubt tangled in Mikoneh's head. He'd always trusted them...

They had their reasons, no matter what. Don't doubt that for a moment, you dunce.

Ter pressed a finger to his long, pointed ear, clearing his throat. "The fairies have agreed to give us sanctuary while we recover our strength. They will also give us supplies."

Penn snorted. "We may need something in a larger size than anything they use."

A nearby fairy chortled. "Fear not, handsome one. We are not without human offerings."

That sounded more foreboding than helpful, but Mikoneh held his tongue.

"You can bathe and sleep in the great oak," said a familiar, bell-like voice. Mikoneh scanned the air until he spotted Cisharri flitting closer.

"We thank you for your hospitality," Maya said, dipping into a curtsy.

The cluster of fairies tittered, but it didn't sound malicious.

"We would love for the twins to stay forever," one fairy piped up.

"Oh, yes, please! We are ever so fond of dra—"

"Enough," said Ter, batting the nearest fairy away with a waving hand. "We are weary, hungry, and in need of quiet, if you please."

The golden-haired fairy harrumphed while Cisharri darted toward a thick, looming oak. "This way," she said. "Come along." She lit upon Minno's shoulder and planted a kiss on his jaw. "Lead us, please."

Minno moved toward the oak, his steps slow and careful. He might have found his feet again, but he still looked spent. Dark shadows hung below his gray eyes, and his skin was a shade too pale.

He's that way because he saved me.

From what fate, Mikoneh didn't know—and he didn't think he wanted to find out.

Doesn't matter. Ask what you can. Learn what you must. Even if you don't like it.

As Mikoneh passed the smaller trees, he lifted his gaze to the towering oak. His step faltered, but he corrected himself and moved faster, taking in the elegant human-sized house carved into the stretching branches as though it had grown that way. Except that was impossible. The tall five-story structure had windows and a distinct door at the top of twining stairs. Soft yellow light effused from the windows as though a fire flickered within, but that would be absurd.

Maya pressed her hands together before her lips, eyes kindled with light. "It's so lovely."

A nearby fairy flitted closer to the young woman. "We *knew* you had excellent taste."

Maya laughed, shaking her head. "If I were blind, I'd still *feel* the magic of this place. It's...it's beyond words."

The fairies fluted out more laughter, and several zipped up the stairs to pull the door open. "Come in. Come see. We prepared a bath!"

Maya rushed up the steps ahead of Minno, and Mikoneh nearly raced after her, but he stopped himself and took the stairs in his turn. He needed to stop being so overprotective. She'd been well for months now, and Ter had brought them to the Moon Veil because it was safe. No Dark Mage or agent of Lord Drayve would find them in such a place.

He entered the treehouse and stared at the intricate, carved interior. Polished oak surfaces gleamed around him, from walls and ceiling to furniture carved from the thick boughs. A delicate stairway led up in a spiral to the next story, and he caught a glimpse of Maya's hair fluttering over the stair's banister before she vanished above.

He snorted. "Please forgive my twin. She doesn't mean to be rude—she just gets excited."

Cisharri chuckled. "No offense is taken, my lord. We're delighted with her."

He couldn't quite hide his smile. Most people were quickly smitten with his twin. While she had no idea how lithe and lovely she was—with her dark hair, bright golden eyes rimmed with dark lashes, and full lips wearing a genuine smile—her kindness and compassion won people over more than her physical qualities. She'd always had a knack for healing others, with herbs and words alike. Mikoneh would readily admit to anyone that he was proud of her, perhaps now more than ever, since she'd crawled back from a dark, broken place.

"Stay in whichever of the rooms you like," a fairy told Ter. "The bath is in that room there. We'll bring food shortly."

"We thank you heartily," Ter replied with a bow of his head.

Mikoneh moved toward a chair, bones too heavy to think of exploring the interior of the treehouse. He'd let his twin tell him everything with her usual enthusiasm. He intended to spend the last of his energy on the questions he needed to have answered, while he waited for his turn in the bath.

Slumping down on the polished oak chair, he was impressed by its comfort. The wood felt strangely plush and soft like velvet. His muscles loosened until they ached with relief. His eyelids drooped, and the room fell away, a distant, unimportant thing.

Someone was whispering. "We should let him rest until morning. I suspect the blood Sathe stole is taking its toll."

Darkness shut out the soft, warm light. Mikoneh tried to peel his eyes open, but his mind spun in a slow whirlpool, taking him with it. When had he last slept? In Drayve's dungeon, wasn't it? Two days ago, maybe longer.

His head fell forward, and the last of his consciousness snuffed out like a weak candle flame.

CHAPTER 10

THE MUSIC OF WIND

"A handful of Light Mages, as we must now call them, defied their queen after the king's heartbreaking death. Alas, their defiance ended in a worse fate than the lesser Mages now slumbering in their foul warrens beneath the ground."

- From Athonen d'Ereth's *The Fall of Mages in the Age of Dragons*

Following a hot bath, Maya found a small balcony on the topmost level of the treehouse. Though she hadn't slept in two days, her mind was too replete with wonder and questions to seek out slumber. Fairies. Honest to glory fairies, here, in a moonlit realm that stretched across a thick forest mirroring Simynshin in springtime.

She leaned over the balustrade, drinking in the warm night air, basking in the stillness and the charge of power on the wind. The breeze almost seemed to whisper to her, divulging the charming secrets of the Moon Veil. Did she imagine the scent of smoking ham, roasted nuts, and succulent squashes?

Music swelled on the air, and the wind tugged on her drying tresses. She turned her attention from the branches to the path she'd recently walked with her companions. There. A parade of fairies flew toward the treehouse, guiding enormous platters of food before them, perhaps hovering by magic strings, or by fairies hidden beneath the platters. Their soft music seemed to charge the air more, and fingers of wind raked across Maya's locks, untangling them.

She turned from the balustrade to enter the treehouse, but a faint, discordant note fluted over the air, and she turned back, staring out into the forest. All seemed quiet, but her stomach tightened.

"What is it?" she whispered.

'Hunters. Coming. 'Ware.'

Startled, she glanced around for a fairy, but the voice hadn't been bell-like or small.

"Where are you?" she asked.

'Here. There. All places.'

The wind tugged on her hair until she dragged her locks behind her. She searched the night sky beneath the large moon. "*What* are you?"

Was the wind laughing? *'We are what we are. What are you?'*

She tensed. "Are you the wind?"

'We are of wind, over wind, within wind.' Gales of laughter roared through her ears.

"I'm sorry." She clutched her sleeve tight. "I don't understand magic."

'But you are *magic. Of. Over. Within.'*

"I don't..." She inhaled. "Are you invisible?"

'*You cannot yet see?*' The flute-like voice sounded disappointed. '*Open your eyes. Open them. Then you will see...*'

Maya shook her head. "I'm so sorry. I don't know how to open magical eyes. I'm human, you see."

The wind howled with laughter again. '*Human, she says. Human!*'

'*Not human.*'

'*More. Much more.*'

'*Much deeper.*'

'*Much bigger.*'

Maya glanced in every direction, seeking a source for the chorus of mocking voices. Her heart clambered in her chest.

"I don't underst—" She broke off as boots thudded in the room adjacent to the small balcony. Turning around, she found Penn approaching. Exhaling a low breath, she ran toward him to escape the voices. "I assume you're here to tell me the food has arrived?"

He blinked. "Ah, you must've seen from there. Yes, and it's quite the feast."

"Well." She threaded her hand around his good arm and pulled close, glad of his warmth and familiarity. His pleasant fragrance was frosted by the clean scent of fresh lavender soap. "Shall we go down?"

"Let's. Your brother's still asleep. I was going to wake him after I got out of the bath, but he looks so peaceful." Penn started to tug her past an empty bed covered in gossamer blankets, toward the room's far door, but he paused. "You're trembling, Maya. Are you—"

"Fine," she said over her humming nerves. "Just tired, and a little faint with hunger. When was the last time we ate, do you suppose?" She didn't know whether to tell Penn what she'd heard, a little afraid that her mind was making things up.

He guided her toward the door. "That trapper's burrow, I think."

Maya didn't risk a final glance at the balcony, glad that Penn guided her into the hallway and shut the door. They took the spiral staircase slowly, Maya in the lead at Penn's quiet insistence. The aroma of food wafted over her, easing her tension, until she could almost dismiss the disembodied voices—

She halted. Except, hadn't they been trying to warn her about something?

Think, Maya! She tried to push down her exhaustion. *It felt urgent. And Mikoneh recently claimed he could hear voices, too. We can't both be crazy.*

Beware of hunters. Did they mean the Mages?

Penn leaned in close to meet her gaze. "Maya?"

She caught her lip between her teeth. "Something strange happened to me above. I don't know quite how to explain."

"Should we wake Mikoneh?" His voice, so gentle, so kind, soothed Maya's fears better than the scent of food.

She shook her head. "No, let's eat. When he wakes up, I'll explain. It's rare he lets himself sleep before anyone else."

The viscount nodded and took her arm again, conducting her into the front room where a table had been conjured up—perhaps literally—and spread with an assortment of foods that made Maya's mouth water.

Beyond the table, Mikoneh was curled up on a chair. A pale green, diaphanous blanket had been placed around his shoulders. The troubles of the past few weeks had vanished from his slumbering brow, and he looked more like his old self, before the woes of rebellion and the loss of their parents.

Maya sat in the delicate wooden chair Penn pulled out for her and heaped her plate with a variety of meats, squashes, and fruits. Each bite melted in her mouth, and her muscles eased.

The spices were unique, and the sauces were divine. If only she could cook like this!

She ate more than she should before she set aside her fork and sat back with an appreciative sigh. Penn scraped his plate clean, too.

Rejuvenated, Maya glanced around. "Where are Ter and Minno?"

Penn dabbed his mouth with a cloth napkin and shoved his empty plate back. "The fairies insisted Minno go with them somewhere, to a—a Moonbeam March, I think they called it. Ter hopped off alone after that, not saying a word. Food arrived just afterward."

She nodded, turning her gaze back to her twin. His long blue-black hair sprawled across his shoulders, free of its tieback, like some admiring fairy had laid it that way on purpose. In the soft light, it gleamed, the blue highlights prominent.

"Penn."

"Yes, Maya?"

She twisted back to face him. "What do we do from here? I mean, I know we'll head for the Rokahn war camp since that's what Fa wanted. But we've lost our home, our cause, and our freedom. We can't go back to Oceana. Yet..."

Penn sat still, waiting with his infinite patience.

With her fork, she pushed ham juices across her empty plate. "Mikoneh can't be aimless. It's outside his character. He'll need a new cause, and I'm...worried."

Penn's palm fell over her hand, his strong fingers curling tight around hers. "I understand. But I think you're worried about the wrong thing. Mikoneh doesn't see his cause as lost, not really. He'll wish to return to Oceana, if not now, then someday. He'll not rest until Drayve meets justice. Just wait and see."

"But our army is gone."

He nodded. "Yeah, which means Mikoneh will need to raise a new one."

She sucked in a breath. "Do you think he'll aim to elevate himself in the Dragon King's army, and eventually win the right to march on Drayve?"

"It's a strong possibility." Penn shrugged. "I've considered it myself, and your twin is always five steps ahead of me." He tilted his head, and long, blond strands of hair fell into his chocolate eyes. "He'll do what he feels is right, no matter what. But I promise I'll do what I can to protect him." His mouth quirked. "It's not much comfort, but—"

"Don't." She cupped her other hand over his knuckles. "It's plenty, Penn. Don't belittle your worth—to both of us. We're lucky to count you as our friend." She glanced around the room. "Especially now, when we're so alone and far from home."

"I'll never desert you, Maya," he whispered.

Warmth crept up her cheeks, and she turned her eyes away, seeking Mikoneh. She couldn't meet Penn's gaze. He always, always said such things, planting false hope in her heart, but she wouldn't let the roots take. She wouldn't dare. He saw her only as a friend, nothing more.

"Thank you, Penn. We both know it." Slipping her hand from his grasp, she stood, scooting back her chair. "We really need to sleep, though my stomach's rather full." She grimaced. "I think my eyelids are winning out despite my best efforts."

Penn rose from his chair. "There are several beds. Pick whichever you please. I suppose we should leave Mikoneh here, though he'd no doubt prefer a bed."

"He'll be fine." Maya risked turning back to meet Penn's eyes as the heat ebbed from her face. "He can sleep just about anywhere when he's tired enough."

"True. Once I found him dangling upside-down from the

side of his cot." He glanced toward the stairs. "Go on up. I'll just…" He glanced around. "Well, I'd put out the lights, but I can't seem to find their source."

"Magic," she laughed.

"Right. Magic." Penn shook his head. "I tried for years to set aside my childhood daydreams to face manhood, only to find out the two intersect."

She shrugged, dragging a lock of hair over her pointed ear. "Your childhood isn't for nothing, you know." She stifled a yawn. "Well, I'm off. Goodnight." Something tugged at her mind, but weariness pulled her toward sleep. The burdens of the day dimmed and fell out of reach. Whatever nagging thoughts could wait.

Penn's voice followed her up the stairs. "Sleep well, Maya."

INTERLUDE I

EMERALD-GREEN EYES

"In her eyes I found the world."

- From the Corpse Poet's 22nd Sonnet

THE WOODS WERE TINGED BLUE. Ancient trees stood in watchful reverence as he passed beneath them. The wide-standing beech trees reached toward each other, their boughs tangled above him. At his feet, ripples cascaded along the watery path he trod, his feet staying above the glowing water's surface as though it were solid. Bluebells and delicate white flowers he had no name for lined the pathway, adding to the hues of blue that shone across the twilight air.

The soft splash of water turned him around. A figure approached, cloaked in white, cowl pulled low over a hidden face.

He stopped and waited, a smile tugging at his lips. "There you are."

The figure lifted its head, and a flash of emerald-green eyes sparkled out at him.

"I've been here all along," said a soft, familiar voice. "I'll be here until you come in truth."

Something snapped in a distant tree, and the flutter of startled birds broke the stillness.

He turned toward the noise. The white-clad figure did likewise, then the emerald eyes danced back to his face.

"Something stalks you. Awaken, Mikoneh."

CHAPTER 11

DANCING LIKE EMBERS

"There was no trace of the Light Mages remaining. Not even a bone or a smear upon the ground. Nothing is known of their families either."

- From Athonen d'Ereth's *The Fall of Mages in the Age of Dragons*

Mikoneh's eyes snapped open. He sat up, heart clattering in his ears. The stillness around him was palpable. A sleek blanket slipped from his shoulders to the polished oak floor before his seat.

Something was wrong.

His dream. The warning.

He could barely remember it—but it left him unsettled. His hand fell to his hip where Fa's sword usually hung, and his chest throbbed. Gone, perhaps forever. That couldn't matter right now. He stood up, legs unsteady beneath him. Checking his surroundings, he reoriented himself. Fairy ring. Treehouse. *Mages.*

He trotted to a window near the front door. The forest had shifted from a bright blue moonlit glow to a blazing amber hue. Horror lifted Mikoneh's fine hairs. His flesh prickled.

A forest fire.

He darted around a table where tureens of food sat, partially eaten. "Maya! Penn!"

No one answered.

"May—"

The front door crashed open. He whirled to find Minno standing like a gray cutout against the amber light.

"Fire." Minno's voice was soft and low.

"I know." Mikoneh turned back to the stairs. "Maya! Penn!"

Doors above swung open, and feet stamped to the spiraling staircase. "What is it?" Penn yelled.

"Forest fire. Get Maya."

"I'm here!" called his twin.

"We need to go!" Mikoneh leaned against the stair railing.

"Just one moment." The soft pad of Maya's feet faded off. A few breaths later, she and Penn thundered down the steps and came into view, both fully dressed, clutching their few belongings. They must've barely gone to bed moments before Mikoneh woke up.

"What about Ter?" Maya asked.

Minno slipped up next to Mikoneh without a sound. "He asked me to come here. We must head southwest. He'll meet us soon."

Mikoneh caught up the gossamer blanket he'd dropped and rolled it into a lump. He could get it wet and wrap it around Maya if need be. "Let's go."

Maya snatched up a few small fruits from the table and stuffed them into her dress pockets as they moved toward the front door on Minno's heels. Since the gray boy knew more about the Moon Veil than any of the others, Mikoneh let him lead out. They descended the tree's front steps in quick succession, and Minno turned southwest at the bottom, not sparing a glance at the fiery sky.

"What about the fairies?" Maya whispered.

"They'll be fine, surely," Penn answered. "They can fly."

"But their homes." The pain in her words sent a fresh twinge through Mikoneh's chest. The twins knew the devastation of losing everything to fire too well. Everything except each other—and for a while, even that.

Mikoneh reached his hand back, keeping his eyes forward. Maya's fingers slipped between his. He squeezed, and she squeezed back. Their steps never slowed.

A distant roar rolled closer, all too familiar, sending flashes of memory across Mikoneh's mind. Violet flames. Cold snow. Silence from the cottage where Drayve's men had anticipated screams.

And afterward—ashes. Two huddled corpses locked in chains.

He pinched his eyes shut, letting his other senses guide his feet.

Don't dwell on it. Focus.

Minno plunged into a denser part of the old forest. The air wafted with the fragrance of moss and strange flowers. Shadows drew patterns across the patches of moonlight along the narrowing path.

Mikoneh eyed the gray boy's back. "Have you recovered?"

Minno didn't miss a step as he glanced over his shoulder. "Enough for now. I merely overextended my magic. Unless we must make another daring escape, I'll be fine." His eyes narrowed. "Just don't be stupid, and we'll all be fine."

"I definitely don't plan on getting caught."

"Good." Minno turned back around.

They moved deeper into the trees, and the glow of the sky fell away under the thick boughs hanging close to Mikoneh's head. Leaves brushed his hair.

"Do you think the fire was caused by Mages?" asked Penn.

"Seems likely," Mikoneh said.

"It's the only explanation," Minno piped up. "Fairies, as a rule, don't cause forest fires." As he glanced behind him again, his eyes caught the moonlight. "Of course, a Fire Elementalist could battle the flames and save the Moon Veil—if he were adept."

Mikoneh's faint grimace fell into a scowl. "Meaning me?"

"No. I said *adept.*"

Minno scraped on Mikoneh's nerves like flint on steel. Sparks of temper stirred within Mikoneh's chest, but a squeeze of Maya's fingers stilled him.

"You could try," she whispered.

His muscles tightened. He stopped walking, forcing everyone to halt. Turning to his twin, he silently begged her not to ask that of him. He couldn't wield fire, not again, not even in trying to suppress it. Not after what it had robbed from them.

She held his gaze steadily. A faint smile touched her lips, compassionate but faith-filled. Somehow, she'd come to believe he could do anything, anything at all, if he only tried his best.

This is beyond me. Please, Maya.

She squeezed his fingers again. "If you could've saved them, you would've done anything—no matter what." Her eyes flicked toward the far-off forest fire. "What would Fa do?"

Those words cut deep. As children, the twins had always used them to keep the other in check in a moment of wrath or mischief. Usually, Mikoneh was the one to ask, reining in his sister's impulses.

He inhaled, gently extracted his hand from his twin's, then dashed back the way they'd come. He didn't know how to calm a forest fire. He had no idea how to summon fire spirits like those he'd seen in Bone Cove. All he could do was try—because Fa would. Because it was the right thing to do.

He jumped over a root, conquering the trail fast. The amber glow appeared above the thinning tree boughs. Adrenaline seared his veins, pushing him onward. Fire. Fire spirits. Elementalist. He barely understood anything anymore, but his fingertips prickled like they had on the execution platform.

Did he imagine tiny fiery figures dancing like embers across the air before him?

No, this is real. You aren't crazy.

He drew a breath. The trees fell away at the borders of the clearing near the oak treehouse. Tongues of fire raged above the forest, coughing up sparks and ashes, while animals darted from the heart of the conflagration. Birds beat against the orange-soaked sky. Rabbits dove into the sinuous river. A buck leapt over a fallen log, then stopped to stare at Mikoneh, its eyes bright in the firelight. One ear twitched, then the deer dipped its antlered head as though it bowed to him. White tail flicking, it darted into the dark trees opposite the growing blaze.

Shaking himself, Mikoneh turned toward his adversary. Flames roared in his sharp ears. Smoke scarred the stars, blotting out the diamond glow.

He placed his legs wide apart. Wispy fire spirits floated toward him. Real, not imagined.

How do I do this?

These weren't like the violet flames that had consumed his cottage. Those had burned high and cold—colder than winter. This was a bright hot blaze—devouring, destroying—but not Magery.

A fire spirit landed on his shoulder, its form almost human, wings of flame fluttering on its back.

"Help me, please," he whispered.

The spirit nodded, and its shape flickered into a reptilian creature with spikes along its back and two horns on its head. A dragon. Mikoneh recognized the mythical beast straight away. He'd seen tapestries depicting the mighty creatures at the annual fairs in Relvin Province.

The fire spirit, longer and slenderer than the fairies, flickered back into a humanoid shape. It lifted its hands. Flames dripped from its tiny fingers like sparking liquid.

'Command,' it crackled. *'We will obey.'*

Sucking in air, Mikoneh nodded. "Please. Tame the fire."

The spirit hopped from his shoulder and rode the wind, up and up. Other fire spirits rose toward the first, floating like hundreds of lanterns unleashed into the skies above the wildfire. They twirled around the first spirit, turning into a wreath of flame. Under their power, the forest fire pulled inward, drawing away from the trees, rolling into itself, shrinking to a single pillar that lifted toward the fire spirits mustered above.

Mesmerized, Mikoneh held his breath—until a voice broke across his mind like a thunderclap in the dead of a dark winter night.

That's right, Firebrand. Tame the blaze. Prove your heritage.

Invisible fingers of dread seized him like ice crusting his bones. Breath exploded from his lungs in a plume visible before his mouth, as though the mild spring night, charged with hot fire, had turned into a frigid snowscape.

His soul shuddered. His eyes searched the shadows cast by the dying flames as they shrank, shrank, shrank under the spirits' direction.

You can't escape me, Firebrand.

The icy fingers dug deeper, biting, ripping. Mikoneh's lungs hitched.

We are destined for greatness, you and I. Find my Revenant. Allow him to bring you to me, Firebrand. Let us begin our work!

The ice climbed up his face, crackling against his flesh. His breath plumed thicker on the air, and his body trembled with a cold so deep it almost burned. He tried to move. Tried to call out. The forest fire was almost extinguished. The fire spirits continued their slow dance, turning, quieting the flames beneath them. Smoke clung to the charred forest surrounding them, and the trees stood like black markers for all the lives that had ended in the frenzy.

No sign of fairies. No hint of Ter.

No one to help Mikoneh escape the prison of ice encasing his flesh, bones, and soul.

He ground his teeth. *Am I a Fire Elementalist or not?* His jaw was heavy with cold. He couldn't find his voice. *Not acceptable, Mikoneh,* he told himself. *Speak!*

He wrenched his lips apart. "Come to me!"

The fire spirits wheeling above didn't so much as slow, yet fresh fire obeyed his summons, bursting over him, rolling across his frame and clothes and hair. The new fire spirits cackled with laughter, banishing the chill all at once, warming him through.

He slumped to his knees, sweat dripping from his chin. His frame continued shaking. The fire engulfing him vanished as though it had never filled him up.

Someone shouted nearby, and the crunch of running footsteps followed. He didn't have the strength to lift his head, but his gut assured him that his twin approached. A moment later, she flung herself down beside him.

"Are you all right?" She caught his chin and dragged his head around until their gold eyes met.

He tried a smile, but it crooked in his weariness. "Not really." He didn't have the energy to lie.

She let out a breath and dropped her forehead to his shoulder. "You did it, though. You extinguished the fire by yourself."

His eyes slid to the slowly wheeling spirits. "Not quite alone."

She pulled back to search his face. "You're shaking like you have a fever."

"He may just," said Minno. "That was a lot of energy to use all at once, and only his second time wielding flames properly. Early on, most Elementalists become ill by pushing themselves."

Something in the gray boy's words caught in Mikoneh's mind. He turned a narrow stare on Minno who stood beside Penn a few paces off. "How did you know that?"

"Know what?" Minno blinked like an owl.

"About me wielding fire once before. Who are you? Why did the Mages capture you?"

The boy considered him for a long moment. "That's complicated." He shrugged. "And irrelevant. We must still leave. Whoever set fire to the Moon Veil is your enemy and still at large—and that aside, Ter intends to meet us in the southwest wood."

He's right. We need to go. Mikoneh tried to stand, but halfway to his feet, he collapsed. Pebbles dug into his trousers.

"He can't walk." Maya's voice was firm. "If only we hadn't been forced to leave our horses behind, poor things."

It *was* lamentable. Hopefully the horses had had the good

sense to leave the caverns and find their way to a more fertile farm than what Relvin Province offered. It would be a pity if Lord Drayve got his black stallion back.

"Far too late to worry about that now," Minno said. "Fairies have few uses for beasts of burden, so don't bother asking for help from them."

"Drat, that was my next plan." Maya's tones carried a trace of sarcasm. She stooped to brush her fingers through Mikoneh's hair. "Don't worry. Penn and I will think of something."

He nodded faintly, distracted by the sensation of floating that had settled over him. The creak of the nearby trees, the rubbing of branches, the odor of woodsmoke and wilted verdure—it all sank into his weary bones. A faint mist gathered around him, tinting the world blue, but he couldn't be sure if it was only his tired eyes that conjured it.

Maya was speaking with Penn, their tones quiet. Did Penn offer to carry Mikoneh? With a broken arm?

Not gonna happen.

Minno heaved a sigh. "It seems there is only one thing for it." He motioned to the other two, beckoning them to stand beside Mikoneh. They heeded him, both looking wary and anxious.

"Clasp hands," Minno said. "You, touch your brother's head with your free hand."

Maya obeyed, while Minno pinched the hem of Penn's tunic. The gray boy slid his boot over to touch its toe to Mikoneh's leg. Something pulsed out from Minno. Magic. It must be.

The world turned aqua-blue, then tipped sidelong, before righting itself. Mikoneh slumped onto his side, head pounding. Lying in a soft bed of wild grass, he stared askew at a sight grander than any he'd ever seen.

Ruins stretched before him, tall, stately, overgrown with vines and redwoods. Once, in a long-ago age, this must've been a kingdom unto itself. The pale pink stone seemed to be lit from within, as though it held a secret flame of gold.

Magic. A world filled with magic. The twins' lives would truly never be the same.

CHAPTER 12

THE CITADEL OF HYANYTHON

"The Keeper of Memory will not divulge the fate of those brave Light Mages, but the look in his eye is enough to confirm what I feel in my heart. Their suffering is not over."

- From Athonen d'Ereth's *The Fall of Mages in the Age of Dragons*

Gritting his teeth, Mikoneh managed to sit up. His body felt leaden. His twin knelt in the tall grass beside him to let him prop himself against her.

"Thanks," he whispered.

She offered him a bright smile, then turned her gaze toward the ruinous city tiered before them among the wild trees. "Where are we, Minno?"

"The Citadel of Hyanython," Minno said. "Hopefully, Ter will find us here—though it's not a direct path to the Rokahn war camp."

"Why bring us here?" Penn asked.

"Close Void transportation is imprecise," Minno said. "Had I tried to take us anywhere that is less of a beacon, we might have ended up in the deep ocean, and you would be drowning right now. Certainly, had I tried to aim for Owenekiras Rokahn's camp—which is a very great distance from the Moon Veil and has no direct opening—we would have been magically diverted to a beacon closer and stronger— and much worse than here. Possibly TeshRelle itself."

Maya tensed. Penn paled.

Mikoneh started to scoff but stopped himself.

TeshRelle was a place of horrors, and until now, a land he'd considered a legend. A place he, Maya, and the village children near their home had included in their childhood games of knights and maidens. The villain always dwelt in the ruins of TeshRelle.

Better not assume anything anymore. You obviously know a lot less than you ever thought.

"What's Void transportation?" Penn asked, though his eyes roved over every detail of Hyanython.

"You want a magic lesson?" Minno tipped his head. "*Now?*"

"Are we in a rush?" asked Penn. "I thought we had to wait for Ter, and Mikoneh can't readily move."

The gray boy's eyes slid to Mikoneh. He huffed out a sigh. "Let's enter the ruins first. We're exposed out here. Mages are everywhere these days."

Maya shifted to face the boy. "Are the ruins safe?"

"Safer than out here," Minno said. "So long as we don't disturb the dead. I assume you can support your twin?" He started for the glittering buildings without them.

Maya laughed and helped Mikoneh to his wavering feet. "He's a rather presumptuous child, isn't he?"

"I think you mean rude," Penn said, though he spoke without malice. "Still, we owe him a great deal."

Her smile weakened. "I wonder what he wants. Why is he staying with us? He'd be safer on his own, wouldn't he?"

"Possibly not," Mikoneh said. "He was Sathe's captive, too, don't forget." Though Mikoneh still didn't understand how or why Minno had been so, considering he'd easily helped them to escape. Minno was obviously very powerful.

Penn fingered his sling. "We'd better catch up to him. I'd hate to get lost in a place this huge."

As they followed the gray boy—Mikoneh leaning heavily on both his twin and his friend—he studied the grandeur of the ruined citadel above a massive crumbling wall and two shattered gates. Beyond the fallen fortification, huge columns of glittering pink stone veined with gold lined a road paved with similar stone unlike anything Mikoneh had ever seen. The buildings themselves were ornate, massive, and domed with gold. Overgrown vines clung to the lighted stone walls.

"What happened to the citadel?" Penn asked when they drew closer to Minno within the stronghold.

"It fell."

"I assumed as much," Penn said patiently. "But how? It looks so...mighty."

Minno halted, then turned to face him with a flat expression. "So is Mage magic."

"Mages did this?" Penn's face lost its color. "And that's our enemy? How can we beat them?"

"Alone, you can't." Minno shrugged. "Why do you think Ter wants to get you to Owenekiras Rokahn? He's your best hope, especially with Sathe having some of your friend's blood." His gray eyes flicked to Mikoneh. "Even the Dragon King will have some difficulty breaking that connection. You may be doomed."

Heat climbed Mikoneh's face. He scowled to hide the flood of fear that swept through him. "I didn't know how to fend him off. We don't even know what he was after."

Minno gave his slow blink. "He's a Dark Mage of the higher echelons—as evidenced by him still wearing his skin—and he's hunting you. Do you really need to know particulars? I expected you to be a little brighter than you are. That's unfortunate, but I suppose you can't help it."

The heat scorched Mikoneh's insides. "You really aren't a pleasant person, you know that?"

"Noticed, did you? At least you're not a complete idiot. Owenekiras will be relieved to know it. We should keep moving." Minno pivoted in a graceful motion and started up the wide, paved street.

"What's his problem?" muttered Mikoneh.

"I think he's trying to keep his distance," Maya whispered. "He seems to be doing it on purpose."

"If you say so." Dizziness painted spots before his vision, and Mikoneh stumbled over his own feet. "Wherever we're going, I hope we get there fast. I..." He shivered. "I need to rest."

"You're burning up." She adjusted his arm around her neck. "I can feel it through your sleeve. Just try to keep walking. Nothing else."

He concentrated on his feet; one, then the other. Repeat. Each motion jolted through him like he stomped along the road. Sweat trickled down his back. Waves of ice and fire took turns coiling through his veins.

At last, Minno turned a corner, entering a shorter street that widened into a circle before a grand estate made of the same glowing pink stone, topped by a dome of gold and jewels that winked and shone beneath a bright setting moon.

"How long has Hyanython been empty?" asked Penn.

"Twenty thousand years," Minno answered. "Since the end of the Age of Dragons. This was one of the last forest strongholds on the main continent to stand against a Dread Mage called Suld. Through the sacrifice of its denizens, and that of others, he was ultimately sealed in TeshRelle." The boy's step faltered. "I've heard rumors he's escaped, but there may be nothing to them. Then again, if Sathe is active, it might be true. Suld and Sathe are brothers."

Shivers stampeded up Mikoneh's spine, pinching his shoulder blades. One creature like Sathe was more than enough. Another such Mage—but capable of wiping out a citadel—was more than he dared to imagine.

Dare or not, you can't bury your head in clay.

Minno moved down the side street, heading for the looming estate. The others kept up as well as they could, though Mikoneh knew he was burdening them. He tried to take his own weight several times, but his legs had turned to straw. When he tried a third time, Maya emitted a low growl. He stopped trying to help after that.

Minno pushed the ornate front door open. The ancient wooden barrier swung aside on silent hinges, revealing a vestibule larger than Drayve's courtroom. At the back of the wide, high chamber, two opposing staircases swept up to the second level. Vases stood in pristine condition. Tapestries hung untouched by time.

Does magic preserve them? It was all that made sense.

"Take him into the library." Minno pointed at a door to the right inlaid with golden runes and bedecked in gems of red and yellow.

Penn and Maya led Mikoneh between them. The room beyond was clear of dust, tapestries, and vases. Gray bedding had been rolled out in the center of the long, dim chamber. Above the makeshift bed, a light fixture hung down. Its gilt arms ended where crystal orbs perched, their light soft as dying candles.

As the three entered the chamber, the orbs flared up, producing a warm glow bright enough to chase away every shadow to the farthest recesses. A tall, curtained window was drawn shut. High shelves were built into the walls, but no books or scrolls remained.

Penn led the way to the bedroll and helped Mikoneh ease down on it. For a bed on the hard flagstone floor, it was comfortable enough. Straightening, Penn massaged his slung arm while he stared around the chamber. "I'm guessing Minno's stayed here before."

"Correct." The gray boy stood in the open doorway. He clutched a satchel in one hand. "When I've had reasons to stay hidden, this has been one haven. Now that you've come, I will likely never use it again, but that's just as well. Become too comfortable and you become too lax." He entered the chamber and set the satchel down. "This is the last of my food stores. Eat. I'll go hunting at dawn. We may be here a few days before Ter finds us."

"Why are you helping us?" Penn asked.

"Not that we're not grateful," Maya chimed in. "We truly are. But you seem so...disdainful. I can't understand your motives."

Minno offered up his owl stare. "You expect me to explain myself?"

"Well, yes," she pushed back. "I think we need to understand each other to build trust."

"Trust?" His head slowly tipped to one side. "Why do we need to build trust? You would be foolish to trust me."

Mikoneh snorted. "You're a blunt one." He shifted on the bedroll, then laid down with a groan. Every muscle screamed. His swimming mind pounded against his skull. He hadn't had a chance to bathe in the Moon Veil, and every bit of him was itchy, but he needed sleep more. "We at least need to trust that you won't stab us in the dark." He settled against the flat pillow and shut his eyes.

"I have no reason to stab you," Minno said, "just as you have no reason to stab me yet. That isn't to say I like you. In fact, I might even loathe you. I haven't decided yet."

A dry smile twitched at Mikoneh's lips. "Well, when you figure it out, let me know, 'kay?"

"Mikoneh," Penn hissed. "Let's not encourage in-fighting."

"I'm not. Minno's an honest jerk, and I respect that. Right, Minno?"

"Yes," came the monotone reply. His voice grew muted, suggesting he'd shifted away from the bedroll. "You two should eat. As Penn said, there's no rush."

"Will you explain about Void transportation then?" asked the inquisitive viscount.

Minno sighed from a great distance. "Perhaps later. I would rather sleep myself."

What Penn's response was, Mikoneh didn't catch. He plunged into darkness, glad to escape his burning body and spinning thoughts.

Interlude II

Lapping Water

"A day without you is a riverbed in drought."

- From the Corpse Poet's 5th Sonnet

LITTLE WHITE FLOWERS CROWNED HIS HEAD. Laying on his back in a patch of grass beside the watery path, he stared at the netting of branches above. The lapping water soothed his mind, calming troubled thoughts he couldn't quite grasp.

"Do you remember their name?"

He rolled onto his side, smiling as the white-cloaked woman appeared from among the tall, ancient trees. The long shimmering material whispered across the foliage behind her.

"Whose name?" he asked.

"The flowers."

His eyes dropped to the delicate little flowers with tiny white petals. "I...don't. That's odd."

"Don't press your mind too much. It may return on its own."

His smile deepened. "You won't tell me?"

The lady knelt beside him, cloak pooling around her. Emerald-green eyes within her pale cowl caught his gaze. "I could, but you would only forget again." She reached out a slender hand and ran her fingers across his cheek. "Be patient, my friend."

Pain wrenched through him. He ducked his head. "For how long? I can't—"

The lady tensed and whirled in a fluid motion that brought her to her feet. A delicate, slender sword materialized in her hand. "Mikoneh, the Revenant has found you in Hyanython."

He jumped to his boots. Fury lit in his stomach, and his fingers prickled with sparks of fire. "I won't leave you, my lady."

She peered at him from the corner of one glittering eye. "Yet you must. If he captures your body, Sathe will have tremendous power over you. The destruction he could wreak... best not to weigh it. Go. Awaken and fight."

He tried to protest, but a force seized his spirit, dragging him from the blue-tinted wood and the lapping water.

CHAPTER 13

THE FREE WIND

- From Athonen d'Ereth's *The Fall of Mages in the Age of Dragons*

Mikoneh jerked awake.

A hand covered his mouth. "Don't shout." Penn's voice. "Mages are inside the citadel."

Mikoneh nodded, and Penn pulled his hand away. Sitting up, Mikoneh glanced around the gloomy chamber. Predawn light filtered in between half-drawn curtains hanging from a window. Both Maya and Minno were gone. He turned an inquiring glance on Penn.

"They're on the roof," whispered the young man. "Minno said your sister could help him somehow. I protested, but Maya put her foot down. I can't fight her when she does that."

Mikoneh snorted. "Who can?" He shoved dark tresses from his face and stood up. The fever that had wracked his frame was gone. Weakness still hounded his bones, but he could stand on his own. That was a welcome improvement.

His fingers itched for Fa's sword. Sathe had also stripped him of his boot knife and anything else he might've used as a weapon.

"Here." Penn pressed a cool metal object into his hand. An ornate dagger. "Minno left each of us one. He said not to die if we can help it."

Mikoneh gave another snort. "He's a strange one."

"Definitely." Penn nodded toward the adjacent vestibule. "Should we go out there?"

"Better to fight in a larger space. Plus, there's no feasible escape route in here." A scuffing outside the house arrested Mikoneh's attention. He crept to the tall window and peeked between the blue velvet curtains. A handful of cloaked skeletons came down the street, heading for the front door.

He swore under his breath. "They're right outside." He turned toward his friend.

Penn met his gaze and offered a curt nod. "I suppose it's well Maya's not here. Minno may be able to keep her hidden."

Something loosened in Mikoneh's chest. The viscount had a good point. "It's some consolation, anyway." He turned toward the vestibule. "Shall we?"

His dream was a mere fragment now, but he recalled the sparks of fire on his fingertips. He reached for the same sensation—the same pull of magma within him. Anger had stirred before, churning it up. He could summon that feeling well enough. It was always near the surface, ready to respond. Ready to guard him from deeper, heavier emotions.

As the clack of bones ascended the steps outside, he moved into the vestibule. Penn was right on his heels, dagger clutched in his good hand, his useless arm still caught in its sling.

We won't last a quarter turn if Sathe decides to kill us.

But Mikoneh knew Sathe's intention was to *use* him. He was probably safe enough for the time being—but not Penn. Penn was expendable.

I won't let them take either of us alive.

Mikoneh faced the closed front doors. He set his feet wide apart and flexed his fingers against his dagger hilt, reaffirming his hold on the pathetic weapon. A tiny diamond winked on the dagger's pommel, and the blade flashed in a strand of light filtering through a stained-glass window above the front doors.

Those doors burst from their hinges. A strange tang sparked over the air. Magic.

Five Mages draped in rotting cloaks poured into the vestibule.

Sparks shot down Mikoneh's dagger. Touching the magma inside, he lifted his weapon. Fire blasted from the blade's tip, even as wind roared outside.

MAYA CROUCHED beside Minno on the flat section of roof surrounding the dome. A walkway had been built into the structure, running around the dome in a full square. A sturdy balustrade, made of the same pale pink stone as everything else, ran the length of the walkway.

Minno peered between the balustrade supports to study the mass of Mages below. A handful turned onto the side street leading to their hideaway.

"We'll be captured or killed," Minno said. "Unless you can awaken your element."

She wrenched her eyes from the streets to stare at Minno. "My—"

"I'd rather not take the time for useless confirmations, but yes, your element. Wind. Isn't it obvious? Your twin has fire, you have wind. Did you think you had nothing? Silly."

Her lips parted. "But—" It made sense upon consideration. The wind must've been what spoke to her in the Moon Veil. If only she hadn't been so tired, she might've connected the pieces and warned the fairies in time about the fire.

"I will coach you as best I can," Minno went on, "though I'm not a Wind Master. We'll find you and your twin better teachers later, provided we purchase the chance. Do you understand?"

She bobbed a hasty nod.

"Good. Listen well, and don't hesitate. Your instincts will guide you. Rokahnian blood would allow for nothing less. You're a thoroughbred, understand?"

She nodded again.

"Excellent." Minno shifted his weight against his knees. "Wind is one of the easiest elements to harness since it's always close by. Even non-Elementalists can sometimes perceive its laughter. You should be able to hear the wind spirits if you listen. Shut out doubt. It will only hinder you. Listen instead for music. The music of life, of laughter, of memory. Do you hear it?"

She closed her eyes, and opened her ears. She'd always loved the sound of wind, the feel of it in her hair—and how it was always close, bringing the fragrance of folk from faraway lands.

It stirred now, as though it was happy that she sought it out. Laughter played in her ears. A humming tune followed, and fingers of wind raked through her long hair.

'Ah, you found us.'

'Open your eyes.'

'Hurry, hurry!'

She cracked one eye open. A hand-span humanoid shape hovered, like a hummingbird, before her. It was iridescent and translucent, wispy like a half-formed thought, with a face that beamed without full definition of features.

The wind spirit darted closer and rested two tiny hands on her nose, forcing her to cross her eyes. *'Hello, Mayanaleh. We are so happy you can see and hear us. We are the free wind of Sirinhigha.'*

A smile spread across Maya's face unbidden, and a giddy sort of joy filled her up. She nearly squeaked in her delight but managed to stifle the sound before she alerted the Mages below to her location. As bizarre as the sight of this tiny spectral creature should have been, all Maya could focus on was how *right* it was. How complete she felt.

She lifted her hand, palm up, and the figure lighted upon it. It weighed nothing, yet the cool sensation was grounding. Maya's hair stirred faster, rippling as other wind spirits flittered toward her across the gray dawn sky.

"You see them, I presume," said Minno in his flat tones. "Good. Now, you must ask for their help."

She tore her eyes from the little spirits to find the boy. "Right. Mages—or whatever those undead things are." Reality settled in like a damp cloak. She shivered. "How can they—I— how can we help?" Scanning the street below, she found the detachment of Mages had reached the manor house.

"Wind spirits are good at collision. Ask them to marshal and descend upon the Mages. Create chaos. Give your twin and friend a chance to fight."

She relayed the message word for word. The lead wind spirit hopped from her palm, twirled over the air, and at a chime, gathered the growing forces of iridescent shapes. They coalesced into a cyclone—then plunged from the heights to charge the Mages.

The front doors burst apart. Maya leaned out past the balustrade, but Minno yanked her back.

"Be sensible," he whispered with slight vehemence.

Heat curled up her neck and bloomed across her cheeks. She hunched down and lifted a prayer to heaven that Mikoneh and Penn would survive.

She'd done all she could—and far more than she might've guessed.

Let it be enough.

She frowned. "You said Sathe is a higher echelon Mage because he has his skin. Are those skeletons—are they Mages or something else?"

"They're Mages of the lowest stratum," said Minno with a hint of disgust. "In the Age of Dragons, they sold their souls to the Dark Mage generals for more power—and when the Mage armies were soundly beaten by the old alliances, these hapless forms slinked back into their warrens. The higher Dark Mages have promised them that once they rise again and enslave the world, the fleshless ones will regain their living states. Which is a lie. Even the Mage Queen isn't that powerful."

The Mage Queen. Another title from legends.

"Is Sathe immortal?"

"Not yet." Minno sighed. "But he's hard to kill."

"What did he want with you?" Maya asked.

Minno gave her a slow blink, then risked a glance over the balustrade. "More are coming." He inhaled sharply. "Not *that.*"

Inexplicably, a strange sort of sorrow crept under Maya's skin. She shifted to glance over the railing. "What is—"

Minno yanked her back by her hair. "Don't be a fool. Throw all your wind spirits at those lesser Mages. Keep them outside the building. Concentrate." He lifted his hand. Lightning crackled above his palm. "And don't look."

He hurled the lightning bolt. It struck below, shaking the foundations of the citadel.

CHAPTER 14

THIS OTHERWORLDLY BARRAGE

"When dragons were first attacked, it was in isolated regions, where the great creatures preferred to keep to themselves."

- From Athonen d'Ereth's *The Fall of Mages in the Age of Dragons*

Lighting struck outside, painting the world white.

The skeletal Mages scattered under the force of the wind.

Mikoneh raced toward the three enemies who veered left. Flames unfurled before him. The taste of fire—a spicy, euphoric flavor—prickled on his tongue. He found himself grinning. Every sense, from sight to smell to touch, had been heightened by the blood pounding in his ears. He lifted his dagger. Fire spewed from its end, lengthening the blade into a sword.

He swung hard. The fire flashed white hot.

It rolled through the first Mage's chest, melting bone. The

skeletal creature screamed, then collapsed into dust. Mikoneh spun and lunged at the next Mage. This one lifted a spear, but Mikoneh's flames swept through the tip, and the metal turned to liquid. The skeleton buckled in a heap of ancient dust, its piercing wail drifting away.

He started after the third, wind whistling through his ears—almost laughing. The flames dancing along his dagger blade cackled in reply.

Penn was wrestling the other two Mages across the vestibule, having much less success fending them off. Mikoneh's grin faded. He must hurry.

His target fell back.

Mikoneh drew on his fury. His flaming blade spit out hotter embers. He darted after the retreating skeleton.

Fa had taught him combat growing up. As a retired soldier, Jonatten had believed that understanding war facilitated peace—and his children had been raised accordingly. All he'd taught them, they'd honed fighting against Drayve's tyranny, first under Fa's command, and then without him.

But he never taught me anything about fighting undead monsters.

Penn cried out.

Mikoneh sent flames rippling over his opponent, then swung to answer his friend's distress. Penn was knocked backward. His dagger spun away. He shielded himself with one arm as the looming Mage aimed his spear.

Mikoneh swiped his blade across the air. Fire roared over the stone floor to slam into the skeleton. The Mage lurched sideways, then disintegrated into primeval dust.

"Behind you!" Penn cried.

Mikoneh wheeled around, lifting his dagger. Flames rolled up the sharp edge, illuminating the figure charging him. Not a Mage.

Chills spidered up Mikoneh's arms, despite the fire spilling off him. Despite the heat of his own fury.

The *thing* was tall, taller by far than a full-grown man, though it wore the general shape of one beneath a crimson cloak with a deep cowl. It was faintly translucent, emanating a reddish hue that twisted and writhed like sentient shadows around its feet. The being—if being it was—reached out a hand bearing too-long, too-slender fingers. It seemed ready to touch Mikoneh's cheek.

He stumbled back, trembling as his gut screamed at him to flee. Why, he didn't know. What about this thing terrified him so much, he couldn't say. He longed to obey—to grab Penn and escape—but under the creature's looming influence, he had no strength.

This is the Revenant.

The fact struck him like a blow. This was the thing that hunted him on Sathe's behalf. The thing his dream had warned him about.

How can I fight such a creature?

He couldn't. He knew it as well as he knew his own name. His body trembled harder, pummeled by the aura surrounding the Revenant.

The creature drew nearer. Mikoneh's knees weakened.

Something like a whisper caressed his ears. Something deep, like the slow rumble of earth—not words—but a sorrow so sharp, tears pricked his eyes. He inhaled, crashing to his knees. He stared up at the looming figure, and his heart felt ready to break.

"Please." The single word fell from his lips, a faint, low plea. Not his. Somehow, it belonged to someone else. He didn't know who. Not Penn. Not the Mages that rallied at the creature's back.

Something else.

Surrender, Firebrand. Give in to the Revenant.

Sathe's voice coiled around Mikoneh like a snake made of ice and nightmares. It rattled him from the spell entrapping his limbs and senses. He shook himself, gritting his teeth, willing the fire to shield him. The spirits answered, and flames shot up like pillars between him and the looming figure.

The Revenant shrank back, hand retreating as though Mikoneh had struck him. Did Mikoneh imagine the trace of sorrow thrumming a note of pain? Did it come from the Revenant?

It couldn't matter. He squared his shoulders and rose as strength returned to his limbs. He must fight; must protect those he could still defend. He pointed the blazing dagger at the creature. "Tell your master I won't be joining him. Not now. Not ever."

The Revenant rippled. Then it stretched higher and tinged darker like fresh blood poured down its cloak. *Come,* it seemed to beckon, though no voice breathed out words.

Something like a compulsion tore at Mikoneh's body, urging him to obey. He shook his head. "I *won't.*" His tones pitched into a growl.

The Revenant rippled again—then unleashed a soul-piercing wail that shook the solid walls. Mikoneh staggered backward, dropping his dagger to cover his ears. The wail rose higher—higher—higher. The flagstones beneath Mikoneh shuddered. Pebbles skittered before his boots. The noise curled between his fingers, penetrating his skull, digging in until madness gripped the edges of his mind. Surely nothing could long stand up under this otherworldly barrage.

He squeezed his eyes shut, sank back to his knees, and folded forward.

The keen climbed higher—then cut off.

CHAPTER 15

A WAYSTOP

*"The Dragon King, young and untested, didn't know to seek out
his silent brethren in the Andyan Mountains."*

- From Athonen d'Ereth's *The Fall of Mages in the Age of Dragons*

L ight cuffed Mikoneh's closed eyes. As though he'd
been coiled within the keening noise, his muscles
slackened. He melted against the floor, gasping. The
light grew brighter.

"Come," said a voice, upbeat and familiar. A hand caught
his shoulder, small but strong. "Come, Mikoneh. Up, up."

He peeled his eyes open and peered into large blue eyes in a
childlike face. Ter's. The Ephe'ahn beamed at him, though one
corner of his mouth strained. The woodelf seemed to glow, or
had the room been drenched in golden sunlight?

"Hurry, now," Ter said gently. "We have little time. Up, my
lad."

Mikoneh unfolded himself. Minno and Maya stood just beyond Ter. Further away, the remaining Mages stood in an unnatural stillness, spears lifted like they'd halted mid-motion. Reluctantly, Mikoneh glanced toward the Revenant. It was gone.

He froze. How? It had been all-encompassing. All-consuming. It meant to eat him up.

Ter's hand stretched before his eyes. "Up, Mikoneh, if you can manage it. We must go."

Shaking himself, Mikoneh nodded. He wiped sweat from his brow and staggered upright without Ter's aid. Penn was also rising, a dazed look on his face. Blood dripped from his slung arm where a spear-point must have struck him. That he'd deflected a fatal blow and directed injury toward a place already wounded attested to his combat skills.

Maya strode forward, her hair cascading behind her like it was caught in its own breeze. Something about her eyes had changed. A strange sort of molten quality cast rainbows among the golden sheen of her irises. She reached Mikoneh and tucked her arm around his elbow.

"Lean on me," she whispered.

He didn't argue, though he was careful not to give her all the weight she expected.

"I'm all right, Maya," he whispered. "Just a little in shock."

She locked eyes with him. "Understandably."

"The *Dayonryse* will not last," Ter said. One long ear twitched. "Horses are just outside. We must go now. Quickly, if you please."

They moved together. Minno positioned himself at the woodelf's side.

"We didn't expect you so soon," the gray boy said.

"Ah," said Ter with a faint smile. "I thought certainly I should have to stay in the Moon Veil longer—but someone put out the forest fire, and I was able to set off for Oceana much sooner than expected."

They stepped outside. Dawn light filtered through the tall trees, brushing fingers of sunshine across the glittering pink stone structures. Birds trilled in the treetops. Along the paved road, horses stood waiting. Familiar horses. Mikoneh gaped.

Rook flicked his black tail, restless to be underway. Penn's horse Aspen was there, along with Maya's nameless silver mare, and two ponies. All were saddled. Maya nearly abandoned her twin to run down the steps, but sense must have kicked in. Her straining arm relaxed.

"They're all right," she whispered. "Heaven be thanked."

"Yeah, Ter be thanked, too," Mikoneh said. He eyed the Ephe'ahn who took the stairs two at a time in graceful bounds.

At the bottom, Ter reached up to stroke Rook's muzzle. "This one is very clever, and loyal, it seems. He led his fellows from Bone Cove, aiming for Simynshin. Incredible, is it not, how intuitive animals can be? It seems he likes you a great deal." Ter's blue eyes settled on Mikoneh. "Much better than his last master, in fact."

"You understand horses?" asked Maya.

Ter's ears twitched. "After a fashion. It's not speech, mind. More feeling and instinct. Deeper." He canted his head. "Well, mount up. We've little time left."

Maya guided Mikoneh down the steps. "Can you ride on your own?"

"I think so. Let me try, at least."

She grimaced. "Will you be honest if you can't?"

"Maya, yes." He rolled his eyes. "I don't happen to like the idea of falling off and cracking my skull open."

A grin flashed over her lips. "No chance of that. It's too thick."

He snorted.

As they reached Rook's side, a glint of metal caught his eye. Within a sheath strapped to the black leather saddle, a familiar blade sat. Fa's sword, safe and sound. Mikoneh whirled to find Ter standing near a cream and brown painted pony.

"Thank you." His voice was husky with emotion. His fingers stroked the sheath. "For this. Thank you."

Ter's eyes brightened in the dawn light. "It is a clever sword, you know. Now, up you get. Our borrowed time is running very low." He swung into his pony's saddle and took up the reins.

Maya helped Mikoneh heft himself into Rook's fine saddle with a reassuring creak of leather, then she moved to examine Penn's arm.

"It's shallow. I can tend to it later. Up you get." She helped Penn onto Aspen's brown leather saddle. Minno was already seated on his shaggy pony before Maya had reached her silver mare. She swung up with an easy grace, then drew her hair back. Her tresses fell against her shoulders in a slow breeze. Her molten eyes danced as she caught up her reins.

Ter clicked his tongue, and the pony took the lead. The company moved into a trot, passing by more frozen Mages in their dark cloaks—all caught in motion like they'd been suspended in time.

The horses headed for the wide highway leading westward through the citadel. Mikoneh had to hold Rook back, lest the warhorse overtake Ter in the lead. His eyes traveled over the ancient stronghold. He'd never seen anything so grand, nor so alien. Compared to the thatched cottages and the hulking castle where Drayve dwelt, these structures were graceful and lithe. The domes were delicate things. Though made of stone, and empty of people, Hyanython seemed strangely fluid—almost alive.

It has a heartbeat.

Could stone breathe? Did it house a soul?

I'm more tired than I thought.

It wasn't that, and he knew it. The Revenant's heart-wrenching wail had unsettled him to his core. He couldn't quiet his nerves, and though the light Ter had summoned had chased off the sorrowful creature, a finely honed instinct—something Mikoneh had developed in his battles against Drayve's forces—assured him the Revenant would return.

How can I defeat something like that?

He studied Ter's back. Setting his jaw, Mikoneh gave Rook the reins. In a few graceful bounds, the warhorse came level with Ter. Before he could outdistance the company, Mikoneh eased Rook into a canter beside the Ephe'ahn.

"What was that thing?" His voice was just loud enough to carry above the clatter of hooves on paving stones.

Ter's eyes slid toward him, then darted ahead. His yellow-blond hair danced in the streaming wind. A frown touched the edges of his mouth. "A Revenant."

"That much I know—though what it means..."

Ter sighed. "It is not a tale for the road, Mikoneh. Let us wait until we are in safer lands, with more distance between us and the Mages in Hyanython, hm?"

The unanswered questions would do nothing to settle Mikoneh's nerves, but he nodded. "All right. I'll let it be for now, but I won't forget."

Ter's lips dipped down. "No, I dare say you will not. None could."

That was true. None could—not in a fortnight, a year, or a lifetime.

THE CITADEL STRETCHED ON LONGER than a full turn. The dim morning light never changed as they galloped beneath the sentinel buildings. Dawn remained until the shattered walls fell away behind them, and forested land rose high and tangled in its stead. As though the sun had been waiting for them to leave the empty stronghold, it slid upward at last—until dark clouds scudded in.

The sky grumbled. The clouds churned and frothed like vapors in a hearthwife's cauldron, and the air carried the scent of the south sea. Fingers of wind tugged on Mikoneh's black hair, tossing loose strands into his face. He dragged the tresses away just as the clouds broke. Rain drummed the world, smearing the vibrant colors of the ancient forest. Puddles collected along the overgrown highway.

Mikoneh didn't bother pulling his cloak over his head. It was too late to keep dry, and the cloth would be sopping soon anyway. Besides, it was the nearest thing he'd had to a bath in over a week. He studied the moss-laden trees, trying to keep his thoughts on his objective rather than on what stalked them. Still, his back felt exposed.

Throughout the morning, Mikoneh had slowly fallen back behind Ter's pony. His twin rode to his left, looking pale and withdrawn, while Penn rode just behind. Minno held the rear. The formation never changed, even when they took brief respites. During their lunch rest, Maya took a few moments to patch Penn's wound. After that, they rode on. When the highway curved southwest, Ter turned his pony north, slipping between the trees. The rest followed him off the road.

The rain backed off toward evening, then returned with vehemence, pounding the earth along the narrow track until it churned up slick mud. The horses' hooves remained steady. Knowing what followed them, no one voiced a desire to stop.

They traveled until the clouds blackened at dusk. Wind

whipped up the path. The horses didn't complain, but even Rook was weary from the long day's ride. Beside Mikoneh, Maya faintly groaned.

He glanced at his twin. Her face was deathly white, and she wobbled in the saddle.

Urgency flooded Mikoneh. He nudged Rook forward. "Ter, please stop."

The Ephe'ahn glanced back. "Are you ill, Maya?"

She hefted her chin and tried a smile that wilted at once. "A little."

Penn and Minno reined up just behind them. The gray boy murmured, "Ah."

Mikoneh shot him a sharp look. "What's 'ah' mean?"

"She used too much energy when she summoned her element earlier. I hadn't thought..." He shrugged. "It will pass, but she needs rest."

"When she *what*?"

"Oh." Maya tried to smile. "I meant to tell you, I'm a Wind Elementalist, it seems. Isn't that wonderful?"

"Completely wonderful." Mikoneh turned a glower on Minno. "You could've mentioned something sooner."

Minno met his gaze with a deadpan expression, unblinking. "As I said, in all the commotion, I hadn't thought. Besides, it's been centuries since I experienced such a reaction."

Centuries?

Ter clucked his tongue. "Even so, Minno, *you* ought to remember well. Did Mikoneh not show signs in the Moon Veil after dousing that forest fire?"

How Ter knew that Mikoneh didn't bother to ask.

The gray boy shrugged. "I didn't think to remember."

"Rather than debate," Penn chimed in, "perhaps we should find shelter?"

The Ephe'ahn tapped a knuckle to his lips, then glanced up

the trail. "There is a waystop perhaps a mile farther. Shall we make for it, or shall we stop here?"

"I—I can keep on," Maya said, "if it's only a mile."

Mikoneh reached across the space between their horses to catch her damp cloak. "You sure?"

She nodded. "You could, so I can."

He sighed, trying to stifle the wry smile that caught his lips. "Stubborn as your mother."

"Why, thank you, Mikoneh," she laughed. "That might be the kindest thing you've ever accused me of."

A grin bloomed against his will. "I'll need to work on that."

"See that you do."

They turned as one to face Ter.

"Let's keep on," said Mikoneh.

The childlike Ephe'ahn glanced between them, then nodded and tightened his reins. "Very well." He nudged his pony into motion.

Mikoneh steered Rook closer to Maya in case she slipped off her saddle. He tried not to think about how fragile she looked, and how much it reminded him of her previous condition not so long ago.

"I'm here, Maya," he said.

Glancing at him, she smiled. "I know, Mikoneh. You always are."

Chapter 16

Soul Puppet

"The taint of Dark Magery was a slow poison seeping into the blood of Sirinhigha.

- From Athonen d'Ereth's *The Fall of Mages in the Age of Dragons*

Despite Mikoneh's fears, Maya held on, and the last mile flew by in a blur of trees and rain. Ter slowed when a tiny structure came into view on the right side of the narrow path. It was a dilapidated thing; barely what anyone could call a stone hut. The thatched roof looked on the verge of collapse. Ter guided his pony to the lean-to near the sagging front door and swung down, in a motion that showed no hint of weariness.

"Bring the lass inside," Ter said. "I will see to the horses once we've settled in."

Mikoneh eased himself from his saddle with a wince, his muscles screaming. An entire day in the saddle left him sore.

With a grimace, he limped over to Maya, on her silver mare, and helped her slide down. She stumbled into his arms, shivering.

"Maybe tomorrow I'll walk," she whispered.

He softly snorted. "Not if you don't want to get captured by those skeletal horrors. C'mon." They limped toward the lean-to, neither very steady. Penn was hardly in better shape, with his broken and patched arm.

A stream burbled behind the saggy structure, and Mikoneh made a mental note to duck out and scrub himself properly after Maya was cared for. Minno traipsed inside ahead of them. Within the damp one-room construction, moldy blankets were heaped against the far wall, and a firepit took up the center of the room. Thatching was strewn about the dirt floor. Ter gathered kindling from a soggy box beside a neat stack of wood.

"What is this place?" asked Penn, more curious than disgusted, judging by his wondering expression.

"A waystop," Minno said flatly.

"I mean—"

"It was built for hunters," Ter cut in, striking a flame over the kindling. "Specifically, for those who hunt fae. Fortunately, such hunters do not come so far into these woods any longer. Now it is used *by* fae to hide. Within its magicked boundaries, no one may find us. If you stepped out onto the road, you would see no hint of a fire. No sign of our horses' hooves. It looks utterly abandoned."

Mikoneh helped Maya to the fire ring, then crouched beside the tiny flames. At once, they leapt up high and cheerful.

"Why, thank you." Ter smiled at him. "That is most helpful."

Mikoneh shifted uncomfortably, still reluctant to embrace his newfound elemental powers.

"What happens if the Mages check inside?" asked Penn.

"They likely will not," Ter said. "The magic repels their sort—very subtly. They will probably not notice the structure at all."

Penn huffed out a laugh. "Maybe we should stay here."

"You could," Minno said. "And slowly starve to death."

"Alas," said Ter, throwing logs onto the cheery fire, "Minno is correct."

"That usually bodes ill," Minno said in monotone. "My being right."

Ter didn't argue, though his smile sloped into something like pity. "We must make for Owenekiras's camp at first light if Lady Maya is up for it."

"I will be," she said with a weary smile. "I just need a little sleep."

"I did suspect your element had awakened." Ter settled back against his hands and crossed his legs before him. "Your appearance has altered. The wind spirits have fully embraced you."

"My appearance? How?" She touched a hand to her cheek.

"Nothing bad," Penn piped up. "Your eyes. They're... brighter. And your hair stirs in its own breeze."

Mikoneh stifled a snort. Leave it to Penn to notice.

"Indeed, both true." Ter nodded sagely. "Few Wind Elementalists show immediate changes. Your swift alteration promises a great deal of power once you master your gift."

Maya glanced at her twin. "Like you."

"Me?" He stiffened. "Did my appearance change, too?"

She nodded. "Subtly. Your eyes ring with fire when you conjure flames. And you feel especially warm. Not hot, but warm. All the time."

A pit grew in his stomach. He didn't want to claim fire. He wanted nothing to do with it. Yes, it had come in handy more than once. He knew he should feel grateful, and yet...

Fire killed them.

He stared into the ring of flames. "Can you tell us about the Revenant now, Ter?"

"And Void transportation," Penn chimed in. "You reclaimed our horses from Oceana in a mere day's time. You must've traveled using magic, just like Minno did to bring us to that citadel. How?"

Ter chuckled. "Very well, but after we eat. Settle your-selves." He dug into a satchel at his side. "I have fresh cheese and bread left, as well as a few dried fruits. Eat your fill. We will reach a village tomorrow evening and can restock there."

While the rest ate, Mikoneh slipped out to wash up. He stripped down to his smalls, then plunged into the stream. It barely felt cold. Once he'd scrubbed off every particle of grime from scalp to toes, he climbed into his soaked clothes and trudged back into the lean-to, feeling a little more refreshed. Ter glanced at him, then turned to stare into the flames. Mikoneh tried to ignore the fire spirits dancing and cackling within the blaze. He sat beside Maya and munched on cheese and bread, dismissing the fruits. He didn't care for sweet things.

Despite the pounding rain puddling near one wall of the hut, and the rumbling thunder—despite the weariness of travel and the intensity of the morning—the food and warmth seeped into the group, easing aches, quieting fears.

At last, Ter stirred. "Void isn't magic, quite. It is more like the fabric of life, the channel through which magic *flows*. The *between* of the Universe. It keeps all things in balance. At least, half of everything. Its aura is an aqua shade of blue."

Minno scoffed but didn't speak whatever was on his mind.

Ter went on, ignoring him. "Its underside—its darker half —is called Hollow, which has a violet hue when used. The two are in a constant, endless war against the other, and their friction keeps a tenuous balance in the Universe. Sort of the warp and weft, crossing under, over, and between each other to hold all things together."

"And...it's used for travel?" Penn asked.

"No. Well, rarely." Ter's ear twitched like a rabbit. "Hmmm. Perhaps I should say that a rare few can use either in that way. As I said, the Void and Hollow create channels, and those channels can be used to go from place to place, where doors exist. To create a new door within that realm is nearly impossible. We must use what exists where anchors have been placed. Some tools allow us to punch temporary holes through the fabric—such as your little blue stone did— but such tools are uncommon. To try to open a portal without a tool or established anchor would make precision nearly impossible. Some can manage it. Fewer still are allowed.

"I traveled to Oceana using an already existing Void door. I then had to use a different means to locate the horses, then return to that same door, and come to Hyanython. Luckily, Minno left a trail I could follow."

Mikoneh tensed. "Isn't that dangerous? Did the Mages use the same—"

"They cannot," Ter said gently. "Dark Mages—and only the most powerful of their number—use Hollow to travel. Hollow is the underside of this tenuous balance. Dark Mages cannot use Void. It would burn them—not destroy them, mind you. Not easily, at least." His smile crooked. "If I were to tap into Hollow, however, it would taint me, like a slow poison, or a corrupting of my mindset into something darker. It's dangerous at best."

"And there's no direct passage—no doorway—to the Dragon King's camp." Mikoneh broke off a piece of cheese. "That's what Minno implied, I think."

"Correct." Ter tossed another log onto the flames. "If there had been such a door, Owenekiras would have stoppered it. He has the skill and the foresight to accomplish such a task, though at a dear cost."

Penn was rubbing his chin. "Can someone learn to use the Void? Could I?"

Ter considered the nobleman. "If the aptitude is there, yes. I would need to test you. But likely you could not use it for travel. That is a very rare talent."

"What about an element?" Penn pressed. "Might I have one?"

"Most do if they bother to awaken it," Minno chimed in flatly. "But few on such a level as the twins." His eyes flicked to Mikoneh, then away. "Few, indeed, become true Elementalists."

"How many elements are there?" Penn shifted to face both Ter and Minno. "And what do I need to do to discover mine?"

"There are five main elements," Minno said. "Fire, wind, and water are the most common. Rarer is earth, and rarest of all is the element of spirit—at least the wielding of it. Spirit of spirit encompasses all things, wrapping around Void and Hollow alike, keeping them vital. There are tests to determine your element and your strength in it."

Ter nodded. "Once we reach Owenekiras's camp, we can try these tests, Lord Penn. If you wish."

"Penn." Mikoneh frowned at his friend. "Stop it."

"Stop what?"

"You don't need to push yourself."

The viscount shook his head. "But I do. You and Maya aren't going to fight for Oceana without me. I need to keep up." He clenched his free hand. "I won't stand by and helplessly watch while others fight my battles using magic."

Mikoneh frowned. Penn was right. Going back to Oceana without magic was a death sentence. But that meant he needed to master fire to end Drayve's tyranny, and he wasn't prepared to do that.

"Something to discuss once you know your aptitude," Ter said, one ear twitching idly.

Penn's hand relaxed against his leg. "You're right. I needn't get ahead of myself." He turned his gaze away. "I just want to contribute."

"You do," Maya said. "Don't be so hard on yourself."

Penn frowned. "But I've failed my people."

Mikoneh bowed his head. His friend felt the same weight he did.

"Oh, Penn. You haven't..." Maya tried to move, but slumped forward, barely catching herself with her palm against the dirt floor.

"Idiot." Mikoneh faintly smiled, then shifted to her side and let her prop herself against him. "Did you forget you're weak as a kitten?"

"For a moment I did," she laughed, then sighed. "Don't think this conversation is over for long, Penn. I'll properly chide you once I get my strength back."

The viscount grinned. "I wouldn't dream of escaping your wrath."

Mikoneh dragged his eyes back to Ter. "What about the Revenant?"

"Ah." Ter's ears drooped. "As to that...I know very little of the particulars."

"Shocking," said Minno. "Aren't you Ter the Ever-Present? The all-knowing sage?"

"Eh heh." Ter's ears drooped further as his expression turned sheepish. "A common misconception, my dear Minno. Heaven alone knows all things."

"Also a debatable point," Minno mumbled.

"I said heaven, not the Celes." Ter's ears lifted a little. "Gracious, Minno. When did you become so cynical?"

The gray boy shrugged. "Twenty thousand years ago, give or take a day." His bland stare narrowed into something glittering with anger. "As you well know."

"Are you really that old?" asked Maya. "How is that poss…" Her eyes widened, catching the fire's gleam. "Are you a Nijaal?"

Minno fell so still, he resembled a stone statue. Slowly, very slowly, he shook his head. "No, I'm too short."

"Among other things," Ter chuckled. "No, no. Minno here is—is Minno. Really, there isn't a better word for him." One pointed ear flicked.

"True." Minno nodded. "I'm nothing important."

Ter's smile gentled. "Don't say that."

Maya—never able to help herself—cut in. "But Nijaal *do* exist, don't they?" She sounded certain. "If fairies and wood-elves and Mages exist, surely the Ancient Ones do."

"Right you are," Ter said. "The Nijaal do indeed exist, and perhaps the legends of them are more accurate than one would expect. They are tall, lithe, and graceful. Many of them are wise."

"And many more are foolish," Minno added blandly.

Ter's large blue eyes settled on the gray boy for a long moment, then he heaved a deep sigh. "True, many have been foolish. The Age of Dragons was a time of tremendous upheaval. Alliances shifted, and many betrayed their own."

"Why was it called the Age of Dragons?" asked Maya. "I've always wondered."

"Hush," Mikoneh whispered. "If you keep asking questions, the answers will be too many to keep up with."

Her cheeks flushed, but she leaned forward. "Are they gods,

Master Ter? The Nijaal, I mean. Most folk in Oceana believe so. We have churches and shrines for them."

The Ephe'ahn's smile fell like a stone tumbling over a cliff. "No, child. They're not gods, nor were they ever such. They are old. Among the oldest beings to live upon Sirinhigha—perhaps even in the Universe itself. Certainly, Lady Katanni is."

Minno stirred, snaring Mikoneh's eye. The gray boy shifted away from the group clustered around the fire. Light and shadow played against his back, while he tucked his knees to his chest and buried his head. Despite the emotionless tones of his voice and the flat stare he threw around, Mikoneh sensed a deep, bitter pain within the ancient child.

Maya was rattling off more questions, and Mikoneh dragged his attention from Minno to clamp a hand to her mouth. "That's enough," he said. "We'll be traveling for a while, and Ter can answer our questions a few at a time. Focus." He cracked a smile. "Better still, go to sleep. You're tired, remember?"

She opened her mouth to protest, then drooped against his shoulder. "You're right. I'm exhausted."

He rested his chin against her head, then pinned his gaze on Ter. "You know *something* about the Revenant. You mentioned a tale."

The pop of the burning logs filled the silence. A single fire spirit hefted its head, then hopped onto a large log to dance among the higher flames. Mikoneh found himself entranced by the contorting blaze.

"Of *this* Revenant, I know little." Ter's voice was soft, a mere scraping of sound. "In fact, nothing. But with similar creatures, I've had several encounters. Enough to know *what* they are, though not who." He folded his legs before him, then rested his hands on his knees. "They are souls, trapped."

Penn flinched back. "Necromancy?"

"A form of it," Ter said with a subtle nod. "But it is not reanimation of the dead. This is..." He dragged in a breath like he was in terrible pain. "It is enslaving a living soul. Extracting it from someone still alive—though that life is all but snuffed out. From all I understand—and mind you, my knowledge is limited on this subject—not one of these poor souls has been successfully returned to their body to live a full life once they have been pulled from it. A Revenant is a soul puppet wielding supernatural powers, and the only way to defeat it is to kill the body to which it once belonged."

"That's horrible," murmured Maya.

Mikoneh wrapped an arm around his twin. "It's bad news for us, too. How do we outrun a hunter like that?"

Ter shook his head. "Outrunning it would prove impossible. We must outsmart it."

"Like with the waystops," Penn said. "We keep out of sight, using magic."

"Yes, like that." Ter poked a stick at the fire. The dancing spirit leapt onto the stick and cackled with laughter as Ter withdrew the burning implement. The Ephe'ahn blew on the flame, and the fire spirit flung free in a somersault, giggling madly. It landed near Minno's hunching form, then turned and headed toward Mikoneh in a flirtatious, sashaying walk.

Mikoneh flinched back, memories of Kevva's flirting playing across his mind. Anger swelled up to stifle the panic. He'd managed to put the woman out of his mind—not difficult to do when a much greater threat was chasing him and his companions. Still, the sting of her betrayal ran deep.

The fire spirit reached his leg and jumped up, its ill-defined face wearing a prominent smile. He stared at the tiny creature, uncertain he wanted to interact with it.

They helped you back in Hyanython and in the Moon Veil. Don't you owe them?

He forced the corner of his mouth to lift. "Uh, Ter? Do—do the fire spirits—do they have feelings?"

Ter chuckled, eyes losing their haunted glaze. "Ah, yes. Certainly, they do. They're very complex. Fire spirits are one of the Spirits Elemental. Guardians, you might say, of the life around us. They are content to ignore us unless they sense that we can see them. Are the fire spirits teasing you?"

Mikoneh nodded vigorously. "One is anyway."

"They're a mischievous lot—though wind spirits are more so, in their flighty way. Fire and wind are the most social of the five common types. Earth is much quieter and fiercely loyal. Water is elusive and very selective of those they accept as Master Elementalists. Spirit is less definable. More ethereal." He turned his gaze on Minno. "Would you not agree?"

Minno made a non-committal sound, keeping his back to the group.

"Minno uses spirit of spirit?" asked Mikoneh.

"Yes, most deftly. He's among its oldest wielders. Aren't you, Minno?"

The gray boy didn't bother answering.

The fire spirit climbed up onto Mikoneh's free wrist. It studied him with flaming eyes, its hair a long mane of fire that danced around its slender ankles.

"It's looking at me," he said.

"For one of its kind, you're of greatest interest in this hut," said Ter. "A Fire Elementalist—especially an inherently strong one—will attract them. Most dwell deep in the earth, but they will answer if you call them. Even the heat of your own body can produce the spark needed to summon a spirit or two. More when you're stronger."

Mikoneh frowned, curling one finger toward the spirit. It turned and rested its tiny hands on his fingertip. "Did either of my parents wield fire?"

A beat of hesitation followed, then Ter nodded. "Yes, your father. It goes deeper than that—but 'tisn't my tale to tell."

"When has that ever stopped you?" Minno asked, glancing over his shoulder. "Another name for this one is Meddler."

Ter gave a sheepish laugh. "True, that. I've heard myself so named." He shrugged. "But we all of us have detractors." His smile vanished. He turned his gaze back to Mikoneh. "That Sathe has taken such great interest in you is—if not surprising—certainly distressing. We must get you and your twin safely to Owenekiras Rokahn soon. He alone can protect you."

A grimace twisted Mikoneh's lips. "I understand what you're saying, but I'm not seeking the Dragon King for protection. I need his help. Oceana is on the verge of civil war. The provinces are controlled by tyrants who don't heed King Nilo's laws. We're taxed nearly to death. People are starving. And now I know Lord Drayve—who's the central figure in the slow-brewing revolution against the king—is allied with Dark Mage forces."

Ter's ears drooped. "Ah. The state of the world is a dreary one, that's so. Your story is much like affairs in Cimin ten years ago, though perhaps yours is not so far along. And Simynshin has its own great struggles. Rokahn—alas—may have it worst of all. I do not mean to diminish your concern, nor your cause, my friend. But Lord Rokahn cannot split his army asunder to answer the needs of every nation. He must muster one great force to take down the heart of the corruption."

"Where is that, Master Ter?" asked Penn. "In Rokahn?"

"That is one great pocket of it, yes. The other is in the high northern mountains."

Mikoneh dropped his eyes to the fire spirit. It had changed its shape to a single flame no bigger than a candle, and it hovered above his fingernail. Irritation twisted in his stomach. He'd expected an answer like that. He wasn't naïve enough to think a great warlord would answer his country's plea merely because once, long ago, two of his generals had served him well and now their children appeared out of the blue.

But if he can't help, what can we do to save Oceana?

Mikoneh pushed his thoughts from his kingdom's struggles, toward something more immediately troubling. It was the thought that came back again and again. "Ter, what would Sathe be able to do if he caught and kept us for long?"

That same silence fell like a blanket to smother the room.

Mikoneh dragged his eyes from the hovering flame. He frowned at Ter, waiting. The Ephe'ahn's ears trembled, and his lips worked as though he couldn't quite spit the words out.

"I'll tell him," Minno said.

"Do not." Ter's voice was firm. "It isn't your place, nor is it mine. That explanation belongs solely to another."

"It's so obvious, I can't believe he hasn't sorted it for himself." Minno sighed. "If we fail to deliver the twins to Owen, you'll regret not telling them."

"We will not fail." Ter's ears shot up, and his eyes brightened. "That is all there is to it." He nodded, as though to himself, and prodded the fire again. As the flames rose in answer, the fire spirit slid back into a humanoid form and vaulted onto the logs. Other fire spirits formed and clasped hands to dance in a circle.

Ter rose to his feet. "Sleep is in order, I think. We must rest while we can. Lord Rokahn's camp is a long way yet from here. Good slumber, my friends." He moved to the pile of blankets and dug through to find a few less moldy than the others. He handed them out, then excused himself to tend to the horses.

Mikoneh wrapped his green gossamer blanket around Maya. He didn't take one for himself. He wasn't cold.

The drumming rainfall lulled the company toward sleep, all except Mikoneh who remained seated at the fire, staring at the spirits playing in its center. The deep, even breaths of his companions filled the damp air.

Sleep never found him, though his very bones were weary. Every time he closed his eyes, he saw the Revenant as clearly as though it stood before him now.

Against that nightmare, he had no hope of slumbering.

None at all.

Chapter 17

Snatches of Distant Lands

"Mages had long been involved in interkingdom politics, usually as a voice of reason. No one questioned their good sense."

- From Athonen d'Ereth's *The Fall of Mages in the Age of Dragons*

Maya pried her eyes open to find cracks of dawn light streaming through the thatching. The interior of the sagging hut sparkled with droplets of rain.

She was lying on her side, with her head propped against her twin's warm lap. She didn't need to look up to know it. With a faint squeak, she stretched and rolled onto her back to find Mikoneh's face. Dark circles rimmed his eyes, and he stared off into nothing. She'd seen the same look on his face often since their parents' deaths, especially after a skirmish that killed friends and neighbors. He didn't sleep as often as he should. He sometimes didn't eat, giving her his portion no matter how she protested.

Mikoneh was the sort of person who had to do *something*, always. He needed a cause and some action he could take to achieve it. Sometimes, Maya was the only cause he could touch —and she always let him. She owed him that and more, after what she'd done...

She pushed a smile to her lips. "G'morning."

He looked down to meet her gaze. "Feeling better?"

"Much. The fever's gone." She stifled a yawn, then rolled over and knelt beside him. "You didn't sleep?"

"Couldn't." He shrugged. "That Revenant burned its image into my eyeballs."

Maya shuddered. "Understandable. I only saw it from the watchtower for a moment, yet I don't know how I didn't dream about it last night."

"Too tired, I suspect." His eyes traveled to the pulsing embers in the fire ring. Whether or not he meant to, the flames sparked at his notice, then shot up into a fire that needed no fuel to burn. Mikoneh tensed, lips turning down. An accident then.

Controlling fire does disturb him, just as I thought.

Maya jumped to her feet, caught the gossamer blanket before it hit the ground, and handed it to her twin with a grateful smile. She then stretched her muscles ahead of the day's long ride in the saddle. Her backside hurt at the very idea.

"They like you," Mikoneh murmured.

"Who?" She found Ter huddled in the far corner, and Penn curled up near the door. But no sign of Minno. She scanned the tiny hut again.

Maybe he's out taking care of the horses.

"The fire spirits."

She blinked, twisting toward her twin. "Really?"

"Yeah. One just floated up to peck your cheek."

She pressed her fingers to the spot she fancied it had kissed her. "That's so sweet. I expected anything related to fire to be fierce and temperamental—like you." She flashed him a grin.

He rolled his eyes, then nodded toward the doorway. "He's gone, I think. Minno is. He slipped out this morning, and I heard hooves retreating."

Maya's gut twisted. "Will he be all right on his own? The Mages wanted him, too, didn't they?"

"Seems so, though Sathe appeared to be losing patience with him. I wondered what they'd want with a child, but...I suppose Minno's older than he looks."

"By a considerable measure." Ter's voice was soft but chipper. "Do not let those big gray eyes fool you. Minno is a force to be reckoned with." He stood on the far side of the fire. Maya hadn't heard him stir at all—and her hearing was much better than that of most people.

At least, in Oceana it is.

"What did Sathe want with him, do you know?" asked Mikoneh.

Ter's ear twitched. "Knowing Minno, it's just possible the Mages didn't know who he was when they caught him—and they regretted their success."

"He was strapped to a wall in a room with an altar, then broke out simply because he wanted to," Mikoneh said.

Another twitch of the ear. "Yes, well, Mages are greedy. Minno's blood has certain peculiarities that could be immensely useful if one learned how to harvest them. Fortunately, that is no simple task, not even for a powerful Dark Mage. Which Sathe must've learned in that moment." The Ephe'ahn clapped his hands together and rubbed them. "Shall we carry on, my little friends? We burn daylight even now."

"Yeah." Mikoneh rose and shook his cloak straight. "We can eat en route. Penn, time to wake up."

THEY WERE MOUNTED and trotting along the narrow dirt path within a quarter turn. Penn still looked half asleep, cradling his freshly bandaged arm in a proper sling Ter had provided. As Maya munched on a plum she'd taken from the Moon Veil, she gazed around at the old forest in Simynshin. The trees were like those in Oceana. Strictly speaking, it was all the same forest running down from the north, broken up only by rivers and mountain ranges. But here —so near the old citadel, filled with fairies and Mages—the trees seemed to *breathe.*

She finished her plum, then tossed the pit alongside the path and licked her fingers. The clop of hooves was a welcome rhythm in her head. For now, she could focus on the present, rather than what lay behind them.

Wind. Since Minno had guided her yesterday, she could see the wind spirits all around her. They hovered on branches or flitted around the wild rose brambles whose petals had shriveled weeks ago in the late summer heat.

More wind spirits twirled around her, playing with her long hair, or tossing the silver mare's tail. They were like elongated, mischievous fairies, though less solid, and opalescent. Some looked human. Others wore the shapes of birds or butterflies, fluttering and flitting about with a busyness that seemed to accomplish exactly nothing. They didn't seem to care, either. It wasn't about attending to tasks—it was about being alive and loving every moment of that aliveness.

She found herself grinning. A new strength had stirred within her when she'd tapped this gift—except for that brief bout of fever. Where before, the fragrance of faraway things had enticed a distant sort of joy, now the wind spirits flung more than the scents of the sea or trees or loam at her. They brought stories. Songs. Snatches of distant lives in far-off lands. Little of it made sense, as fast as they gabbled, but their raw energy—their irrepressible enthusiasm—charged Maya's soul.

For the first time since Fa and Mama died, she drank in life with real vigor, rather than grasping at any distraction from the pain.

A wind spirit resembling a hummingbird darted into her view, then zipped away, drawing her eye toward her twin. Her smile weakened a little. He rode with his eyes fastened ahead, a rigidity in his back, his jaw set with a stubborn determination —probably to stay awake despite his sleepless night.

Fire. Why did his element have to be fire?

She couldn't imagine coping with that—trying to wield the very thing that had murdered their parents.

The fire didn't do it. Drayve's men did, at his command. It was Drayve—and Sathe—not fire at all.

Saying that, even to herself, meant nothing. A tiny voice in the back of her mind—one she wished she could snuff out— asked a question. *Could Mikoneh have saved Fa and Mama, had he known about his gift?*

It wasn't fair to ask. It was too late to wonder.

She must find a way to silence the question forever.

Mikoneh was already angry at himself for far too many things beyond his control—and that was just the trouble. He hated not being in control.

She squeezed her reins tighter and banished her dismal thoughts. They would be there later to reflect on—that much she could count on. Instead, she sought the wind spirits and lifted one hand to beckon them. A hundred or more answered, twirling into a cyclone around her, drying the last of yesterday's damp. The silver mare whickered and shuffled backward, but Maya soothed the horse with a pat. "Easy there, Fairy. Easy." Wind spirits pitched her hair into her face, and she spat out several strands.

Penn's voice came from behind her. "You named your horse?"

Maya glanced back. "She needs a name, doesn't she? But I'm just trying it on. Does Fairy fit, do you think?"

The handsome viscount smiled and nodded. "It does. I like it."

"Will the fairies, I wonder?" Mikoneh mused.

Maya's cheeks warmed. "I think so. What's not to like? She's a beautiful horse, all silvery like the light in the Moon Veil. It feels right to me."

Her twin shrugged. "Do what you want."

"Well, it's better than Rook. Why name a horse after a bird?"

He snorted. "Don't blame me. I didn't name him."

"Is naming my horse after a tree a problem?" asked Penn with a thread of amusement in his tone.

"At least it's a majestic tree," she allowed. "Aspens remind me of diadems."

"They're like milkweeds in the tree kingdom," Mikoneh said. "Sprouting up where they're not wanted. Crowding other foliage out. Making a mess after a windstorm."

She cast him a disdainful glance. "You're only saying that to rile me."

"They can spread tree rot like rodents spread disease." He shrugged. "But I guess that fits with your imagery, too. A diadem of gold to hide the disease of nobility."

"Why do you have to be such a killjoy?" She nudged Fairy closer to her twin, rolling her eyes. "Not all nobility is like

Drayve, you know. Look at Penn. He's humbler and kinder than *you* any day in a fortnight!"

Mikoneh's lips twitched, the edges of mirth threatening to overcome his determined stoicism.

"Admit it, Mikoneh, son of Jonatten," she said. "You like aspens, but you think you can't say so because it's not a manly thing to confess."

"I like aspens," Penn chimed in.

"Not helping her cause, you know." Mikoneh flashed a grin before he could suppress it.

Penn coughed out a laugh. "Why do you insist on being a bully, young man?"

"To keep you humbler and kinder than me, of course."

The nobleman laughed heartily at that. "Maybe so. Honestly, I think meekness would ruin you. Truly, you're far better off as you are: moody and intense. It adds character."

Mikoneh snorted again.

"He wasn't always this way." Maya hadn't meant to blurt that out. Why did her tongue have to be so eager to wag? She ducked her head, afraid to meet her twin's eyes. He didn't like reminders of *before*.

The thud of hoofbeats filled the silence. A heavy sigh followed. She glanced at Mikoneh to find him scratching at his scalp with vigor, his tresses a tangle around his fingers. He always did that when he was trying to solve a problem.

"She's right, I wasn't always," Mikoneh said. "Sorry, Penn. I really don't mean to be rude. I was just teasing."

"I didn't take it as rudeness," Penn said gently. "Nor do I blame you for bouts of moodiness. We all have them. I'd hate to hold you to a higher standard than I do myself."

"Thanks, Penn. For the record, I like aspens too. They're among my favorite kinds of trees."

The silence grew more comfortable, and heat bled from

Maya's face back into her veins. She reached out a hand, and Mikoneh caught it in his strong, callused fingers. They said nothing while their horses rode side by side.

No matter how stubborn or angry or hurt, they always forgave each other.

CHAPTER 18

KENOOSHIN

"Simynshin was the first to embrace the baleful advice of a Dark Mage ambassador, and where it led, other kingdoms followed."

- From Athonen d'Ereth's *The Fall of Mages in the Age of Dragons*

Toward dusk, a cold wind swept across the trail.

Steering Rook with one hand, Mikoneh drew his cloak closer with the other, surprised to feel the chill. He hadn't experienced one since he'd tapped his fire element—except when Dark Mages were nearby. Grimacing, he urged the stallion closer to Ter in the lead.

"We may have a problem," he shouted above the whistling wind.

Ter glanced at him, tight-lipped, and nodded. He knew. With a whip of his reins, his pony flew faster down the path toward the village he'd promised they would reach around nightfall.

The idea of people living so deep within the old forest surprised Mikoneh—but then, the world was a strange place full of peculiar folk, and his experiences were limited to a tiny province in the backwater kingdom of Oceana. The wide world of Sirinhigha took no notice of a country that clung to its southern neighbor, Lintha, like a child hiding behind its mother's skirts.

A frigid breath like winter's chill nipped at Mikoneh's ears. He hunched deeper into his cloak and tugged his cowl lower over his face.

Did lights bob among the giant trees ahead?

Ter guided his pony around a bend, and the dense forest fell away all at once to reveal a strange village. Massive oak roots had lifted out of the ground to create cozy child-sized houses underneath the enormous trunks ringing a clearing. Moss grew over the roots to cover the little homes, cradling lighted windows not yet shuttered for the night. The cold lessened, as though Mikoneh had crossed a threshold into a warm house.

Clusters of children ranging from five up to twelve stood in what must be the village green. At the center of the sward, a well twined out of the ground, more tree than anything else, with leaves and branches hanging over a bucket waiting to be lowered into the hollow trunk.

Not children, Mikoneh realized. *Ephe'ahn.*

The woodelves watched them solemnly from either side of the path. Ter's pony slowed, then halted. The group followed suit.

Ter swung from his saddle with a sigh. "Welcome to Kenooshin, the first Ephe'ahn village of Simynshin when traveling from the south." His smile was abnormally stiff.

Mikoneh glanced around at the childlike fae, reading wonder and fear in their youthful faces. He frowned. "Are we really welcome?"

Ter's pointed ear twitched. "Indeed, you are. My folk would never turn aside Rokahnian refugees. We owe the Dragon King too great a debt." His large eyes skimmed the village, and several woodelves flinched back as though he'd struck them.

One Ephe'ahn, with bronzed skin and brunet hair, stepped forward. He looked like an older child, perhaps eleven. A quiver of arrows hung from his back. "We bid you hearty welcome, Lord Ter."

Ter's smile flickered, and his ears quivered. "Lord isn't necessary, Kem. Truly it's not, if you please."

Kem inclined his head. "The night is touched with Mages' rime. Do you seek shelter?"

"We do, indeed." Ter glanced at the trees.

Mikoneh tracked that gaze and startled. In the higher branches of the ancient oaks, wooden structures hung like oversized, ivy-covered birdhouses, lit up from within.

"The Frozen One seeks them." Ter gestured toward the twins as Mikoneh helped Maya from Fairy's back. Mikoneh kept one hand on the sheathed sword he'd strapped to his belt.

Kem's eyes narrowed. "Are they—"

"Yes." Ter's tone was hasty. "So they are. Shall we go inside the hostel?"

"Of course. This way." Kem motioned toward a large oak lighted by a dozen hanging chambers circling its trunk high overhead. At its base was a structure made from protruding roots. Penn slipped to Maya's other side, and the three followed Ter and Kem. Other childlike fae moved to guide the horses away. Mikoneh tried to picture a stable growing from the trees but shook off his curiosity and hurried to catch up to Ter.

"Aren't we putting your folk in danger?" He kept his voice low.

"The risk is minimal, as the Ephe'ahn are watched over by

the Sword," Ter said. "If Mages—or worse—try to break through the wards protecting this village, the vile things will bring upon themselves something they're not ready to reckon with."

Mages or worse. Mikoneh's mind flashed to the Revenant. *Don't think about it.*

"Was the Moon Veil not as well protected?" Mikoneh asked.

Ter's step faltered. "It was far more protected than Kenooshin." He sighed. "Only a traitor from within could have caused that fire—or let in what did. The fairies must see to that issue. Rest assured, Mikoneh, not a single living Ephe'ahn would side with Dark Mages."

"What about dead ones?"

Ter halted and glanced at him. "Those wouldn't be allowed in the village either." He rested a hand on Mikoneh's forearm. "Hurry, now. Into the light."

Mikoneh ducked through the small doorway and entered a room that looked much like an Oceanean tavern—but in miniature, and far cozier than the stark stone poverty of Relvin Province. Warm lanterns brightened a cheery room where seven tables stood. Several were occupied with male and female Ephe'ahn clutching steaming mugs or devouring food from small plates. Their skin and hair tones ranged from dark brown to pale hues, though all seemed to have the same large blue eyes that took in everything around them. They were clad in woodland garb much like Ter's: earthy tones, with bows and arrows close at hand.

One female woodelf—with rich brown skin and honey-gold hair—slopped her mug as she lifted it to her mouth. Her eyes collided with Mikoneh's. She lowered the mug, mouth gaping, long pointed ears twitching. She looked no older than ten. Her drinking companions sat with their backs to the door, but the girl mouthed something, and they craned to ogle the newcomers. Blue eyes widened. A hush fell over the warm chamber. The studious gazes traveled over the three humans, only to dart away once they reached Ter.

They're afraid of him. Why?

Kem lifted a hand, gathering the quiet stares to himself. "Our travelers seek sanctuary from the vile ones. They will be given every courtesy."

No one argued. No one stirred.

"This way, honored ones." Kem motioned to a set of stairs at the back of the tavern room where the trunk stretched upward. The stairs jutted from the polished bark, twining up toward the higher rooms hanging from thick, sturdy branches. "Choose whichever lodgings you wish. None are occupied. We have no other guests at present." Kem bowed his head to Ter. "Seek me if you require anything."

"Dinner, perhaps?" Ter's ears trembled. "And we shall need fresh supplies for the road. The Moon Veil was attacked whilst we were there, and we couldn't stock up all that was needful. We must head for Lord Rokahn's camp as swiftly as possible."

Kem nodded. "It will be accomplished, Lord Ter."

"Only Ter, thank you." Ter's ears quavered again. "After you, Maya."

She swept up the stairs without hesitation, and Mikoneh followed close. He didn't expect any danger to meet them, but his twin had so little regard for herself that she could get into trouble in a trice.

The stairs gave way to a deck that circled the massive trunk, and tiny vine-twined ramps branched out to offer passage to the individual hanging chambers. Maya crossed to the closest with a laugh and ducked into the free-hanging lodging held up by intricately woven, chainlike branches. Mikoneh caught up, startled to find the structure didn't sway under their combined weight.

The room was of a modest size, with a bed spacious enough for a rather broad human, crowding most of the space. Mikoneh halted to take in the cozy feel of a chamber bursting with life, from flowering ivy climbing the walls, to a tapestry rug woven from bright flowers, to oversized glowing mushrooms—a source of light that required no flame. Several fireflies hovered close to the mushrooms, pulsing with their own light.

"It's perfect." Maya pressed her fingertips to her lips. "I could stay here forever."

"Like it better than the Moon Veil?"

She shrugged. "I love both."

"Of course you do." He moved to the bed and pressed his hand against the strangely woven bedding. It was made from some kind of fern, soft and delicate. The mattress itself was plush, whatever it was stuffed with. He eased himself onto it, glad to be sitting on something besides a saddle. His soreness had persisted and likely would for days yet. How Maya could ignore it to study every cranny of the room, he didn't know. A smile edged his lips.

"Do you want this room?" he asked. "Or do you want to keep exploring the others to find the perfect one?"

Maya froze with one hand extended toward a firefly. She whirled toward him. "By myself?" Her voice was a squeak.

His smile slipped. "I can stay with you if you want."

She nodded. "Please. I...I don't want to dream about the Revenant—or those awful skeletons."

So, they'd shaken her as much as they had him. He hadn't been sure.

"I'll stay." He unbelted his sword, then spread across the

bed with a groan, closing his eyes. "I don't want to move yet anyway."

Her footsteps padded near, then the mattress sank under her weight. Warm fingers ran through his hair, gentle, tentative. "Are you well, Mikoneh?"

"Yeah," he murmured. "Just weary."

"That man—Sathe—using your blood, is he draining you somehow?"

"Dunno." He cracked his eyes open to find his twin looking down at him with open concern, the fear bright in her golden eyes. "Don't worry so much, Maya. We'll make it to the Dragon King's camp. He can help us. He can explain what's possible. We'll be safe there."

"I suppose. But what if the legends are right? What if war has changed him, and now he's bloodthirsty like people say? I mean, Fa and Mama hadn't seen him in years... We've been wrong about everything else. What if—"

Someone near the door chuckled.

Mikoneh turned his head to find the source of the sound. He expected Ter, but it was Penn. The viscount was leaning against the doorframe, a grin plastered to his face. His hand supported his slung arm.

"With all we've seen, I think we can rule out nearly everything we ever heard in Oceana. I'm beginning to think the Dragon King's a saint in disguise rather than a warlord." Penn's mirth faded, and his eyes drifted to the glowing mushrooms. "My—er—lodging is the next one over southward." He pointed through the vine-curtained window. "It's not much different, only the colors of the flowers and the glowing hue of the mushrooms. And it has a very large butterfly." His grin returned. "I'll bid you a good rest and see you at dinner."

"Do you mind being alone after that Revenant?" Maya asked.

Penn shrugged. "You'll both be close by, and this village feels safe enough. I'll be fine." He inclined his head, then strode down the little ramp, cradling his injured arm.

Maya trotted across the short expanse of floor and pulled a door made from vines over the opening. She turned back to Mikoneh, the fear back in her eyes. "I know Ter said we're safe here, but the wind is restless and...I feel hunted."

"I feel the same way." Mikoneh dragged the sword onto the bed. "I'll keep this close. But we'll be okay. Remember that Ter said the Dark Mages won't risk entering this place and upsetting the wards."

"Wards." She gave a choking laugh. "Fairies. Dragons. Undead Mages. Ghosts. It's all so much. Lovely, some of it. And wondrous. But terrifying, too. I wish Fa and Mama had prepared us a little more for all this."

"I know." He patted the bedding. "Get some rest until dinner. Anticipating a bad thing never made it easier to bear."

She crawled into the bed, curling up close. He propped himself up on plush pillows, keeping his sword nearby. The sleepless night had caught up with him, and he dozed almost at once.

His dreams were strange, restless, with the cries of an ancient battle ringing in his pointed ears.

CHAPTER 19

THE BARRIER

*"Among the human countries, only Rokahn stood against the
Mage Queen's demands in the end."*

- From Athonen d'Ereth's *The Fall of Mages in the Age of Dragons*

A hand fell over Mikoneh's mouth.

His eyes snapped open. Ter stood above him, blue eyes illuminated in the mushrooms' glow, one finger pressed to his lips. Slowly, the Ephe'ahn removed his hand from Mikoneh's face, then stepped back.

'Come,' he mouthed. 'Quietly.'

Sitting up, Mikoneh shoved his long, loose hair behind his back, and stared around the dim room. Maya was gone. He looked sharply at Ter, who tapped his lips with the finger still lifted, then beckoned toward the open door leading from the hanging guestroom. Urgency filled the woodelf's large blue eyes.

Adrenaline spiked. Mikoneh slid from the bed, one hand groping for his sword. His fingers met the leaf-woven blanket. He glanced down. Fa's sword was gone. His alarm pitched higher.

Ter caught his arm. "Maya has it." His voice was the faintest whisper.

That struck Mikoneh as odd. How had she left without waking him, and with the sword he'd been clutching before he fell asleep?

I must be wearier than I thought.

At a tug from the woodelf, Mikoneh followed Ter to the door. A chill seized him at the head of the ramp. He shivered and drew the cloak tighter around his shoulders. Had the wards around Kenooshin failed? The two descended the ramp, Ter leading. On the tree's circular deck, Mikoneh's eyes darted to the next hanging enclosure. Was Penn already gone, too? The enclosure glistened like it was coated in frost. Mikoneh stepped toward it.

Ter caught his cloak. "This way." Still the faintest whisper.

As Mikoneh turned, he glimpsed frost covering the bark of the tree trunk. It glittered in the dim light emanating from below. He dropped his gaze to the ground beneath their perch, and his eyes widened. The entire village was encrusted in blue rime.

The Mages attacked after all?

All was still. Like the very wind held its breath.

He sought out any sign of Maya or Penn below. Nothing. No indication of any of the Ephe'ahn either, like they all slept through the cold that crept across their forest home.

We can't abandon them to the Mages.

He trailed Ter toward the spiraling stairs jutting from the tree, and they descended on swift, silent feet. Within the hostel, all was still and dark. No blaze in the hearth, no mushrooms to light the tables.

He watched Ter's back. Something needled him in the recesses of his head.

Something's wrong.

He halted. "Ter?"

The Ephe'ahn turned toward him. "Quickly, now. We haven't time." He gestured toward the door leading out onto the village green.

Mikoneh shook his head. "I don't think—"

"It's you Sathe wants. Do not let him claim you. Make haste."

"I—" That something screamed at him, but he couldn't understand what it was trying to say.

Ter's eyes flashed violet. He shot out his hand and snatched Mikoneh's wrist. "Stop dawdling. Do you want him to catch your sister?" His grip tightened like a vise.

Mikoneh hissed, adrenaline spiking higher. "That hurts, Ter."

This is wrong.

"Come along, *now.*" Ter yanked him toward the door.

'*Mikoneh, stop.*' The voice breathed against his back, sharp, urgent. He faltered, but Ter's strength was surprising.

This isn't right. He tried to pull free, but Ter's fingers curled tighter, bruising him.

"Stop." His voice cracked, like he hadn't used it in a hundred years. "Ter. Stop it! Let me go."

"Not until we're free of the village."

'*Mikoneh!*'

That voice. Mikoneh knew it. Was it Sathe? The Mage had talked to him in his head before.

Frigid urgency flooded through him, dimming all but one thought: *Ter's right. We need to run.*

He lurched forward, and Ter stumbled under the sudden release of resistance. They blinked at each other, then straightened and raced out the door.

'*Wake up. Please!*'

Wake up? He was already awake, wasn't he? Breath plumed from his lips. He jogged toward the trees on Ter's heels. Ahead —those were the horses, weren't they? And Maya and Penn beside them?

Just a little farther.

This isn't right, something in him said again. *Think, Mikoneh. Think!*

Icicles dripped in the tree branches. Cold slithered up his spine, seeping into his bones.

Run faster.

No, think! he told himself. But he kept running.

Almost to the trees, something snatched Mikoneh's arm. He wrenched to a halt, slipping free of Ter's grasp.

'*Snap out of it!*'

He shuddered.

The Ephe'ahn staggered to a stop and whirled, blue eyes wide. "Hurry!"

"I—I can't." He tugged against an invisible force. "I'm caught." Panic swirled in his stomach, rising like bile in his throat, choking him. If the Mages caught him, what could he do to resist? Minno was gone. Fire couldn't stop a Revenant.

Ter's eyes flashed violet again. His image shimmered, and something crouched behind it; a huge, ugly, toad-like thing. A monster.

Mikoneh flinched back. "What are you?"

The image of Ter solidified again. The woodelf's smile was bright as sunshine. "I'm myself, of course. Come. Hurry. Your twin is waiting."

"What about Penn?"

Ter's smile wavered. "What about him? Useless. Utterly." The Ephe'ahn flinched. "No, he's waiting, too. Come, *hurry*." He reached out.

Mikoneh backed up again, pressing against whatever force held him. "No. You're not Ter. This isn't real, is it? I'm dreaming."

Think, Mikoneh, he told himself. *Think through the haze.*

The Ephe'ahn's laugh was a burbling, hacking thing, like a stray cat coughing up a hairball. "Don't be foolish, Mikoneh. This is your only chance. Come now, or you will suffer."

"No."

"What about your twin? Will you leave her to us, then? All alone?"

Mikoneh's shoulders pinched. Fury blazed in his chest. "Don't you *dare* hurt her!"

*'**Fight, Mikoneh.**'* The familiar voice broke through from far, far away.

He stood frozen. What should he do? He couldn't surrender to this imposter wearing Ter's skin—nor could he leave Maya to a fate worse than death. Would she become a Revenant? What *wouldn't* Sathe do to her?

The thing that had snatched him back gripped him harder, stronger, whirling him away from Ter. *'**Mikoneh, it's me! Wake up now. Please!**'*

He stared into the empty air where someone should be standing. The frozen village, still as death, spread before him.

"There's no going back," Ter said. "They're all dead. Only your sister remains."

No, that was wrong. The Ephe'ahn's words rang false. The voice...the voice trying to stop him from making a mistake...he knew that voice...

"Don't you dare!" shouted Ter—and yet it didn't *sound* like Ter.

Think, Mikoneh!

"Penn." He whispered the name. As though somehow that single action shattered a looking glass, Penn stood before him. Both hands gripped Mikoneh's shoulders, his sling hanging forgotten around his neck. Fear had driven the blood from the viscount's face, but his brown eyes were nearly amber, bright with determination.

"P—Penn?" Mikoneh choked out, drenched in sweat, trembling from head to toe like he'd run a dozen leagues.

They stood on the outskirts of the village, but where before all had been frozen, now dewdrops sparkled on the cheery little houses nestled among the roots of the ancient trees. Dawn light stretched beams across the sward to scatter shadows. A few Ephe'ahn had stirred from their homes to peek out, their big eyes pinned on Mikoneh and Penn. Glancing around, Mikoneh found no sign of Ter, nor any hideous monsters.

"You can see me?" Penn let out a rush of air. "Thank the Nijaal—you can see me." His hands shook, still clutching Mikoneh tight. "I've been trying to get you to stop for...I don't know how long!" His eyes darted to the trees, then back to Mikoneh's face. "You were in a trance."

Weariness poured through Mikoneh's body in a flood. His knees wobbled, and he let himself slump to the ground. His heart pounded in his ears. "I...I think it was a sort of dream. I was following Ter. The Mages infiltrated..." He dragged a hand over his damp face. "I don't want to think what might've happened if..."

"You would have crossed the barrier." Ter's voice, subdued.

Mikoneh snapped his eyes up to find the Ephe'ahn. With the real Ter standing before him, it was easy to tell the difference. This Ter's eyes were brighter. His countenance, too. He was somehow more tangible. The other had been cold and strangely lifeless.

The hunching thing behind him was real enough, though definitely not human or—or fae. Mikoneh shuddered.

"There's a barrier?" asked Penn.

Ter nodded. "Yes. It protects this and other fae villages in the south. Most fae live in the High North beyond the mountains. Had Mikoneh crossed the barrier, it would've been a willing action, based on the barrier's parameters, and the alarm would not have been raised. The Mages could have snatched him without anyone being the wiser." The Ephe'ahn canted his head. "How did you know to stop him?"

Penn shrugged. "I couldn't sleep. I was roaming the tree decks and saw Mikoneh leave his room. He was moving as though he were running from something—so I followed. I realized something was wrong when he started arguing with someone I couldn't see."

Mikoneh's hands were still shaking. Staring down at them, he marveled at how close he'd come to placing himself in Sathe's clutches. The Mage had clouded Mikoneh's mind, keeping him from thinking clearly. That was obvious now.

Is he out there, watching me from the trees?

Mikoneh didn't dare glance behind him to search the forest. "How do we proceed if the Mages are waiting right outside?"

The woodelf shook his head, sighing. "We cannot travel by the same path. We must call for help."

"Is that possible?" Penn asked.

"Difficult to say," said Ter. "We can issue a summons, but there may be none available to answer. The Mages keep out of this village, and others like it, for a risk that is not certain, but remains too likely to prod at."

"Clear as mud," Mikoneh muttered, too drained to keep his tongue civil.

Ter's chuckle was unexpected, but perhaps that surprise

was residue of his encounter with the imposter. Still, it only worsened Mikoneh's mood.

"What's so funny?"

"It's just..." Ter's smile broadened. "You're so much the Fire Elementalist. That temper is refreshing, I confess. Very different from...well, never mind." He bounded closer and offered a hand up.

With a grimace, Mikoneh accepted. Despite the woodelf's diminutive height, he was strong. Pulling Mikoneh to his feet was hardly an effort for the little fellow. Ter's ears twitched absently as he tapped a finger to his chin.

"Long ago, the League of the Sword protected Ephe'ahn villages under solemn oath," Ter said after a moment. "That oath remains in force, but the danger has largely passed. If the barrier is ever breached, someone from the Sword is honor-bound to answer the summons, but it's possible none are stationed at the Watch. It is many years since there was true need of it—and the Dragon King must use all his men in his current struggle."

"The Sword." Penn's voice was breathless. "You mean—they're real?"

"Why not?" Mikoneh wavered on his feet. "Everything else is." Still, he couldn't ignore the awe that prickled up his arms. The League of the Sword. The elite group of knights whose skill with a blade was second to none save their master: Owenekiras Rokahn himself. Stories had reached Oceana about their fearlessness and their invincibility. He'd be willing to lay odds they weren't *quite* so untouchable as that, but even so, he'd love to glimpse one of their number in action.

If my father served as the Dragon King's general, was he part of the Sword, too?

"Indeed, they are real," Ter said. "And quite as fierce as the stories say—though not so immortal, alas."

Penn glanced at the trees surrounding Kenooshin. "Should we sound the alarm and see what happens?"

"That's a big risk, Penn." Mikoneh took a step toward Ter. "If the Mages are watching, and activating the barrier does nothing, won't they attack this village?"

Ter nodded. "Most definitely, yes. It is a great risk."

"Then what do we do?" Maya's voice came from beyond Ter. She clutched Fa's sword in both hands, hugging the sheathed blade to her chest. Mikoneh moved to meet her and accepted the sword when she offered it. He belted it to his waist, then turned back to Ter.

"You understand all this better than we do," he said. "It's your call."

Ter offered a mirthless smile. "So be it." He pivoted to take in the village, turning slowly, until he faced forward again. "I will speak with Kem. The villagers should have a say in what happens."

"None of this is fair to them," Maya murmured. "They didn't ask for this danger. Perhaps we should try to sneak away unseen."

"Impossible, I'm afraid." Ter shook his head. "Mikoneh's blood in Sathe's possession can track your brother anywhere. No matter where we run, his minions will find us. We are not safe until we reach Lord Rokahn's camp."

"What makes his camp safe?" asked Penn.

Ter blinked at him. "Why, because it's already hidden from the Mages."

"Better than the Moon Veil?" the viscount challenged.

"Indeed. Fairy enchantments are strong, but they are nothing next to the Dragon King's mastery of stealth. Excuse me a moment." Ter bowed his head, then moved off toward a growing cluster of Ephe'ahn near the hostel. Kem stood among them, waiting.

An insistent itch rubbed at Mikoneh's mind. A desire to run—by himself—to spare the village, his twin, his friend, and their guide.

It's me he wants.

But that was foolhardy. Despite how little Mikoneh understood about the Mages and their politics, there was no doubt they were vile, selfish creatures out to destroy what was good in the world. In their hands, what would Mikoneh be forced to do for their cause?

How many homes filled with parents and children might I be forced to torch?

He couldn't risk that. He wouldn't become a tool for evil.

CHAPTER 20

THE CUSTOMS OF THE WORLD

"Her vile plot might have won out—the Mage Queen might have ruled the entire world—but she miscalculated two things."

- From Athonen d'Ereth's *The Fall of Mages in the Age of Dragons*

Mikoneh didn't force his way into the meeting with the Ephe'ahn, though part of him wanted to be involved. Instead, he, his twin, and Penn retreated to the nearest hanging chamber above the hostel, where they seated themselves on the bed and ate berries, mushrooms, and a kind of sweet creamy pudding. One bite of the last was enough to sour Mikoneh's weak appetite, so he used an oil cloth some helpful villager had left and polished his sword.

His nerves were as taut as a bowstring. Every creak of the tree boughs, every breath of wind, every raised voice drifting from the hostel, sent his heart rate soaring. Swells of dizziness rolled across his mind. As he rubbed his blade, his fingers trembled. He desperately needed to lie still and recover from his nightmare. But he was terrified Sathe might get into his mind again.

Since his attempt to compel me failed, what will he try instead?

Another puzzle was how Ter intended to bring the Sword here. Did he have a tool like the blue stone to punch a hole through the Void?

If he did have such a tool, he could get us out of here, couldn't he?

Even if it wasn't precise, it could still put space between them and Sathe.

Then it can't be that.

He scowled and tucked his oilcloth away. Sheathing his sword, he glanced at Maya and Penn, who eyed him back.

"What?" His tone was sharper than he'd intended.

Penn shook his head. "You just look…"

"Pale," Maya said. "Shouldn't you lie down?"

Mikoneh sighed and buckled his sword on again. "Not until we know what's going on—unless you want me sleepwalking through the village again, strolling to my doom."

"In your defense," Penn said, "you weren't really strolling. More like galloping, then bucking, then galloping again."

Mikoneh tried to suppress a snort but failed. He rolled his eyes to dampen his amusement. "Thank you. I feel much better with that image stuck in my head."

"It's what I'm here for." Penn's eyes sparkled, but then he looked away, fingering his sling.

"Stop that." Mikoneh spoke at the same time Maya said, "We need you, Penn."

The viscount heaved a sigh. "Forgive me, but I feel like an encumbrance."

"Oh, yeah?" Mikoneh folded his arms. "I can see that. You

definitely didn't just keep me out of the Mages' hands. Not that."

"I'm glad I did," Penn said. "But I need to be able to do more. It's a much bigger world than we knew—with *magic*. If I just had some magic…"

"Penn," Maya said gently, "we're running for our lives because Mages want our magic. If anything, Mikoneh and I are the burdens you and Ter are putting up with. *We're* causing the danger."

Mikoneh grunted his agreement.

"I understand that perspective," Penn said, "but with that same magic, you could both really help Oceana like we never dreamed."

"How?" Mikoneh's tone was a low growl. "By torching people to death? Great idea."

"Don't get grouchy," Penn said. "You know what I mean."

"He's just tired." Maya shot Mikoneh a glare. "And needs to *sleep*. We can tie you up, Mikoneh. Keep you from galloping anywhere."

"Sure. Because ropes won't hinder my slumber at all."

"Mikoneh, *try*. We'll keep a watch."

He raked a hand over his scalp. Tresses snagged on his fingers. "I know. I want to, but I can't. Not until—"

"It's all settled." Ter was in the doorway, almost as though he'd appeared there.

Mikoneh's heart slammed against his ribcage. His hand caught his sword hilt. "Don't *do* that."

Ter's ears fluttered. "Apologies. The village council has agreed to let us sound the alarm. We shall soon see if the Sword is able to respond."

"How?" Mikoneh cringed at his sharp tone. He made a point to soften his voice. "Will they come quickly? Do they have stones like the one we used to summon you?"

"Ah." Ter's smile widened. "It is an old Void anchor that can only be opened under very strict conditions."

"Will we know straight away if it works?" Penn asked.

Ter's large eyes settled on the noble. "You have a most inquisitive mind, which reminds me of a very dear pupil of mine. That will serve you well, Master Penn, if it doesn't get you skinned first. The cost of curiosity can be a high one."

Penn smiled. "Will we know soon?"

"Yes, quite soon."

"Were the villagers really all right with this?" asked Maya.

"Oh, yes." Ter's smile tightened—or did Mikoneh imagine it? "They are most fiercely loyal to Owenekiras. He has done much for my people."

That was an itch Mikoneh had to scratch. "The Ephe'ahn debt to the Dragon King includes us? Why?"

"Because as Jonatten and Seranni's children, you fall under his protection. They acknowledge that. Thus, they consider the failure to protect what the Dragon King claims as a grave dishonor. They would never forgive themselves."

The idea remained strange to Mikoneh, but then, Mama had often declared the customs of the world to be bizarre and mottled. She'd laughed about it, shaking her head like all of Sirinhigha was a place of madness.

I'm beginning to understand.

He inhaled a long breath, settling his nerves. "Very well, we accept—with reservations. I hate the idea of putting anyone in danger for my sake." He avoided glancing at his twin. For her, on the other hand, he would do nearly anything. They both knew it. Her eyes bored into him, sharp as daggers.

Ter offered up his usual chuckle. "Well, then, it is decided. We will know soon if the old oaths are still binding."

"If not..." Mikoneh shifted his grip. "If no one comes and

the Mages realize they can enter, are your people prepared to fight?"

Ter's smile slanted into a half-frown. "The Ephe'ahn as a rule do not fight. They hunt—yes—but only for sustenance, never sport. They are...ill-prepared for battle. That is one reason why the Dragon King protects them still. My people are a most gentle sort."

Mikoneh frowned. "That changes things."

"No. No, no. It changes nothing," said Ter. "They have chosen, and an Ephe'ahn does not shrink from his choice once made. They will all protect you if they must. Spirits willing, it will not come to that."

Mikoneh rubbed his thumb along the pommel of his sword. "Will Lord Rokahn be upset if we sound this alarm when the village isn't really in danger?"

"But it is," said Maya. "Isn't it, Ter? The Mages are surrounding the Ephe'ahn as much as us. They'll strike if they think they can, and meanwhile, we're under siege."

"Right you are," Ter said. "We have no choice, and that is how the village council sees it. I doubt very much many of the other Ephe'ahn will disagree. We are small, and perhaps generally timid, but we are also a most level-headed people. Now, that's settled. I'm off to witness the summons."

Mikoneh took a step forward. "We'll come, too, if that's all right."

Ter bobbed a nod and motioned for them to follow.

The four left the hanging chamber, moved down the ramp, then walked toward the spiral stairs. As Mikoneh started down the steps, dizziness crashed into his skull. He staggered. A hand snatched him back, away from the edge.

"Maybe you shouldn't go anywhere," Penn murmured.

"I agree." Maya was digging through her herb pouch. "Take him back to the bed, Penn. I'll stay with him."

"That's not..." A fresh wave of dizziness overtook Mikoneh, and he slumped against Penn, closing his eyes. "I'm fine."

Mikoneh didn't need to peel his eyes open to know they were glaring at him. He grimaced. Obviously, he wasn't fine, and for once, he wouldn't try to convince himself otherwise.

You can't even walk, dolt.

"Fine." The word scraped up his throat. "Take me back."

Mikoneh.

He lurched upright, startling Penn enough that the young man lost his grip on him. Mikoneh dropped, slamming his knees against the gleaming deck. His bones ached as though rime crawled over them, freezing his joints, slowing his heart to almost nothing.

It's only a matter of time. We will break through to reach you soon. Spare everyone the effort and heartache, Firebrand. Come to me now, or I'll claim your twin instead.

"N-not a chance." His words were the barest whisper.

Laughter crackled like ice breaking across a river, filling his head. He exhaled a shuddering breath, and vapor plumed before his mouth.

Voices surrounded him. Someone was hauling him upright. He couldn't focus on them; he couldn't do more than breathe, and even that was an effort. The cold tightened around his lungs. Panic seared his mind, spiking his heart.

Get out of my head!

Laughter boomed, tremoring through his frame. Someone laid him across a soft, green-smelling surface.

The bed, he thought distantly. *I'm still there. Sathe doesn't have me. Get out...*

You will be mine, Firebrand. Forever.

He ground his teeth. *Get out of my head!*

That's not enough, Firebrand. You're not nearly angry—not nearly strong—enough.

GET OUT! Fire surged through him, eating up the cold, devouring it. Flames licked at the edges of his dim vision, and the growing blackness curled away. The fire remained when the chill retreated.

Wait. Are those...?

He bolted upright. Flames consumed the bed around him. Penn and Maya had retreated down the ramp, and Ter alone stood within the conflagration.

"Breathe, Mikoneh," he said in soothing tones. "Call the fire back in, as you might draw in a breath."

Sweat rolled down Mikoneh's cheeks, beading on his chin. Fire spirits flickered and flitted around him, riding the sparks and curling flames. He inhaled—tried to center himself—the way Fa had taught him before each sword drill.

Don't panic. Stop panicking.

Fire roared and cackled in his ears.

Stop that.

A fire spirit tugged at his hair.

Stop. You'll burn everything I love.

One whispered in his ear. 'Come play.'

"GO AWAY!" He shot to his feet, clutching his sword, gasping for air. Panic gnawed at his skull and pounded through his scorching blood.

The fire spirits reared, pulsing with hurt feelings. All at once, the flames died. The room stood in tatters, the giant mushrooms shriveled and crisped. The bedding was a tangle of ash and char.

He slumped onto the bed's edge and covered his damp face in his hands. Groaning, he collapsed onto his side and fell into disjointed dreams, with Fa and Mama on fire, while Maya became a skeleton, cloaked, with eyes that blazed with violet light.

A great hand formed from ice and snow, reaching down from a wintry sky to cage him.

He screamed and tried to run, but Sathe caught him.

You're mine, Firebrand. Mine.

Forever.

Chapter 21

Adrift in the Great Waters

"Firstly, the Dragon King is a creature of justice. And she had wounded too many souls for him to disregard her sins."

- From Athonen d'Ereth's *The Fall of Mages in the Age of Dragons*

"It's not quite a fever. Or at least, nothing like those I've treated." Maya dipped her cloth in cool water, then dabbed at Mikoneh's face again. "Is it whatever Sathe is doing to him?"

"That is a contributor, I would guess." Ter stood at the foot of the bed within the new cage-like enclosure where they'd moved. The Ephe'ahn's arms were folded, his ears drooping like a wounded puppy. His frown did something to age him, though his physique remained that of an eight-year-old. "More than that," Ter went on, "he rejected his element. That is a grave mistake to make. Reversible, but difficult."

She chewed her lip, then sighed. "It's not his fault, you know. It's...our parents..."

"They were burned alive, locked within their cottage," Penn said. He was standing on the other side of the bed like Mikoneh's personal guard.

Maya smiled weakly at him, grateful he'd kept her from saying it. She couldn't. Not yet.

"Ah." Ter's ears wilted further. "That is truly sad. You harbor my deepest sympathies, Lady Maya."

She tensed. "Oh. I'm not a lady." Heat climbed her cheeks. "I don't have any titles."

"Indeed? Yet you behave like one."

Her head ducked, and she concentrated hard on her twin's face. His pallor was gray, his breaths labored, and he tossed as though caught in a fever dream, but his skin was as cold as the high northern reaches.

Penn shifted, fixing a narrowed look on Ter. "Shouldn't you be summoning help, Master Ter?"

The Ephe'ahn's ears trembled. For a moment, that was his only movement. Then he sighed. "We cannot proceed as we planned."

Maya clenched the damp cloth tighter. "Why not? Can he not move? Is my brother dying?"

"Easy, easy." Ter's smile became all sympathy and kindness. "He is not dying—but Sathe's hold on him is stronger than I'd expected. If we bring your twin to Owenekiras's camp, the Mages may be able to breach those borders, no matter the wards placed there. I suspect that it is Mikoneh's unfortunate connection to Sathe that caused that forest fire in the Moon Veil to begin with. Sathe made your brother subconsciously start that fire, if I am not mistaken. It's with deep regret that I say this, but we must find a means of severing this link *now*, or we risk great harm to Sirinhigha's best hope against its darkest adversary."

"But..." Penn hesitated. "The Mages haven't breached *these* borders despite that connection. Is this village better protected than the Dragon King's forces?"

"Ah, that is a well-considered argument, Lord Penn. But they are two separate issues. The Dragon King's camp is hidden. Its location is undetectable. While Sathe would like to burn an Ephe'ahn village down for no better reason than Mage cruelty, it is not a high priority, and the Mages here are few. They risk a great deal if we do manage to summon aid. They aren't willing to take that step. Yet.

"If, on the other hand, they could pinpoint the location of Owenekiras Rokahn's camp through Mikoneh, they would surely muster a force large enough to swallow it whole—and hang the hazards. It is a much more important target than a small village and one young man, no matter his blood." Ter sighed again, shaking his head. "We must break Sathe's blood link before we can go further."

"How?" Maya asked.

"I had hoped your brother would free himself. He certainly tried. A hot enough elemental fire can purge the blood of magical contagions—although not indefinitely. Had Mikoneh broken the link long enough for us to flee into the Dragon King's camp and made his—hm—*aura* vanish, Sathe would have had trouble finding him to reestablish the connection."

"But he didn't." Penn's voice was soft. "So, what can we do?"

"There are several options to weigh, though none are without risk. Ideally, we could travel north and seek the Nijaal. Lady Katanni—their spiritual advisor, you might call her—she could help in some way. Her woodland realm is a place of healing." The Ephe'ahn tapped his chin. "But getting there alive is the great trouble. Short of that, we can still summon aid. Rather than go to the war camp, we could enlist soldiers to protect us while I guide Mikoneh to burn out the Mage contagion. It might not work—not with his mental block—but it is an option."

Maya dropped the cloth into the basin of water. Ripples cascaded across its surface. "Neither of those is very promising."

"No, indeed not." Ter stepped away from the bed and began to pace. "Perhaps Lord Owenekiras himself would answer. Certainly, he would if he were able. It's a matter of what he's currently doing."

"I don't want to cause trouble." Maya fished out the cloth and wrang it like it was Sathe's throat. "But I'll accept help from anyone we can trust."

Ter shook his head. "Minno *might* have been of some help. Why must he always scamper off? He must've..." Whatever Minno *must've*, Ter never said, trailing off into a fading mutterance. His pacing ceased. "Yes, that might be the thing to try first." He turned toward the bed and rested his gaze on Maya. "I will seek Owenekiras Rokahn. On my own, untracked, it may be possible—and I can travel faster by myself. I will return as soon as I am able. Keep your brother abed. Keep him unconscious if possible. If all goes well, I will return in a twig or two."

The Ephe'ahn bounded from the room, down the ramp, and out of sight. Maya stared at the open doorway, a prayer hanging on her lips. She shook herself and turned to Penn.

"Do you think the Dragon King will actually come?" she asked.

Penn shook his head. "I really don't know. I hope so, for your brother's sake."

"So do I."

Cut adrift in the great waters of a war-torn world, they needed allies more desperately than ever.

She shifted. "Any idea how much time a twig is?"

"Absolutely none."

INTERLUDE III
ALL CLOAKED AND HOODED

- From the Corpse Poet's 12th Sonnet

THE BLUE-HUED WORLD WAS DIFFERENT THIS TIME.

Mikoneh walked among hundreds of soldiers, all cloaked and hooded, traveling through the ancient High North woods with bows, arrows, swords, spears, and other weapons whose names brushed against Mikoneh's memory—just out of reach.

Beside him, three figures walked; two with long, steady strides; one with shorter, graceful lopes. They were his companions. He knew that instinctively. He would trust them with his life, and they felt the same.

Tension hummed on the air. They were moving toward a battlefield.

He turned to find the white-cloaked woman at his side.

Perhaps sensing his glance, she turned her cowl until he could see her emerald eyes.

A sorrowful smile touched her lips. "I'm glad you're here, my shadow friend. It's some comfort. Many will die this day, I fear."

He reached for her hand.

She reached for his.

CHAPTER 22

WITH A FEW DROPS OF BLOOD

"The Mage Queen's second mistake was her effort to gain power over more than the world. When she targeted the very fabric of time and space—the cloak of Mithrinn itself—she gained the attention of those who didn't often involve themselves."

- From Athonen d'Ereth's *The Fall of Mages in the Age of Dragons*

Mikoneh jolted awake. A soft breeze caressed his face and blew back his hair.

The air around his bed was tinged blue.

Am I still dreaming?

He shifted until a heavy weight caught his blanket, pinning him. He glanced left to find his twin kneeling beside the bed, her face tucked into her arms on the edge of the mattress, asleep. He rested his hand on her tangled hair. She hardly stirred, too deeply held by her dreams. The day had surrendered to night. He'd slept a long time.

The soft blue light came from a stand of mushrooms near the closed door. On the floor in one corner, Penn slumbered, a vine-woven blanket wrapped up to his shoulders. Fa's sword was clutched in the viscount's hand.

Mikoneh smiled faintly. They'd done all they could to protect him.

From what?

The memories triggered. He shuddered under the force of Sathe's voice, and the subsequent fire that had consumed their previous quarters.

Why did it have to be fire?

He brushed back his loose hair, then gently slipped from the bed. Bare feet touched wood slats. He stood up, glad his balance was stable. Dragging his hair behind his back, he knotted it to keep it out of his way. A window offered him a dusky view of the village below. Shadows moved around the hanging lanterns of Kenooshin. Patrols, probably.

He studied them, habitually memorizing the patrol patterns. He didn't plan to escape into the night, though the idea pressed on him. He remained resolved not to give Sathe any power in the war waging across the continent.

What should I do instead?

Had Ter summoned the League of the Sword as he'd intended? Had it worked?

Mikoneh placed his knuckle in his mouth and gently gnawed, running through what he knew. So little. Too little. He'd never seen himself as a big fish in the proverbial lake of Oceana, but here he was hardly a tadpole in the great oceans of Sirinhigha.

We're so far out of our depth, I don't know how to act.

A single shadow moved differently from the Ephe'ahn patrols, almost formless. Small, though—not a full-sized man.

Is that Minno?

He caught the fragrance of cedarwood and patchouli. Definitely Minno.

Why did he come here?

The gray boy slipped into the hostel where light still streamed from the windows.

Mikoneh strode over to Penn and gently tugged his sheathed sword from his friend's fingers. Belting it on, he slipped out the door and down the ramp. When he reached the main stairs leading to the deck where their room was, Minno was already halfway up the spiraling climb.

Waiting, Mikoneh let the night breeze tease strands of his dark hair. His thumb rubbed the pommel of his sword. Minno reached him, gray eyes fixed on Mikoneh. If the boy was surprised to see Mikoneh up and waiting, he didn't show it. He only nodded. He clutched his long tunic near his abdomen where something swelled beneath the gray cloth.

"A pleasant night," Minno said without a hint of inflection.

"I suppose." Mikoneh arched a brow. "What brought you back?"

"Mages. They're crawling across the woods like violet vermin."

"How did you get into Kenooshin without them seeing you?"

"They saw me. But they couldn't stop me."

Was that really surprising? Already, Minno had proven himself powerful in ways Mikoneh didn't understand. "Did you push yourself too much again?"

Minno shook his head. "I was careful. I came to warn you. There is nowhere you can flee. Ter had best summon the Sword using the old channels."

"We were discussing that. I'm not sure if he has yet, though."

"He hasn't. They would come at once. The Sword has recently been alerted to increasing anti-fae sentiment. The old oaths are renewed."

"Anti-fae sentiment? From whom? Mages?"

Minno shrugged. "They likely started it up again, but humans are growing less tolerant of fae encroaching on what they consider to be their lands. The story has never changed much, not even after twenty-thousand years." A faint grimace touched his face. "Why should it? No need to change a narrative that still works to manipulate weak minds."

"You mean prejudice." It wasn't really a question.

"I do," Minno said anyway. "Works well to start a war. And few are innocent of experiencing some level of that irrational hatred in their lives."

"You're rather cynical," Mikoneh said.

"Convince me I'm wrong then." Minno moved closer, still clutching the swell in his tunic. "After encountering Dark Mages, do you harbor no prejudice toward them?"

"Are you telling me there are Dark Mages worth protecting or respecting?" asked Mikoneh dryly.

The boy hesitated at that. "Perhaps not. Very well. What are your feelings toward nobility?"

Caught. Mikoneh bobbed his own shrug. "Point taken." He inclined his head. "What do you have there?"

"Ah, this. This is why I left rather hastily. I feared Sathe might need dinner. I didn't want..." He grimaced again. "Let it remain unsaid."

Mikoneh's brows flew up. "Do Mages need to eat?"

"The ones with flesh do. I suppose 'need' is the wrong word, though. They don't require sustenance of the type you do, as they sold themselves for a pathetic kind of immortality. But they still enjoy food, which seems reasonable if it's cooked well."

"Right. So, you...stole their dinner?"

Minno shook his head. "I rescued what they might have perceived as their dinner."

"So, it's a rabbit."

Minno gave his slow blink. "Your creativity astounds."

Despite the bland tone, Mikoneh recognized the boy's sarcasm. He rolled his eyes. "You know what, it doesn't matter. I really don't care."

"Good." Minno nodded toward the first hanging room, drawing Mikoneh's attention for the first time to its charred remains. "Lost control, did you?" The gray boy's lack of inflection somehow made the question worse.

Heat kissed Mikoneh's cheeks. His tongue burned with a retort—but truth was truth. His temper withered until he sighed, letting his shoulders slump. "It appears so."

"Ah." Minno's eyes drifted toward the second hanging enclosure. "Is Ter in there?"

"No."

"Well, then. I will go back down to find—" His voice cut off as a distinct *quack* sounded from under his tunic.

They both stared at it.

"Is that...a duck?" Mikoneh asked.

"Is what a duck?"

"That." Mikoneh nodded to the swell.

"That what?"

"Your lump."

"What about it?"

"Did it quack?"

"Did what quack?"

"Is the lump in your tunic a duck?" Mikoneh nearly shouted the question—though why he cared to argue over something so trivial, he'd never know.

"Certainly not." Minno slow-blinked. "What is *causing* the lump is a duck."

Annoyance gnawed at Mikoneh's stomach, but he inhaled and nodded. "Thanks for your clarity. If you don't mind, I'm going back to sleep."

"I don't mind. In fact, I don't care."

Mikoneh turned around and marched toward the ramp, shaking his head. What a frustrating child.

At the door to the hanging chamber, Penn stuck out his head. His eyes were sharp with worry until he spotted Mikoneh, then he relaxed. "There you are."

"Here I am." Mikoneh held out his hands to either side, then slapped them against his thighs. "In the flesh." He flinched at his curt tone.

Don't take it out on Penn. He's not the one who rubbed you wrong.

The nobleman took Mikoneh's tones in stride—like he always did. A smile slid onto his lips. "You must be feeling better. You're not staggering like a drunken sailor anymore."

"I feel fine. I don't understand why I collapsed..." His words died off. Maybe he didn't understand *how*, but Sathe had attacked him. Overwhelmed him.

He got inside my head with a few drops of blood. What could he do with even more?

A shudder racked his bones. He didn't want to know. Not ever.

"Was that Minno?" Penn had moved closer in Mikoneh's preoccupation.

He shook himself into the present. "Yeah. He brought a duck."

"A...duck. For breakfast?"

"No, to spare it, I think. Funny, I didn't take him for the sort to save an animal."

"Me neither." Penn tracked Minno's descent down the spiraling stairs. "But then, he did save *you*, didn't he?"

Mikoneh snorted. "Thanks, Penn."

"You're most welcome, good sir." Penn flashed a winsome grin—the sort that had made the women in camp weak-kneed. "Back to bed with you, my friend." He took Mikoneh's elbow to steer him toward the ramp.

"I was coming on my own," Mikoneh said. "Just now. In case you didn't notice."

Penn shrugged. "Now you'll be sure to make it without planting your face on the lovely, polished wood beneath your feet."

Mikoneh rolled his eyes but didn't debate the man further. Why waste energy? He seemed to have precious little of late. Crossing the ramp, he tried to guide his thoughts away from his current struggles, but that only plunged him into memories of Oceana. Of his dead soldiers. Of Kevva's betrayal.

Don't think about it.

A sour taste settled in his mouth. The sparks of his fury—so quick to catch flame—stirred.

Don't think about it. Stop.

He never wanted to think about Kevva again.

About Drayve.

About Oceana.

His home, his past—his heartbreak.

If I never went back, would that be so terrible?

He knew the answer. He knew he could never abandon his homeland—if not the country of his birth, still the country of his heart. He couldn't let Drayve overthrow King Nilo, using Sathe's Magery as a weapon more terrifying than anything the twins had guessed possible.

Mikoneh would return, one day, hopefully not too far in the future. He must destroy Drayve's plans.

How? He has a Mage in his pocket, and that Mage is hunting you.

Penn guided him into the enclosure and across the short stretch of floor to the bed. Maya was spread across the coverlet, likely moved there by Penn before the man had gone in search of her twin.

"You're a good man, Penn." The words were barely audible, but Mikoneh meant them.

Too good. How did you spring up from a man like Drayve?

Penn chuckled and patted the bed. "So are you, Mikoneh. One of the best." He took the sword from Mikoneh's hand.

Scoffing, Mikoneh sank back to stretch out across the comfortable mattress. "We're in over our heads, you know."

Silence, then: "I know."

"What are we gonna do?"

"Endure." Penn's voice was quiet but firm.

"Right. It's what we're good at."

"Yes."

Mikoneh shut his eyes. Almost at once, he fell into the blue-hued world where friends—strange, nameless friends in a faraway life—waged battle against Mages. Dragons winged across the sky. Fire, ice, wind, or water exploded from their mighty maws in destructive torrents, while jewel-like wings sparkled and flashed with immense fury.

He longed to fly with them—to soar free.

To carry his lady with the emerald eyes far from danger.

But he couldn't flee the war. Not now. Not in such an important moment.

Perhaps not ever.

Chapter 23

The Color of Liquid Silver

"The treacherous Mage Queen was doomed the moment the Dragon King allied himself with the Lady of the North."

- From Athonen d'Ereth's *The Fall of Mages in the Age of Dragons*

Frigid cold struck Mikoneh like a dagger in his chest. He sat upright, seeking the source of the chill. Sathe! Sathe had come for him. He'd broken through the village barrier.

A tall, imposing figure stood in the doorway. Sunlight flooded the path before the dark silhouette, though it did nothing to banish the cold or reveal the face hidden in shadow. The figure strode into the chamber. Leather creaked, and chainmail softly clinked. The fragrance of winter wafted over the air—fresh wind, high peaks, and cloudy skies.

It's not Sathe. They're both wintry, but this is the cleansing cold of untouched snow.

Mikoneh shrank back, nonetheless. This stranger was pure power, carefully controlled, and agelessness, perfectly preserved.

A shaft of sunlight fell across the stranger's brow, revealing the man's visage, well sculpted as if carved from stone by a master sculptor. He was a stoic man, with eyes the color of liquid silver, and hair of blue-black caught in a long tail down his back. His armor was the shade of glossy obsidian, cut in a style both sleek and deadly. His boots, sword, and gauntlets were likewise raven-dark. A cape made of black scales flowed down his back, finishing the portrait of a hardened, vigilant warrior.

A name thundered across Mikoneh's mind. Owenekiras Rokahn: The Dragon King.

Mikoneh climbed from the bed, glad Penn hadn't covered him up. Where Penn and Maya had gone, he didn't know— nor could it matter just now. He stood before the warlord as straight-backed as he could, unwilling to bow to a king of a foreign country, no matter his roots.

He was also your parents' leader.

Mikoneh hesitated, then clicked his heels together and threw his hands behind his back. "My lord." It was all the deference he would offer.

Owenekiras halted several feet away. His hand fell to his sword, but the motion seemed natural, not threatening. Still, Mikoneh's nerves tingled. His fingers throbbed for Fa's blade wherever Penn had placed it—out of reach. A curse settled on Mikoneh's tongue, unspoken.

Owenekiras's silver gaze flicked up and down the length of him. "You're Mikoneh." The voice was low and cold as smooth ice. It held authority without the rumbling shouts of Oceana's nobility.

Mikoneh hefted his chin higher. "I am." He waited only a

heartbeat. "I didn't expect to meet you here. Did Ter summon you?"

"He fetched me. Your connection to Sathe has been explained to me." The man's cool expression didn't change, though he tilted his head slightly, seeming to examine Mikoneh deeper than his skin. "Unfortunately, your blood link is not a simple matter to correct."

Something within Mikoneh's chest deflated. "I was afraid of that. Can anything be done safely?"

"Safely." The man's voice curled over the word, as though experiencing it for the first time. "No. This will require risk no matter how we proceed. To you, most of all. To me as well. And to any whom we involve."

"Not my sister." The words came out in a rush. Mikoneh curled his hands into fists. "She must be kept safe. Please."

Owenekiras nodded like a lord granting a boon. "She will be kept so. To do otherwise would be to double the danger of Sathe gaining what he desires. He has set his sights on you, but he might use your twin as well. Not as directly, but it's still too great a chance. Your sister will be escorted to my camp."

Mikoneh's heart hammered against his chest. "And me? Where will I be taken?" While he was relieved that Maya would be safe, he hated to part from his twin, even for a little while.

"That depends upon the course we choose." Owenekiras gestured toward the doorway. "If you're well enough, will you join us below? Ter is prepared to lay out our options, and you will select our path. It is just that you do so, as your soul is under the greatest threat."

Mikoneh started forward, then halted. "Why does he want me, my lord? Couldn't—couldn't he find another strong Fire Elementalist?"

"He could, yes." Owenekiras's tones remained level. "But your other, latent gifts are what make you so tempting. Ter told me you've rejected your element. He also guessed why." A faint line appeared on the Dragon King's brow. "Jonatten and Seranni were exceptional folk—extremely clever warriors—and they were my friends. Their deaths wound me. Your loss is a deep one, and for that, I offer my sympathies. Your reasons for rejecting fire are understandable." He turned toward the door and marched across the floor, cape billowing behind him. "However, even if you never accepted your element again, Sathe would still have terrible uses for you."

The man's blows had been many and sharp. Mikoneh teetered as he absorbed every word, then he gathered himself up and followed Owenekiras. He let his inner kilns fire—not his element, not that—but he let his irritation toward Sathe purge every uncertainty. Whatever those latent gifts, he wouldn't let the Dark Mage have them.

Some of that irritation spilled over, aimed at Owenekiras— the man his parents had served. He was alive, and they were dead.

"I don't need your sympathies." His voice was soft. "They're not helpful after the fact."

Owenekiras paused at the bottom of the ramp, cape slithering around his ankles. He didn't look back but nodded. "True. They are dead."

Those words rammed into Mikoneh like a glaive. He stood frozen while Owenekiras moved toward the spiraling stair.

Move. Move, drat you!

His legs obeyed. He ran after the Dragon King, then slowed as the latter began his descent. The man's every motion was power and grace in harmony. Drawing steadying breaths, Mikoneh followed, keeping space between him and the imposing man.

They reached the bottom of the stairs and entered the tavern-style room. A handful of Ephe'ahn—Ter among them—

as well as Penn and Maya, stood before a child-sized table. Grim eyes and taut mouths suggested they'd settled nothing and fretted a great deal about the current situation. Several of the Ephe'ahn bowed their heads to Owenekiras while something between awe and terror scrawled across their faces.

We shouldn't have come here. We've endangered too many innocent people.

Mikoneh's fists clenched tighter. He hated to involve others in his problems. Things had gotten so much worse, and far more unfathomable, since escaping Drayve's clutches.

Who'd have thought anything could be worse than being burned at the stake?

He uncurled his fingers, reluctant to reveal how frightened he was. Maya could already read him too easily. She caught his eye and offered up a smile strained with worry. He answered with a toothy grin before he remembered that would only make her fret more. The harder he tried to assure her, the easier it was for her to see the unease brewing beneath. Sure enough, her smile fell dead away. He let his grin drop, too, and his customary grimace fell into place, while his attention shifted to the table.

Somehow, he'd expected to find maps—but the table was laden with food and goblets of mead. Nothing else. Several of the Ephe'ahn were eating, even as they wore grim expressions like they'd assembled for a wake.

The cluster of folk parted to let Owenekiras stand at the head of the tiny table. He didn't glance at the food. Instead, his gaze roved the chamber, taking in those gathered, along with the fireplace; the glowing mushrooms; the cheery blooms crawling up the beams that seemed to grow from the roots cradling the room. His eyes then settled on Mikoneh.

"Proceed, Ter." The Dragon King's voice was soft like a breeze just stirring.

Among the child-sized woodelves, Ter pushed his way to the fore. Minno positioned himself directly beside Ter, the boy's gray eyes fastened on Owenekiras.

Ter's ears fluttered, and he wore a crooked smile. "As you wish, Lord Rokahn." His big blue eyes swept the room, then landed on Mikoneh. "Our options are few—and none is ideal. The first: We attempt to break your mental block on your element and guide you on how to burn away Sathe's hold long enough to get you to Lord Rokahn's war encampment. Once there, the wards in place should shield you from Sathe's influence, but the moment you step beyond its boundaries, he will find you readily enough."

No, that didn't sound ideal.

"And the other options?" asked Mikoneh.

"Well." Ter's ears drooped. "We could step from this village, lure Sathe to you, and steal the drop of blood from him directly. The risks in that are, I should think, quite obvious."

"Risks?" muttered Penn. "It's madness."

Mikoneh exhaled through a hitch in his lungs. "Any other options?"

"Yes, though they are less certain," said Ter. "We could try flying to Lady Katanni's lands, northward, and hope Sathe and his followers do not pursue us aloft."

"Aloft?" asked Maya.

"Indeed." Ter slid a glance toward the Dragon King. "We are not without transportation now. But neither is the enemy. And setting that aside, the element of time isn't in our favor. It's possible that en route Sathe will gain a firm enough grasp on your mind, Mikoneh, that you will step straight off our ride's back and plummet to the ground at his order."

A lump lodged in Mikoneh's throat.

"That's no option at all," Penn said.

No, it's not.

"Would he kill me if he can't cage me?" asked Mikoneh in tones too thin to really belong to him.

Don't lose your nerve.

"Most probably." Ter's innocent voice held a grimness no child could carry.

"What do we do?" Maya looked pale.

"I would counsel you to select one of the first two options," Owenekiras said. A hush followed the statement, then he spoke on. "Any other possibility risks too much to too many. A fourth alternative is to flee this very moment and—if you are fortunate enough to avoid Sathe's scouts—hide yourselves for the rest of your lives, or until Sathe discovers and uses you up. Perhaps all of you, but certainly Mikoneh."

Mikoneh rested his palms on the low table and leaned against it. Why did Sathe want him in particular? Everyone kept skipping over that answer, like they were afraid to state the nature of his latent gifts out loud. Some part of him wanted to demand the answer outright, but another part of him hesitated. Was it so dangerous that he shouldn't even know its nature? Did they avoid telling him for *his* sake?

That's not the most pressing question right now anyway. Maya comes first.

The aroma of food turned his stomach. Which was the smartest choice? How could he best protect his twin? Going to Owenekiras's camp would ensure her safety, but then what?

It amounts to the same thing. He straightened up. *The end result doesn't change. Going to the encampment—assuming I can burn away Sathe's influence anyway—is only a detour.*

"We should seek Sathe—heading northward like we're aiming for the Nijaal," Mikoneh said. "If he doesn't take the bait, we'll reach your fae lady after all. But I don't want Penn and Maya to come."

They both began to object, but he held up his hand. "Hear me out. Please."

Silence settled in. He turned to his twin, holding her gaze. "If he gets us both, he wins. At that point, I'd do anything he wanted to spare you. But if he *doesn't* catch you, then even in the worst possible scenario I can fight him, by fang and claw if necessary. I need you to stay safe."

She took a step closer, every muscle tense, her eyes pleading. Her lips parted like she meant to argue, but Penn caught her hand and squeezed.

The fight bled from her body, and she nodded. "I don't like it, but I'll respect your decision. He wants you most."

Relief roared through Mikoneh. "Thank you, Maya. Believe me—I don't want Sathe to catch me, and for more than just my own wellbeing. I hate to think what he might use me to accomplish."

He turned toward the Dragon King. "Going to your encampment would only delay what sounds inevitable. We need to find Sathe, now or later."

Owenekiras Rokahn inclined his head. "Then it's decided. We must plan our first move." He angled himself to address Ter and Mikoneh at the same time. "I propose we move from the village as soon as may be feasible to avoid unnecessary danger to these good folk. A brief flight would be advisable. Outside I can shield the boy for a single turn, but no longer. His companions will be safe enough here."

Ter rubbed his chin. "Hm, yes. I believe we can be ready to depart Kenooshin in half a twig."

That measurement meant nothing to Mikoneh or his companions, but he could guess it wasn't longer than half a sandglass turn. He glanced at Owenekiras. "You'll be joining us?"

The warlord nodded.

Mikoneh turned to his twin. "Would you and Penn gather my belongings upstairs? I need to be ready to leave whenever."

"Are you up for this so soon?" Maya reached for his forehead, but he caught her wrist and gently pulled it down.

"I'll be fine—and I should move before I'm crippled again."

She searched his face, then sighed and pulled free. Together, she and Penn moved toward the stairs, while the Ephe'ahn villagers shuffled toward the hostel's front door, leaving Mikoneh alone with Owenekiras, Ter, and Minno. In the stillness, the pop and hiss of the cheery fire filled Mikoneh's senses like a distant taunt.

Your decision makes sense, he told himself. *It's not an excuse to avoid your element.*

Mostly, he believed that. But it certainly helped to avoid the looming issue. He'd blocked himself. He didn't want to tap into the core of fire inside him ever again. And yet...somehow a hollow place had been carved into his chest where fire had warmed him, soothing the cold that harbored in wounded places deeper than flesh and bone.

Ter plucked up a pale green fruit from the table and rotated it between his fingers. His blue eyes flitted between Minno and Mikoneh, only lighting on the imposing form of Owenekiras once or twice while the woodelf seemed to debate something in his head. Minno stole a handful of nuts and seeds from a bowl, and crouched close to the ground, presumably to feed his duck.

Since neither of them seemed inclined to illuminate what would happen next, Mikoneh moved closer to the Dragon King. Did he imagine a chill emanating from Owenekiras's obsidian armor?

"How many will come with us?"

"Only those assembled here," answered Owenekiras, his eyes pinned on Ter's rotating fruit.

"Sathe may have dozens of lesser Mages with him."

Owenekiras nodded. "The perils do not lie in numbers, young one." His gaze slid to meet Mikoneh's. "I don't like our odds, but we've little choice under the circumstances."

Fear crept up around Mikoneh's lungs. "You're talking about the Revenant, aren't you?"

Though Owenekiras's expression remained stony, a darkness leached into his slitted eyes. "That is another issue, unfortunately, though no less grim."

Ter's fingers halted. The Ephe'ahn's youthful face looked almost gaunt. "It troubles me as well." He rotated the fruit again. "I know of a certainty that it isn't Cal, though the wards at TeshRelle have been breached."

Owenekiras frowned. "Agreed. I would know if Cal had been bound in such a manner. He's no longer on these shores."

"That is good," Ter murmured. "Yet Suld's freedom is confirmed?"

"Yes. He's been causing all manner of mischief in the North, but Reteris and his folk are assisting in that fight."

"Ah." Ter's ears perked up. "That is good news. Firedrakes ought not to be idle." He seemed to shake himself, then turned his focus on Mikoneh. "Despite matters being what they are, we will do all we can to keep you safe. Heed us and things will go better all 'round."

Mikoneh arched his brow. "Is there some reason I wouldn't heed you?"

"Only the foibles of youth." Ter looked him up and down as he idly began peeling the green fruit. "But then, despite your age, you seem an old soul at moments."

"The cost of loss," Minno said somewhere near the floor, hidden behind the table.

"Indeed." One of Ter's ears sagged, then straightened.

"One last important question: Are you afraid of heights, Mikoneh?"

He shook his head.

"Good. I thought not—considering—but it's always best to ask." The woodelf issued an airy laugh, then pried open the fruit. It resembled a citrus. Mikoneh had tried a tropical fruit —an orange one—at the fair he'd attended with his family several years before. Ter now plopped a slice in his mouth and winced. "A tad tart, but good for the nerves." He swallowed and proffered a slice.

Mikoneh took it with murmured thanks, and munched with appreciation as he considered the present company. Swallowing, he asked, "Why is Minno coming?"

The gray boy poked his head up from beyond the table. "Because I want to."

"Despite appearances," Owenekiras said, "Minno is capable of wielding several types of magic with proficiency and is therefore helpful against Dark Mages." His head canted so that he could slide a narrow look on Minno. "When he desires to be, at least."

"I desire to be," Minno answered flatly, then stood up, hefting a green-headed mallard in his arms. The duck looked decidedly resigned. "And perhaps my lord will be generous in return."

Ter's answering laugh was wry. "None here will let you see Lady Katanni, Minno."

The boy shrugged. "You may change your mind."

"Doubtful," Ter said, still smiling.

Owenekiras turned toward the spiral stairs a single breath before Mikoneh registered the scuff of boots descending. Penn and Maya entered through the back door, the latter clutching a satchel. The girl brought it forth, while Penn hung back to let

Maya have the first goodbye. The viscount studied Owenekiras, his expression a mixture of curiosity and wariness.

Mikoneh took the satchel from his twin, rummaged through it, then pulled out the Ashwood box with the pendants and key. "Keep this with you, just in case."

She took it, nodding.

Mikoneh set the satchel at his feet and pulled her in for a hug. She embraced him hard, burrowing her face against his neck.

"Be safe." Her voice was a feeble whisper.

"I'll try," he murmured.

She clung to him for several more breaths, then drew back. Her golden eyes shimmered with brimming tears, but she wiped them away and applied the brightest smile she could. It was dazzling.

Mikoneh rapped a knuckle against her cheek, making her laugh, then he hitched his satchel over his shoulder.

Penn stepped forward and proffered Fa's sword. "Wield it well."

"Always." Mikoneh flashed him a tight grin, then his gaze found Owenekiras. "I'm ready."

"Very well." The Dragon King pulled something from a pouch at his belt. He turned his hand palm-up, revealing an amber gem that seemed to glow of its own accord. "Keep this on your person, Mikoneh."

"That isn't a Warding Gem—not quite," said Minno, listing his head sideways. His duck quacked as though in agreement.

"No," Owenekiras said. "Though its use is similar. Warding Gems cannot protect Mikoneh while Sathe has his blood—but this one is more of a cloak than a shield. It will scatter the ties that bind Mikoneh to said blood. Unfortunately, this gem alone hasn't the strength to protect him much longer than one full turn. Two at most."

"I see." Minno prodded the gem with one finger. "Still useful."

The duck quacked again.

"You'll need to stay here, Duck," Minno said, setting the mallard on the table. "The villagers won't eat you, I promise."

Owenekiras stretched out his hand, and Mikoneh pinched the gem between two fingers. A tingle raced up his arm and pressure settled against his shoulders, just like a winter cloak. He glanced at Maya, wondering if he'd winked out of sight, but she eyed him with a thoughtful frown.

"I still see him," she said.

"Yes," said Ter, "but were you to try, you'd not be able to scent him or trace him in any long-range manner."

Relief brightened the girl's eyes. She gave Mikoneh a last hug, then Ter motioned Minno, Owenekiras, and Mikoneh outside the hostel. Every woodelf within the village had gathered to see them off—likely to catch a glimpse of the legendary Dragon King—but they parted as Ter bounded ahead of the company toward the edge of the forest clearing. A song rose from the crowd, the words foreign and subdued like the folk sang a funeral dirge.

That's cheery.

Mikoneh thumbed the amber gem, then slid it into a pocket in his trousers. He glanced back once to wave a final time at Maya, unable to shake the haunting impression that he would never see his twin again.

Then he stepped into the trees.

CHAPTER 24

LIKE A GREAT BLACK SWAN

"The Mage Queen refused to foresee her own defeat."

- From Athonen d'Ereth's *The Fall of Mages in the Age of Dragons*

Ter led Owenekiras, Mikoneh, and Minno along a path the Ephe'ahn seldom used, judging by the roots and weeds tangled across it. The trees leaned close on either side, stretching their boughs low to tickle the top of Mikoneh's head. The fragrance of dense verdure and leaf mold mingled with an autumn chill that nipped at his flesh. His immunity to cold must've died when he rejected his element.

No one spoke. The villagers' song had rooted inside Mikoneh's head, playing over and over, the jumble of foreign words like a taunt.

He fastened his eyes on Owenekiras's back. The cape wrapped around the man's powerful shoulders seemed to shimmer and slither around his ankles, rejecting any path of light that filtered through the dense canopy.

He's like a Mage, yet completely different.

Mikoneh didn't understand why that feeling persisted. Nothing about Owenekiras's fair skin or aura said undead or corpse-like. It must be the power emanating from him that put Mikoneh in mind of Sathe. Both were cold, impenetrable fortresses.

Even so, Mikoneh wouldn't let the Dragon King intimidate him. He needed to work with this man, not avoid asking questions or discussing their plan. Squaring his shoulders, Mikoneh moved up to fall in beside the warlord, leaving Minno alone in the rear.

"Mind if I ask a few questions while this ward is working?"

Owenekiras's gaze didn't stray from the path ahead. "No."

"The Revenant. What do you—"

Owenekiras halted. He twisted toward Mikoneh, and the cold pulsing from him struck like a sudden wall of ice. "Best not to mention that being in the open. I will explain more about it if we reach a haven where it cannot sense us."

Mikoneh blinked. "I thought the ward—"

"It's enough against Sathe. Not against...such tragedy." Owenekiras turned and continued along the path, catching up to Ter within a few lengthy strides, though the woodelf hadn't slowed.

Mikoneh followed fast, slipping one hand into his pocket to finger the gem. He frowned, weighing the Dragon King's words. They fit within the sensations—the instincts—he'd experienced when facing the atrocity in Hyanython.

Steeling himself, he caught up to Owenekiras again and matched the man's pace with an effort.

"How will we go north?"

"By dragon."

Mikoneh's step hitched, but he corrected himself and kept up.

A dragon. Don't they eat people? Is that why he's called the Dragon King—because he can tame them?

"How far a flight is it to the High North?"

"From here, five days," the man answered.

Mikoneh glanced over his shoulder. Minno was watching them with an almost hungering stare. Turning back around, Mikoneh dodged a jutting root. "Aren't you trying to keep *that one* away from this Katanni person?"

"If we are fortunate enough to make it so far unmolested," said Owenekiras, "I will be certain Minno doesn't remain with us."

"But that's unlikely." It wasn't really a question. Facing off against Sathe seemed inevitable. Mikoneh fought against a shiver. "You mentioned TeshRelle. What is that place, exactly? I've heard stories, but...I don't know what to believe."

"As the stories say, it is a blackened realm now," Owenekiras said. "Not unlike the Blighted Land in Cimin— but even more tainted. It was the place where we sealed one of the most powerful Mages who ever lived."

"The one called Suld, right? And now he's free."

"Yes." The Dragon King frowned. "But that is a conflict for others to wage. We must focus on Sathe." His eyes flicked to Mikoneh and skewered him with a weighty look. "Suld and Sathe are brothers. Their powers are not dissimilar. They are among the Mage Queen's greatest generals."

"Minno mentioned them being brothers. I've heard of the Mage Queen. She's part of the old stories. But I never expected her to be real. Is this the *same* Mage Queen, or a descendant?"

Minno piped up. "She's the one from the legends. Like most of that dark breed, she's been asleep. After the Age of Dragons, they slinked into their tunnels and holed up, recovering from their countless losses. The more powerful ones are perfectly preserved in their slumber, the less powerful rotting away but still alive. For these many ages they have been recuperating, and now at last they are strong again and stirring in great numbers. Perhaps stronger than ever."

"Indeed," said Owenekiras. "They have an advantage they didn't last time."

"What's that?" asked Mikoneh.

"Void and Hollow."

"The fabric of—everything?"

"The *lesser* fabric," Minno muttered.

Owenekiras inclined his head. "It is a poor man's patchwork cloak holding back a flood. During the Age of Dragons, the substance—the stitching—called *Complété* was shattered, and time and dimensions nearly collapsed. In a desperate act, Lady Katanni and others forged Hollow and Void to replace it. They are unstable substitutes—fragile at best—but it was all we could do."

"We?" Mikoneh arched his brow. "You were there?" Was this another ageless man? That couldn't be right. Tales of Owenekiras's childhood spent as a pirate, defying his royal parents, had reached as far as Oceana.

"That is complicated." The Dragon King rested a gauntleted hand over his armored sternum. "And irrelevant."

"You're just being modest," Minno said blandly.

Mikoneh didn't push the issue. Frankly, it wasn't his business—and he had enough to digest without cramming more information into his skull. He focused on the path, turning their upcoming goal over and over in his mind.

"How far away is the—dragon?" He stumbled over the word.

"We're nearly there," Owenekiras said.

A real-life dragon. Mikoneh was about to see one. Did they look how hearth stories described? Did they really breathe fire?

He mentioned firedrakes challenging the Mage called Suld. Are those also dragons or something like them?

In his provincial corner of the world, Mikoneh had been accustomed to knowing more than the stablehand and blacksmith, the baker and chandler, the butcher and wheelwright—all the people who had spent their days on one trade. Fa and Mama had traveled, seen things, experienced life, and they'd taught their children what they knew. At least some of it.

Maybe a tenth of it.

It was hard to swallow, but Mikoneh must. He wouldn't lie to himself. He'd never supposed he knew more than a king or a ship captain did—but even so, he knew much less than he'd suspected.

Better get used to that taste. You've entered the wide waters.

The trees seemed to straighten up, as though to honor the Dragon King walking beneath them. The trunks thinned out, growing wide apart, letting in dappled sunshine, until they fell away entirely, surrendering to a lake. Upon the gleaming water, a scaled beast waited, folded like a great black swan. Its eyes—a bright, glowing red—studied the company as they stepped beyond the trees. Glossy scales winked in the broad sunlight. Spikes rode the dragon's back and huge, lithe tail. A mane of reddish black cascaded down its long neck. Smoke drifted from the nostrils on its enormous maw.

Stunned, Mikoneh fell still, barely breathing. Beneath that ancient, feral gaze, he was a mere speck. Why would dragons care to eat people at all? They were nothing, *nothing* against the grandeur; the graceful, deadly power; the sheer weightiness of this magnificent creature.

The dragon's slitted eyes slid from Mikoneh to land on

Owenekiras, and the mighty beast bowed its head. Scales flashed red, then back to black.

"This is Larkynven," said the Dragon King. "He has agreed to aid us."

"Hello, Lark," Minno said, striding forward, unperturbed by the disconcerting presence. "How are your daughters?"

If the dragon answered, Mikoneh heard nothing. Not even the rumble he'd anticipated. Nevertheless, Minno nodded.

"Glad to hear it," the gray boy said gravely. "They must be very beautiful by now."

Again, silence. Then the dragon shifted its attention back to Mikoneh, and a voice filled his mind like crackling fire and roaring winds.

'Greetings, Mikoneh of the Flame.'

He staggered backward, heart in his throat. He stared into those inhuman eyes and found—intelligence, wisdom, understanding. This wasn't a monster wreaking havoc and destroying livestock. This was grace, purpose, and perfect control.

Mikoneh hesitated, then straightened up. He swallowed down the lump in his throat and inclined his head. "Greetings, Larkynven."

The dragon's maw dropped into a grin, revealing two rows of white fangs. Huge, terrible—and fascinating. **'He recovers well.'** The voice filled Mikoneh's mind again, but not as loud as before.

"Good thing," Minno said. "Considering everything."

Mikoneh tensed. Minno was right—he was supposed to *ride* this dragon in a moment. Assessing its size, the four of them could ride easily. Likely, Larkynven wouldn't even feel them on his back through that thick hide.

But how do we stay aboard?

The dragon shifted in the water, then unfolded one enormous, scaled wing, revealing red membrane beneath. The scales on the outer wing flashed red and black as it stretched toward shore. The motion also revealed a saddle—a long, multi-person saddle—strapped to the dragon's back.

Oh.

Something stirred within Mikoneh. A sensation. An... excitement.

I'm going to fly.

For a moment, he forgot all about Sathe, Mages, wielding fire, even sorrowful Revenants.

He was going to *fly*.

At Owenekiras's gesture, Ter bounded up the dragon's wing. Minno went next. Mikoneh hesitated only an instant—more from wonder than fear—then he hurried up the sleek scales, glad he kept his feet and didn't stumble in front of this mighty creature.

Larkynven's eyes tracked him, long neck craning, until Mikoneh settled into the saddle in front of Minno and Ter. The foremost seat was empty, awaiting Owenekiras Rokahn—Dragon King.

I'm gonna fly!

CHAPTER 25

CRACKLING SILVER

"The battles in the Age of Dragons were countless, the losses incalculable."

- From Athonen d'Ereth's *The Fall of Mages in the Age of Dragons*

Flight was the most wonderful thing Mikoneh had experienced in his life.

The thrill of takeoff filled his bones with light. He found himself laughing as water poured off Larkynven's glistening scales. Mighty, batlike wings beat the air, stirring up wind currents that lashed Mikoneh's hair. Power and control curled off the dragon's massive, sinuous body as it climbed higher, higher—above the trees, into the wide, cloudless sky.

He whooped. Every single care burdening his body and soul tumbled away, lost in the intoxication of leaving solid ground. In breathing the crisp air. In *flight*. He felt more like himself than he ever had, as though he'd been born for this moment. He needed it to last. To stretch on for eternity.

The wings carried the dragon's passengers across the wide forest. Trees whipped past, small, almost insignificant so far below these great, endless heights. The Andyan Mountains stood dead ahead, cloaked in snow and ice, breathing cold across the continent. The wind stirred something deep within him—not like the voices of the Spirits Elemental—but a deeper, ancient voice within his soul. It whispered and roared in a medley of songs that flamed across him, urging him to step from Larkynven's back. To fly under his own power.

He almost obeyed. Impulse nearly hurled him from the saddle—but sense caught up.

That's madness. You'd die.

He tightened his grip on the leather handles fastened to his saddle seat and tried to block out the windsong beckoning to his soul.

None of the others seemed inclined to jump. Owenekiras stood rather than sat on the foremost part of the saddle, clutching reins that circled Larkynven's long neck. How the dragon felt the man's guiding touch through those scales—or whether that mattered—Mikoneh didn't know.

He sat next in the row of seats, with Ter behind, and Minno—as always—in the rear. Glancing back, Mikoneh read nothing of intoxication in either face. Ter seemed solemn, while Minno gripped the saddle with white knuckles. He looked a little green.

Twisting forward, Mikoneh tried to recapture the sheer joy of flight, without letting his compulsion return.

"You could, you know." Ter's voice was a shout above the wind noise.

Mikoneh glanced over his shoulder. "Talking to me?"

Ter nodded. "Yes, but forget what I said. It isn't my

place…" Did pain draw lines across his youthful face? He looked older than before, almost careworn. "Not anymore."

Facing forward, Mikoneh frowned. He'd fallen in with strange companions, each wielding secrets he couldn't guess at, and he wasn't certain he wanted to.

Violet lightning struck the dragon's left wing. Larkynven lurched right, smoke curling from the wounded membrane on the wing's underside. Owenekiras dropped the reins and darted up the dragon's neck, using its flowing mane for handholds. His motions were swift, fluid, and he reached the dragon's head in a few heartbeats. There, he planted his feet and called out instructions to his great mount.

More lightning bolts streaked the sky, coming from the forest below.

Sathe had found them. It must be him.

"Stay down!" Ter called, though Mikoneh had no idiot notions about sticking his head out for an easy target. He hunched into himself, keeping an eye on Owenekiras standing between the dragon's horns, clutching threads of mane, cape billowing like a black standard.

How long can Larkynven stay airborne with his injury?

Owenekiras lifted one hand. The silken threads of mane slipped from his fingers, then an orb of crackling silver formed above his open palm. It swelled, larger, larger, until it was the size of a knight's helm. Owenekiras stretched his arm over his head and flung the orb toward the forest.

The sound of rumbling broke over the air. The orb burst asunder. Silver lightning struck from that core, meeting fresh bolts of violet electricity racing for the heavens. The two colors clashed, painting the world in shades of purple, gray, and white.

Mikoneh flinched back, shading his eyes.

The Dragon King unleashed another crackling orb. It met

a fresh stream of violet lightning. A tang touched Mikoneh's mouth, sharp on his tongue. His hair lifted a little from the charge that filled the sky.

Larkynven wheeled, using his right wing to keep a tight circle over the section of forest where Sathe's minions mounted their attack. If the dragon was in pain, he gave no sign. His fierce eyes were fastened on the unseen enemy below the trees.

Can't keep this up forever. We must escape.

But that wasn't the plan. They needed to confront Sathe. To take him alive or steal the drop of blood back.

Or kill him if necessary.

Was that even possible?

The dragon swiveled west. A third orb of silver wiped out a new attack—but a second string of violet lightning shot from the forest to the east.

"Watch out!" Mikoneh's cry was drowned out by the strike of lightning against Larkynven's hide. Smoke curled away, but it hadn't seemed to damage the dragon like the first hit. Even so, Larkynven flowed out of his spin, slithering over the air like a serpent. His jaw opened. Fire poured from his great mouth. Mikoneh imagined the forest turning to char under the scorching barrage—but the flame was controlled, a thin spiral that pierced the canopy of trees. An aura of violet light had been growing from that quarter, but it was snuffed out.

They're trying to knock us to the ground. But isn't that where we need to be?

He sought out Owenekiras, still atop the dragon's skull. The man threw another orb, then whirled around. His silver gaze connected with Mikoneh. His expression was stony.

"Now, Minno." The man's command carried.

"Understood." The boy's voice held its steady monotone. A hand seized Mikoneh, then shoved him from the saddle and off the dragon's back. Into the sky. Air cradled Mikoneh's body. His stomach somersaulted—then he found himself grinning, oddly unafraid as trees and earth rose to meet him, promising death. His shoulder blades burned.

What's wrong with me?

He twisted to face the sky and the dragon shrinking in his wide field of sight. His eyes collided with Minno's. The gray boy had fallen with him. If the plummet frightened Minno, the boy gave no indication.

Mikoneh had expected to hit the leafy canopy by now, but the air seemed to be holding him up, slowing his descent. He twisted around just as his body halted to hover immediately above the foliage. The forest odors assailed his senses, life and rot and animal smells, mingled.

Minno came level with him, kneeling upon the air as though it were solid. "Owen will drop us in a moment. Be ready."

"Wha—"

The solid air dissolved. Mikoneh crashed into the oak tree, branches thwacking his face and limbs. Scratching. Snagging. Bruising. He snatched at a thick bough. His fingers slipped, and he rammed against a lower branch where he—thankfully—caught himself. Every muscle throbbed. He groaned and spat out leaves. Twigs clung to his hair, which had come loose from its knot to hang down his back in a curtain of tangles.

He gingerly sat up. A hitch in his ribs made him flinch, but he scanned his surroundings, trying to ignore the pulsing pain in his bones. He'd managed to avoid eight feet of tumbling. The ground was that close.

A grimace twisted his lips. *Great plan, that. Now what?*

Minno padded into sight below. "You're not very graceful when you fall."

"Somehow or other, I find it difficult to practice regularly."

The boy eyed him blandly. "You're really nothing like him. At all."

"Like who—" A chill skittered up Mikoneh's back. He jumped from the swaying branch and slid his sword from its sheath, grateful he hadn't lost it on the way down. Minno turned to eye the direction he faced: east.

The shadows beneath the trees darkened, and a coldness seeped into the air, more bitter than the deep snows of midwinter. Leaves curled, tingeing blue and brown like frostbite had laid its merciless fingers on them.

"Revenant." Minno's voice was disturbingly calm.

That thing. The creature made of nightmares and sorrow. A prisoner of Magery.

"We didn't discuss how to deal with this," he whispered.

"That's because there's no way to plan for it." Minno shook his head. "No one defeats a Revenant—at least no one like you or me."

Mikoneh swallowed. His hands shook. He eased himself into a defensive stance and flexed his fingers against his hilt to fight the sudden slickness of the metal.

Be calm. Don't panic.

The Revenant stepped from the trees. Its aura rattled Mikoneh to his center. That same sorrow struck marrow deep. It was as though the Revenant absorbed every speck of heartbreak from the world around him, then reflected it back, magnified tenfold. Flashes of memory—the burning cottage, the huddled corpses, the subsequent battles—all flickered across Mikoneh's mind. Beside him, Minno exhaled sharply.

Give in, Firebrand. Sathe's voice boomed in his head. **Surrender to my Revenant.**

Mikoneh clenched his jaw. *Never.*

He didn't dare say anything out loud. He needed every shred of strength to fend off the Revenant's assault. The flickering horrors running over his head. The dread nicking at his soul.

"Mikoneh." Minno's voice was soft.

He glanced at the boy. Minno's face had lost its color. He stood like a limp doll held up by strings.

"Owen trusted me to protect you." That monotone was broken. Something in Minno's body language spoke of defeat. "He always trusts me more than he should, you know. One of his few weaknesses. I promised him."

The dread bit deeper. "What are you—"

"Shut up and listen." Minno drew his eyes from the Revenant. "I promised him I would protect you until he arrived. But I lied. He trusts me more than he should." The boy swallowed. "He won't find this place quickly. I made certain. It's because of you, you know. It's your fault. No one else knows—only me. I know. I always do."

"Minno." Mikoneh couldn't pretend to understand what the boy was saying, but he sensed enough to be afraid. "It's not too late. Fix what you've done, and we'll take on Sathe together. All of us. Don't do this, please."

"Too late." Minno shook his head, not meeting his eyes. "I hate you. That's why. That's why I'll betray him. You robbed me of both of them. And I hate you for that."

Knots tightened up and down Mikoneh's insides. Minno wasn't making sense, but that hardly mattered. Not right now. His heart thudded against his ribs. "Please, Minno. Call the others."

Minno hefted his head, locking his gaze onto Mikoneh's. "It's your fault. But you can blame me if you must. I don't mind." He held up an amber gem, like the one meant to cloak Mikoneh. It had been broken into two pieces, worthless. Mikoneh didn't need to check his pocket to know it was his, and somehow the gray boy had stolen it.

Twigs snapped. Cloaks rustled. Draped Mages moved from the trees.

The Revenant slinked closer.

"You don't understand," Minno whispered. "I realize that, too. But one day...one day you will. And then you'll—well, you'll probably still blame me. Mages aren't kind. Believe me, I know. Goodbye, Mikoneh." He turned away.

The Revenant came nearer still, snaring Mikoneh's attention like a hook reeling in a fish. He turned against his will to face the tall, slender figure. Slitted eyes met his from beneath the dark red cowl.

Memories burst across Mikoneh's head—all the things he didn't want to remember. His sword fell into the leaf mold with a faint thud.

He fell into those memories, unable to resist. Betrayed. Again.

CHAPTER 26

SINCE THE FIRE

"More than Dark Mages fought on her side. The foulest creatures imaginable deemed the Mage Queen's cause their own."

- From Athonen d'Ereth's *The Fall of Mages in the Age of Dragons*

Maya lay upon the cot like a limp ragdoll, black hair tangled around her arms. With firm, deliberate steps, Mikoneh conquered the rug-strewn ground, half-conscious of the tent walls quivering in the fierce snowstorm outside. A gale rose, high and shrieking.

He knelt beside the cot and took up her ice-cold hand. She didn't stir.

"Maya, can you hear me?" His voice cracked. *Please, God, don't take her from me, too.*

"She's been like that since the cottage fire."

The voice jolted through Mikoneh like an arrow struck his

back. He twisted without rising to seek out the familiar presence.

"Kevva." Why did that name—why did that face—wound him?

She stood in a snow-dusted cloak, the cowl pushed back to reveal her vibrant auburn curls and vivid green eyes. Those eyes were bright with an inner flame, a fierce will, and something that stirred grief and wrath within him. Why?

Kevva moved forward, graceful as a cat. Her patched skirts rippled behind her. Her full lips twitched toward a smile that flickered and died as fast as it came. "I'll do what I can, but Mikoneh...it's up to her if she wants to come back."

He shook his head. "She's not injured." He knew that much. He'd made sure she was safe before he'd lured the knights after him, away from his men, away from his twin. To keep them all safe. He'd given Drayve's knights a long chase, even as he'd tried to deny the violet flames and what they'd stolen from him.

"No, she's not injured." Kevva stepped beside him and rested a hand on his shoulder. "Not *outside*."

He turned his gaze back to his twin's slack face. "I don't..." He drew a deep breath. "I don't understand."

"No, you wouldn't." Kevva crouched and caught his face in her hands. Her nearness made him want to flee, but he wrestled it down, planting himself firmly in place. Kevva's eyes searched his. "You will never understand giving up."

"She isn't giving—"

"Not completely, no," Kevva whispered. "Perhaps giving *in* is a more appropriate word for it. But you—you don't understand even that much. Not you. Your will—your sense of *right* —won't allow you to cave, to surrender, even if it's the sensible thing. You don't know how to fail."

He scowled. "I fail every day."

"Not when it truly matters."

Heat scored his face and flashed across his chest. He wrenched away and pushed to his feet. "My parents are *dead*, Kevva. I'd say that signifies failure." His voice was a low, guttural sound.

She eyed him, then scoffed and rose. "Yours, or theirs?"

"How dare—"

"I don't mean to be harsh," she said, lifting a hand. "I know it's insensitive, after..." She shrugged. "And really, it's not important right now. What matters is caring for her." The woman's eyes fell on Maya. "She needs you."

Mikoneh dragged a hand down his face. "I know. I'll stay with her. I won't let her crumble."

"And if she does crumble, Mikoneh? If she's not as strong as you—will you forgive her for being mortal?"

"That's not—" Pain burst across his frame, flaring through his bones, his marrow, his muscles. He arced back with a scream, then staggered and sank to his knees. His vision spotted.

Up, Firebrand. Awaken. Your master calls.

CHAPTER 27

ACT OF DEFIANCE

"Others fought for Darkness against their will."

- From Athonen d'Ereth's *The Fall of Mages in the Age of Dragons*

P ain burst across Mikoneh's chest. He arced backward, and his head slammed against stone. Spots bloomed before his eyes. He sucked in a breath, trying to resist —but there was nothing to fend off. Nothing to fight.

He screamed again—this time in defiance.

"Good," said a frosty voice. "Better. Much better. Now stand."

The pain eased but didn't leave. Mikoneh sat up, trembling. Sweat trickled down his face, and his breaths came in short gasps. Every muscle spasmed.

He sat within a cave—or perhaps it was part of the tunnels. The chamber was crude, not carved out like a proper room, and the air was dank with the odors of minerals and lichens.

"I said stand." The voice took on a low, commanding tone.

Mikoneh shifted to glower at Sathe. "Working on it."

The man gave him a frigid smile. "I do so admire that inner flame of yours. Impressive, considering that you deny your element." Sathe drifted forward, robes dragging behind him. His too-smooth, too-pale face hinted at none of his thoughts. Mere inches away, he crouched and reached out, stroking Mikoneh's cheek. "Don't worry. I will help you overcome that irrational mental block of yours. Together, we will do *unspeakable things.*"

Mikoneh lurched back. "Don't *touch* me."

Sathe's smile broadened, lighting his eyes like twin torches, gleeful—like a child tormenting a cat and finding it fun. "You're mine now—and by the most delightful of twists, wouldn't you say? The very boy who rescued you from me before, betraying the great Owenekiras Rokahn to rid himself of you." The Mage chuckled. "I confess, I didn't expect it. But then, Minno is an oddity. One of a kind, you know. If I'd realized what I had..." He rose to his feet. "Enough of that. Stand, my Firebrand. We've a ceremony to attend, you and I."

Mikoneh remained seated. Why *had* Minno betrayed him, after helping him before? It didn't make sense.

Is this part of Owenekiras's plan?

No. That made even less sense. Not communicating that would be—

Pain bloomed across his body. He jerked back, growling. Sathe's frosty laughter filled his ears. Wrenching himself straight, Mikoneh glared at the Mage with every ounce of hatred he could dredge up. This was the man responsible for robbing him and Maya of their parents, and now the man meant to use him to hurt others.

I won't let you. I'll die *first!*

Sathe sighed and shook his head. "The more strength you

use up now, the better for me. Make your choice, then do please abide by it, at all costs." His smile split into a grin that revealed straight teeth. "Just know this: The more you fight, the more it pleases me."

Mikoneh managed a strangled laugh. "You *have* to say that, but we'll see which of us galls the other most before all this is done." He pushed to his feet, then wobbled until he found his balance. "I'll find a way out, Sathe. That's a promise."

The Mage considered him with glittering eyes. "That fighting spirit—it's most refreshing. I do so dearly admire your bloodline. None can compare. *None*." He pivoted and moved toward the cavern maw. "Come, my Firebrand. We've work to begin in the next room."

"No." Mikoneh leaned against the back wall.

Sathe paused, then glanced over his shoulder. Those glittering eyes grew colder. "Admirable, but now isn't the time. We have so little of it at present. The moon does not wait for its servants. Come, *now*."

"No." Mikoneh locked his jaw and folded his arms. It was a pathetic showing, no matter how he examined it—but he would use whatever weapon he could.

Sathe sighed. "Very well. Revenant, bring him."

Cold swept through Mikoneh. He lurched away from the back wall as the tall, eerie, crimson-cloaked figure slipped through the porous stones. Beneath its stare, Mikoneh shuddered again. A compulsion to follow Sathe filled him—filled him up—until he choked. Even so, he shook his head. He would *not* cave.

The Revenant reached out a hand. Dark memories slithered across Mikoneh's mind, swelling every feeling of hopelessness, despair, heartache... He clapped his hands to his head and cried out, shaking himself, trying to escape.

"Will you come quietly?" asked Sathe. "I can make him stop...if you come."

"No!" Mikoneh's voice exploded from him, full of heat and hatred. The memories came faster—death, war, massacres. Things he didn't understand. Ages of time he hadn't lived, yet he felt as though he were part of it all. Part of the living, part of the fighting—doomed to exist when all else died around him.

He fell to his knees, striking the ground hard. A tear squeezed from one eye. He swallowed back bile, trying to resist. The Revenant came closer, drowning him, pounding him with every dark thought, deed, wish—until Mikoneh folded forward, screaming, fighting against a madness clawing at his soul.

Sathe was laughing, somewhere far away.

Consciousness flickered in and out. Emerald green eyes found him.

'My shadow, fight on. Fight as long as you can.'

He tried, how dearly he tried.

"Bring him to the altar," Sathe commanded across the annals of time.

Hands, cold and sharp, lifted him. The memories assaulted him, even then. Destruction. Betrayal. Mayhem. Greed. Thousands of years of everything broken and dark.

He was placed across cold, smooth stone. The icy hands retreated.

"Bind his body."

Frozen cords slithered across his frame. Somewhere far away.

Dead eyes. Broken houses. Empty cities. Swallowed continents.

'Fight. Fight on, my shadow.'

He trembled beneath the crushing weight of the world's blackest sins.

"Enough, my Revenant."

The pressure lifted. The memories fell away. Mikoneh gasped, shaking harder. He stared up into Sathe's hungering eyes. Tears spilled down Mikoneh's face, and he sought his voice, but he couldn't find it.

The Mage leaned close. One clawed finger stroked Mikoneh's cheek. "Now is the time, my Firebrand. From this moment, we will become greater than you can fathom—you and I, together. You do not understand—not yet. But you will very soon."

"I—won't—" It was all he could choke out, but the mere act of defiance lent him strength. He lunged against his restraints. Not ropes. These were cords of violet light, wrapped around his body like two dozen serpents.

With a snap and a fizzle, the cords sent a jolt through his body, biting deep. He arced back, slamming his head against the stone altar.

"Resist if you must." Sathe drew an amethyst-encrusted dagger from one voluminous sleeve. "It will do you no good."

"Stop."

The Mage laughed. He bent close and touched the blade tip against Mikoneh's sternum where the laces of his jerkin were loose. The dagger bit into flesh, stinging. Mikoneh sucked in a breath between clenched teeth. He lurched against his bonds, but the viperous cords tightened, holding him fast.

"How I've ached for this day," Sathe whispered. "Long have I sought you—and when I thought I'd found you...I had to be sure." His blade bit deeper. Icy cold spread from the point, seeping into Mikoneh's bloodstream.

"W-why?" he gasped out.

"Ah. As to that." Sathe's cold eyes met his. "You've no idea who—*what*—you are. It's almost a pity. You will never know the freedom of your blood. Only enslavement. But then, that might be what spares you from madness." A slanted smile caught his lips. He drew the dagger away. "Waking your blood in this manner is cruel, that's regrettable. But necessary. Very necessary." Sathe tucked the blade into his sleeve, then rested his cold fingers on the beads of blood spilled across Mikoneh's chest. "It's for the best, you know. No one should be denied what they were *meant* to be." His laughter could freeze fire.

Violet light pulsed from Sathe's fingers. A chant rose around him. Figures draped in blacks and purples moved into view, closing in on the altar. Runes carved into the stone ceiling flared into life. The chant rose higher.

Fire—icy cold, blisteringly hot—scored through Mikoneh. He threw his head back and screamed. His body convulsed, wrenching against the cords. The taste of copper blossomed on his tongue. His head knocked against the altar.

On and on, agony filled him, carving through bone and sinew, burrowing into every recess of his body, his mind—his soul. His senses heightened. Scent overwhelmed him until he gagged on the odor and taste of mildew, minerals, rotten flesh. His eyes peeled open, and he made out the grains and ridges in the stone ceiling. The colors. Every hue and shape. The chant drummed in his ears, so loud—too loud. Skin brushed against stone that had seemed smooth before, but now he felt the imperfections. Every slight variation in the planes.

Sathe stepped into his view again. Every flaw, every pore, every hint of the man stood unveiled before Mikoneh. His frigid scent—unique to him—filled Mikoneh's nostrils.

The Mage spoke in a language like flowing liquid. The patter of rainfall. The rush of a brook. The gurgle of a stream. The roar of a waterfall. The crash of the ocean. His syllables ran together, lulling Mikoneh into a strange, ethereal realm.

Consciousness wavered. The blue-hued world fell in

around him, and *she* stood in her white cloak, emerald eyes boring into him. '*Fight, my shadow.*'

He screamed on, body thrashing, soul writhing.

Sathe's voice filled his mind, cracking through every ward, every defense. Every ounce of will. The blue hues shattered, revealing a cage of black and violet lightning. The woman with the green eyes vanished.

Pain ripped at his back, drawing another scream. He thrashed more, resisting—but he didn't know how to fight. This was magic, tearing apart his soul, sending needles of ice and fire across his mind. His body was racked as surely as if Drayve's torturers had applied their craft.

Help me! His scream filled the void of his mind. He wouldn't give Sathe the satisfaction of shouting aloud. *Someone, please!*

Laughter answered. Cold, pricking. A great hand seized his mind and filled him with darkness like a flood.

No one will help you now, Firebrand. No one can.

You are mine.

Chapter 28

Blood Waking

"It was on the Elemeer Plain that the Dragon King realized the extent of the Mage Queen's evil."

- From Athonen d'Ereth's *The Fall of Mages in the Age of Dragons*

The Ephe'ahn song in the trees did nothing to ease Maya's distress. She paced near the edge of the village, gnawing the pad of her thumb.

Something was wrong. She could feel it as surely as the wind spirit caressing her cheek. Several more wind spirits had settled on her shoulders, and one perched upon her head. All seemed intent on soothing her—but she would *not* be soothed. Not until she learned what had happened.

It's Mikoneh, I know it. He's in trouble.

She whirled toward Penn, who'd stationed himself between her and the village border. His brown eyes were amber in the lantern light. Dusk had fallen across Sirinhigha, snuffing out the last embers of hope that she was overreacting.

"What can we do?" she asked.

Penn shook his head. "Nothing. There's nothing." His voice was gentle.

She turned away, fighting a mist in her eyes.

Don't fall apart. You can't do that to him again.

She resumed chewing on the pad of her thumb and pacing. Surely, Ter would return soon, along with the imposing Owenekiras and the blasé Minno—and Mikoneh would be with them. All would be well. She was only letting her imagination run away with her in the dark.

You know better than that.

She couldn't fool herself. She needed to be braced—braced for *something*.

Please let the answers come, at least. I can't abide the not knowing!

The Ephe'ahn song faded away, then a new musical strain drifted up. They'd been singing since sundown, at first boasting a cheery variety, then slowly drifting into more melancholy refrains. She didn't understand the words, but the atmosphere and tone were enough to convey their somber message.

Are they as worried as I am?

Owenekiras Rokahn was an impressive man, and when she'd looked into his metallic eyes, she'd felt such reassurance. They would succeed. His strength, his power, would allow for nothing less.

He never promised, though. He was as grim as any of us. He knew the peril was great.

Besides, there was no guarantee that the Dragon King had been spared whatever trouble. He might be dead or...or worse...

She pressed her palms against her face, fending off the hopelessness with a squeak of frustration. "Stop it, stop it."

"Maya?"

She turned back to her friend. "I'm all right—" Movement among the trees silenced her. The shuffle of footsteps filled her ears, then Minno's cedarwood scent followed. Relief hummed in her head, and she darted toward the gray boy. "They're back—"

Minno stepped from the forest. Alone. His shoulders were hunched, and his head hung like a stuffed doll. His stride was erratic, as though he moved under someone else's influence. Maya halted. Penn planted himself in front of her, drawing a sword the Ephe'ahn had gifted to him. The blade gleamed in the lantern glow.

Is Minno being controlled? Maya wondered.

"That's far enough." Penn's voice was a firm command.

Minno paused and hefted his head like it weighed a thousand pounds. The usual blasé expression on his face had cracked, revealing something broken. His gaze drifted from Penn, landing on Maya. Lingering. Then his face hardened. His posture tensed up. Did hatred blaze in those gray eyes?

"I'm myself," Minno said in the same monotone he always wielded. "Don't waste your strength on me."

"Where are the others?" Penn lowered his blade, but slowly.

"Are they well?" asked Maya, pressing a fist against her stuttering heart.

Minno heaved a sigh. "We were separated in the fight. I don't know where—"

The song of the Ephe'ahn cut short. Voices hummed from the hostel. Doors flung open, pouring light onto the village pathways, while child-sized bodies stepped outside.

"The dragon returns!" Someone stabbed a finger at the starry sky.

Maya looked up just as giant wings snuffed out the moon.

Wind spirits hooted and spun in invisible eddies, then the moon reappeared, and two figures leapt from the back of the great, wheeling creature.

A dragon. A real dragon!

Her attention snapped to the figures when they landed.

The shorter one—Ter N'Avea—raced forward. He passed Maya, then seized Minno by his shoulders.

"What happened? Where is Mikoneh?" Ter demanded.

Minno shook his head. "I—"

Owenekiras strode forward. Maya's lungs pinched. In one hand, he clutched Fa's sword. "Minno."

The gray boy froze, then ducked his head.

Maya glanced between them. "He said you were all separated. Is Mikoneh...? Did he...?" She couldn't bring herself to ask. The answer was obvious. Mikoneh wouldn't have dropped Fa's sword idly.

Owenekiras maintained his gaze on Minno. "You promised me." His voice was low, almost soft.

The boy hunched into himself further. "I said I would try."

"Did you?" Owenekiras took a step toward him. "Minno, did you try?"

Minno shuddered, flinching back—then he fell perfectly still. Inhaled a long breath. Lifted his head and turned toward the Dragon King. "No. I didn't try. I didn't *want* to try. The Revenant came and—" His eyes narrowed. "I needn't answer to you."

"No," Owenekiras said. "But you *will*."

"Please," Maya said, heart in her throat. "Tell us what happened."

"Be silent." Minno's voice scraped over his lips, harsh, almost vehement. He didn't glance at her. "I'll tell you nothing, Owen. Not unless you give me what I want."

"Is Mikoneh your hostage, then?" asked Ter, tipping his head to one side.

"No." Minno didn't look at him either. His eyes were fastened on Owenekiras. "Tell me how to reach *her*."

The Dragon King eyed him for a long moment, then he took another step forward. "What happened, Minno? You gave your oath."

The boy took a step back. "I—" He scowled, his mask breaking altogether. "I'll explain *nothing*, until you answer me. Do you not listen? You must grant me access to Katanni first."

"You know I can't and won't." Owenekiras took another step. "Minno, where is Mikoneh?"

"Gone. Gone! That's all I'll say." Minno staggered back another step, madness tingeing his eyes.

"Then Sathe has caught him," Ter murmured.

Cold fingers clutched Maya's heart, squeezing. Her breath hitched. *No. Oh, no. Please, no.*

"Monster!" Penn lifted his sword. "Take us to Mikoneh, or I'll cut you in two!" He started forward, but Owenekiras stepped into his path.

"Do not engage Minno. You cannot defeat him. Few can."

"I refuse to back down—"

"Be sensible, Lord Penn," Owenekiras said. "Stand down. Minno can kill you with a touch."

"I don't care!"

Maya staggered to Penn's side, trying to see him through her tears. "Penn, please. I don't want to lose you, too."

His muscles were tight under Maya's touch, but Penn held still, breathing heavily. She could feel his rapid heartbeat through her fingers, matching her own quick pulse.

Owenekiras turned back to the gray boy. "You've betrayed me, Minno." His voice was soft, almost...wounded.

Minno's eyes widened. His chin fell to his chest.

The Dragon King heaved a weighty sigh. "Leave us, Minno. Please. Before I do what I would regret." He turned from the boy, finding Ter. "We must assume the very worst. Sathe will awaken Mikoneh's blood, and they will bond. He'll settle for no other arrangement."

Ter wrung his hands. "What can be done?"

Maya stared between them. They'd dismissed Minno. No punishment, nothing but banishment. That was all?

What's done is done. The priority is finding my brother.

Silence breathed over the air. Even the wind spirits had stilled, as though awaiting the Dragon King's decision. Finally, Owenekiras stirred. "First, we must ensure Maya's safety." Owenekiras turned toward her, his eyes glittering orange in the lantern light. "You must come to my war camp. There, you will be under the protection of every Rokahnian ward, and eight hundred thousand soldiers."

She shook her head. "I don't want to be tucked away somewhere safe. I need to find Mikoneh—"

"As Lord Owenekiras said," Penn broke in, "we must be sensible, Maya. Getting yourself caught by Mages will only make matters worse, especially for your twin."

"Lord Penn is right." Ter stepped forward several feet. His ears twitched down. "We cannot give the Mages any greater leverage than they already have."

Maya frowned, trying to comprehend what they were saying through the horror dancing across her bones. "I won't pretend to understand any of this, about blood waking, or b-bonding." Her chin quivered. A fresh sob caught in her throat. "I just want to save my brother."

"We will." Owenekiras's voice was a soft rumble. "But the damage has been done. Resign yourself to that. He will be tortured, in every imaginable—and unimaginable—way. Mages are not kind to dragons. Not any longer."

Maya stilled. His words sank in, reverberating off her soul. "Dragons?" Her voice was a faint whisper, nearly inaudible. What was he saying?

The Dragon King heard her whisper. "Yes. All Rokahnians are descended from dragons, and the noble lines have not been diluted—only put to sleep. You and your brother are of the Old Blood. You're dragons." He brushed a gloved finger through the blue-black of his hair. "It is evident in your appearance to the few who understand."

Dragons. The word drummed against Maya's skull, trying to penetrate. Trying to make sense through the haze of fear, of worry...of growing anger.

Ter's ears flicked up, then down. "Alas, Sathe is among those few. He knows the look."

"He ought," Owenekiras growled. "More than once, a Rokahn has given him scars he cannot easily hide. But that isn't important now. We must leave for my encampment. When you're made safe, Maya, we will begin the hunt to find your twin. I swear to you, we will not rest until I uproot every Mage warren underground and within the Andyan mountains. He will be found."

"Thank you." Tears spilled down her cheeks, though she felt hollow. The piece of her where Mikoneh resided had been carved out, and she was empty, bereft. He should be here, learning about their heritage alongside her. *Dragons.* "Will he be able to endure—what—what they do?" She could barely ask the awful question.

Penn caught her arm. "He's the strongest man I know. If anyone can, it's him."

"Just so." Ter hopped closer and offered her a bright smile. "Of the many souls in this old world, he is truly among the great. You will see."

Minno scoffed, still standing there, despite Owenekiras's command to leave.

Maya shot the gray boy a glower, her anger mounting. "You don't believe it? No, perhaps not. I don't know how you betrayed my brother—what specific promise you broke—or why. But this much I can tell you: He won't fall. Mikoneh is stronger than anyone. Whatever Sathe tries to do, Mikoneh will beat him before we ever find him. Mikoneh doesn't lose. He pivots."

"Is that so?" Minno's eyes narrowed. "All the more reason to despise him."

Biting down her anger and helplessness, Maya whirled toward Owenekiras. "We should go. The sooner we reach your camp, the sooner you can seek out Mikoneh, right?"

"Yes." The Dragon King nodded. "Let us be underway." He started east, then paused and looked toward Minno. "Don't follow us, Minno. Don't come near my camp."

The gray boy flinched as though Owenekiras had struck him. "I had no intention of doing so. I need to find Duck anyway."

"Have a care with yourself, Minno." Owenekiras moved off, and Maya and Penn hastened to follow. Ter loped after them.

"You're letting him go?" asked Penn, his voice tight. "Can you not defeat him either?"

"I cannot," Owenekiras said. "Though my reasons are different."

Maya studied Owenekiras, indignation churning in her chest. She wanted to pounce on Minno and throttle him. Tear his eyes out. Destroy him if necessary. Anything to make him give back her twin.

But I can't. I don't have that power. Not yet.

She was a dragon. Could she harness that power? Could she free herself from feeling powerless ever again?

If Mikoneh's a dragon, can't he get stronger, too? Can't he defeat Sathe?

Or would the Dark Mage bind her brother too tight, and use that dragon blood as a weapon against the world?

She shuddered, fresh tears spilling down her cheeks.

They strode toward the village boundary, but after a moment the Dragon King turned to her. He proffered Fa's sword. "We will find your brother. My oath on it."

CHAPTER 29

SWORN TO SILENCE

*"When at last, he understood what the Mage Queen had done,
fury poured forth like a storm."*

- From Athonen d'Ereth's *The Fall of Mages in the Age of Dragons*

They *flew.*

At first, Maya couldn't focus her thoughts enough to conjure up the questions that should be foremost on her mind—questions about Mikoneh's capture, and her revealed heritage. The influence of wind filled her up, pushing out every worry and every fear. It was a kind of intoxication, and part of her embraced it.

No, stop that. Think about Mikoneh! Don't lose yourself to the wind's pull.

She tried to ground herself on the dragon's back. To center herself on Mikoneh's capture and the horrors meant for him. At last, she grasped the terrible thought, making it tangible, and reality pinned her down. The dragon—Larkynven—bore them northeasterly, towards the distant plains of Simynshin.

Clutching Fa's sword close, the blade now wrapped in a cloak Ter had lent her, Maya leaned forward to speak above the wind noise. "Why did our parents never tell us we were dragons?"

"They were sworn to silence." Owenekiras never looked over his shoulder, but his voice rose, strong without becoming a shout. "It was for your safety."

She frowned. "But if we're dragons..." A dozen questions flitted across her mind. "Can we turn into..." She glanced at the scales glistening beneath the moon.

"Yes, though you're young. You would fit into my arms in your true form, no more."

She sat back to digest that. "Then...what could Sathe possibly want with Mikoneh? He's too tiny to—to wreak havoc." A pinprick of hope shot through her.

Owenekiras shook his head. "Sathe doesn't need raw destructive power. That he has in plenty."

What destruction could a dragon wreak that wasn't raw and colossal?

It's all so much.

She ached for a distraction from Mikoneh's situation and her own feebleness. Anything to keep from collapsing under her fear and grief. Yet giving into the flight's intoxication again felt wrong. "May I ask a few more questions?"

"We have leagues yet to cross," he answered mildly.

Maya collected her thoughts. "All right, start with dragons. Mikoneh and I have already come of age. Why are we so small in our true forms?"

"Dragons live for centuries," the man answered. "In those years, you are mere infants."

"Oh." She mulled that over. "Then...do dragons my age not marry?"

Did his cheek twitch because he cracked a smile?

Maya shook herself. "Never mind. That's not important—"

"Women of your age often wed, whether dragon or otherwise. Once you've experienced a human existence, your maturity quickens. The true Rokahnian blood has been long dormant. Few of our people even recall their heritage."

"They forgot they're dragons?" She couldn't fathom such a thing. "Didn't they ever chronicle their histories?"

"Much was lost in the aftermath of the Dragon Wars." His voice dipped lower. "Too much."

"But—you're a prince of Rokahn, and *you* know what you are. Why didn't you tell your people?"

"I learned of my heritage after I left Rokahn. I, too, grew up thinking I was human."

"Oh." She'd forgotten about the stories of his banishment. It must all be true. But those questions—everything about Rokahn—could wait. More pressing matters crowded back into her head. "There's something I don't understand..." She hesitated, fear prickling through her—but she needed to know. "If my parents were dragons, why didn't they use their true forms to beat Lord Drayve or—or to save themselves? Did they not know their birthright?"

He didn't answer for a moment, then the barest hint of a sigh escaped his lips. "Jonatten and Seranni were the best of people. Fiercely loyal and strong warriors. But they weren't dragons."

Maya jerked back. "But they had to be. Do you mean they were too dormant to tap—to—to become—"

"I mean what I say," Owenekiras said gently. "They weren't dragons."

Her mind reeled, unable to settle on the implications. She leaned against her saddleback, letting the night air pull her thoughts from his meaning. Away. Far away. The lines of the world blurred, fading.

A hand fell on her shoulder. Ter's voice was soft. "Do not let the wind seduce you, young one. It will take you into itself. You will lose your corporeal shape. Coming back from that is most difficult."

She shuddered. Lines reformed around her, and she seemed to fall back into her body. She turned Owenekiras's words over and over again, trying to breathe through the tightening vise around her lungs. She bowed her head and focused on each breath. In. Out. In.

Ask.

She couldn't find the words.

You need to ask.

How could she?

"You were placed in their care as toddlers." Owenekiras spoke slowly, as though to soothe her. He didn't turn around. His eyes were trained ahead, where wisps of the dragon's mane trailed across the starry heavens. "It was to protect you. They were quick to agree, as they couldn't have children of their own. Two more worthy parents I've never known."

Her lips trembled. Emotions swelled up, too complicated to sort. The questions eddying around her mind drained away, unimportant. The joy of flight vanished.

Only one question stayed, and she didn't dare ask it.

Not yet. Perhaps not ever.

Chapter 30

Scaled Wings

"The Dark Mages had enslaved dragons, corrupting the sacred war bond."

- From Athonen d'Ereth's *The Fall of Mages in the Age of Dragons*

Mikoneh hung by his arms from chains anchored to the porous rock ceiling. Pain throbbed across his body, except for his manacled hands. Those were too numb to feel anymore. If he stretched his bare toes, he could just brush the rock floor in the center of the room. He still wore his trousers, but his jerkin, boots, and socks were gone.

Torches set in brackets around the dome-shaped chamber flickered with violet flames. They didn't put off heat. The room was cold enough to turn his breaths into wisps of cloud.

He couldn't remember why he was in such a predicament. His mind was blank, as though a wall had been erected between memory and the present moment. He allowed it, glad of the reprieve. The icy-cold pain deep within his exposed chest was enough to combat against. If he pushed, he felt certain he would recall everything, and he wasn't ready for that.

Not just yet. Give yourself a moment. Just breathe.

The scrape of approaching footsteps jolted him. He tensed, and the pain flared higher.

I'm coming, my Firebrand.

The words thundered through Mikoneh's head, rattling bone, tearing at his soul. Adrenaline surged up, roaring in his ears. His fingers itched to draw his sword, but his sheath was empty. He'd dropped Fa's sword in the old forest. Instead, he pinned a glare on the doorway at the far end of the chamber. A handful of cloaked figures entered. Mages.

The memories settled into Mikoneh's mind, sharp, edged, but not overwhelming. Sathe had bound him somehow. Bound him so tight, he couldn't escape.

The foremost figure drew back his cowl. Mikoneh wasn't surprised to find Sathe's face revealed. "Those chains must be uncomfortable for you," the Mage said in soft tones. He trod closer. "I will release you once I'm certain you'll not escape."

"If not now," Mikoneh growled, "I will eventually. My oath on it."

Sathe's chuckle was like crusted ice. "Your family's stubbornness is second to none—and I admire you for that birthright. But you speak of what you don't understand. We're bonded, you and me. There's no escape from that."

Panic pitched across Mikoneh's mind. Instinct assured him that Sathe wasn't lying, though how Mikoneh knew that much he couldn't guess. No, he didn't *want* to guess.

Sathe studied him, dark eyes glittering in the violet light. "Release him."

Mikoneh scowled. "Thought you weren't going to risk that."

The Mage didn't answer.

A second cloaked figure moved forward. Though the Mage never lifted a hand toward the chains, the manacles snapped, dropping Mikoneh. He crashed to his knees, and blood rushed back into his arms like streaming fire. He hunched forward, shuddering beneath the protests of his body.

"I will demonstrate for you what our bond means, Firebrand. Pay attention. The lesson is important." Sathe's voice crowded Mikoneh's mind. ***Rise.***

Mikoneh scoffed—but his body obeyed. Despite the agony pelting his muscles, the fire prickling at his arms, and the tearing throb against his shoulder blades, he stood on his feet.

Now, draw out your wings.

The words made no sense, yet the throb between his shoulders heightened. Flesh shifted, bones jutted out, and wings slid from his human body as though they'd always been there. He cried out, startled, frightened. The large, midnight-blue, scaled wings stretched above him, glittering in the torches' glow. He staggered forward, as though to escape, but caught himself.

Don't panic. Be calm, idiot. Stay calm.

Sathe stepped forward. "Now, a test." His eyes flashed with cold fire, and something like fingers tugged on Mikoneh's insides, peeling essence from his soul. He wrenched back, but the fingering persisted. Sathe's irises turned golden, sparkling, and his pupils slitted.

"Ahhh." The Mage closed those eyes slowly and tipped his head back, like he relished a pleasant taste. "It's been far too long since I drew on a dragon's power." His eyes opened wide. "Nothing is so raw, so potent, as your bloodline." He dropped his chin to meet Mikoneh's stare. "Child, you know not what greatness we will achieve together."

The Mage's glittering eyes narrowed. "Now, the final test and the final proof." He reached out, caught Mikoneh's chin between his fingers, and sent a command through the channel between them.

Summon flame.

Mikoneh lurched back, scrambling to throw up a mental shield against the order. But his *soul* obeyed. Flames burst from his body, wreathing him, not consuming his trousers or flesh. It was a mere tickle—and an agony. His soul quaked. His heart screamed.

Sathe laughed, a mad, crackling, searing sound.

"You see, Firebrand?" A grin slashed Sathe's lips and he jerked Mikoneh's chin up. "You're mine. You can hide nothing—resist nothing—*be* nothing without me. We are one."

A deep, rumbling fire stirred within Mikoneh—one that had nothing to do with Sathe's command. He spat at the Mage's face, and Sathe flinched back, losing his hold on Mikoneh's chin.

"You may have me chained, body and soul—but I'm not yours, Sathe. I never will be! I'll escape from this. I gave my oath and I'll *keep* it."

Sathe wiped the spittle from his cheek with one sleeve, then lowered his arm. He settled a stare on Mikoneh. "Defiance will spare you the brokenness of most captive creatures. But I will still hurt you when you resist."

A faint twitch of Sathe's eyes, and claws raked across Mikoneh's soul. He buckled to his knees. A cry tore from his throat, and he folded forward to huddle on the ground. White light bled across his vision. All he knew was pain.

Beg me to stop, came the taunting voice. Not a command.

Never. Never! Not under my own power, that I swear.

Agony heightened. Pain wrapped itself around him.

He fell into it, became lost in it.
The world blackened.

INTERLUDE IV

THEY WITNESS IT ALL

"Time cannot sunder what we have."

- From the Corpse Poet's 39th Sonnet

"THE TREES ALWAYS REMEMBER."

He stood beneath them, cradled in the blue hues of memory. She stood at his side, gowned in white. Her hood had been drawn back, revealing long, straight wheat-blonde hair. Her head turned, and those emerald eyes met his gaze. Her smile was warm.

"What do they remember?" he asked.

"Everything. The grief, the loss, the warfare. The laughter, the growth, the endurance. They witness it all. They never forget."

"Why am I here?" he asked softly.

For a moment, she didn't answer. Her eyes turned skyward. "You retreated into yourself. It was essential."

"But why do I keep coming *here*?"

"Ah." She turned away and reached out to finger a bush laden with ripe red berries. "I can't answer that, my shadow friend."

"Who are you?"

"You cannot yet remember."

He turned toward the nearest elm. Its graceful branches spread wide, shading the watery ground around it. Ripples cascaded when he stepped forward. "But the trees—they remember."

"They do." Her voice was gentle.

The memory of pain sliced through him, and he shuddered. "Must I return? Can't I stay here?"

"It's not possible." The woman turned toward him. Her eyes were filled with light. "But you will visit this place again. That I don't doubt."

He nodded. He would come back. His heart belonged here.

Chapter 31

Flame and Tendrils

"Many dragons fell to death. Others to madness."

- From Athonen d'Ereth's *The Fall of Mages in the Age of Dragons*

Mikoneh stared blearily at the stone floor plastered to his cheek. The coils of pain had lessened across his body; had faded to a mere hum at the edges of his consciousness. He licked his lips and tasted blood. Inch by inch, he pulled his arms from his sides and heaved himself up to his knees. The chamber was empty. Only a single violet torch blazed near the exit, radiating cold.

He shifted his legs, and chains rattled. Glancing behind him, he found his vision blocked by the large bat-like wings protruding from his shoulder blades. He jerked back, and the wings unfolded in a spasm. His ankle chains clattered. He stared at the looming appendages. Glittering blue scales covered the exterior of the wing, while the underside was a fiery

membrane veined with gold. Black claws—or were they talons?
—protruded from the bend in each wing. The thumb, he
supposed, considering what he knew about bat anatomy. The
sharp tip curved out, gleaming in the violet light.

Wings. *His* wings.

How though? How am I a dragon?

Stranger still, how was he only partly transformed? Wings
aside, he still wore his human skin. Yet he knew what he was.
Some animal instinct, deep within, called him by name:
Dragon.

He tried to flex one wing. It obeyed as surely as if he'd
willed his finger to twitch. The vibrant orange, red, and yellow
colors of the underwing shone like true flame, rippling and
contorting as the wing stretched wide, fanning out. He
counted four long fingers of bone spaced across the membrane
surface, just like a bat. His mouth curled up in an incredulous
smile.

It's not possible. Is it?

He spread the other wing, craning his head to watch it
expand. The length of each wing was at least eighteen hands,
and its height from top to bottom was at least ten. The fiery
membrane flickered and flashed, mesmerizing. Gingerly, he
folded his wings up, and they tucked against his back, show-
casing the blue scales of the outer wings. Deep, glittering, like
precious gems.

He reached over his shoulder and brushed a finger against
the scales. Hard as steel, yet warm to the touch. They were the
size of small silver coins, but far thicker.

I'm a dragon.

Questions assailed his mind. Why Fa and Mama hadn't
told their children. Why they hadn't transformed to save themselves. Why Sathe wanted a dragon—particularly him. Why no
one knew that Rokahnians were dragons. How dragons had

become legends in the first place. How he could move with such large—yet flexible—appendages.

The last thought brought laughter. He tipped his head back, letting the wry mirth engulf him, until his eyes welled with tears.

No. No tears. Don't give Sathe the pleasure.

Laughter answered—not his own. The crackling sound filled his head, reverberating off his soul. He hunched beneath its weight and stature. Cold seized his limbs.

You are mine. If I choose, I can hear every thought. Feel every emotion. You cannot hide.

Mikoneh shuddered, curling into himself. Fear slithered into every space within him.

This was worse than death. Far, far worse.

Doesn't matter. Fight. Don't let him win.

A small voice in the back of his mind whispered back, 'He already has.'

Mikoneh shut that voice off at once. He refused to lose. Instead, he would pivot.

He was left alone in the domed chamber until he couldn't count the turns of time. Once, a skeletal Mage brought him food, dark amusement dripping from its ceaseless grin. The meal was tasteless, but not rotten like he'd half-expected. A few boiled turnips, a wedge of cheese, and a stalk of some green he couldn't identify. He ate, determined to keep up his strength, while he contemplated his next step.

If Sathe could read his mind—and that was confirmed—well, Mikoneh couldn't imagine the Mage would really choose to do so *all* the time. Surely, a Mage general had important matters to focus his energy on. The tricky part was knowing when the monster was listening in. It might not be something Mikoneh could detect, but then again, perhaps he could. Sathe's presence was always accompanied by wintry touches. With Mikoneh's element forced awake again, he shouldn't feel the cold, unless Sathe was intruding.

I'll need to pay careful attention.

He'd tested the manacles clamped to his ankles. The chains were thick and bright, no sign of rust to promise escape. Still...

If I can use fire, maybe...

He considered his palms. Should he risk summoning the fire spirits? He'd rejected them and hurt their feelings. If they didn't answer, he wouldn't blame them.

I should apologize either way.

Even if he hated wielding flame, that wasn't on them—at least, he didn't think it was.

Do the Spirits Elemental choose the wielder?

He might never see Ter again to ask. His heart throbbed, and he bowed his head, envisioning Maya's horror when she learned that Mikoneh had been captured. Would anyone know that Minno was the culprit? Mikoneh almost didn't believe it himself. Not after the gray boy had rescued them in the first place.

Something had changed...standing before the Revenant, Minno had sunk into himself. Had his own memories over-whelmed him, crushing something within?

I might never find out now—and if I do get out of here, I'll probably just wring his scrawny little neck.

Mikoneh sighed, aware he was just delaying his decision. Drawing a breath, he reached inside until he found the core of heat at his center. Breathing in to calm himself had extinguished his flame before. Would breathing out draw on it instead? He closed his eyes, centering on that core, pulling on it as he exhaled a low breath.

Flames curled up from his fingers. His eyes snapped open. A single fire spirit flickered above his palm, its shape human.

"You came." His voice was hoarse.

The fire spirit considered him. It folded its slender arms, then tossed its head.

Mikoneh grimaced. "About before...I'm sorry."

The spirit maintained its stance, chin up.

A faint, rasping sigh escaped Mikoneh's lips. "I didn't mean to offend or hurt any of you. I wasn't thinking. I—panicked." He shifted to rattle the chains on his ankles. "For good reason, by the way. The Mages caught me."

His words were having some effect. The fire spirit's chin lowered bit by bit, and it slowly unfolded its wispy arms.

His grimace softened. "But that's no excuse to lash out. I have a bad temper sometimes." He scowled at himself. "Most times. Sorry." When he issued the last, solitary word, the spirit jumped up and rested its slender little hands on his nose. The creature—all flame and tendrils—stared into his eyes and canted its head.

'*We forgive you. We all forgive you, dragon.*' The flames crackled higher, and dozens of spirits sparked into shape before him, hovering in the air, suspended on nothing but their own flame. The fire spirit before his eyes drew back to let him take in the sight.

He sat against his ankles and stared at the wonder before him. For the first time, he let himself soak in the fact of their existence. The reality of magical life beyond human sight. A smile tugged at his mouth, spreading slowly toward a grin.

"You're amazing." He didn't intend to speak out loud.

Several spirits turned into wheels of flame that bounced around the room, as pleased by his compliment as he was to admire them.

The lead fire spirit settled on his palm. '*We answer to you, Dragon Prince.*'

He blinked and turned his gaze on the little creature. "I'm not a prince."

The spirit cackled and sparked. Its form flickered into a dragon shape. '*You know so little, so little. Trust us. You must trust us.*'

He frowned. "I don't trust very well."

'*Choose. Choose to trust. We will prove ourselves.*' The spirit lifted itself on fiery wings. '*And we will choose to trust you in return.*'

"Can you help me escape?" He dragged his legs forward, rattling the chains. "Can you melt the metal?"

The fire spirit flickered back into its human form and lit on the chains. Spreading its arms, it walked along the metal links like a tightrope, then sighed and brightened, spreading wings like his while maintaining its humanoid shape. It flew to his palm, and he lifted his arm.

'*Magery. Difficult to melt. Difficult to heat at all.*'

"I was afraid of that." Mikoneh used his free hand to scratch at his scalp. "I have to escape somehow."

'*Patience. We will help.*'

'*Help,*' chirped another spirit.

'*Help.*'

'*Yes, help.*'

They all chorused out a final '*We will help!*'

Mikoneh found himself smiling. "Thank you. We'll need to be very careful. No mistakes." A shiver ran up his back. He stiffened. "Go. Go now, please."

The spirits winked out.

Sathe's laughter filled him up like a blizzard. **Don't think I don't know what you're attempting. It won't work, but I commend your stubbornness. I'll be visiting you**

shortly, Firebrand. Wait for me. Wait, and dread my coming.

The cold retreated, leaving Mikoneh damp with sweat. He drew his knees to his chest, hugged his legs, and focused on deep breaths. The panic leveled out and bled away. He didn't know what Sathe might do to him—might require of him—but he would fight. It was all he could do.

It was all he knew how to do.

～ (‖) ～

THE MAGE CAME when Mikoneh had drifted into a semi-doze. Sathe was suddenly present, standing before Mikoneh, looming like a great pillar of ice.

"Rise." Sathe's tone was firm, but the command didn't resound through Mikoneh like before.

He's testing me. Mikoneh didn't move.

Sathe clicked his tongue. ***Rise, Firebrand.***

The compulsion seized him, and Mikoneh dragged himself upright. Chains clattered around his bare feet. The Mage reached out and took his chin between a cold, pale finger and thumb. Those eyes—once black pits, now gold, glittering, and slitted like a feral cat—bored into Mikoneh as though exposing him, flesh, bone, and soul.

"You tolerate pain well. Better than most, worse than a few. But that is only one kind. I will teach all of them to you, drop by drop, until you are acquainted well with each. Not just pain of the body. All of them, Mikoneh. Every kind."

Mikoneh trembled, despite his efforts to stand tall and defiant.

I won't be here that long.

Sathe chuckled, then the Mage's hand moved like a flash, releasing his chin, to strike his cheek. Mikoneh's head jerked to one side, and he stumbled. His cheek flared with cold rather than heat, and the frost spread.

"You will be with me *forever.*"

Mikoneh turned a glower on the Mage. He said nothing. Let the man delude himself. Let him believe what he liked.

You won't break me. Not you. Not ever.

Sathe's lips tugged into a rictus grin. "Foolish, very foolish." He caught a strand of Mikoneh's hair and looped it behind his pointed ear. The Mage's fingers hovered on the pointed tip Mikoneh always hid from Oceaneans at Fa and Mama's insistence. No one in Oceana had pointed ears. Sathe's fingers stroked that point. "I have always admired dragons. Of all the fae, they are the fiercest and—oddly—the gentlest. You breathe out the elements like weapons, conquer the skies, inspire fear—and yet none can craft so well. You are poets, explorers, justicers, kings. So much to admire. And you, so young, yet so strong. Truly, you are a most worthy heir." His grin stretched into a cruel, deadly thing. "Alas, you will never rule."

Mikoneh jerked back. "Stop touching me, you lunatic. I'm not whoever you seem to think I am."

Sathe lowered his hand with a faint scoff. "Willfully blind, too. This will be dear fun for me. I had thought to break you in slowly, but...I think not. We begin now."

CHAPTER 32

BORN OF THE BLOOD

*"The Dragon King raced to find some means of severing the
corrupted bonds, but time was against him."*

- From Athonen d'Ereth's *The Fall of Mages in the Age of Dragons*

The Prince of Rokahn's camp spread out across a vast green plain, surrounded by palisades. Within that great sheltering wall, orderly rows of tents, smithies, corrals, pavilions, and even wells, boasted of Owenekiras's meticulous attention to detail.

Maya drank it all in as she leaned out from Larkynven's saddle while the dragon tipped to one side, turning in a wide circle above the encampment. Penn eagerly leaned out as well, taking in the view with a keen eye.

Red and blue pennants snapped above a tall black tent centered among the rows of smaller silver tents. A second pass allowed Maya to make out the heraldry: A black dragon, wings spread wide, clutching two crossed swords. How appropriate. She recalled seeing that crest among the pendants in the little Ashwood box she kept close.

Larkynven swooped westward and glided low over the open ground outside the palisades. The dragon landed with surprising grace and tucked one wing in, while the east-facing wing stretched out to give his passengers an exit. Owenekiras rose and moved down the wing on steady, practiced feet. His cape—which glimmered like obsidian scales in the sunlight—flowed around his leather boots.

Maya and Penn followed quickly, with Ter close behind. Maya reached the tall grass of the Simynshinian plain and bleakness cloaked her, grounding her to the earth. The fears she'd valiantly batted away in the air settled in to nibble at her heart. Tears welled in her eyes, but she blinked them back, determined not to cave...like she had before.

I'll be strong for you, Mikoneh. Like you were for me.

How tenderly he'd nursed her when she fell into herself a year ago. She remembered nothing of her collapse. Only that the horror and grief of that night—that last terrible moment shared with her parents—had shattered her. She'd fled. Fled into the recesses of her soul, knowing nothing, feeling nothing. She'd first come back to herself six months afterward. Mikoneh had carried her from their shared tent quarters, out into the sun on one of those rare warm days in early spring. It was a quiet afternoon, and the gentle caress of the pleasant wind had stirred her senses.

She'd opened her eyes, and for the first time in her recollection, she'd watched her twin weep.

Returning to full strength had been difficult. She'd wasted away to almost nothing in her illness. Fortunately, Mikoneh was all patience and understanding—without letting her wallow. He'd forced her to rise each day; then to take a few steps; then to walk across the tent; across the camp; to the horses. He'd pushed her, gently but firmly, and she'd slowly regained her desire to live. Watching him—knowing he carried the burden of their grief without complaint, that he commanded the rebel army inherited from their parents, that he hardly slept, and was the last to eat—it made her ashamed of her feebleness. Of her cowardice. But he never blamed her or shamed her for falling ill. No matter his temper, no matter his weariness—he never once called her weak.

In her convalescence, she'd realized that Mikoneh was the strongest person she knew. It might not be fair to put all her faith in her twin, yet he'd proven himself again and again. The trouble Mikoneh had was a trouble different from most people: He didn't know how to give up. It wasn't in his soul, even when he thought he'd failed.

Was it any wonder, really, that he wielded fire? Blow on flames, and they only grow higher and hotter. She fervently believed he would defeat Sathe—though her nibbling fears said otherwise.

Even Mikoneh had his limits.

Yes, he'd been strong enough to stand upright and keep moving after their parents—*they* are *my parents*—after Fa and Mama died. But he'd still changed. Gone was the smiling youth with a sparkle in his golden eyes and a ready quip on his tongue. He'd grown into a brooding, often angry man, though he tried to keep that in check.

She missed what he once was—but then, he likely missed her, too. Neither of them was the same.

We'll never be able to go back.

Especially not now. He was a captive of beings darker and more depraved than Drayve, surrounded by tainted magic, tormented by fire he didn't want to wield. Somewhere far away, and no doubt frightened. And they were both dragons, not born of the blood of those they'd been raised by.

Nothing is the same.

Ahead, the log palisades loomed, sturdy and imposing. Four sentries paced outside the gates where Owenekiras aimed his steps. At his approach, the sentries turned from their uniform march and stood tall. Their helms and breastplates gleamed in the broad sunlight. Their spears jutted toward the sky.

One sentry lifted his voice. "The Crown Prince of Rokahn comes!"

A cheer rose from beyond the camp. It must've been a traditional announcement since Maya couldn't imagine anyone had missed the massive dragon wheeling overhead.

The gates drew aside, and the sentries shifted into two short columns, giving their leader passage. Eyes followed Maya and Penn inside the encampment, and Ter greeted one of the sentries by name, then the gates were drawn shut by a handful of men.

Maya paused to study her surroundings. Fa had done his best to run an orderly camp within the forest hideout, but tents had been pitched wherever the tree roots allowed, and their provisions had been shabby. By contrast, this was pristine. Soldiers marched past in perfect formation, clad in proper armor polished to reflect the world like a looking glass. They paused to salute their prince, then moved on again at his nod.

Owenekiras glanced back, then motioned toward the aisle between the neat rows of tents. She obeyed his silent direction, staying close to Penn. The grass had been pounded down by thousands of feet, but it remained green and lush, carpeting the paths through the encampment.

Maybe an Earth Elementalist helps keep the grass vital? She could only guess what each Elementalist skillset encompassed, but that ability made sense.

It was a long walk to the central black tent. Penn wore a patient grimace, cradling his broken arm close. She offered him a pain-relieving herb, and he accepted, chewing quietly though his lips puckered.

At last, they neared the tall, stately structure. The fabric walls were thick, black-on-black, in a seamless damask pattern. Sentries guarded the entrance. Nearby, a handful of men in light armor and white capes had stationed themselves to watch their prince's approach. Each wore the simple heraldry of a broadsword on their silver breastplates.

One stepped forward. He looked to be in his mid-twenties, with tousled white hair, vivid green eyes, and pointed ears. A ready smile touched his lips, and he bowed with a level of informality that suggested camaraderie with the Dragon King. He was a fit man, with a lean, muscular frame.

"My lord, welcome back. I trust everything went..." His smile slipped as he read Owenekiras's face, as though he could see past the stony expression to what lay beneath. His hand fell to his sword. "Tell me where to go, and I shall leave at once."

"Not yet, Captain," Owenekiras said. "This will require all our cunning. Call my generals for council this evening. I will brook no delay."

"As you command, my lord, so shall it be." The captain nodded, then turned—but his gaze fell on Maya, and he faltered. A smile returned to his lips, warm and welcoming. He inclined his head, then moved off without a word to heed his lord's order.

Ter moved up beside Maya and Penn. "That is Captain Akonn, leader of the Sword."

Maya wrenched her gaze from the man's retreating form.

"He's their leader? So young?" She flushed, thinking of Mikoneh leading Fa's forces at a similar age.

"The Sword follows their strongest fighter—so long as he is honorable." Ter's ears fluttered. "None could be more so than Captain Akonn, first knight of the Sword. He's also excellent with a quarterstaff—and not nearly so young as he appears."

"I'd love a bout with him." Penn's eyes gleamed with interest.

Maya shot the viscount a warning look. "Not until your arm's fully mended."

He sighed. "Why did I have to break a bone right before meeting up with legends?"

Sensing eyes on her, she shifted to find Owenekiras. He lifted his hand toward the tent. "You're likely fatigued," he said. "Akonn's assignment will take a while to complete. There's a chaise lounge within. Rest yourselves. I will have food and drink brought."

Her cheeks warmed. "I thank you, my lord."

Tugging on Penn's arm, she led him into the black tent. Despite the dark, heavy walls, the interior was a pleasant temperature. The trappings were elegant but not gaudy. Delicate stands curved into hooks where lanterns burned with a soft, blue glow. Several plush chairs and the chaise lounge were positioned over a wide, silver-threaded area rug bearing an ornate pattern. Small tables were placed strategically around the chamber to hold food or keepsakes as needed.

One table displayed a Fang and Claw board arranged with delicate golden pieces sparkling with tiny gems. Maya had never seen such an exquisite set. Mikoneh would be drooling. She started toward the display but stopped herself. She shouldn't be roaming a lord's lodgings.

Instead, she padded onto the rug, welcoming the reprieve from the direct sunlight of the warm autumn day. Penn sighed, then moved to a chair and stood beside it, waiting in lordly fashion. She made for the chaise lounge and sat. He allowed himself to sit in the chair.

The main tent flap opened, and Owenekiras entered with Ter at his side. Penn started to rise, but the Dragon King waved him back into his seat.

"Refreshments will arrive shortly." Owenekiras turned to Ter. "Will you be staying?"

"Yes." The Ephe'ahn frowned. "I feel responsible. I should have read Minno's mood better."

"Are you an oracle now?" asked Owenekiras, smiling dryly.

Ter's ears twitched. "Ah, no. But—"

"We both failed." Owenekiras turned toward a bureau set against the wall near the front entrance. He opened it and rummaged for a moment, then withdrew a rolled map. "Now we must repair what has been done."

Ter followed the imposing man across the room, toward a second chamber beyond a set of flaps. Owenekiras parted the flaps, then glanced back to settle his glittering eyes on Maya. "Rest. There is time." He slipped into the compartment beyond, and Ter followed close. The flaps fell back into place, hiding them.

Maya turned to Penn. "He's right. We should try to rest."

The viscount leaned back and heaved a sigh. "I just...feel guilty."

"Me, too." She plucked at her smudged skirts and tried not to dwell on Mikoneh's predicament. She would accomplish nothing by fretting—but she didn't know how to stop.

THE POUNDING of boots and din of soft voices pulled Maya from dreams of musty tunnels and violet torches. She sat up and blinked in the tent's gloom. Red light from the setting sun pooled at the tent flaps where two dozen men and women had congregated.

Akonn of the Sword stood in the opening, his white hair dyed crimson hues in the setting sun. He'd changed from light armor into a white shirt, a cream vest with finely stitched embroidery, and brown boots and trousers. Belts crisscrossed his chest, wrapping around his shoulders, and he wore a sword at his hip. Gold trimmed the ensemble, including earrings dangling from his pointed ears. Maya had never seen a wardrobe so elaborate before—except among the nobility in Drayve's fortress and Lord Owenekiras's black clothing.

The leader of the Sword stepped aside to admit the others, and each entered wearing similarly ornate clothing. Some wore the same uniform as Akonn, while others wore different military outfits with diverse embroidered patterns hemming jerkins and cloaks. Whatever the situation on the battlefield, these leaders—and the entire camp—showed no sign of poverty and struggle.

Their leader is the Dragon King. Perhaps it's true, what the hearthwives say in Oceana: Dragons hoard wealth.

She sat up straighter. Hadn't she and Mikoneh been lured to the river within the Moon Veil by gems? Hadn't she struggled to keep from taking a handful or two for herself? Hadn't Mikoneh experienced the same strange sensation?

We really are dragons!

Shaking herself, Maya quietly rose from the chaise lounge, smoothed her shabby skirts, and tacked on a smile. Penn remained asleep in his plush chair, and Maya didn't intend to disturb him. As the generals and officers gathered within the chamber, their attention fell on her, and a ripple of bows followed. She curtsied in reply.

"My lords and ladies," Akonn said, "this way." He gestured

to the back chamber, perhaps as a gentle reminder that they'd been requested urgently.

They shuffled, then lined up and moved into the back room. Akonn took up the rear, tossing Maya a winsome smile before he dipped under the flaps and let them fall behind him. She hesitated, uncertain whether she was invited to the meeting or not. Should she ask? Should she wait?

"Maya?" Ter's voice preceded his head peeking through the flaps. "You are welcome to join us if you wish."

She started forward, then paused and glanced at Penn. Should she wake him?

Of course I should. He already feels useless. We must do whatever we can.

She shook Penn, and he jerked upright, a snarl on his lips. Then he blinked. "Maya. Sorry. I was having a bad dream, I think."

"The council is underway. We've been invited."

He dragged a hand down his face, nodding, then rose and smoothed back his long, tangled blond hair. "Let's go."

She led the way to the back flap where Ter still poked his head out, wearing that warm smile of his. He parted the flaps to give them passage, and Maya stepped into a chamber lit by more glowing blue lanterns. They were turned up bright, casting clear light on the men and women assembled around a circular table made of marbled obsidian. Owenekiras's map lay across it. A quill was perched in his hand, and he noted a location near the southwestern edge of the large parchment. His gaze, however, was pinned on Maya.

"Please, come in." His voice was cool and level. "Sit."

She obeyed, taking the closest available carved stone chair. Stone! How did they transport such heavy belongings?

She blinked, recalling Larkynven.

Penn sat beside her, picking at the frayed hem of his sling

while his brown eyes circled the table, absorbing the faces around them. Nearly everyone was watching Maya with stoic expressions, revealing nothing of their thoughts. Akonn alone smiled at her, then turned back to the map. She was glad for one friendly face, at least.

Glancing at Ter, she returned his beaming grin. Make that two friendly faces.

Owenekiras tapped his quill to the parchment, recapturing every eye. "Let us begin."

Ter cleared his throat, apparently delegated to open the council. "I recently answered a blood summons asking for help and stumbled upon Jonatten and Seranni's wards—and their good friend—far from their home in Oceana." Gazes flitted toward Maya and Penn, then away. "Alas, they had fallen into Dark Mage hands. We escaped but were pursued most ardently by the dread Mage Sathe."

Several generals shifted. One swore under her breath.

"He also has a Revenant," Ter added.

That provoked stronger curses.

Maya's chest tightened, recalling the ravaging sorrow of the Revenant. No matter how clever, how could Mikoneh escape from such a—a—force?

"Unfortunately, Sathe recaptured Mikoneh, the lady's twin brother." Ter's hand motioned toward Maya. "By now, he must already be bonded to Sathe. We must find the young man before permanent damage is done."

Those last words rammed through Maya's heart like a spear. She flinched back. Tears welled in her eyes, blurring the blue lantern glow. Ducking her head, she hoped no one had noticed.

A deep voice spoke up. "Your news is grave indeed, Master Ter. What would my lord have us do to find him?"

"Tear every hole apart," Owenekiras said in cold tones.

"Uproot every warren. Our battlefield has shifted for the time being to the underground. Sathe will likely attempt to move North. With his new weapon, he'll look toward the lands of the Nijaal, now or later. Mikoneh's potential is vast. Sathe will recognize that quickly and wish to employ it before Lady Katanni sees them coming. Beyond that, I don't believe I need to highlight how this could affect our war efforts."

Maya tried to wipe her eyes discreetly until Penn passed her a clean handkerchief. She offered a watery smile. He returned it with a drier one.

"Can we warn the Lady of the Wood, Master Ter?" asked Akonn.

"We can try," answered Ter. "Alas, she's been silent for some time, dealing with urgent matters of a most delicate nature."

"Is she even in the North?" asked a woman seated near Penn.

"Had the Lady left her lands," Owenekiras said softly, "she would have informed me."

No one argued. It was the most civil council Maya had ever been privy to. Even when Fa had gathered his officers, discord had been inevitable. Debates had ensued. Insults had been bandied.

Not here.

Are they too afraid to express their opinions? Surely, they must wonder why they will go to such lengths for one man. A coldness settled in her lungs. *Is Mikoneh capable of becoming such a terrible weapon that they all see it that clearly?*

Her head swam. She caught the edge of the table, pinning her borrowed handkerchief between her palm and the smooth stone ledge. Bile burned up her throat.

"Maya?" Penn's voice was faint. His hand brushed her arm.

"I—I'm just scared. By the Nijaal, I'm so terrified."

His fingers squeezed her wrist, warm and reassuring. "I understand."

Voices surrounded them. Tactics were laid out. Akonn volunteered to take a force into the nearest known tunnels marked on Owenekiras's map, but Ter's light voice discouraged him. The debates began at last, but no one lifted their voices in a moment of heat. Everyone remained calm, level-headed, hashing out their plans with such composure that they might've been discussing a local festival on a bright spring day.

No, even that would encourage discord.

Beneath the Dragon King's cold silver gaze, all were respectful and pragmatic.

A twist of hope lodged in Maya's chest. If anyone could rescue her brother, surely it would be a band such as this.

Surely, they had a chance.

CHAPTER 33

PRISONERS OF DARKNESS

"Despite the Mage Queen's efforts to secure all dragons for her cause, she underestimated her opponent."

- From Athonen d'Ereth's *The Fall of Mages in the Age of Dragons*

He stared into his goblet of water, mesmerized by the ripples caused by his trembling hand. His throat was parched, his muscles burned, and his stomach wrenched with hunger—but he ignored all of it. Just sat and stared.

A hand rested on his head and stroked his hair, then Sathe leaned close. "Drink, Firebrand. I won't let you escape that way either."

The idea hadn't entered Mikoneh's head. Somehow, he didn't have the will to lift his goblet.

Do it anyway.

Was that his voice or Sathe's?

Whichever it was, he obeyed. The cool liquid slid down his throat, soothing the discomfort. He was tired—that was half his struggle. Day or night, he couldn't keep track. Full turns closed in on him, endless, pain-filled.

He hadn't stopped resisting. Not once had he caved to Sathe unless the man forced him by using their bond. Mikoneh had discovered it was a two-way connection. Several times, he'd found the Mage's thoughts invading his mind when Sathe hadn't meant to speak with him. Frustration had bubbled up —not his own. But the Mage had much more control over their link, and he made certain Mikoneh knew it.

Drawing his hand back, Sathe adjusted his robe and drifted toward the bedchamber door. He'd left his bed unmade, and yesterday's robes were tossed across the floor, ready for Mikoneh to tidy once the Mage was gone. Never beforehand— that had been made crystal clear. Not that Mikoneh was eager to play maid to the tyrant.

Sathe paused at the stone doors and glanced back, wearing a wicked smile that gleamed in the violet torchlight. "Rest while you can, my Firebrand. We'll carry on when I return." The doors swung open at his silent command, then he stepped out, and they boomed shut.

Mikoneh let the echoes of the noise settle before he moved from his chair. He drained his goblet, though the water tasted like minerals and dirt, then set it on the tray with his untouched breakfast.

He padded to the bed, arranged the black coverlet until every wrinkle was smoothed, then he fetched his clothes folded on a chest at the foot of the monstrous four-poster. All but his empty sheath, and boots. Those hadn't been returned to him, the latter likely meant as a deterrent if he decided to bolt. Sathe had ordered him to strip whenever he was in the Mage's presence. Part of his torture, his humiliation. It made the work of breaking his spirit easier for the Mage if he was already naked.

At least Sathe had taught him how to draw his wings back into his spine. How such enormous appendages fit into his lean human body, he couldn't guess. Yet somehow, he could still feel them, like they existed between body and soul, folded, waiting for him to pull them out.

Dressed, Mikoneh stooped, picked up Sathe's robes, and shook out the wrinkles. He returned the clothes to the wardrobe where the rest of the Mage's tasteless robes hung. A fleeting desire to burn every article in that wardrobe skittered across his mind. Mikoneh hesitated, then batted it down.

Don't make things worse.

He knew what he needed to do. It defied everything he was —all that he believed—but it was the only answer he could lean on. He had to fight by giving in. Not all at once, and not altogether. Inch by tiny inch, he must become sedate. Malleable. He must give ground until Sathe believed he was tamed.

The trouble was Sathe knew that was his plan. It was a battle of wills and a slow one. Somehow, Mikoneh must convince the Mage he'd broken without really breaking. Without giving himself away.

It felt impossible.

He had to try anyway.

He padded back across the room and paused, torn between the chair and the pallet Sathe had provided for his bed. Should he try to sleep? He didn't trust Sathe to stay away long. The Mage returned randomly, keeping Mikoneh on his toes. If Sathe found him asleep, the Mage woke him with pain. Sathe's methods varied, but they were always cruel.

Weariness tugged on Mikoneh's mind, dragging him toward the makeshift bed. He heeded the pull, his vision swimming. Climbing onto the thin pallet, he curled up. His body shook from recent torture. Sathe rarely employed methods that marred his skin. He saved that for Mikoneh's more defiant moments. The Mage said that was because even dragons healed too slowly to bother with such techniques. Besides, blood was precious, Sathe claimed. Too precious to waste outside of his rituals.

Huddled among the ragged bedding, breathing in the cold scents of mineral rock and rich earth, Mikoneh tried to center himself and escape the vestiges of pain. His mind flowed past the memories, escaping the humiliation. The hurt. The horror.

It won't last. One way or another, it won't last.

He had to believe that. Mostly, he did.

Licking his lips, he tried to ignore his thirst. Sathe had given him only one goblet of water. If he wanted to drink anything more today, it would be wine. That he refused to do. He'd not fuzzy his mind to make Sathe's work that much easier. Nor did he want to become reliant on the alcohol to dull his pain.

Eat, at least.

He knew he should, but the effort...

He dragged himself upright and slid off the pallet, caught the tray up, and staggered to his chair.

It can't last forever. One way or another...

He choked down his plain fare, one dry bite at a time. Then he crawled back onto his pallet to steal a few precious turns of sleep.

Ice crawled across his eyeballs, his lungs, his bones, making him as brittle as glass. Driving the fire from his blood. Turning him into winter.

He jerked upright, gasping. Sathe stood before him, wearing that cold, frosty grin.

"Awake, Firebrand? Good. Let us commence."

Perhaps a week had passed since he'd been captured. Perhaps a year. Time didn't matter within the Mage tunnels. All that mattered was Mikoneh's private war.

At last, Sathe gave him leave to wander the tunnels beyond the Mage's private suite. Not alone, though. Mikoneh was accompanied by one of the skeletal Mages draped in a rotted cloak that smelled of mold and maggots.

Together, they moved along the wide, dismal tunnels, passing by the evenly spaced violet torches at a steady clip. Warmed by his own inner fire, Mikoneh was surprised the first time he'd investigated the violet flames. No fire spirits danced within them, and his constant little spirit companions leaned away from the blaze, sputtering like the violet light weakened them. Mikoneh felt chilled in the torch's vicinity, as though it were made of Sathe's cold soul. Perhaps that was really the case.

Most of the tunnels veered and curved as though giant worms had paved the paths pell-mell over eons, and the Mages had simply moved in. He hated to imagine what Mages kept for pets in these dank halls.

And then he met one.

He turned left at an intersection, trying to ignore the smell of rot. There, he came face to face with a creature—a *thing*—half his height, three times as wide, with the face of a deeply sorrowful toad.

He lurched back, throwing a hand over his nose. *It's the thing I saw outside Kenooshin...* The monster that had stood behind the fake Ter. The creature's reek was enough to make his eyes water. He spun away and found himself facing his skeletal guard instead. The combined odors of rot, death, and bog water made him gag.

A deep, rumbling, basso roar sounded behind him. Mikoneh whirled back around, fingers sparking with fire in case the toad-like creature decided to pounce. Its eyes—huge, unblinking things—regarded him with intense interest. The drooping layers of flesh lifted, tightening its rubbery jowls, until its massive lips split to reveal four rows of sharp, crooked teeth. That leer sent chills racing down Mikoneh's back.

The skeletal Mage rested bony fingers on his shoulder. Mikoneh nearly jumped out of his skin.

"Come," said the Mage in an astoundingly human voice. How it spoke at all, without organs, muscles, or flesh, was utterly beyond Mikoneh. Worse, somehow, was that the tones were light and high like a female.

He jerked back from that hand, veered around the Mage, and stalked back up the tunnel. Trying not to run, trying not to panic. Though the toadish monster had been more disgusting than horrific, he found himself trembling, utterly afraid.

"What was that thing?" he asked softly, uncertain if the Mage would answer, uncertain if he wanted to know.

His escort didn't reply.

Just as well.

He moved steadily away from the creature, though its image stained his memory. He didn't care where he went, turning down passage after passage, confident the Mage would stop him if he wasn't supposed to wander down certain corridors. It—she—seemed content to let him walk aimlessly.

A long channel gave way to an arched entrance without doors. Beyond that lay a wide chamber. At the center of the room, a single violet flame flickered above an ornate vase. The vase was painted a dazzling silver, with deep shades of purple in patterns that looked symmetrical yet felt distinctly unbalanced. His equilibrium teetered.

It's not the vase causing that. It's the flame.

The cool light conjured shivers that marched up Mikoneh's arms and lifted the fine hairs on his neck. He scowled, angry that everything down here frightened him. He hated that. Hated that such disgusting, vile, maggoty people—and their filthy abode—set his teeth on edge.

He spun toward the Mage. "You won't win. Owenekiras and those like him won't let you conquer this world."

The grinning skull considered him, eyeless, heartless. She said nothing.

Scowl deepening, Mikoneh turned and marched across the chamber, steering clear of the vase, but unwilling to shrink from the cold, guttering flame. Afraid, he might be. A coward? Never.

The Mage followed, eerily silent beneath the befouled robes.

They stepped into a wider tunnel—made of rock instead of packed earth. The scents grew more metallic and drier, less moldy. The change was welcome.

Mikoneh pressed up the passage, letting curiosity and defiance lead his steps. Whatever else he might discover—toad monster or dizzying flames—it was still better than staying in Sathe's chambers. He was grateful just to walk, to make *some* choices for himself. For a moment, he could escape from the private horrors Sathe inflicted.

So, stop thinking about them. Let them go.

He quickened his pace. The Mage kept up.

A pebble bit into his bare foot. He winced, but strode on, cramming that tiny pain in with the rest he'd locked away.

The passage sloped down. The torches placed at intervals

gave way to pitch blackness. He hesitated, then lifted his palm and summoned a fire spirit, using the heat of his body. The spirit sparked into life, wearing the shape of a proper flame. It seemed content to hover above his palm, scattering darkness.

Squaring his shoulders, Mikoneh plunged deeper into the tunnel. Did the Mage hesitate? The pause was brief, then she followed him, her steps muted. Both walked more slowly, taking care in the dim light of the single orange flame.

Cold swept up the channel, nipping at Mikoneh's flesh despite his element. An unnatural, familiar cold.

The Revenant.

His step faltered.

Breath plumed before his lips.

Turn back.

But he wouldn't. He'd cowered too much, and with his mustered defiance, he would challenge hell itself. Lifting his chin, he pushed ahead. Was the Revenant guarding this tunnel? Or was this where the trapped soul dwelt when Sathe wasn't commanding it?

The cold deepened. Mikoneh's nerves prickled, but he wouldn't falter.

He. Would. Not.

Crimson light flickered ahead. Mikoneh's lungs pinched. He forced out a long breath, inching forward, keeping his hovering flame bright. Just a little farther.

Pebbles skittered before his toes. The ground had grown rougher, as if the passage hadn't been smoothed as carefully as others. He took greater care with each step to avoid face-planting.

The whisper of robes behind him ceased. He glanced over his shoulder, lifting his palm higher to illuminate the shadows. The Mage had paused two yards back. The guttering flame revealed her endless grin, but somehow an eerie grimness was etched into that bleached skull.

The Mage's evident terror only emboldened Mikoneh.

Will she not follow? Is this my chance?

If he faced the Revenant and didn't cave, could he find an exit?

Don't be stupid. The Revenant won't let you run any more than she will.

Yet the reckless, foundless hope endured. He pressed on, ignoring the pounding of his heart and the sweat gathering on his brow. His palms were slick, but the fire spirit remained a steady glow, unflinching in the growing crimson light. Flecks of black dwelt in that red candescence, like dark fingers smearing blood into the very stones.

Cheery thought.

The tunnel curved. That explained where the eerie glow came from. He followed the turn and stepped into a square room filled with crimson light. His blood froze. Tears pricked his eyes. An altar sat at the center of the small chamber. It wasn't empty.

A body lay across the carved stone slat: a man, with pale hair painted red by the sourceless glow. The Revenant was nowhere in view. If the bound soul was here, it had no form at present.

This is his body. I know it.

It made sense. Ter had explained that the Revenant was trapped because his body was captured and imprisoned, not dead, never alive. The same horrible sadness he'd felt in Hyanython, and again in the forest when Mikoneh was captured, filled the room—more solid, more tangible than the crimson glow.

Mikoneh inhaled, steeling himself, then he marched into the chamber proper. In the red light, everything felt off-kilter, like the world was tipped slightly sideways. His steps were drunken, but he persisted, making his way to the altar. Cold streamed around him, wrapping fingers across his body. He ignored them.

He halted at the edge of the stone slab, fixing his stare on the prone figure garbed in fine raiment, pristine, like he'd only dressed this morning and lain down for a brief rest. Not a wrinkle, not a tear, not a hint of time touched the sleeping man or his garments. He was beautiful, like a fae lord from hearth legends. High cheekbones; angular jaw; elegant, pointed ears; long, straight hair, perhaps snowy white; thick lashes brushing pale cheeks; ornate clothes in a style Mikoneh didn't recognize —but it was certainly the garb of a high lord or a wealthy king.

This was the Revenant as he had been. Someone of importance, captured, forced into eternal slumber, and chained. A wretched soul in servitude.

Will this be my fate someday?

Once Sathe had used him for whatever he intended, would Mikoneh sleep in a state where he could never rest? The idea sent more chills down his frame. He locked his jaw, resolving to die before that happened—but escape first if possible.

He shook himself of those dismal thoughts, refocusing on the prisoner before him. The altar looked the same as those Mikoneh had seen before, but he wasn't certain what that meant. He didn't know enough about Dark Magery to understand the magic at play.

There were runes carved into the floor and ceiling when Sathe forced our bond. Those must be what specifies the form of captivity.

He glanced up. If runes existed in the red-stained stone, he saw no sign of them. But then, this chamber was tiny. A group of Mages would be hard-pressed to surround the altar here.

The ceremony was probably performed elsewhere, and the body deposited here afterward.

He stepped backward to study the altar. Complex, bone-chilling symbols and runes were carved into the block of stone. He reached out his hand—but couldn't bring himself to touch the carvings. Shivers gnawed at his flesh. He drew his hand back, and instead committed the symbols to memory. Ter claimed no one had found a way to free a soul once they'd become a Revenant, but if Mikoneh could do nothing else in this forsaken realm, he could pour all his effort into rescuing a fellow sufferer. Hopeless as that likely was, it was a cause, and Mikoneh didn't know how to live without one.

He circled the altar, memorizing every single shape, every single flaw. The off-kilter light made him stagger, but he persisted until he'd gone full circle. Then he went around again, making certain he'd missed nothing. The symbols were foreign—yet he *almost* understood them, like they whispered in a tongue not quite Sirinhighan Common, but a corrupted form of it.

In any case, he found himself fascinated by the sleeping lord. He knew nothing about the man except the look of his face and the terror and sorrow inspired by his captive soul, but Mikoneh decided he liked him. If nothing else, they were on equal footing: prisoners of darkness.

Mikoneh wasn't alone.

The thought comforted him.

The crimson glow heightened. Fresh chills pattered up his back. He tensed, then exhaled a long breath, loosening his taut muscles. He turned, slowly, carefully, so he didn't lose his balance.

Cloaked in sorrow and menacing light, the Revenant loomed before him.

CHAPTER 34

SOMETHING TO FIGHT FOR

"Just like in a game of Fang and Claw, a player can change the outcome with a single brilliant move."

- From Athonen d'Ereth's *The Fall of Mages in the Age of Dragons*

For a moment, Mikoneh couldn't move. The force of the Revenant's presence imprisoned him as surely as his bond with Sathe. But then, the aura seemed to ease. The sorrow pulsed stronger than the terror.

Mikoneh pressed a dry smile to his lips. "I didn't mean to intrude."

The imposing figure didn't twitch.

"I'm Mikoneh, which you already know. Still." He shrugged. "It's polite to say as much."

Nothing. No voice. No movement.

"I owe you," Mikoneh said, keeping his tones deliberately

light. "This is the one chamber where I could be alone. Except for the matter of your body."

That stirred the air. The sorrow grew, pricking at Mikoneh's eyes as though it dug for his tears.

"Yes," he whispered. "I know it's you. Ter N'Avea told me what you are—what they've done to you." He drew a steadying breath, trying to bat down the dizziness from the unsteady light. "I don't blame you for capturing me. It's not your fault. I just...wanted you to know that." He managed a wry laugh. "Not that I came here to deliver that message. I didn't know where to find you. I was just walking."

You're rambling. Shut up.

He fell still, keeping a crooked smile tacked to his face.

The Revenant shifted at last. Its arm raised, hand hidden in the voluminous folds of its crimson cloak. The figure reached toward Mikoneh. It was everything the latter could do not to flinch. He maintained his smile with every fiber of stubbornness. A finger—made of shadow and eerie light—stuck from the fabric of that cloak. It stretched toward Mikoneh's face.

He clenched his jaw and didn't move.

The Revenant's finger touched his cheek. Cold shot through Mikoneh like ice in his veins—but he was accustomed to bracing against Sathe's torture, and he held his ground. The finger wasn't solid, but it wasn't intangible either. Sensation surrounded that finger until it could almost be flesh.

Words filled Mikoneh's mind.

'*You are a dragon.*'

He hesitated, then choked out, "Yes. I am."

The sorrow exploded over the air, knocking Mikoneh backward until he struck the altar. He gasped out. Tears—not his own—spilled down his face.

'*I am sorry.*' The words rumbled through him, though the Revenant wasn't touching him anymore.

Mikoneh shuddered, cold sweat trickling down his back. With one sleeve, he swiped at the foreign tears. "Not...your...fault."

They stared at each other for several moments. Mikoneh managed to stem the flow of tears, though the sorrow still clung to the air like a vapor.

"Tell me who you are," he whispered.

The Revenant fell so still, even the flickering light around him seemed to cease. Then he shook his cowled head. '*I cannot say.*'

"Can't? Sathe won't let you?"

The Revenant hesitated. '*I cannot say.*'

Nodding, Mikoneh groped for any questions he thought the being *could* answer. Were there any? Soul-captive as he was, did the Revenant know anything beyond his imprisonment?

"How long have you been with the Mages?"

'*I do not know,*' was the mournful reply.

"Years?"

'*Longer.*'

"Decades?"

'*Longer.*'

Mikoneh scoffed. "Apparently, it's fashionable to live forever in magical circles." He winced. "Sorry if that was insensitive. I know you're not...that you didn't *choose* this fate."

The Revenant drifted closer. Swirls of red light brushed against Mikoneh's face and hands. Tendrils curled around his feet. The air grew denser, almost humid, and sorrow lanced Mikoneh's eyes again. He wrestled back the tears.

"Do you have a name?"

'*I cannot say.*'

"Is there a way to free you?"

'*None that I know.*'

Mikoneh tapped a knuckle to his lips, contemplating.

"That's what Ter said, too. But where there's a way into something, there's always a way out."

'*Not if the way is destroyed.*'

"Maybe." Mikoneh folded his arms. "But that doesn't seem rational. If someone can simply do something using magic, then prevent its undoing—ever—this world would've been destroyed long ago. Maybe the Mages shrouded the answer to your liberation, but they couldn't prevent it wholly."

'*My soul could move on,*' said the Revenant.

Mikoneh flinched. "Possibly that's the only way—but I'd like to pursue other avenues before we settle on the morbid one."

'*Why?*'

Mikoneh flashed a grin. "Prefer doom and gloom, do you?"

'*Why help me?*'

"Two reasons." Mikoneh made himself look into the shadowed cowl. "First, it's unjust—what they've done to you. Whoever you were, whatever they've forced you to do, no one deserves such a fate." He paused. "Almost no one. And second, I need something to focus on. If I don't...Sathe will win. Give me your cause to fight for and I'll stay strong, for both of us."

'*As you please.*'

"Thank you." He let his smile quirk higher. "You need a name. I'm not good at giving them, though."

'*I don't mind.*'

"You might regret that." He cupped his hands behind his back and inched out of the Revenant's path to pace the rock floor. His gaze traveled to the slumbering lord upon the altar. "That *is* you, isn't it?"

'*It used to be.*'

Mikoneh circled the altar to stand across from the Revenant and the doorway. He studied the slumbering face. The flawless planes and facets. Maya would blush and stutter in such a man's presence. She was always developing feelings for the handsomest man around.

A pang flashed over his chest. Maya. She must be in agony. *Let her be strong. Please, let her stay strong.*

"I don't know any good lordly names," he said to distract himself. "Would you hate it if I just called you Reven? It's not good, I admit."

'*Reven is fine.*'

Mikoneh looked up and lifted an eyebrow. "If you hate it, say so. Polite dishonesty doesn't serve anyone."

'*I am grateful for any name.*'

"Oh? Maybe I'll just call you Lizard, then. Or Rabbit."

Silence. Then, '*Reven is better.*'

Mikoneh snorted. "Glad you do have an opinion. Reven it is." He moved around the altar. "With that settled, I have a few more pressing questions. Are you able to leave the tunnels?"

An explosion of icy pain shot through Mikoneh's head. He gasped and slammed to his knees, his vision turning white as a blizzard.

'**Firebrand, return to me.**'

The pain ceased, and he found himself sprawled across the small room. Reven loomed over him, sorrow palpable.

Mikoneh shuddered, trying to find enough strength to rise. The command rang through his head, seizing his limbs. He rose, strong enough or not. Sweat stuck his shirt to his back. He panted for air, trying to dislodge his thoughts from the clutter in his mind.

"I...have to go..." he whispered hoarsely.

The Revenant drifted aside to give him passage from the chamber. '*The answer is yes. I can leave the tunnels. Not often, but sometimes.*'

Mikoneh vaguely recalled asking about that. He nodded. "We'll discuss more on that later—I hope. Goodbye, Reven."

'*Fight, dragon.*'

HE STAGGERED into Sathe's bedchamber, half-blind with pain. Twice en route, he'd been attacked by Sathe's wrathful ice. The skeletal Mage had been waiting outside the Revenant's quarters and had wordlessly set its bony fingers on his elbow to guide his steps—yet they hadn't traveled fast enough for Sathe.

"You *summoned*," Mikoneh choked out, leaning heavily against the doorframe.

"Making friends?" asked Sathe. His eyes gleamed like rime in starlight. "How bold you are. Yet the Revenant cannot save you. He is more of a prisoner than you."

"Then what's the problem?" asked Mikoneh.

The Mage's eyes narrowed. Fresh pain exploded behind Mikoneh's skull, sending him backward. He crashed against the corridor floor, pressing his palms to his face. Screams tore from his throat.

The pain lifted in the next heartbeat.

He lay stunned, trembling.

Sathe stepped into view above him. "No defiance today, my Firebrand. I'm not in the mood."

Something happened to set him off. The realization brought with it a flood of hope before Mikoneh could dam it up.

The pain burst back into life. His screams heightened.

Do not rejoice, fool. This means nothing for you. Do you understand?

Mikoneh managed a nod and choked out some sort of assent. The pain fell away. He was curled up, sobbing. His hair clung to his face and shoulders like a net, broken free from its leather binding.

Sathe stooped and stroked his cheek. "Why are bravery and foolishness always companions to the bold?"

He leaned forward and whispered in Mikoneh's ear. The words were harsh, cruel, horrible. Mikoneh tried to block them out, but the Mage fed them into his soul, pouring his filth deep, deep inside.

Lying still, taking shallow breaths, Mikoneh endured it. He must. He would. He had a cause, something to fight for, something beyond himself. Sathe wouldn't win.

CHAPTER 35

NO SMALL FEAT

"The very shape of the land changed in the Dragon Wars. When enormous powers clash, oceans rise and mountains are ground to dust."

- From Athonen d'Ereth's *The Fall of Mages in the Age of Dragons*

Tearing her gaze from the diamond sky, Maya smiled at Captain Akonn standing before her. In the moonlight, his white hair looked silver, and his green eyes shone like pale jewels. The faint noise of the nearby stream burbled behind him.

"Good evening, my lady." He motioned to the patch of grass beside her. "May I sit a moment?"

"Please."

He settled next to her, keeping a respectful distance, and tipped back his head to consider the starry firmament. "Breathtaking."

"It is. You bring news?"

"I do—though no sign of your twin yet."

Her heart sank. Two weeks had passed since Mikoneh's capture, and though Owenekiras's forces had been scouring the land for tunnels since the council meeting—and several warrens had been breached—no sign, no hint of her brother had resulted from their efforts. Meanwhile, she'd been stuck in the main camp on the plains of Simynshin, sharing a multi-room tent with Penn. She often snuck away at night to be alone.

She twisted a lock of her dark hair. "What news do you bring, Captain?" She kept her tones bright.

"We've found a new tunnel system further north. It's still inhabited."

That *was* news. They'd driven hordes of lesser Mages from the south during the first week of attacks, uprooting channels full of the undead creatures, sending them scurrying north-ward. But after that, the tunnels they'd found had already been cleared. Such was inevitable. Even Maya could've foreseen that once the Mages heard of Owenekiras's augmented aggression, they would move quickly to stay ahead of the Dragon King's wrath.

Surely, Sathe saw this coming. If Mikoneh is so useful, Lord Owenekiras would have to answer.

She still didn't understand why her twin was so coveted a weapon that a Mage would risk wrath and ruin to keep him. It frightened her to consider how many soldiers were sacri-ficing their lives to rescue him. She'd expected to hear grum-bling behind Owenekiras's back; soldiers were often disgruntled, no matter how worthy the cause, and this mission was ambiguous compared to others—at least from Maya's point of view. They didn't care about Mikoneh like she did.

They all understand something I don't, and no one will tell me what it is.

They always tiptoed around the facts. Even Ter had taken to dodging her when she marched toward him, determined to wring out the answers, no matter who suffered. Only Penn and Akonn approached her willingly, the former unfazed by her determination since he knew as little as she did. The latter had to approach because he'd been assigned to protect her—but he wouldn't answer the question burning in her mind.

"Any word on Sathe?" she asked.

Akonn shook his head. "Lord Owenekiras believes we were led to this tunnel network to keep us from the right path—so we're going to try a different strategy."

She shifted to face him full-on.

His smile was gentle. "Lord Penn requested an audience with the Dragon King this morning. He presented irrefutable proof that Sathe is a prominent fixture in the Mage network of Oceana—and not just within Drayve's court."

She blinked. "How did Penn manage that?"

"He offered up several important names at the Royal Court in Nauttia." Akonn paused. "That *is* the name of Oceana's capital, right?"

"It is, yes."

"Penn suspected that several of the ambassadors whispering in King Nilo's ear were working with the Earl of Relvin, and thus, perhaps Sathe. He was right. Two of the names Penn provided belong to well-known Mage captains serving under Sathe. That proves the Mage general has infiltrated Oceana as deeply as he needs to move freely."

"What does that signify?" she asked.

Akonn shrugged. "We'd already suspected Sathe would take your brother to his own nest, rather than to where bitter rivalries wage frequently in the Mage Queen's court. At least until your brother is fully under his control—no small feat where a dragon is concerned. We didn't know where that nest might be, but Penn is certain it's in Oceana."

Maya's lips parted. She drew a delayed breath. "That makes sense. Drayve gained a lot of footing through Sathe's power, though few believed Penn on that point, even among our forces. We just...didn't believe in magic. But Penn did."

The fae captain nodded. "I've heard Oceana takes its cues from Lintha, and that foolish old kingdom would much rather believe in its own merchants than anything else. Magic? Never."

She flushed, embarrassed for the home of her childhood. "King Nilo is a good man but easily led by the whispers of others."

"Ah, yes. 'A good man swayed always by others becomes a blind tyrant,' so the fae saying goes." Akonn sighed. "But then, upheaval and discord swell across every border into every kingdom. Cimin's king was assassinated by his own cousin ten years ago, and the rightful heir is missing. Lintha is controlled by the merchant guilds while its figure-head king—a mere infant— will no doubt be raised brainwashed and useless. And Rokahn..." He sighed. "Ruled by a tyrant in league with the Mages. Only Simynshin has a stable monarchy at present. But the Mages are trying to infiltrate where they can."

"Purging all these tunnels will help prevent that, won't it?" asked Maya.

"We hope so, though the underground is so riddled with Mage warrens, it will be hard to keep them guarded from new infestations."

"Can't Earth Elementalists fill in the tunnels to keep that from happening?"

Akonn shook his head. "Dark Magery permeates the tunnels, magically keeping them from caving in during earthquakes or Elementalist attacks. It would take an army of the most skilled Elementalists to do more than collapse weakened sections here or there. That, or we would need to directly kill the Dread Mage whose magic fortified those tunnels. Not a simple feat. Our best hope is to defeat the Mage Queen herself, and that's no easy task in itself."

"Is she well hidden?"

Akonn nodded. "And more—she's well protected. Sathe and Suld aren't the only powerful Dread Mages, and dark forces beyond Mages are equally interested in guarding her for their own ends."

"It sounds like a ghastly challenge." She shivered.

A wind spirit landed on her skirts and whistled an inquiry: '*Are you well?*'

She smiled and nodded. "Well enough."

Akonn's smile brightened. "They care for you a great deal."

Maya blinked. "You see the wind spirits?"

"Of course." He flashed a grin that revealed his white teeth. "I'm a Wind Elementalist as well." His hair stirred, and more wind spirits appeared to spin around his forehead like a circlet.

"You should've said something! Will you teach me?"

He held up his hands. "Swordsmanship and the use of a quarterstaff, I'll gladly teach to anyone with the aptitude. Wind —that is something else. You need a proper instructor. And I know just the man for the job—a real Wind Master. In fact, he's due to arrive from Elenth almost any day now. Owenekiras asked him to come."

Elenth, the capital of Simynshin. It was a thriving city in the northwest where Princess Latta dwelt with her father, Prince Atlanse, heir to the throne. Maya had often dreamed of visiting if only to catch a glimpse of the Songbird Princess herself.

"I'd love to receive instruction from a Wind Master," Maya

breathed. She could ask him all sorts of questions about the royal family of Simynshin, alongside learning to control her element. Then, perhaps she'd be allowed to join in the search for Mikoneh.

I won't stay powerless.

"I should warn you," Akonn said, his eyes sparkling. "Hilker's an odd fellow—but good at heart."

"Since leaving Oceana, nothing's been normal." She grinned. "And I'm not sure what sort of recommendation that is for normalcy, truth be told."

He chuckled. "Well said. Most wish to escape a mediocre life. Few get the chance. You're among the lucky—though the cost is rather high."

"Did you lead a normal life once, Captain Akonn?"

"Normal for my people, perhaps."

"You're fae, aren't you?" She grinned. "I always thought fae were little fairies who granted wishes—but then, I also thought they were only stories."

"Fae encompasses all magical life which possess—or can take on—human form," Akonn said. "That includes dragons, gryphons, unicorns, pegasi, fairies, elves. The list is long, and some of the names on it are hard to explain."

"It's amazing—most of all to accept that *I'm* on that list."

Akonn's smile deepened. "Not just on it. Dragons top the list, setting aside the Nijaal."

"So, they *are* considered fae. The Nijaal, I mean."

"Yes, certainly. They were the first."

Maya fell still, contemplating the difference between truth and legend. Somehow, the knowledge that Nijaal weren't gods was satisfying. She hadn't been raised to worship them, of course. Fa and Mama hadn't subscribed to any specific religion, and they'd tended to scorn local superstitions tied to faith. On the other hand, they hadn't discouraged Maya and Mikoneh from believing what they chose to put their faith in. Maya liked to believe in a higher power, but even the Nijaal had seemed too...abstract...too world-bound to be proper deities. She needed to believe in something far more vast, more powerful.

She wished she could ask her parents what they'd *really* believed now that she knew more about the outside world.

Her breath hitched. *Adoptive or not, they* were *the parents who raised us.*

The knowledge that she came from Rokahnian blood, *dragon blood*, and Jonatten and Seranni didn't...well, she must come to accept it. Until this moment, the unasked question had plagued her: Who were her real parents? She didn't want to ask. But really, it changed little when it came right to the root of things. She needed to learn about her true heritage, and once she did, she would accept and embrace both bloodlines. Both connections. Wasn't more always better?

"They're amazing," Akonn said. "You've never seen one, have you?"

Maya started, then glanced at him. What had they been discussing?

Oh, yes. Nijaal.

"No," she said. "I haven't. I've only heard hearth stories." An idea fell into her head. She leaned toward the captain. "Are *you* Nijaalin?"

Akonn stiffened, blinking rapidly, then he laughed. It was a clear, bright sound. "Oh, no. Not me. I'm a lesser fae by far." He inclined his head. "Forgive me for laughing."

Heat climbed her face, up to the pointed tips of her ears, but she grinned through her embarrassment. "Don't apologize. I always jump to the silliest conclusions. I'm a bit impulsive. Not like Mikoneh. He thinks everything through."

Except when his temper gets the best of him. But she wouldn't say so out loud.

"Penn speaks highly of your brother as well," Akonn said. "I look forward to meeting him." His smile softened. "But don't discount your own abilities, my lady. There's a time for quick decisions as much as for sensible caution."

Her flush deepened at his kindness. She didn't know how to reply, so she shifted her thoughts back to her twin. "You'll like Mikoneh. Everyone does—once they get used to him. I think even his enemies respect him, just like they did our father. He's a bit sullen these days, and his temper is sharp, but he's firm in doing what's right. And when he lets that wall of his down...you couldn't find a gentler soul." Tears sparkled in her vision, then rolled down her cheeks, warm and wet.

Stop crying. Don't cry!

Heedless, the tears continued to fall.

Akonn drew a handkerchief from a pouch at his hip. "We'll find him. We'll save him."

She accepted the pristine cloth with murmured thanks. Dabbing at her eyes, she stared at the palisade looming a few yards before her. Somewhere beyond that wall, Mikoneh suffered, alone, afraid, but brave as he was always brave.

"I know you will," she whispered. "And he'll still be strong. Wait and see. Nothing can break my brother."

Chapter 36

Inner Forges

*"The battle to seal the Dread Mage Suld in TeshRelle was costly,
but in the end, the Lady's forces won out."*

- From Athonen d'Ereth's *The Fall of Mages in the Age of Dragons*

Cracks. They filled his vision and weaved through his thoughts.

Huddled on the pallet that was his bed, covered in a lumpy, ragged blanket to hide his naked body, he shivered in a cocoon of ice that his element couldn't touch. The fire at his center had cooled, almost snuffed out. Sathe wouldn't let it die completely—not that. The Mage needed his flame...for some reason.

Reason. That was cracked, too.

He drew deep breaths, waiting to come back to himself. It was important—he knew that much.

Take your time. He shuddered and pulled in closer to himself. *Just breathe. Everything can wait.*

But not for long. He knew he needed to seal the cracks, needed to find himself and rise.

Not yet.

He stayed still, swimming in the thawing river of pain and fear. Sathe had been so angry. Almost mad with it.

He quaked at the memory.

Step away. No reason to remember.

Just breathe.

He inhaled, drinking in the stale, mineral air. Letting it fill his nostrils, his throat, his lungs. His body floated along the river, shedding the pain drop by drop, back into its source and out of his soul.

He might have wept. His face was damp.

How long have I been lying here?

He didn't know. There was only pain, then the easing of it. Far worse than Sathe's torture was his gentleness afterward. The soft whispers, the light caresses, the empty promises that the suffering would soon end. It never did. The torture continued each time Sathe was angry. Each time he reappeared. Each time he made fresh cracks in the mind and soul.

Usually, the cracks closed after a while. This time, they were worse. Sathe had been so angry.

That's good. It means something. It means...something.

He shifted. The pain flared higher, then softened. His environment settled in around him beyond the faint odors in the air and the sensation of his scratchy blanket.

Mikoneh. My name is Mikoneh.

His mind snapped awake. He stirred from the river of his soul, rolling onto his back. The rough stone ceiling of Sathe's private chambers rose above him, flickering with violet light. Pale lichens climbed that misshapen surface. Mikoneh studied the textures, so clear with his newfound dragon sight. He'd always been able to see in darker spaces better than most people could, but now he hardly needed a torch. Honestly, he suspected he would see better without one.

If I'm a dragon, can I transform into one like Larkynven? Would that trap me in a space too small for my bulk, or could I break the walls and free myself?

He'd wondered the same thing before, but he hadn't dared experiment.

Would Reven know more?

He hadn't sought out the Revenant since that first encounter. Sathe had been angry then, too. Very angry.

Though not as angry as this time.

What had caused Sathe's most recent tantrum, he didn't know, but it promised a win for the Mages' enemies. That was heartening. He had to embrace every shred of hope he could snatch.

Breathe.

How long had Mikoneh been trapped in his pain? Sathe had mentioned he would be gone longer than usual, but had that been turns ago or days? At first, Mikoneh had cursed himself for making Sathe mad—for making the sessions of torture so much worse—but then the Mage had hurt him for something far removed from their private war. If Sathe would injure him no matter what he did, well, that meant Mikoneh needed to fight harder. That way, he might escape, and at least the pain would be warranted.

He laughed aloud. The sound was hoarse and feeble.

Slowly, the mirth faded.

Hefting himself upright, ripples of pain cascaded over his flesh. He gasped, tasting copper. Sathe had left welts and abrasions, wounding him inside and out. A cloud settled over

Mikoneh's thoughts, but he breathed deeply until it cleared. He had things to do. He couldn't let anything stop him.

Climbing to his feet was difficult. His breath grew labored, rattling in his sensitive ears. He leaned against the wall. As he willed himself to stand upright, the inner forges of his element flared, thawing the remnants of Sathe's icy touch. Somehow, that gave him renewed strength.

He lifted his hand, turned his palm up, and summoned flame. A fire spirit sprang into life, wielding a humanoid shape with wings to match Mikoneh's. The reminder of his wings brought an awareness of them, beneath his skin, ready to unfurl at a thought.

Useless. He fixed his eyes on the hovering spirit. "Can you sense the Revenant?"

The fire spirit hesitated, stretching its senses, which heightened Mikoneh's. He tasted the violet flame, aware of the cold air currents, tracing them along the passages of the underground warren. There. Less than a league away, the crimson cold of the spectral Revenant haunted the air, changing the currents.

Mikoneh dressed, gasping as his muscles stretched, reopening several lacerations. Then he started off, letting the fire spirit guide his steps along the gloomy channels. No cloaked escort waited outside Sathe's chambers today. Perhaps the Mage general had assumed Mikoneh would be too injured to explore.

That brought a grin to Mikoneh's face and an urgency to his steps.

Stray pebbles nipped at his toes, but he hardly noticed. On he pressed, glad the crimson presence remained stationary. The tunnels wended, crisscrossed, some made of packed earth, others of solid stone. All carried the cold, metallic taint of Hollow. He knew the magic for what it was now. He'd slipped into Sathe's mind several times during their more intimate sessions, learning terms, sometimes even names. He committed it all to memory, hoping against hope he could hand it over to the Dragon King one day.

Soon. Let it be soon.

The fire spirit sputtered. The tunnels began to rumble. Rocks and clumps of dirt rained from the earthen ceiling. Mikoneh staggered sideways, slamming into the wall. He hissed out a curse, his mind going numb against the spreading pain.

Shouts sounded down the passage. A quick glance revealed a side channel, and he slipped into it. At the same moment, the distant crimson shade drifted away.

He cursed again under his breath.

Clacking bones sprinted along the neighboring tunnel, and he glimpsed a handful of cloaked figures racing by, clutching spears, swords, and several unfamiliar weapons.

They're under attack. Owenekiras?

His chest fluttered with hope. His wings throbbed to be pulled free.

Don't be foolish. Running pell-mell into the fray will only draw Sathe's notice. I'll never make it.

He should chase down the Revenant instead. If the imprisoned soul was going topside to fight, he might reveal an exit the Mages weren't using. It wasn't a solid plan. For all Mikoneh knew, the Revenant didn't need to use physical paths. Perhaps he could slip through the stone itself to reach the surface. Hadn't he done that before, or had Mikoneh dreamed that?

Better than sitting still.

Mikoneh counted to twenty, then stepped back out into the wide tunnel. The fire spirit jabbed a wispy hand toward the retreating crimson form somewhere out of sight. Mikoneh stalked after it, not trying to stay silent. The passage groaned. Pebbles skittered.

He licked his dry lips and focused on keeping his feet along the bucking tunnel. The Revenant was moving slowly, but so was he. If the tunnel collapsed, he might find himself no better off than the lonely soul he sought. He tried to pick up his pace. In a way, running was easier. He only staggered into the walls twice.

The passage vomited clods of dirt and roots. Mikoneh tried to dodge the random upheavals. Clouds of dust coated his hair, clothes, and skin. The fire spirit seemed to enjoy the chaos. It cackled and somersaulted, spitting embers from its flaming wisps of hair.

Mikoneh reached a crossroads and stumbled to a halt. Panting for breath, he tried to reach out and sense what the fire spirit did. *Left turn.* He threw himself in that direction, ignoring the protests of his battered body. The violet torches had gone out along the earthen corridor. Perhaps the quakes had smothered them with dirt, or maybe this was a seldom-used passage.

Didn't matter. Mikoneh's eyes adjusted to the darkness better than he'd hoped. He could see the grit along the floor, and the lichens almost glowing where they climbed the rock walls. The tunnel was sturdier than those made from dirt and silt. The tremors were fainter here.

Where are you going, Reven?

In the commotion, with the threat of tunnels collapsing, Mikoneh wondered if the Revenant would return to his slumbering body, to protect his shell from being crushed. But if Mikoneh could trust his sense of direction at all in this underground world, he was plunging further away from that tiny chamber and the imprisoned lord.

He couldn't tell if the tunnel was taking him up or down. It rose and fell indiscriminately, and after a hundred paces, it began weaving back and forth. Still, the tremors *were* weaker in this section. Mikoneh didn't struggle to stay upright when they struck.

All at once the tunnel tipped sharply up. Stairs were carved into the stone floor. He faltered, trying to catch his breath. Strands of hair clung to his face and neck. His tunic stuck to his back.

Fresh air crashed into his senses.

An exit.

Freedom.

The fire spirit chirped and pointed up.

Thank you, God.

He gulped down several greedy breaths, then started the climb. There. A circle of distant light, perhaps a hundred yards above. He made for it, scrambling up the steep stairs with careless haste.

Almost there. Keep going.

Really, Firebrand? You think it so easy?

The voice slammed into his head, shattering the delicate wings of his faith. He lost his footing and slid down several steps before he caught himself. His skull throbbed, his muscles screamed. The flame of hope died in his chest, and the fire spirit vanished with a pop into the fresh air.

Return to my chambers immediately.

Several cracks reopened in his mind. The Mage's will seized him. Mikoneh made his way down the steps, taking care not to slip again. He could still sense Reven above, far above, far away from him. Somewhere in the open world of Sirinhigha.

It was almost enough to make him sob. But he wouldn't give Sathe the satisfaction.

He reached the flat floor, turned, and hobbled back toward his warden, through the trembling corridors of his dark underground prison.

CHAPTER 37

RHYTHM OF THE FIGHT

"At the center of it all, the Mage Queen's goal remained: destroying the Complété itself."

- From Athonen d'Ereth's *The Fall of Mages in the Age of Dragons*

Staggering backward, Maya adjusted her hold on her quarterstaff. She planted her boots in the dirt, whipped her long braid behind her, and considered her enemy. But that was just the trouble. Ter wasn't an enemy, and he *looked* like a child.

Raised by warriors, Maya had been taught how to sword fight, shoot a bow, and—her favorite—wield a quarterstaff. She was particularly good at the last, able to hold her own even against a stronger foe.

But she had no stomach for dueling a child, even for training.

Ter eyed her with a smile, his quarterstaff still lifted, ears perched at mid-level like he was listening for her next move.

He'd returned at sunset from some mission unrelated to the search for Mikoneh. He appeared so grim and solemn, Maya tried to cheer him up with food, but the Ephe'ahn only grew quieter and quieter. At last, she'd given up and moved off for her evening training session with Akonn and a few other knights of the Sword. They'd been happy to give her pointers and had been equally swift to offer praise when she impressed them. During a bout against Trinn, Akonn's right-hand man, Ter had arrived and issued a jovial challenge. She'd been so relieved to see him smiling, she'd accepted—but he was still so tiny, and she didn't want to hurt him.

Not that he showed any sign of a child's weakness.

Indeed, she found herself driven back more than she had been against Trinn. Maybe the knight had been holding back a little, but Ter certainly wasn't. His hits were quick and hard, ramming against her staff with measured strokes. She barely shielded herself, unwilling to commit to the fight. Her bones felt brittle from the ceaseless barrage.

But holding back wasn't fair to him. He was obviously taking out some hidden frustration in this duel.

"Are we finished then?" asked Ter, canting his head.

She shook her own, wiping her hand against her leather jerkin. She'd exchanged her dresses for more practical clothes since coming to the Dragon King's camp. A female general named Larta wore a similar size.

If Ter needs to vent, well—so do I. Stop holding back.

She adjusted her grip again and swept forward. Their staffs met with a thud. She advanced, then retreated. They answered each other well, strokes rapid and heavy. Maya lost herself in the rhythm of the fight. With each attack, with every defense, her tension bled away, bit by bit. Her fears faded.

Then Ter halted and lowered his quarterstaff.

Maya stumbled to a stop mid-swing, blinking, her breaths heavy.

"We've lost the sun." Ter glanced at the torches that had been lit around the training field to chase off the night. "Best pick this up another time, hm?" One ear twitched.

Maya swallowed, nodding. She wiped sweat from the side of her face. A crowd had gathered to watch them spar. Akonn stood grinning at the fore of the chattering soldiers.

"That was wonderfully done," he said.

Penn trotted over from the other side of the crowd. His arm was still in a sling, though the bone was mending well. His brown eyes caught the torchlight and burned orange. "I never knew you were so good with that." He nodded toward the quarterstaff.

Maya's cheeks warmed. She'd made a point not to let him know, afraid he might see her as less feminine. She pressed a smile to her lips. "Well, I had to defend myself against Mikoneh somehow." The smile quavered. The jest died in her heart.

Penn brushed his fingers against her arm. Thankfully, he didn't try to soothe her. She'd heard every assurance, every promise, and none helped.

"If it is any comfort," Ter said, "my business in the North confirmed the Mage Queen remains somewhere in the Andyans, and Sathe has not yet reached her. That means your twin is not in her clutches. A huge blessing, to be sure."

"Is it?" asked Maya. Didn't that mean they still had no clear method of narrowing down where he was?

"Oh, certainly," said the Ephe'ahn. "It backs up what Lord Penn conjectured, does it not?"

She nodded. "So, he really might be in Oceana."

"It does lend confirmation." Ter padded closer. "It also

means Sathe is out for his own ends, rather than delivering Mikoneh to his queen. That is encouraging in its way."

Akonn approached, expression pensive. "Discord among the ranks."

"Precisely." Ter's ears perked up. "My source is confident of that much, whether Sathe is among the dissenters or not. Indeed, he claims that Suld's fortress has fallen, and the Mage is vanquished."

Maya started. Sathe's brother was dead?

Akonn inhaled a sharp breath. "That's impossible."

"No, no." Ter shook his head. "It seems that Lord Reteris and his kin ravaged the fortress, and an adept Elementalist razed it to the ground. Suld is no more."

"They're certain?" asked Akonn. "Suld's body was recovered from the rubble?"

"Yes, so my source says." Ter frowned.

"Yet you seem grim." Maya studied his face. "You did when you arrived, too."

The Ephe'ahn's frown twisted into a grimace. "Ah, that is about...something else. Not important to any of you." He blinked. "That sounded very rude. Forgive me." His smile dawned bright and warm. "It is a private matter, that is all. It pertains to a far-off friend who isn't well just now." He clapped a hand to his stomach. "I am half-starved. Anyone else?"

Maya's stomach rumbled in reply. She laughed. "Me, too. Let's see what might be left in the mess tent."

Ter offered his arm. "Allow me to escort you, fair lady."

"Lead on, good sir." She looped her arm around his, bending slightly.

They moved toward the large tent, their steps teetering as they each tried to compensate for the other's height difference. Akonn and Penn followed, chuckling all the way.

A MIST CLUNG to the early morning, lingering around the tents, bringing a chill that reminded Maya of winter's approach. She moved through the writhing vapor, steps soft in the stillness of the camp. Her dreams had been troubled, and she'd not been able to banish them. Defeated, she rose, determined to shed the heaviness in her soul.

She'd first gone to Penn's room to speak with him, to bleed away some of her tension in his warm conversation, but the viscount wasn't in there. Where he'd gone off to so early, she didn't know. He'd been doing that a lot lately, perhaps just as restless as she was in his worry for Mikoneh.

On the north end of the large camp, not far from her quarters, a stream ran within the palisade boundary. A shallow place in the flowing water would allow her to ford it, and she could sit on the other side, to feel somewhat apart from the commotion of camp. Thankfully, in the dawn hour she was almost alone. The distant ring of the smithy forges and the shouts from someone near the corrals were all that broke the quiet.

Reaching the stream, she slipped off her boots and plunged into the cold water. A wind spirit swooped by above the churning mists. It chirped, shaping into a bird, before it whisked away on some pressing whim.

Maya climbed from the stream, the bottom of her breeches dripping. She sat among the frostbitten wildflowers along the bank. Her lips tugged toward a smile, though it was feeble. She drank in the crisp air, trying to settle her soul.

It's not going to work. You can't just sit here while others rescue Mikoneh.

Yet what else could she do? They'd made it clear she was in danger if she joined them—that Sathe might try to catch her, too, and use her. Mages were always looking for vulnerable dragons.

Dragons! She, a dragon. She still didn't know how to swallow that news, though it was more exciting than scary.

Mikoneh didn't know. Has Sathe shown him what he really is? He must be so afraid.

Stop! Stop, stop, stop.

She knuckled her temple to dislodge that train of thought.

Wind spirits materialized above her head, snatched up her loose tresses, and tossed them in her face. They laughed and rolled across the air, pleased with themselves. She spat out strands of hair and batted them aside.

"Mischievous this morning, are you? I appreciate the distraction."

"Ah, so you're the flighty kind. That makes this simpler." The unfamiliar voice was deep and severe. The fragrance of moss and honey accompanied that voice.

Maya straightened her spine and turned to find a figure moving toward her in a fluid, almost floating motion— No. The figure *was* floating. His feet were several inches above the grass, yet he walked as though upon solid ground.

And then she saw why. Wind spirits had wrapped around his boots, cushioning him, holding him aloft. They seemed to find the task diverting, like a wonderful joke. She dragged her eyes from the peculiar sight, up to the stranger's face.

He was a man in his late fifties, with shoulder-length salt-and-pepper hair and eyes whose irises were a deep, striking burgundy hue. He wore a frown, studying her just as she studied him. He clutched a poleaxe that was propped over one shoulder. His clothes consisted of a patched gray cloak over a plain brown tunic, gray pants, with well-worn leather boots. Her gaze fell on the wind spirits still giggling where they held the man above the dewy grass.

"Hello," she said. "You must be the Wind Elementalist Captain Akonn spoke of."

"And you must be the dragoness," he replied, rubbing the stubble on his chin. "A beauty, too, even among your kind."

Heat rushed over Maya's cheeks. She'd never thought of herself as a beauty. Dressed in rags and taller than most girls, she'd assumed she was a gangling thing. Certainly, comparing herself to her twin—whom everyone said looked a great deal like her—she'd secretly feared that she looked too masculine.

"Well," the man said. "You'll do."

She blinked up at him. "For what?"

"Training. I don't train lost causes, but you've the instinct and the disposition for wind. The spirits favor you—though that can be an impediment. Keep that in mind." He scowled. "Don't just sit there. Stand up. Show respect for your elder."

She scrambled to her feet, bewildered and intrigued in equal measures. "So, you'll train me to become a proper Wind Elementalist?"

"Said so, didn't I?" He rubbed his chin with greater vigor, looking her up and down. "True Rokahnian blood, too. Thoroughbred."

Her flush deepened. "I'm not a horse, you know." Her tone was mild. After all, Akonn had warned her the man was eccentric.

He jerked his eyes back to her face. "Not a—of course not." A grin stretched over his face. "Oh, aye. Yes. Sorry—I seldom see people as people."

"And what of seeing dragons as horses?" She let herself smile.

His grin grew wider. "That depends on the age, darlin'. You're awfully small for a dragon yet."

"I'm not likely to grow bigger in this skin."

"No." He folded his arms without losing his grip on the

poleaxe. "Suppose not. But you'll grow in leaps in dragon form, assuming you don't get your fool neck broke first. Many a baby dragon has got themselves killed for no better reason than to see the world, same as other young folk."

She tipped her head to one side, trying to read him better. "Do you know much about dragons?"

"More than some, less than the Dragon King."

"That's a broad scale."

He shrugged.

Maya took a step forward. "There are two questions I haven't dared ask, but I really need to know."

The man's smile dipped into a wry smirk. "Definitely the flighty type. All right, ask your questions, dragoness—then we get to work."

She shook her head. "You said you'd train me. I haven't said yet that I'll let you."

"Oh-ho?" He chuckled. "Barely outta your egg and already so bossy. *She-dragons*." He shook his head, but his grin was wide again.

"There—that's one of my questions. Was I hatched from an egg?"

The man eyed her for a long moment, then he tossed back his head and roared with laughter. "Of all the—" He hooted and slapped his free hand against his thigh. "D'you think I was there, youngling? D'you think I witnessed you—" He burst into renewed laughter.

Unflinching, Maya waited for him to calm down. "You can laugh," she said, "but I know even less than you, and it's myself we're discussing. What I want to know is: Are dragons hatched from eggs? Are the stories right on that count?"

The man's gales slowed, then he wiped at his eyes. "Ah, yes. I see your meaning. But, lass, you should warn an old man before you startle him so. I worry over your second question."

"You're not old," she said. "And I'll only ask my second question once you've answered my first."

"Sure, sure." He dropped into the grass, and the wind spirits that were wrapped around his boots whisked away. He placed his poleaxe beside him and patted the ground. "Sit. Let's talk. I'm Hilker, by the by. What's your name, dragoness?"

"Maya." She sat cross-legged beside him. "Are you human, with those eyes?"

He snorted. "When you say two questions, do you mean thirty?"

"Sorry." She really wasn't. "My brother says I talk faster than the northern winds can blow at Wintertide."

"Your brother's an astute fellow. And I'm half-human, half-fae. The human half is winning out, but that's a story for another time." He scratched at his stubble. "You want to know if you were hatched from an egg. Well. Back in the Age of Dragons, odds were good you might be so—but now, with few dragons knowing what they be, you were more probably birthed like any human child. So, probably no. You weren't hatched from an egg."

She nodded, plucking at the hem of her jerkin. "I wondered."

"Evidently."

Ignoring his sarcasm, she shifted her mind to her next question.

"The Dragon King. He's a dragon, right?" She blinked. "That's not my main question. It's a leading question to the, well, the question. Rhetorical too, really, as I already know the answer."

"Go on, then." He motioned with his hand.

"All right. If Owenekiras Rokahn is a dragon—"

"He is."

"If he *is*, then why does he ride a dragon?"

The dam broke, and Hilker dissolved into another fit of laughter. She merely sat still, watching him as he fell back into the grass, overcome by his own amusement. Funny or not, the question was perfectly sensible.

An insect hummed past, darting away from the Master Elementalist.

Hilker slowly regained control of himself, then fell still, chuckling while he stared at the sky. "Why does the king of dragons ride another dragon?" He snorted through his nose. "Well, I suppose that is a funny thing when you stop and look at it. Started in the Age of Dragons, y'know."

"I'm beginning to," she said. "But why?"

"Bonding, lass. Dragons have different kinds of bonds, some for peacetime, some for wartime. And in the latter case, sometimes dragons bond with each other. That's how it started."

"They bonded with each other, and now dragons...can ride on each other's backs?"

Hilker snickered. "No, only the Dragon King and his heirs do. Only the line of Rokahn. Unless commanded or if the need is dire, that is."

She considered that. "Then, my twin and I were allowed to ride on Lord Owenekiras's dragon because he commanded it."

Hilker shot her an intent look. "I suppose so."

"Well." She shrugged. "I guess that's the end of my questions."

"Doubtful." He sat up and brushed blades of grass from his shoulders. "But let's at least get some training in before your next batch conjures itself up, eh?" He flashed her a grin. "Unless you've decided not to let me teach you."

She stood. "Perhaps I'll give you a trial run."

Hilker took his own feet and brushed off more stray grass. "Best start on the right foot then." He lifted his left leg to balance only on his right. As she started to laugh, Hilker snagged her eye. "Catch yourself, lass, if you can."

Wind spirits charged her, swept her upward, then dumped her in the water. Hilker's laughter rang out even beneath the stream's current. She broke free, spluttering and shivering.

"Again." Hilker didn't so much as move his fingers. As though he'd issued a silent command, the wind spirits plucked her up, then tossed her back down in the water. She shrieked, helpless.

As she sat up, gasping for air, she heard the dread word: "Again."

CHAPTER 38

AWAY FROM THE WORLD

They stood above a canyon under a glittering night sky. Mikoneh eyed the lit-up town below, while a gust tossed his ponytail. Sathe stood close, admiring the same distant view.

"Thank you." Mikoneh was surprised by his own words. Sure, Sathe had offered to bring him topside in a rare show of generosity, but Mikoneh didn't believe for one moment that the Mage's motives were kind. Yet, he still felt gratitude. Clean air, open spaces, the sky. All of it filled Mikoneh with wonder like he'd seldom known. No one appreciated freedom as much as one who'd been denied it.

Sathe drew closer. "But of course, Firebrand. You didn't think I'd keep you below ground forever, did you?"

"It crossed my mind."

"Yes, so it did." The Mage snickered. "You know what I value most about you—even above your stubbornness?"

The answer flitted over Mikoneh's thoughts. "My blunt honesty."

"Very good." Sathe's voice was a low coo. "Marvelous how our bond deepens."

A shiver dragged frosty fingers over Mikoneh's skin. He said nothing, keeping his gaze on the town. So close, but not near enough. Sathe would make certain of that.

"So I will," whispered the Mage. "You're a quick study. I'm glad of that, too."

Mikoneh clenched his teeth and stayed still.

"Behave for me, my Firebrand, and I'll have no reason to punish you."

"I did nothing several nights ago, but you still hurt me."

Sathe's silence was like a tomb, cold and empty. "That was something else. Something else..."

He turned away, leaving Mikoneh alone on the ledge overlooking the canyon. A river flowed near the town. Its shape was like a slithering snake from up here, with scales glistening in the moonlight. Mikoneh longed to jump toward it, to plunge into its depths, and let the current carry him where it would.

The Mage's hand settled on his spine between his shoulder blades. "Ready, Firebrand?"

Mikoneh's wings throbbed beneath his skin, eager to pull free. Stubbornness flashed through his chest, but he knew better than to heed it. Yes, Sathe wanted this—but so did Mikoneh. He stepped away from the Mage's touch, pulled his jerkin over his head to avoid ripping it, then allowed his wings to slide from his human back. It was so easy. So exhilarating. Adrenaline spiked, urging him to jump from the cliff—to fly.

"Hold fast," Sathe said, laughing. "Your wings are untried. Don't risk your neck." He stepped up to Mikoneh's side and pointed toward a ledge that jutted out four feet below the top of the canyon brink. "See that? Spread your wings, let the wind fill them, then step off there. You may not fall. Your reflexes are good. But neither of us wants you to die tonight, hm?"

Sathe's friendliness prickled Mikoneh's flesh. He moved away from the Mage in a few quick steps and set his bare toes along the edge. Dropping his jerkin near his feet, he let his thoughts lift from the ground toward the gleaming sky.

He closed his eyes. Wind flowed around him. He unfolded his wings and spread them wide. The wind stroked the webbing, vibrating through him. Instinct snared his soul. Who cared about the jutting ledge below? He wouldn't fall. He would *never* fall.

Trusting his wings, he jumped from the cliff. The breeze caught him, lifting him high, high in the air. He opened his eyes and found himself carried toward the wisps of cloud hovering near the moon. Away from Sathe. Away from the world.

He laughed, free for the first time in...he didn't know how long. He was freer than he'd been in *years*, tied to the ground, caught in Oceana. A prisoner of gravity.

The wind tugged him downward, bringing his focus back to the moment. His smile returned. He let his senses bleed into his wings, absorbing the feeling of cool wind against leathery membrane and hard scales. Strange, how right it felt. As though his wings had always been there. In a way, he supposed, they had. He just hadn't known it.

Drinking in the frigid air, he sent out a command for his wings to beat against the currents. They heeded him, shoving him up in a fluid motion. Laughter cracked from his mouth again. His wings lifted him higher. His tentative smile stretched into a broad grin.

He let his fears go. Beating his wings faster, he thrust himself into the ocean of stars. His wings carried him like he'd spent every day of his life aloft, never failing, always adjusting —the slightest adjustments—to compensate for the fickle winds. At first, he only dared to keep straight, but soon he let himself veer until he wheeled in a full circle, wide, then tighter, tighter, until he could touch his own toes.

Joy. It was unadulterated joy.

He hooted, laughed—almost wept from the pleasure of flight.

Breaking out of his tight spin, he tucked in his wings and tumbled toward the distant cliffs. Not even a flicker of fear sparked.

This was how it was meant to be. This was who he was.

Sathe can't take this from me. Not this moment. Not this identity.

He flung his wings out and caught himself, jerking upward on a current. No matter what, he was a dragon on the wind.

Firebrand, return.

It was a command, but not the kind Mikoneh was compelled to obey with every fiber of his being. Still, he brought himself up short, wings adapting with tiny beats and twists to keep him hovering in place.

Amazing.

Firebrand.

Mikoneh frowned. His gaze flickered west toward Simynshin. He angled east, trying to recognize the land from so high up. Was that the border between Lintha and Oceana? Were they so close to his childhood home?

Should I escape?

Will you try?

Mikoneh grimaced. He knew he couldn't. No matter how far he flew, Sathe could order him to return. As things stood, he was a prisoner even in the air.

A dragon, yes. But a captive one, body and soul.

He curled his hands into fists. He would return. For now, he must.

He attuned his wings and made for the cliffs.

"Mikoneh."

His wings faltered. That voice. That wasn't Sathe.

Searching the horizon, he tried to find some source for the sound that filled his head.

"Mikoneh, show me where you are."

He *knew* that voice somehow. Not Maya or Penn. Not Ter or even the Revenant. It didn't matter. He trusted it. Inhaling, he adjusted his wings again, lifting himself into the sky on a fluid, fast beat. He raced toward the moon, then spun and took in the full view of the dark land below him.

Here. I'm right here.

He drank in every detail he could see. The canyon. Town. River. Trees. Rocks. Hills.

"That will do."

Firebrand, return. *Now!*

Mikoneh's heart lurched. His limbs locked. His wings folded. He plummeted toward the ground. Wind rushed through his ears. Fear raced through him. His wings wouldn't respond. He was falling toward a sudden, deadly impact.

Sathe wouldn't let me die. He wouldn't.

But growing terror gripped his thoughts, paralyzing reason. He couldn't die, not now, not after that speck of hope.

"I'm coming!" he screamed.

The compelling force broke. His body became his own. He spread his wings wide and soared upward on a snatching current. Not pausing to think, he altered his course and swooped toward the cliff where Sathe waited.

The Mage looked like a smear against the dark rocks, growing bigger as Mikoneh aimed for the ground nearby. He slowed his descent, letting reflex guide his motions. Moments later, he landed beside Sathe, breathing heavily, nerves still taut from his fall.

He expected pain. But Sathe regarded him with wide eyes, his soul exuding horror. He strode to Mikoneh, caught his face in both hands, and searched his gaze.

"What happened up there?"

"I—I almost fell." Hadn't Sathe done that?

The Mage shook his head. "Before that. You were—" He broke off, and his expression darkened. The expected anger flared. "What happened right before that?"

"I'm not sure." It wasn't a lie, but if Sathe didn't know...if somehow Sathe couldn't hear that voice... *Don't think about it.*

Sathe's eyes narrowed. "Try to explain."

"I..." How could he shield knowledge of the voice from Sathe? The Mage could read his thoughts.

"Don't toy with me, Firebrand. I can dig into your head if I must."

Mikoneh winced, recalling what that felt like. He lowered his eyes, bracing himself. "I won't tell you. You'll have to force me."

Sathe sneered. "And here I thought we were becoming friends." A sigh followed. "It won't be so easy this time,

Mikoneh. You expect pain. You endure it well. But what of others? What if the innocent suffer?" A thread of glee laced his voice.

Mikoneh jerked his eyes up to meet Sathe's. "Don't you—"

"Dare?" Sathe's lips stretched into an impossibly wide grin, showing nearly all his teeth. "Ah, Mikoneh." His thumb caressed Mikoneh's cheek. "It seems I must." He seized Mikoneh's chin and yanked his head toward the distant torchlight.

Go down there and slaughter every person in that town. Every. Last. One.

Mikoneh's eyes widened. His heart ceased to beat. "No. No, I won't." The compulsion to obey flooded his body, taking control. "No."

Draw your claws and wield your flame. No one survives.

"No." Mikoneh wrestled against his body to the last stitch of his willpower, but Sathe's word was law. His will, absolute. Mikoneh's wings spread wide and lifted him.

Say nothing. Give no warning. Kill everyone. Burn the town to ash.

Mikoneh's lips sealed shut. He winged toward the distant town winking across the river. Tears gathered in his eyes. His fingernails burned, then bladed claws unsheathed, covering his human nails. His vision sharpened. Fire spirits answered his unwilling summons.

He touched down outside the town. Laughter filled the houses. Several were dark, their occupants already gone to bed.

The river roared in his ears.

Please no. Sathe, please don't make me do this. I'll tell you! I'll tell you what happened.

Too late, Firebrand. You must learn absolute obedience.

Mikoneh ground his teeth. His head throbbed in his futile effort to disobey his master.

A tear rolled down his cheek.

He approached the first house on silent human feet. His clawed fingers flexed. Fire hovered at his shoulder.

Help me. Somebody, help. Anyone. Nijaal. God. Anyone!

Forgive me.

CHAPTER 39

A NEW PURPOSE

"Too many humans, fae, and animals vanished like foam in the ocean tides of magic."

- From Athonen d'Ereth's *The Fall of Mages in the Age of Dragons*

"It was necessary, my Firebrand." Sathe's voice was a distant noise, unimportant.

Mikoneh remained curled up on his narrow pallet, staring at the stone wall, his back to the Mage. The smell of blood still filled his nostrils.

"Even so, I understand how difficult your task was."

Task? Mikoneh twitched, a spark of wrath igniting, burning through layers of numbness.

"Rest," Sathe said. "We must leave soon." The rustle of his robes grew louder. A hand settled on Mikoneh's head. "It's unfortunate that you compromised our location, but it can't be helped now. Just refrain from your impulses in the future, hm?"

Mikoneh shuddered. An impulse? It was far more than that. Yes, he'd given that voice a view of his location, and he would do so again.

He'd been forced to tell Sathe everything after he'd returned to his master from slaughtering every man, woman, and child, and torching every building in the town across the river. Dawn had spread its light across the world. His hands had dripped with blood, and he'd stood trembling, sobbing, while Sathe compelled him to explain about the voice and his response to it.

Then he'd blacked out. He'd regained consciousness only moments ago and found himself unable—and unwilling—to move. If he'd been bathed, he didn't know. He didn't care. Let the blood remain, a testament of his sin. Of his guilt.

Bile burned his throat. He shifted, afraid he might retch—but the sensation passed, leaving a sour taste on his tongue.

"You're strong," whispered Sathe. "Stronger than I'd suspected. Truly, Mikoneh, I've come to admire you." His fingers stroked Mikoneh's hair near his ear. "You'll pull through this, and you'll be better for it. War is ugly. A warrior must harden his heart against the sorrow early on, or something in him breaks. Dragons are no different."

Mikoneh twitched again, resisting an urge to roll over and slam his fist into the Mage's jaw. Would the creature never stop talking? Couldn't Sathe leave him alone, let him sink back into oblivion for a time? Forget, just for a little while?

Sathe withdrew his touch, then rose with a whisper of his robes. "I'll return shortly. Prepare to move when I do. We must leave these tunnels."

This would be the second move since Mikoneh's capture.

Following the recent collapse, they'd moved west, by several leagues, to occupy a newer network of tunnels. Mikoneh had assumed they'd been under attack from the Dragon King's forces, but apparently not. A glimpse into Sathe's mind, while the Mage slept, suggested that a distant fortification held by Mage Suld—Sathe's brother—had collapsed under a dragon siege. With Suld's death, his magic had died as well, buckling any tunnel across the continent that had been fortified under his personal seal of Magery.

Sathe's feet padded away. The chamber doors closed. Mikoneh lay motionless and tried to retreat into that dark abyss, far removed from the atrocities he'd committed, but his mind had kicked back into action. He couldn't stay still. He couldn't forget.

Mikoneh sat up. The blanket fell from his shoulders, revealing his bare skin. He searched the room. His clothes were folded on the chest like normal. He wrapped the blanket around his shoulders and stood, his limbs heavy but functioning. He dressed automatically, noting that his hands were clean. So were his trousers. He moved toward the doors. He didn't care if Sathe wanted him to rest. Didn't care what happened to him if the Mage got mad.

You'll care if he makes you hurt people again.

Hurt them. No, not just that.

Kill them.

Mikoneh's eyes pricked, and his throat burned, but he refused to cry. He'd done enough of that on the cliff. Straightening his shoulders, he trod down the earthen passages, stretching his senses for Reven's signature. There, much closer than before, only a few tunnels away.

Every step brought clarity. Each movement pulled him from his darkest thoughts. He'd never be able to forgive himself for slaughtering the villagers, but...it was Sathe's fault, not his. He knew that, despite the guilt burning a hole in his stomach.

You just can't let it happen again. Not ever.

Far more important than escape, Mikoneh had settled on a new purpose.

He would find a way to kill Sathe, no matter what that meant for himself.

~  ~

THE CRIMSON GLOW PAINTING the tunnel ahead brought a strange relief crashing through Mikoneh. His step quickened. He turned the corner and halted.

The Revenant stood at the end of the passage where the walls gave way to an enormous underground chamber. Half of it had collapsed, likely in the aftershock caused by those dragons destroying Suld's fortress in the north. Several pillars of earth held portions of the ceiling that remained, and somehow —despite the ugliness of the Mages' underground lair—the chamber seemed...elegant. Warped, twisted, like their violet magic, yes, but crafted like architecture from another age; an age when people took great care with whatever they created.

The specter's back was to Mikoneh, and he didn't turn, perhaps not noticing him. Steeling his nerves, Mikoneh pressed forward along the tunnel, keeping his steps as quiet as he could. Halfway, the Revenant's cloak rippled, and the cowled being turned toward him.

'Mikoneh.' The voice filled him with the same sorrow, though it didn't strike as hard—perhaps because he'd been prepared for it. Or perhaps because Mikoneh's sorrow was closer to Reven's now.

"Hi, Reven." Mikoneh crooked a smile. "I've been having a...really bad night." Emotions swelled in his throat, choking him, unknotting the numbness that had settled into his soul.

He blinked back the mistiness in his eyes and strode forward. "How are you?"

The Revenant considered him for a long moment, still as death, then turned back to the chamber. *'You should leave. Sathe will be cruel again if he discovers you here.'*

"To you or to me?" asked Mikoneh, coming up beside the cloaked form. "Did he punish you for last time, like he did me?"

'My existence is pain enough. He cannot hurt me more.'

"Then you're worried for me." Mikoneh searched the shadows where Reven's face ought to be. "Thank you. But I'm fine."

'That cannot be.'

"I'm not...great." Mikoneh shrugged and turned his gaze toward the pillars lined before him. "I hate what he does to me. What I..." He swallowed against a lump. "Last night was..." He swallowed again and cleared his throat, blocking the images of the town now turned to ash. "I won't pretend I'm not wounded, but I don't think Sathe needs any reason to lash out. It's all whimsy with him. Worse than the pain is when he's almost kind." A tremor crawled up Mikoneh's frame. "I hate that the most."

Reven's eyes were on him, prickling his skin. Mikoneh kept his gaze forward.

'You are afraid.'

"Yes." Mikoneh coughed out a laugh. "Terrified. And broken, I suspect. But I'm also pragmatic. Fear serves a purpose. I'll use that to stay alert and cautious—but Reven..." He blew out a breath, willing his muscles to relax. "I won't let him keep me caged—and whatever he intends to use me for, I can't allow it to happen. He—he made me..." He couldn't say it out loud. He couldn't confess. Not yet.

Raking a hand through his loose hair, he pinned his gaze on the nearest pillar. "This room feels old somehow."

'It is one of the first tunnels they crafted, long ago, when they first tainted their magic.'

"*They* meaning Dark Mages, right?"

The cowl shifted as Reven nodded.

"Why did they let their magic become tainted?"

'That is a long story.'

Mikoneh shrugged. "I have time, I can't rest, and I desperately need a distraction. Besides, Sathe is gone. Once he returns, we're moving. I don't know when I'll be able to come find you —or if..." He frowned. "Will you stay near here, along with your body, or will they move that?"

'I will come. Sathe keeps me close.'

Mikoneh's heart clenched. *I need to find a way to free him before I kill Sathe.* He recommitted himself to that, though it seemed as impossible as his other resolution. He curled his hands into fists, fortifying every nerve against his coming battle with Sathe.

"A voice came to me. In my head." Mikoneh's words were barely above a whisper. "It asked where I was, and I tried to show it, but I don't know how much good it will do me. Sathe couldn't hear the voice, even though he's in my head, too. It made him furious. He punished me." Mikoneh choked again but pressed on. "That voice scared him—a lot. And now we're moving."

'That voice would scare any Mage.'

Mikoneh jerked his eyes toward the Revenant, heart skipping a beat. "Why?"

'It is a deep bond—deeper than anything a Mage could force. A natural connection exists between each living dragon and their lord: the Dragon King.'

That *was* the voice. Mikoneh recognized it now—cold and

deep, aloof, but not twisted like Sathe's. Mikoneh huffed a laugh. "So, the Dragon King is seeking me. And...and we're bonded too."

'*It is nothing to fear, Mikoneh. It is a natural bond, and one Owenekiras Rokahn would never abuse. That he entered your head without consent is proof of his worry—as well he should. Sathe's plan for you is terrible.*' Reven trailed off.

Mikoneh shivered, unsure whether he should press him to continue or not.

'*In any case,*' Reven went on, '*you may rest assured that if the Dragon King is seeking you personally, he will find you. No matter what defenses Sathe has raised, none can stop such a man if he is determined. Sathe is a fool to forget this.*'

"If I'm bonded to Owenekiras, can he track me anywhere like Sathe could?"

'*The bonds are of two kinds. The Dragon King's is not so intrusive, not so...one-sided. A pure bond, untainted by Dark Magery, is equal. It is a boon to the bonded human, extending their natural years to match the dragon's long life. It is a boon to the dragon, lending a gentler perspective. It is a weight for both and a reward in the sharing of two hearts.*'

"You're one, aren't you?" asked Mikoneh. "A dragon or a bonded."

'*Once, yes. No longer.*'

Mikoneh's instincts whispered at him. He turned fully toward Reven. "You're a dragon, aren't you? But why turn you into...this? Why not force a bond?"

'*They did. But I...shattered. This was the alternative to true death.*'

An inferno scored Mikoneh's insides, burning away the last of his numbness. He shook with anger. To trap this dragon, first in a bond as cruel as Mikoneh's own, and then to turn him into something neither alive nor dead, caught between two worlds—it was too unjust.

"God must really hate people," he found himself saying.

'*It is people who hate people,*' Reven replied. '*We demanded freedom from God, and then misused that freedom to oppress and hurt others. Yet we blame God for that misuse. Is it his fault we go our own way?*'

Mikoneh had no answer for that. He shrugged, still clutching to his anger, letting it give him purpose.

Reven spoke on. '*A good father raises his children well, but he cannot keep them caged. When they are grown, he lets them find their own path, find their own purpose, even if it hurts them. So, too, God gives us choice.*'

"You believe in God, after everything you've endured?" Mikoneh scoffed.

'*He is my one relief.*'

Sorrow flickered beside the anger. Reven had every right to believe in anything that helped him endure his suffering. Mikoneh's fists tightened. "I'll free you, Reven. Somehow, I swear I will."

'*You cannot. It is too late.*'

"No. I refuse to believe that. Absolutely not." Fire spirits sprouted from the ground at Mikoneh's feet, drawn to his fury. He knew he should temper himself. He should contain the flames, to keep Sathe from concentrating on him—but he didn't want to let go of it. Didn't want to return to the pain and fear. The fire could motivate him—keep him focused. Centered.

He closed his eyes and allowed the flames to curl through him, wonderfully alive. He couldn't burn away his bond, though a throb urged him to try. It wouldn't work. Ter had suggested burning away their previous connection *before* it reached this point.

Fine, he couldn't free himself. But what about Reven?

His eyes snapped open. "Magic has rules, doesn't it?"

'*Yes.*'

"Tell me about them. About Magery. In general terms."

Reven nodded. '*Do you need to sit?*'

"No, I'm good. I prefer to stand." He allowed himself a tight smile. "Can you pull back your cowl? Am I allowed to see your face?"

Reven fell still, then rippled a nod. He reached those too-slender fingers up and pulled back the cowl. Mikoneh hadn't known what to expect. The soul's shape was distorted, elongated, not human. Perhaps he'd anticipated something from a nightmare. What he saw was indistinctness. A shadow cradled in crimson light—the mere suggestion of a face—though sad more than frightening. Mikoneh searched that light for a hint of eyes or a mouth; any likeness to the body lying on the altar several tunnels away; any feature to intimate the man he'd once been.

Reven's attention pinned on him, as though the specter had been avoiding his eyes until this moment. Mikoneh tensed. Reven's chill sank deep, gnawing bone and soul alike.

"That's quite the unnerving presence you have, Reven." Mikoneh offered a smile to combat the cold.

'*You handle it well.*'

"What good would screaming do?" He pried his eyes from the unsettling sight. "Tell me about Magery. Anything you know."

'*I will try.*' The Revenant drifted into the chamber proper, crimson cloak raking the packed earth behind him. '*It is scrawl magic at its core—made of sealing runes which indicate specific words or phrases, etched within the confines of a shape. Usually a circle. That amalgamation—sometimes combined with sound, like a chant or song—conjures the force necessary to invoke the spell.'*

"Okay, so can anyone do it, or only Mages? Are Mages human or are they fae?"

'Mages can be of any race, though Magery began with humans. They wished to wield their own magic. Once, they were allies of the fae and fantastic. Now they are power-hungry and afraid.'

"Sounds like humans," Mikoneh muttered, then scowled at his own cynicism. Not everyone was Drayve. Penn was a good man, despite being raised by such a sniveling, greedy creature. Mikoneh rubbed his neck, then flinched, recalling what his hands had recently done.

Don't go there. Focus on now.

"Anything else you know?" he prompted.

Reven was quiet for a moment. *'Dark Magery, like most invasive magic, often requires a true name.'*

Mikoneh frowned. "That's a little vague."

'The Spirits Elemental help to funnel scrawl magic—and other types—keeping it from tainting. But Dark Magery works around that with true names. If I knew your true name—your soul's name rather than your given birth name—I could break through every defense you possess, and I could control you. It is not unlike what Sathe has done, though he employed your dragon blood to enslave you, rather than your true name. The difficulty with Dark Magery is that its wielders have stolen the true names of many things within the natural world—a tree, a mountain peak, a river of water—and what they have discovered, they have twisted. It is a sorrowful thing, most unholy.'

"That's what Sathe did to you, isn't it?" Mikoneh's eyes narrowed, his fury climbing higher. "He stole your true name, so you can't tell it to me."

Reven was still, then a long sigh filled Mikoneh's mind. '*I do not know it.*'

"And you couldn't tell me that fact either?"

'*I can say nothing about it directly.*'

"Seems the word 'it' is indirect enough."

'*You have provided the context, not I.*'

"I can work with that." Mikoneh rubbed a finger along his jaw. "Speaking in hypotheticals for a moment: If Sathe did steal my true name, could it be stolen back?"

'*It could, though I do not know the method to do so.*'

"What can you tell me about yourself, Reven? Do you remember much about your life, before...?"

Again, silence. '*I remember so little. Merely snatches. Colors and scents, most of all.*'

"Nothing of your family?"

'*Nothing.*'

Mikoneh couldn't imagine a life so empty, without Maya, Fa, and Mama. Yes, the memories made the hollowness of now, without them, cut deeper—but he preferred that to a barrenness without those attachments in his heart.

"I'm sorry." The words scraped across his lips. He stared into the shadows before him, letting his thoughts drift from a subject that must bring Reven pain. Instead, he settled again on Magery, and on the few rules he'd learned. How could he steal back a name?

Sathe knows Reven's name—and I'm bonded to him.

Mikoneh turned toward the Revenant. "What happens if two people know someone's true name? For example, if I knew my twin's true name, and Sathe found that knowledge in me, what would that do to Maya? Could our fight over her cause her harm or death or anything like that?"

'*It is my understanding that only one person can possess the true name at any given time.*'

"Is that right?" A grin stretched across Mikoneh's face.

He had no idea how to steal a true name from someone else, yet the fact that he *might* filled him with a giddiness he couldn't suppress. Sathe had bound him, yet that very state might enable Mikoneh to rescue a fellow sufferer. There was a kind of irony in that. A justice that bolstered his resolve and healed a few of the cracks.

"I need to go." He spun away from the chamber. "I'll find you again, Reven. Soon, I hope. Wish me luck."

The Revenant's voice filled his head: '*May the good fortune of the kindly fae guide your steps.*'

Chapter 40

The Interior of Oceana

"Those last battles were desperate campaigns. Some were waged upon land or sea. Others, many others, were waged in the sky."

- From Athonen d'Ereth's *The Fall of Mages in the Age of Dragons*

Maya traced her fingers along the black-on-black damask pattern of Owenekiras's command tent before she slipped through the entrance flaps. It had become something of a ritual, allowing her to brace herself before she learned whatever she'd been summoned to hear.

Within, she waited for Penn, eyeing the game of Fang and Claw set up on one of the small tables. The ornate pieces— dragons, griffins, knights, maidens, catapults, and others—were in different positions each time she saw them, but the stationary pieces—castles, camps, villages, and such—were unmoved, except a few that had obviously been conquered since she last looked. Someone was playing a complex game that was taking a very long time.

Penn joined her shortly, his arm free of its sling, though he still took care not to strain the mended bone. Several camp healers had helped Maya treat the humerus bone, and it had healed faster than any breaks she'd treated before. She wasn't sure whether to chalk that up to magic or a miracle. Or perhaps the two were really one and the same.

"What were you up to all day?" Maya couldn't keep from asking the viscount, curiosity mingling with hurt. He'd been absent more and more lately.

"Oh, just training." He shrugged.

"With your arm still mending?"

He flashed her a mysterious sort of grin. "Not that kind of training."

"Wha—"

Ter poked his head between the second set of flaps and offered his customary ear twitch. "Ah, there you are. Come in, come in."

Forgetting Penn's dodge, Maya hurried forth. Owenekiras Rokahn had rarely been in camp since the search for her twin had commenced. He'd returned late last night, and word had spread across the massive war camp like a wildfire—he'd found the lost dragon near Oceana.

Lost dragon. It was what everyone called Mikoneh. Maya wasn't sure how to feel about the title; it was strangely distancing—but it brought a strong motivation to the teams seeking him out.

Entering the council chamber, Maya expected to find all the war leaders present, but Owenekiras Rokahn stood at the far end of the obsidian table, alone except for Ter. The Rokahnian prince had been stooped over a map spread across the smooth stone surface, but he looked up now, piercing Maya with a cold, penetrating stare. He looked as solemn as ever.

"Is it true?" she asked, setting her fist over her heart. "Did you find him?"

"Briefly, yes." The words were spoken softly. He straightened to his considerable height. "Please sit."

She shook her head. "I can't. I'm too anxious. What happened? Where is he?"

Penn took her arm, saying nothing. His quiet support lent her a sense of calm she couldn't find on her own. Keeping her eyes on the Dragon King, she waited for him to speak.

"Shall I?" asked Ter.

"No," Owenekiras said. "I will explain. As ruler of the dragons, I have a special connection to each. It isn't something to abuse but can be useful in times of distress such as this. I've been reaching out to locate your brother since he was taken, but Sathe has been careful. Fortunately, the stronger a dragon's blood—the more awake—the harder it is to keep them hidden from me. Sathe has been working to bring Mikoneh under his control, which has become a double-edged sword. The Mage general would know the danger, but your brother is useless to him without that dragon blood fully awakened."

Maya frowned. "I thought he didn't want him for his dragon blood."

Owenekiras hesitated. It was a slight thing; she almost missed it. "It's not because he's a dragon, in general, but because of his particular bloodline. Your family is special among dragonkin."

That was one of the puzzle pieces she'd been missing. "So, you found him with this connection?"

"Yes. From a distance. He was flying." Did Owenekiras's lips twitch upward? "The sheer joy of it stirred the deepest of his dragon instincts, and for a moment he was a beacon. I reached out, and he answered. He showed me where he was. My connection to my subjects is unique, and Sathe couldn't intercept our conversation. Unfortunately, Mikoneh's thoughts are not his own, and Sathe can command him to speak. The Mage will know by now that I've located their warren. They'll be on the move." A smile did curl across his lips now. "Which is to our advantage."

Ter chuckled. "True, that. Sathe cannot waste more time trying to secure his control over Mikoneh. He must act, and after Suld's defeat in the North—and the Mage Queen's subsequent flight into deeper mountain holes—Sathe dares not join his fellows in that direction. He must head for the interior of Oceana."

"Ah," Penn said. "You're forcing him to surface where he has fewer Mage allies."

"It's not without risks to us," Owenekiras said. "But yes, that's the general idea." His gaze fell on Maya again. "The greatest threat is Sathe's grip on your twin. If we can separate them, I can sever their connection, but it must be in person. I cannot do it at a distance."

"And," Ter said, his ears drooping, "it must be done before Sathe is killed—or your brother will suffer a blow that is difficult for even the strongest dragon to endure." His voice softened. "Lost bonds are most painful, even those between a Dark Mage and a dragon."

Maya clenched her hands at her sides. "I'm coming. Please. I can't stay here, not knowing whether I'll ever see Mikoneh again. I know it's dangerous, and I promise not to run off and get myself captured. I just...I need to be there. To help somehow."

Ter glanced at Owenekiras whose gaze remained on her.

"Maya," Penn whispered. "This is beyond either of us."

"No," Owenekiras said. "She's right to request this. I intended to bring her."

Penn stiffened. "But—"

"Why?" asked Maya, just as dumbfounded.

"Because you will be safer nowhere else." A hardness entered Owenekiras's eyes. "I allowed your brother outside my view for a matter of moments, and he was captured. I'll not repeat that—not with reports that Minno is near this camp, along with several other unsavory threats."

Maya's heart throbbed. The gray boy had come here? But why? He'd been warned off back in Kenooshin.

"That said," the Dragon King continued, "you must swear on the bones of Jonatten and Seranni that you will do precisely as I say, and under *no* circumstances whatsoever will you leave my view. Not if your twin screams for aid or Penn is dying half a castle away. Do I make myself clear?"

"Pristinely," she said. "I swear to your conditions on my parents' bones, and on my brother's soul. I'll do nothing to jeopardize him or anyone else."

"Thank you." Owenekiras began rolling up the map. "We leave for Oceana in one full turn. Be ready at the southern gate." His gaze flicked to Penn. "You as well. Your knowledge of Oceanean nobility may be required."

"I understand. Thank you." Penn tugged Maya toward the flap. She followed willingly, long legs carrying her across the room.

"We're going to save him," she whispered. "Penn, we're going to save him."

"That we are."

They stepped outside, and Maya faltered. The Wind Master, Hilker, stood with one hand extended, like he'd been about to draw the flaps aside to enter. His crooked smile appeared.

"Ah. Lady of Wind, lovely day for a training bout."

She shook her head. "I'm sorry, Master Hilker. I can't. I'm going to save my twin." She pulled Penn along after her and never looked back.

CHAPTER 41

SEARCHING FOR A STOLEN NAME

"Despite the Nijaalin Council's efforts to block the way into the Complété, the Mage Queen meant to enter that realm at any price."

- From Athonen d'Ereth's *The Fall of Mages in the Age of Dragons*

Sathe guided Mikoneh along the infinite tunnels. Somehow, Mikoneh knew it was nighttime when they left the network he'd become familiar with to travel eastward. Since flying, he could sometimes hear the sky, as though the stars sang to him. Whether that was only in his head didn't matter. He was grateful for any connection to the world above, and to any measurement of time.

A long trail of cloaked Mages followed them, some skeletal, some with varying levels of flesh. If Reven was anywhere nearby, Mikoneh couldn't tell. He wasn't willing to stretch his senses and draw Sathe's notice to his interest in the Revenant.

Nor was he inclined to think about his gnawing hunger. He hadn't eaten more than a few mouthfuls of dry bread in two days—Sathe's latest torture fixation.

Instead, he tried to level his thoughts on the cold dankness around him.

To breathe in the mineral scent and ground himself.

Keep walking. Just walk.

They marched for several turns. None of the Mages showed any weariness. Mikoneh did his best to hide his, but at last, he stumbled. His meager portions of food and water, coupled with Sathe's torture, had weakened him more than he'd suspected. Sinking to his knees, he concentrated on deep breaths. The stale air hung close and confining.

Sathe knelt beside him and snatched a lock of Mikoneh's hair. The Mage tugged it hard. "Tired, are you?"

"Just...need a moment..."

"Thirsty, then?" Sathe whispered in his ear, needling his flesh. "Rise, Firebrand. I will give you water at the next bend."

It was motivation enough. Somehow, Mikoneh pushed to his feet and staggered on. But the next bend didn't come. The tunnel continued straight.

Playing mind games, huh?

He focused on the path, nothing else. One step. Another. His tongue was dry as sand.

Doesn't matter. Listen to the stars.

But when he stretched his senses, he couldn't feel them. Had the sun come up? That was likely. They'd been walking for a long time.

He stumbled on a jutting root in the path.

Roots? We can't be too far beneath the surface, then, right?

He imagined the sun rising directly above him. The world sparkled with dew. Birds sang their dawn greetings to each other, winging across the wide, pale sky. A deer loped across a meadow toward the safe shelter of the trees.

"Enough." Sathe's voice shattered the daydream. "We'll rest here."

Mikoneh blinked in the semi-gloom, readjusting to his night vision.

Sathe pointed at a shadow against the wall. "There's a door. Go inside. Wait for me."

Glad for a chance to sit, Mikoneh found the lever hidden in the stone door and pushed it inward. The room beyond was large, filled with pallets likely meant for prisoners in transit. He moved inside and chose the closest one. Rolling onto his back, he stared at the root-webbed ceiling. The taste of loam settled on his tongue, and the rich fragrance of earth filled his nostrils.

He closed his eyes and let his mind drift where it wished. Sleep took him gently, pulling him into a soft velvet darkness, away from his sore muscles, his hunger, his helplessness.

HE WOKE TO SILENCE. Sitting up, Mikoneh adjusted his eyes and peered around the room. Sathe had taken another pallet, though he'd tossed aside the worn blanket and wore his outer robe like a coverlet. The Mage slept deeply. His chest rose and fell, and Mikoneh felt no sense of awareness from him.

Licking his cracked lips, Mikoneh eased his legs from his pallet and positioned himself to face the Mage. He interlaced his fingers and rested them against his knees, leaned forward, and concentrated.

This wasn't his first attempt to enter the Mage's soul. He didn't dare force his way inside. He had to walk the familiar channels Sathe had carved between their souls. It was delicate work. One wrong spiritual step and he would alert Sathe to his presence. It didn't take a genius to know the punishment for that would be more severe than anything he'd experienced yet. Instead of a town, what might Sathe make him destroy?

Maya. It would be Maya.

He didn't close his eyes. He needed to make certain Sathe stayed asleep, so he let his inner soul work on its own. The sensation was peculiar, as though he were a solitary flame walking corridors made of ice. He didn't belong in Sathe's soul any more than the Mage belonged in his. The wrongness was deep. The bond was twisted and sickening fast.

He didn't know how to go about searching for a stolen name, but if any piece of the Revenant dwelt inside Sathe, surely, Mikoneh would sense the difference; find some piece of his aura.

Will it be like Reven's soul or like his slumbering body?

That Mikoneh didn't know. But he could guess.

A true name suggested one's truest self. Not a tainted form, damaged by years of captivity. He was searching for a bright light in the dark cloisters of Sathe's soul. That gave him renewed hope, and he plunged ahead, determined to search every level one by one.

It won't be near the surface. Sathe wouldn't be that careless.

The passageways of the soul seemed endless, but Mikoneh didn't like to give up. He pressed on, taking corners, descending stairs, searching the darkest nooks. He recognized that his mind was conjuring a realm that he could fathom as he searched. The soul wasn't really made up of hallways and chambers, but he was grateful for the substantiveness of it. Hopefully, it would guide him right.

He slammed into a wall. Black ink bled from the surface, staining his flaming shape. He flinched back, then gasped. Sathe was waking.

He wrenched himself from Sathe, unsure how to avoid

leaving footprints behind. The Mage jerked upright. Mikoneh blinked, trying to center himself on his own body. His limbs tingled.

Sathe turned toward him with narrowed eyes. "Did you—"

"Please," Mikoneh rasped. "I need water." He slumped against the pallet, glad of his faintness. It might spare him a little of Sathe's wrath.

Cold fingers caught his chin. "Did you wander into my soul, little Firebrand?"

So tired. He hadn't expected such a toll. "I didn't...mean to. I was searching for water." He didn't focus on the words, just let them run from his mouth.

Sathe grunted. "Poor thing. You're delirious, aren't you?"

Maybe he was, maybe he wasn't. It hardly mattered. Mikoneh stayed still, waiting for whatever came next. His soul felt heavy in his frail body.

Water trickled into his mouth. He jerked upright, clutching for the container that held it. Sathe relinquished the flask. Mikoneh drank deeply, not caring if it made him sick. The water tasted metallic, but it was cold, and he drained the flask. His stomach lurched, but the water stayed put. Though his body still felt weighed down, he remained vertical and planted his gaze on Sathe.

"Are we leaving soon?"

"Yes, but eat first." Sathe drew a pouch from his outer robe. "I'll give you something more filling when we reach the next stop."

Mikoneh accepted the pouch, scenting beef. He loosened the drawstring and found dried meat within. It took only a few breaths to devour every crumb, then Sathe offered him a second water flask. He drained half of that.

"You need to be more vigilant," Sathe said. "Even if you're tired, wandering into my soul could destroy your mind. Have a care." He frowned. "I will be more vigilant, too."

Mikoneh took another drink, refusing to focus on the Mage's words. He lowered the flask and sloshed it. "We're heading for Oceana, aren't we?"

Sathe said nothing.

"Is the Revenant coming?"

The Mage huffed through his nose. "You're rather fixated on him. Should I be jealous?"

Mikoneh scowled at the floor. "Jealousy is a waste of energy."

The man chuckled. "Such a practical soul for one with so much buried fury." He caught Mikoneh's chin and stared into his eyes, as though he searched for something. "Still...I don't understand."

Mikoneh pulled his head free. "What?"

"What he has against you."

"Who? Minno?"

"No. Never mind." Sathe rose from the pallet and stretched his arms. He then slipped his outer robe back on. "It will be good to feel the sun again. Our next stop will bring us to our destination in a blink. One last long walk, Firebrand—then we're safe."

Mikoneh frowned. His stomach churned again, though the water had settled.

Don't think. Just rest.

His thoughts drifted—until he realized he was in a strange place. Not Sathe's soul. This felt different. The corridors were murkier, less distinct. Strange words and images flashed before him in a peculiar pattern.

Faces, familiar and unfamiliar, danced before him—including himself, sitting like he sat now upon the pallet. He jolted. This was Sathe's mind, rather than his soul.

Maybe this is the answer.

Balancing his attunement, he hovered between his own body and mind, aware of both, half-conscious of each.

Step carefully.

If he could witness what Sathe was thinking about in this moment, maybe he could stir up an answer. He shifted his body. The Mage had moved back to his own pallet, knelt, and was riffling through a satchel Mikoneh hadn't noticed before.

"You didn't answer my question about the Revenant."

Sathe paused but kept his back toward Mikoneh. "Be careful. I am a jealous man, no matter your feelings on the subject."

A crimson glow flickered in the Mage's mind. Mikoneh's vision teetered, torn as he was between two planes. He clenched his hands and persisted. "I'm not trying to gall you," he said. "I just want to know what's going to happen to him."

"Why would anything happen to him?" Sathe turned, his lips twisted in a cruel smile. "He's *mine*, just as you are." There. Something else flickered across the Mage's mind. A shape like wings, silvery in color, chained by crimson tendrils. Was that it?

Mikoneh reached for it, but the image vanished.

Sathe stood up and moved closer. "I can feel you, Mikoneh. Be careful. You'll become trapped if you delve too deep." He squatted before him. "Looking for something specific?"

"You're the one drawing me in," Mikoneh growled. "I don't know what I'm doing or not doing."

Sathe blinked. "I suppose that could be. Still, try a little harder not to pry. I'm a rather private man."

"Yeah? Me, too."

The Mage chuckled. "That fire. How it moves me." He stood up and strode toward the door. "Let's be on our way. You've rested long enough."

Staggering to his feet, Mikoneh tried to maintain the faint

connection between their minds without concentrating on it. It seemed to stay in place, and Sathe didn't notice or didn't care. They moved into the earthen tunnel, and the door closed behind them. The crowd of cloaked Mages stood waiting as though they'd remained there the entire time Mikoneh had slept. Perhaps they had.

He took his place behind Sathe, and the Mage led out.

Mikoneh watched his feet and strode along the dank passage, occupying himself with thoughts of Maya and Penn in their camp days. Even Kevva—despite what she'd done—shared a piece of his fond remembrances. Things hadn't been easy, but they'd been familiar, and he'd settled into a life he could be proud of. The rebels had looked to him upon Fa and Mama's deaths, confident he could pick up where they'd left off. He'd prayed he could, and he'd persevered despite his cosseted doubts.

Maya's illness had been a heartbreaking weight, but she'd fought her way through the darkness. That was a hope he clung to now—that if Maya could come back from something that devastating, he could conquer this. It was nothing to losing their parents.

Penn's friendship had meant a lot, too. At first, Mikoneh had scorned the viscount. Penn had been found wandering in the forest and brought in blindfolded. He'd been so earnest in his request to join the rebels, but few had argued in his favor. Maya had, though. So had Kevva.

Kevva.

The young woman who'd betrayed their army. Sold them out to Drayve—and for what? Some jewels and a chance to play mistress until the lord of the keep discarded her?

Flames sparked in Mikoneh's chest. He'd trusted her above few others. They'd fought together. Laughed together. She'd even claimed to love him—though he'd never returned her feelings. That was what had set her off, and that conditional loyalty infuriated him most. He'd tried to let her down gently; he'd thanked her for her declaration, but he couldn't reciprocate. He'd hoped she could understand.

She'd said she did. That it was fine. She'd only wanted him to know.

And then Drayve's forces had found them. Kevva had been among the lord's soldiers, cloaked in furs, gowned in jewels, looking every bit like the haughty ladies she'd always claimed to despise. Her green eyes had flashed when she'd looked at him, and a sneer had curled her lips, destroying her natural beauty.

Kevva had never said a word, but her message was clear: This had been a personal attack against Mikoneh. She wanted him to suffer for spurning her, no matter what it cost—and the cost had been enormous. From her horse, she'd witnessed Mikoneh and his forces battle, until all but two dozen had fallen within their own camp.

At last, heartsick and furious, Mikoneh had surrendered.

How was she faring now? Did she regret her betrayal, or had she convinced herself that she'd been right to forsake their cause? Had Drayve tired of her yet?

"Fascinating," Sathe said. "I'd wondered about your relationship with that woman." He paused and glanced over his shoulder. The rows of lesser Mages halted and waited in silence. "She swore up and down to Drayve that she'd been earning your trust for months, unable to leave camp until then. She's a convincing liar, I'll allow."

Mikoneh snorted. "Among other things."

"I'm surprised you didn't destroy her when you came into your element." The Mage started to walk again, a swagger in his steps. "I'd have thrown an extra fireball or something and melted her face, at the least."

"I was a little preoccupied with escaping," Mikoneh muttered.

The Mage's chuckle had a little warmth in it. "So I witnessed. You certainly shook Drayve's court. It was quite a spectacle."

"I'm surprised you didn't just claim me at my trial. Or did Drayve refuse to give me to you?"

Sathe shrugged without looking back. "I didn't ask. I had to be certain you were the one I sought. I'd heard about your *parents*, and my source was reliable, but facing certain death has a way of bringing out one's potential. You awakened, and I thought it best you left Relvin before I swooped in. It wouldn't do to let Drayve know all that I am."

"Yet we're returning to Oceana. Plan to hide me from him in the dungeons?"

Sathe scoffed. "That backwater province holds no interest for me now. We're going to King Nilo's court. There, we'll be treated with proper deference."

Mikoneh's step faltered. The king's court?

Sathe spun and caught his chin in one hand. "Just *try* and report that to the voice in your head. See what I do then."

Mikoneh's temper flashed. He knocked Sathe's hand aside. "I get it."

"Good." Sathe's lips curved up in a self-satisfied smile, then he turned around and kept walking. "You know, I'm not opposed to helping you."

"With what?" Mikoneh's voice was a low growl.

"Dragons are the greatest justicers in the universe, you know. It would be a pity not to exact vengeance on that red-haired girl. Kevva, right?"

"Justice and vengeance aren't the same thing."

"Either way." Sathe's voice took on a thread of glee. "I could help."

"Thanks, but no thanks. I'll see to my own debts."

"Suit yourself."

Mikoneh was grateful that Sathe lapsed into silence after that. He returned to his reflections, determined to think of nothing that might amuse the Mage. He settled on battles Fa had taught him—things that were part of history, so, surely, not of interest to Sathe.

He was mulling over a particularly gruesome battle, reviewing the brilliant pincer move he could visualize well enough to believe he was part of the fight. The glowing blue aura of the swaying grass. The gleaming armor and the dark green heraldry of the enemy. The battle horns blowing.

Sathe's boots scuffed the grit, then he whirled, golden eyes bright with something between fear and wonder.

"How do you know of that?"

Mikoneh fumbled for an explanation. "My father taught—"

"Impossible. No one of this age remembers the Battle of the Elemeer Plain—not anymore."

His throat cinched. "But—" His mind stumbled back into memories of Fa's lessons. Along with weapons training, he'd gone over dozens, maybe hundreds of battles and skirmishes.

But none by that name.

His skin bristled. Thinking over it, Fa had never mentioned that battle strategy.

Did I dream it?

Sathe was studying him like he might study a piece of fruit he'd never seen. He stepped closer, intrigue curling the edges of his mouth upward.

"I didn't understand," the Mage whispered. "I still don't. But..." He pressed his fist to his lips. "You *are* a dragon—but still young. Too young." He caught Mikoneh's shoulder and dug his fingers into his sleeve. "You were raised by Jonatten and Seranni, yes?"

"Yes," Mikoneh growled.

"From boyhood?"

"All my life."

"Transform."

"Wha—"

"No." Sathe glanced around the tunnel. "Not here. This way." He dragged Mikoneh after him, quickening their pace. The clacking bones of the lesser Mages' feet grew louder. Sathe's emotions were a tangle Mikoneh couldn't unravel— and wasn't sure he wanted to. Sathe didn't let them stop; they pushed on until the dried meat Mikoneh had eaten had been burned up, and Mikoneh felt on the verge of collapse. But he gritted his teeth and kept moving.

Turns passed. A kind of coolness settled over Mikoneh, like he could feel the sun setting. And then, Sathe turned a sharp corner. Ahead of them, two great monolith doors stretched to a high ceiling, carved in runes glowing deep purple. Flanked by torches that burned with their cold, violet flames. Guarded by Mages whose faces were more flesh than bone, though still rotten.

Sathe quickened his step again, lifting his free arm in a broad wave. The guards turned toward the door and set their mottled hands on encircled runes carved at heart level. The runes flashed bright violet, and the doors rumbled open to admit Sathe's entourage.

Beyond stretched a wide stone chamber. A distant ceiling was held up by beautifully carved pillars in a circle, with two columns of pillars flanking an open corridor leading toward the room's center.

The chamber was brightly lit by torches made of orange

fire, as well as the violet of Hollow. Sathe led Mikoneh across the smooth floor between the columns. Fire spirits turned toward Mikoneh and crackled greetings. He managed a limp smile, too preoccupied by Sathe's peculiar reaction to manage more. Why was the Mage so unsettled by his knowledge—and why did Mikoneh know about an untold battle from a long-ago age on a plain he'd never heard of?

The pillars ended before a broad circular space. The stone floor was decorated with complex runes defining circles within circles, from the edges of the space, all the way to its center where an altar stood.

Mikoneh tensed and pulled at Sathe's grasp. The Mage glanced at him with a devious smile.

"Relax, Firebrand. We're not here for that—not today." Sathe tugged with more gentleness than Mikoneh expected, and he allowed himself to be led to one of the inner circles of runes. Sathe stopped near the altar, outside the deepest rings of scrawl magic.

The contingent of lesser Mages hovered beyond the circular space, keeping to the pillared corridor, as though they sought protection from whatever Sathe had in mind.

The Mage leader pulled Mikoneh's attention back to him with a slight jerk. When their eyes met, Sathe's smile was deceptively kind.

"Now, my Firebrand. Transform."

Mikoneh blinked at him. "You want my wings—"

"No. Change into your true form. We must see the truth."

Mikoneh shook his head. "I don't know—"

"Yes, yes. You don't know how. We don't have time to be cautious, and you've adapted well to everything else. This shouldn't be a struggle. You simply don't understand. That's fine. We'll break through the mind block."

He narrowed his eyes.

Transform into your dragon state.

The rumbling command filled Mikoneh's head. Compulsion seized him. Fire scored his veins. His mindset shifted—his thoughts altered.

The world around him grew larger.

CHAPTER 42

THE BLACK KING

"The climactic battle was waged beyond this mortal sphere, somewhere in the World Between, where the fabric enfolding Mithrinn was weakest."

\- From Athonen d'Ereth's *The Fall of Mages in the Age of Dragons*

Never had Mikoneh's vision been so clear and sharp. He stood far below Sathe, looking up into the Mage's startled face. Mikoneh canted his head sideways and let out an inquiring chirp. A spark of fire crawled up his throat and bloomed over the air, too small to harm anything.

Silence rang in Mikoneh's keen ears. He craned his long, scaled neck to view the Mages hovering outside the runes. Every eye socket was pinned on him. Hunger pounded from their auras.

I'm a dragon.

The thought was more of an observation than a revelation. Of course, he was. What else would he be?

He turned back toward Sathe, and his slender midnight-blue tail curled around his haunches.

Sathe crouched down, and Mikoneh's head came slightly higher than the Mage's knee. "I had honestly expected you to be huge."

Mikoneh cocked his head the other way. Why would the Mage assume that? Instinctively, he knew that dragons grew slowly. He was only twenty years old—an infant in their lifespans.

The Mage rubbed his chin, the wheels in his head turning. Then he shrugged. "Well, that destroys my pet theory, but it hardly matters. Change back."

Mikoneh backed away on all four legs. This was *safer*. He didn't want to return to his human form—to his human thoughts and feelings. Too complex. Too heavy. In this form, he could feel his connection to Sathe like chains wrapped around his scaled body. His wings, folded against his sides, quivered with an urge to fly away—but a coiling instinct insisted he must stay. He was bonded to Sathe whether he liked it or not. He belonged to the Mage.

Sathe's lips quirked up. "Fascinating, the difference in your thoughts as a dragon true, isn't it? I recall *his* mind shifts from long ago."

His meant Reven. The specter's image flashed across Sathe's mind, entering Mikoneh's thoughts. Violence choked the small dragon. His instincts—deep, feral—pressed him to lash out at his master, to serve justice for the shackled Revenant. But the feelings were at war with a sense of loyalty—tainted though it was—to stay with Sathe. Even to protect him.

That's what you want from me. Comprehension struck Mikoneh's mind. *I'm your protector.*

Sathe's eyes flashed with amusement. "Close, my Firebrand. But that is only a perk." He strode forward, stooped, and scooped up the small dragon. Butterflies twirled in Mikoneh's stomach. He fit into Sathe's arms like a large cat.

"If you won't transform, I suppose I'll just have to carry you."

You could command me.

Sathe chuckled. "Where's the fun in that?" They moved to the center of the rune rings, and Sathe planted his feet beside the altar. "Brace yourself, Firebrand. Traveling through Hollow is unpleasant for creatures of light." He tapped his foot, issuing a chanting command. Violet light swallowed them.

Pain screamed across Mikoneh's body, turning the fire in his veins into chunks of black ice. He arched his back, letting out a cry that sounded like a pathetic chirp. The blue world flashed before his vision—along with the woman in the white cloak. Sounds from a faraway place filled his memory. Then the violet light dissolved. The pain vanished. He was still clutched in Sathe's arms, a tiny predator chained to a maniac.

They stood in a wide stone corridor lined with tapestries depicting ocean-scapes: cliffs, bays, ships, and tridents. East-facing windows revealed the real coastline blazing red in a spectacular sunset. Mikoneh's wings throbbed, eager to spring into the open sky, with its plumes of gold, purple, and red clouds.

"Later, my Firebrand." Sathe's voice was a soft coo. He ran his fingers through the dragon's mane of blue-black hair. "First, we have an appointment with the king."

Something of Mikoneh's human brain stirred. A king. And this was the eastern coast. Likely within a castle, judging by the solid fortification and the heraldry depicted in the woven tapestries. They were in Nauttia, the Royal Capital of Oceana. This was King Nilo's home. Sathe hadn't been lying.

Fa had said the king was a good man but weak-willed and

easily swayed. Had Nilo caved to the Mages' demands to guard his kingdom from invasion?

Mikoneh needed to transform. To take back his human thoughts. As a baby dragon, he felt small, helpless, and almost glad of it. Fluttering his wings, he escaped Sathe's arms, then swooped down to land several yards ahead in the corridor. He focused on his human side. Tried to reestablish the sensations of his human shape. To recall flesh. Hands. Every part and piece of himself.

His body stretched. His thoughts shifted. The sensation of bones sliding around, rearranging themselves into a familiar shape, felt as natural as his dragon form. Soon, he stood before Sathe, tall and human. Somehow, he was clad. He swayed, exhaustion crushing his flash of rebellion. He staggered sideways and slumped against the cool stone wall. Even his inner flame was spent.

"Why are we here?" he managed to ask.

Sathe's grin stretched impossibly wide. "I told you. Here, we will be truly safe."

"From what? The Dragon King?"

"You think yourself very clever." Sathe's slitted eyes flashed. "You have cause to fear that man as much as I do now. Perhaps it's time to help you understand." The Mage's anger twisted into a dark, gleaming pleasure. "That *man* is no more human than you or I. He's a beast—a dark, violent brute. The only people who have caused as much harm to this world as the Dragon King are his faithful companions. You think Ter N'Avea an innocent little fae, hm? Not so. He's a brutal murderer. A human-killer. He slaughtered entire villages, and he did it with glee. You disbelieve me, I've no doubt. But if ever you see Ter again, look him in the eye and ask if it's not true. He's at least honest enough, he'll not lie to you."

"What's your point?" asked Mikoneh. "I'm not their liegeman. They helped me to escape you. They asked nothing of me. They didn't throw me in chains."

"They have your sister, don't they?" The man's voice was the soft rumble of distant thunder. "Owenekiras views all dragons as his property. That voice you heard when you flew— that was him. He'll not let you escape. If you chose to stay with me of your own volition, he wouldn't let you."

Mikoneh snorted. "I wouldn't blame him for doubting my lucidity, with all your mind games. I doubt it myself."

"Yet you don't question your innate loyalty to *that* man? You should, you know. It's a dragon's curse to be bound to Owenekiras forever. You can't fight it. That connection has existed since the Age of Dragons."

Mikoneh arched his brow. "I didn't realize you were a lunatic. Owenekiras Rokahn isn't that old." He didn't focus on the fact that others had referred to the same fact. That didn't matter just now. Riling Sathe did.

"Ah, but he was there just the same. He traveled across time itself to meet us in our first engagement."

"Like to make yourself sound special, don't you? It's not good form to ride on someone else's cloak hem." Mikoneh was glad he could muster enough bravado to hide the chills nettling his neck and arms. He didn't know why he felt so shaken. Something in the Mage's words unsettled him, something deep and nameless. He didn't doubt Owenekiras or Ter. They weren't the brutes Sathe claimed. This feeling came from some- thing else...

Sathe backhanded his cheek. Hard. Mikoneh's head jerked back and crashed into the stone wall. His vision flashed, but he straightened up fast, aiming a glower at his captor. They eyed each other for a long moment, neither stirring.

At last, Sathe straightened his shoulders. "Be grateful I'm not a petty man."

"Aren't you?"

"No. Believe that."

Mikoneh's eyes narrowed. "Not possible."

Sathe fluted out a breath. "We really don't have time to banter."

"No? I thought we were safe."

"Come along, Firebrand. The king awaits." Sathe shot him a warning look, then brushed his robes back and started along the corridor.

Mikoneh shook his head, trying to dislodge the pounding headache and growing dizziness. He shoved off the wall and started after Sathe, setting a glare on the man's back. He indulged himself with visions of unsheathing his newfound dragon claws and sinking them into the Mage's spine. If Sathe read his mind and saw, Mikoneh didn't care.

They moved along at a quick pace. Mikoneh eventually forced himself to abandon his daydream and look around. This was Nauttia Castle, after all, the oldest standing structure in Oceana. He'd heard about it all his life. Fa had visited once, though he'd never said what business took him to Nauttia.

Was it on an errand for the Dragon King?

Mikoneh might never know.

Fa had described the castle as functional, strong, and stark. Looking past the tapestries, Mikoneh could see what his father had meant. Compared to the grand architecture of Hyanython or the cozy crafting of Kenooshin, this was blocky and crude in design. But then, Oceana's people were that way; meant for tough winters, grueling summers in the fields, and withstanding the sieges of life. There was little by way of gentility or refinement. Oceana was Lintha's insufferable little brother, patiently endured by the other nations of Sirinhigha.

What would King Nilo be like? Why did Sathe want Mikoneh to meet the man?

Mikoneh halted at a window overlooking a courtyard bursting with autumn colors. He gazed out over Nauttia Proper beyond the castle walls. The city spread wide and flat. The buildings were square, made of stone, gray and purposeful. It seemed a pity, all this military crudeness, set against the sparkling sea beyond the city's boundaries. It was like a man-made scar against the earth.

He grimaced and trotted to catch up to Sathe, who'd slowed but not stopped. They quickened their steps again and soon reached a stairhead. They took the flight of steps downward, reached a half-stair landing, and turned to descend the next set of steps.

Where are the guards? And the servants? There should be servants.

"They're already gathered," Sathe said.

Mikoneh's stomach knotted. Gathered for *what?*

The stairs gave way to a spacious room where Mikoneh spotted guards in polished armor standing at intervals, spears propped in hands, helm visors lowered. Sathe swept past them without any reaction on their part.

He really does own Oceana. So then, he'd really been in Relvin Province only for Mikoneh and his sister. Dread hummed in Mikoneh's mind. He had a sneaking suspicion he was about to find out exactly what the Mage wanted with him.

The wide room came to an end where doors—made of thick oak, purely functional—swung aside to admit them into another chamber. Two guards held the doors. Mikoneh caught one eyeing him from behind his visor.

Dragging his attention ahead, Mikoneh tensed. They'd entered the castle's throne room, packed with knights, nobles, and servants. The castle's staff had been assembled, too, judging by their livery. Sathe caught Mikoneh's arm and sent out a ripple of violet light that parted the crowd. Eyes darted toward them, then away. A few gazes were reverent; most were afraid.

They're hostages.

Sathe's fingers tightened around his arm.

They moved toward the throne where King Nilo sat in state. The man was in his sixties, with graying hair that settled around his shoulders, a weathered face from years of seafaring, and stern blue eyes. He was draped in a navy-blue cape lined with white fur. A silver crown crested in sapphires sparkled in the light from several nearby candelabra and the low-hanging iron chandeliers where hundreds of candles winked. Fire spirits perked up among those flames and waved down at Mikoneh.

Nilo was a solid man, like his subjects, but there was a weakness around his jaw. His eyes settled on Sathe as the two approached, and dread lit those depths. He straightened in his throne, yet he somehow looked small before the dark-robed Mage.

"Master, welcome back." Nilo's voice quavered.

"I informed Ligg I would be here today." The Dark Mage glanced at the crowded chamber. "Weren't you expecting me?"

"We were."

"Yet you seem shaken."

Nilo's mouth worked. "Your presence awes me, always, Master." He inclined his head.

Sathe's delight was a palpable thing. "Always so eloquent." He released Mikoneh and pivoted to take in the room's occupants. "Clear the center of the chamber. Make room!" His voice was like a lashing whip. The Oceaneans flinched back, stumbling, bumping into each other in their haste. Gems flashed on ornate bodices and brocaded vests. Despite the king's austerity, his courtiers seemed to enjoy their regalia—for all the good it did, now that they were slaves to Dark Mages.

When the crowd had crushed as far back as it could, Sathe strode into the center of the chamber. Above him, banners rippled in the stray breezes. The silver trident on a navy-blue field glittered, but it meant nothing. Mikoneh frowned. Oceana was no more. No one had to tell him as much. Without so much as a battle or formal surrender, Nilo had sold his people to the enemy.

Sathe held up his hands. "Two years ago, I came here with a promise—and you in turn swore fealty to my beloved queen. You placed your faith in me. Now, it is time to fulfill that promise." He turned his wintry smile on Mikoneh. "Indeed, the spirits have been most kind to Oceana. Without war or bloodshed, you will become the greatest sovereign nation in Sirinhigha. You will withstand the might of even the Black King himself."

Black King. Did he mean Owenekiras Rokahn?

How can you make that promise? You're insane.

Sathe's smile heightened. **Patience, my Firebrand.**

"You have been faithful to your oaths, but of late"—Sathe's eye swooped across the room, landing on several faces in the crowd, lingering—"some of you have reneged. Several have breathed treason against my queen."

One man in the crowd dropped his head, shuddering.

"But my queen is merciful. She offers more chances than are perhaps deserved." Sathe strode to Mikoneh's side. "I promised you a perfect shield. One that would protect you from Owenekiras Rokahn forever." He rested his hand on Mikoneh's shoulder. "Here he is!"

If that was supposed to hearten the crowd, Sathe had miscalculated. The ocean of nobility, gentry, and staff stared back, blank-faced.

Sathe chuckled. "You doubt. After all my brethren and I have done for you, you doubt me still." He heaved a melodramatic sigh. "Very well, a demonstration, then." He dug his nails into Mikoneh's shoulder.

Pull out your wings.

Mikoneh scowled but drew them from his back. They ripped through his jerkin and spread wide. Someone in the crowd screamed. Every eye was fastened on him. Most looked terrified. Some, fascinated. No one dared to move.

"Behold," Sathe said with a flourish of his hand. "A dragon disguised in human form. Fear not, he's my captive and can do you no harm."

Mikoneh shot him a hard look, but the Mage ignored it.

"This is the way to keep the Black King from your borders. Indeed, it is enough to make the dread warlord surrender." Sathe's teeth flashed in his broad grin. "You wonder how that's possible. I see the doubt growing in your eyes. Allow me to enlighten you." Sathe walked around Mikoneh to address the other side of the chamber. "This is not just any dragon. In this man flows the blood of Owenekiras Rokahn himself: He is the Black King's son and heir!"

No. That was a lie. Mikoneh's fists clenched tight. *You're lying to them.*

Sathe twisted to fix a smug smile on him. **It's no lie, Firebrand. Why do you think he tried keeping you safe from me? What other reason could a man like that possibly have? Jonatten and Seranni were your keepers and protectors...until I destroyed them.**

Shivers raced up Mikoneh's skin. He stared at the deranged man before him, torn between denial and horror. Somehow, he knew it was the truth. Sathe wasn't lying. Why else seek out Mikoneh, bind him, torture him, then put him on display to manipulate the world?

Owenekiras Rokahn was his father.

Sathe resumed speaking to the room. "With the prince of

dragons in our possession, no dragon army will dare mount an attack. Soon, Owenekiras Rokahn will issue a formal surrender to spare his heir. And then, King Nilo's forces—combined with Lintha's armies—will march on the world and find no resistance. Already, Mages have secured Rokahn. With your help, Cimin and Simynshin will soon follow. Victory is at hand, my bold allies." He moved before Mikoneh, hands outstretched like some mystic come to proclaim a message to the world.

Mikoneh stared at the back of the Mage's head, his horror sinking deeper.

I won't let you. No way.

He unsheathed his claws and lunged at Sathe.

Kneel.

Mikoneh crashed to his knees on the flagstone floor, hissing at the pain. He glowered up at Sathe looming before him.

"You see?" Sathe laughed. "Caged, he can hurt no one—though a dragon is never tame. Don't come too near."

Mikoneh felt like one of the wild animals he'd seen on display at the Relvin fairs when he was small. The crowds had oohed and ahhed, half afraid, half inspired. Maya had wept to see it. Mikoneh had been indignant. How could people cage another living soul just to collect a few coins?

If Sathe was attempting to sell the crowd on his scheme like some showman, he was failing. His demeanor was too cold, too remote. But then, perhaps that wasn't his game. He didn't need to inflame passions. He seemed to prefer fostering fear.

The Dark Mage stooped and snatched the hair at the nape of Mikoneh's neck. "A quick mind, but a slow learner. You can do nothing to harm me, my little dragon prince. Nothing."

Mikoneh spat in the Mage's face.

Sathe reeled back, releasing him. Wiping at his face with

one wide sleeve, he shrugged at the crowd. No one had dared to laugh or cheer. They were too cowed for that.

"Now that you each understand," Sathe continued, "it's time to answer the call. Send your men to Lintha, Nilo. We begin today to conquer the world."

A smattering of applause was his only answer. Eyes darted between the Mage and his captive dragon. The invisible chains loosened. Mikoneh climbed to his feet and shoved his dark hair from his face.

Sathe turned to the slave on the throne. "Of course, my dragon and I will remain here to oversee the campaign. We must make certain your people live up to your oaths. In the spring, we will head to the North and reunite with my lady queen."

Nilo nodded, a weariness in the gesture. "You are most welcome, Master. You and your dragon." His eyes flicked toward Mikoneh, then away at once. "Oceana is yours."

Interlude V
All Creatures Have One

"No song shall ever be as fair as the music of her silver soul."

- From the Corpse Poet's 15th Sonnet

THE WORLD WAS QUIET. He stood on the swell of a hill, overlooking the flickering campfires of dozens of armies. She stood at his side, white cloak tinted blue in the soft glow of a midnight sky.

"I can't find his name," Mikoneh whispered.

"Whose?"

"That's just the trouble. I don't know it. It's been stolen."

"Ah. Where are you looking?"

"The Mage's mind." He couldn't recall his captor's name. It was as though the name didn't exist for him in the here and now.

"Don't look there. A name isn't kept in one's mind."

Mikoneh cracked a crooked smile. "Yours is."

She looked at him from beneath her cowl. "Is it?"

He paused. "No. You're right. That's not where to keep a name." He set a hand over his chest. "But what if the Mage doesn't have a heart?"

"All creatures have one." The woman sighed. "But we fill ours with different things. Some with love and kindness. Others with greed and ruin."

"And prisoners." Mikoneh squared his shoulders. "Then I know what to do."

"Always." Her voice was fond.

CHAPTER 43

DRAGONKIN

"The Mage Queen pierced the core—the very heart—of the fabric. The Complété shattered."

\- From Athonen d'Ereth's *The Fall of Mages in the Age of Dragons*

Two days later, Sathe brought Mikoneh to one of the castle turrets to witness the armies marching from Nauttia.

The castle sat on a bluff overlooking the eastern ports. The city was in a crescent shape hugging the gradual slope leading to the castle on the westside. A thick autumnal forest covered the western lands. Nauttia was huge, with flat-roofed structures, market plazas, and roads cut in squares making the city a uniform pattern that led out to deep, high walls. The bluffs on the eastside kept Nauttia secure from a siege from the sea. It was an impressive, if austere, sight.

"Beautiful, isn't it?" the Mage breathed, leaning against an eastern merlon to peer down at the mustering forces.

"It won't work." Mikoneh refused to watch the marching rows pouring from the garrison built near the castle walls.

"What won't, precisely?" Sathe flashed a patient smile edged with frost.

"I'm not a good hostage." Mikoneh shrugged. "Do you really think that a man who didn't even raise me will surrender everything—just give up on his ideals and principles—for his estranged heir? He gave me away, for glory's sake."

Sathe chuckled. "You don't understand dragonkin connections, Firebrand. Least of all your father. Owenekiras Rokahn is *bound* to protect his kin—and he sent you to be raised by his most trusted generals, far, far away from the fighting. That isn't a man who shucked his responsibility because you were an inconvenience."

"That's not in keeping with what you said before." Mikoneh twisted toward him, folding his arms. "You said he was using me and Maya."

Sathe rolled his eyes. "Yes, yes. I *lied*. I had hoped to turn your loyalty, but it occurred to me in the throne room that I'll need to break you another way. Rokahns are just too stubborn."

"I'd say sorry," Mikoneh growled, "but I'm not."

"That I don't doubt."

They turned back to the gleaming rows of armored soldiers far below—thousands of them, bearing the Trident heraldry of Oceana. Gulls sang overhead, speaking of the sea. The scent of brine and autumn flowers filled the mild air. An early winter had descended upon Relvin Province, destroying meager crops, but not here. In Nauttia, the weather was fair, and the trees were fully aflame with golden colors.

"What do you want with Sirinhigha?" asked Mikoneh. He

preferred to dwell on the current issue before him, rather than on the revelations of his heritage. He didn't know where to begin with those.

"Simple. To rule."

Mikoneh rolled his eyes. "You're not a complicated man, are you?"

"No," Sathe agreed. "Complications annoy me."

"I can see that."

"Scorn my goals, Firebrand. I don't care."

"I'm not asking you to." Mikoneh turned from the view and stared out at the eastern ocean. Warships lined the harbors, not set to sail for Lintha until the following day. A few fishing boats were returning from their early morning trawling. "I just don't understand hungering for power."

"Oh, no?" Sathe scoffed. "Yet you did just that in Relvin."

Tightness gripped Mikoneh's chest. "That wasn't the same."

"Wasn't it?"

Mikoneh spun toward Sathe, temper flaring. "I was seeking to end tyranny, not place myself on top. I didn't want to rule."

"You did rule, though. An entire army, in fact."

"By necessity."

Sathe shrugged. "You can't tell me you didn't enjoy commanding your men."

"I *didn't.*" Heat licked at his words. "I hated every command that sent my men to their deaths. If I was proud of anything, it was in our victories—few though they were. They were hard won. And I understand better now why. I wasn't fighting Drayve at all. I was fighting you."

"Astute." Sathe leaned close. "Yes, you played a real-life form of Fang and Claw against me, even then. No board, no pieces—just blood and brains. And it was delightful. At times, you surprised me. Some of your methods were—complex—for one of your experience. Even with Jonatten's training, you shouldn't have done so well. *However*, you're still barely a man. And I've won."

"You cheated."

Sathe blinked. "How?"

Mikoneh leveled a look on him. "I saw your dreams last night. *You* convinced Kevva to sell us out. You promised her power and the opportunity to spite me."

"And it worked. That's not cheating. It's warfare."

"It's dishonorable."

Sathe barked out a laugh that could freeze flame. "You think I care about honor? I'm a *Dark Mage*, Mikoneh Rokahn." He took a step closer and caught the front of Mikoneh's fresh jerkin. Pulling the gray fabric, he dragged Mikoneh near. "The wide world isn't what Jonatten, Thane of Marcress, made it out to be. There are more liars, thieves, and cutthroats than there are honorable folk. It's a harsh lesson, but one I suggest you learn swiftly, my naïve little dragon. We're all out for ourselves. Even you. Yes, yes—your sister matters, but even that's selfish. It's for your sake, for your heart, that you protect her so fiercely. It's all about you."

His grin stretched wide. His breath smelled like snow. "It's all about me, too, Firebrand. And now that you're mine, it will never be about you again—except perhaps in your efforts to preserve yourself and keep your mind intact."

"I'll find a way to kill you, Sathe." Mikoneh hefted his chin. "My oath on that."

Sathe's laugh curled icy breath around Mikoneh's face. "I look forward to your efforts—and doling out my punishments."

A child's voice cut through the tense atmosphere. "I think that would be foolhardy on both your parts, if you seek an outside opinion."

Mikoneh jerked around to blink at Ter. The youthful Ephe'ahn was sitting on a flat merlon along the crenelated turret. His boots swung idly, and his long ears were perked up. His large blue eyes caught the golden sunrise and shone. He was garbed in his customary woodland clothes of green and brown, with a quiver of arrows at his back.

"*You*," hissed Sathe.

Ter's ears twitched. "Me." His tone was chipper.

The Mage dragged Mikoneh behind him. "This dragon is mine. You'll not touch him. Our bond is forged."

"So I see on all counts." Ter's lips curled up. "I wouldn't *dream* of touching him. I'm only here to confirm things."

"You've given yourself away," sneered the Mage.

"Did you truly not expect us to seek you here?" Ter tipped his head to one side. "That was silly of you—and I never took you for the silly sort. My mistake."

Sathe's cheeks flared with the first tinge of color Mikoneh had ever seen there, even when the man was raging. Satisfaction curled in Mikoneh's chest, but he didn't let it grow.

"I'm stuck, Ter," he said. "I can't do anything to disobey him."

"Yes." Ter nodded sagely. "That I also see." His eyes ran between them, as though he followed invisible chains.

"Then flit back and tell your *master*," Sathe said. "Tell him Mikoneh is *mine*, and any attempt to stop the armies of Lintha and Oceana will result in terrible pain for his son and heir."

Ter offered a slow blink, then the blue of his irises flashed red. "So. You told him." Somehow, the rime in his voice was colder than Sathe's tones. "That was foolish."

Sathe snorted. "The hatchling has a right to know his heritage."

"Not from slime, he doesn't." Ter's ears flicked down. "You have no right to a Rokahn at all, you maggot." He bounded from the merlon and marched forward, eyes truly red and burning with wrath. For a moment Ter seemed taller—though still not the height of a grown man. Despite that, the diminutive fae sent Sathe back several steps. Mikoneh had to fall back, too, until he pressed against the crenel behind him, chest tight. Instinct insisted he flee. He ignored it.

"Be very careful, Sathe," Ter growled. "One careless move and you'll *wish* I'd cut your throat this moment rather than left you to Owenekiras's justice. Bear that in mind as you *handle* Mikoneh's soul." He drew back, hopped onto the nearest merlon, and leapt from the turret.

Mage and dragon stared into the air where Ter had disappeared from view. Neither moved for a long moment. Then Sathe whirled on Mikoneh and struck his face hard enough that Mikoneh jerked sideways. His cheek and jaw burned. The tang of copper filled his mouth. He straightened and glared at the Mage, biting back a foul word.

"Get inside," Sathe commanded. "Best not let you out in the open." His eyes darted over the city circling them.

"Scared, Sathe?" Mikoneh wiped blood from a cut on his upper lip.

"Don't mock me." Sathe snagged his collar and yanked him close. "Do *not* infuriate me."

"Ter already did both."

Mikoneh anticipated the icy pain in his veins—but it was still enough to slam him to his knees. His vision turned white. A kick followed, right in his ribs. He grunted, slumping over. A cough followed. His vision seeped back in slowly. He found Sathe's robes pooling before him.

"Up," barked the Mage.

Mikoneh gritted his teeth and hefted himself to his feet. His knees burned beneath his trousers. A scrape on his palm stung. He barely noticed. "I thought you said you were safe here. You told me they wouldn't come."

Sathe ground his teeth, his hand lifting as though he would strike again. Mikoneh willed himself not to flinch. He stood erect and waited, daring the Mage to hit him. A breath later, Sathe lowered his arm.

"I said to go inside. I believe your *father* will hesitate to make a move. Likely Ter was sent only to confirm the extent of our bond. What he saw should suffice. But I'll not take chances."

Mikoneh smirked. "True. Ter did say to be careful."

The blow to his temple struck before he saw it. Black suns exploded before his eyes, but he stayed upright.

You will remain silent.

The command was absolute. Mikoneh sealed his lips, then offered another smirk before he aimed for the trapdoor that led to a spiral staircase. He moved into the shadows of the turret interior, satisfied with his defiance, no matter how dizzy he felt. It was worth it.

He was kept in the bedchamber he shared with Sathe all day. Despite his aching ribs and wrung-out nerves, he couldn't sit still. Instead, he paced, determined to wear out the blue rug that spread across a sitting area. Sathe was content to watch him, perhaps amused by Mikoneh's animal behavior.

I don't care.

It wasn't a lie. He had no energy and no desire to give a single thought to his captor. Let the man rot like his fellows. Let the world burn for a turn or two. Mikoneh needed to think, and he had to do it purely on instinct. So, he paced, turning back, forth, back. Content to let his mind wander where it would.

"You're making me tired." Sathe's voice sliced through him.

"*Good.*" Mikoneh hadn't been sure he could talk yet, but the magic of Sathe's command was apparently gone.

"That lip is swollen. Come here."

Mikoneh stomped harder, quicker. He pivoted and paced the other way. "Is this what my life is going to be now? Hidden away in a castle tower like some hearth-tale's pox-rotted damsel?"

Sathe snorted. "If the damsel had the pox, I doubt very much any self-respecting dread lord would keep her in his tower. She'd be in the dungeon."

"Big difference."

"There is the matter of relative cleanliness."

Mikoneh chose a different section of the large rug to stamp down under his bare feet. "You're dodging my question." He refused to look toward the Mage, even for a breath.

"It's temporary, Firebrand." Sathe's voice was smooth, as though he'd not recently lost his temper. "Once the message of your circumstance sinks in, Owenekiras will send word, agreeing to my terms. He will stand back, at last, to allow a new age to descend upon Sirinhigha." Under his breath, he murmured, "That will satisfy the Mage Queen."

"I don't know how you can be so sure." Mikoneh turned toward the Mage, setting a glare on the pale man. "I'm *one* person."

"We've been over this. You overestimate your sire's sense of honor. He will bend. He's taken such great pains to protect you and your sister."

"But if—" He bit back the words.

Sathe smiled, reading them all the same. "True, Firebrand. He has an heir in your lovely sister—so why bother with you?

Were he a Mage, I would concur. I would have taken Windfall along with you as added insurance. But Owenekiras isn't a Mage. He's a dragon—and dragons *care*. You're his brood. His blood. Possibly, he even loves you."

"He doesn't know me."

"He knew you when you were small. And besides, aren't people sentimental toward those born from their love? Especially if they tragically lose their lover?"

Something twisted inside Mikoneh's chest. A wall rose in his mind. He didn't want to think about that. He didn't want to know. If a woman besides Seranni was his mother—if none of this was rot—he didn't want to know.

Why not? That isn't fair to the woman who birthed you.

Yet the feeling remained, despite his logic. Despite the fleeting nudge of curiosity. Something deeper, stronger, willed him not to know.

"You're an odd one." Sathe lifted a goblet to his lips and sipped.

Mikoneh didn't bother responding. He took up his pace again, hands cupped behind his back. "So, Mages don't care about their young?"

"Most of us don't breed."

"Thank the Nijaal for little blessings," Mikoneh muttered. "But how do you keep your numbers up—"

"We're nearly immortal, or hadn't you noted the fleshless ones?"

"Oh, I noticed." Mikoneh pinched his earlobe, trying not to focus on the underground horrors. His mind landed on a different horror instead. "Why don't you forge an army made up of Revenants? The one you have seems more useful than your emaciated forces in their entirety."

"He's truly a work of art, isn't he? One of my best. Unfortunately, the process is long and costly, so it's not something I can produce on a large scale."

"*Alas*," Mikoneh drawled.

Sathe's chuckle grated on his ears. "Don't fret. I'll have no need to turn you into what he has become, so long as you keep that inner fire of yours blazing."

The echo of an outside heartbeat entered Mikoneh's mind. He let it linger, not touching it. Not letting his mind drift too far into it. But he couldn't stifle a pang of joy.

Sathe set his goblet aside with a thud. "What are you celebrating, Firebrand?"

Mikoneh snatched onto an image of Ter. Of the hope the Ephe'ahn had given him despite himself.

"Poor thing," Sathe cooed, leaning back against the silken settee with a whisper of his robes. "Ter can do nothing for you."

"We'll see." Mikoneh slowed his paces, then allowed himself to drift toward the narrow bed brought into the chamber for his use. He spread across it sideways, letting his head dangle off the edge. His eyes closed. His mind drifted.

"Weary, my Firebrand?" whispered Sathe, too close.

Mikoneh tensed but didn't open his eyes.

"Very well. Sleep. When you wake, we will strengthen our bond."

Shivers raced down Mikoneh's spine, but he stayed motionless and leveled his nerves with deep breaths. Let it all go. Push the world away. Keep the heartbeat that had come into his mind. Drift toward it. Slip inside.

He entered blackness.

CHAPTER 44

THIS INKY DARKNESS

"The Star Sword should have killed the Lady of the North. Only the Dragon King's sacrifice spared her."

- From Athonen d'Ereth's *The Fall of Mages in the Age of Dragons*

Mikoneh thought he knew what true evil was. The concept wasn't far-fetched, from all he'd seen Drayve subject Relvin Province to. Heavy taxes were the least of that man's sins. Burning houses with occupants inside; taking the daughters of farmers for his private pleasure, then discarding them; executing innocent people in a fit of tantrum; wining and dining while his people starved. Drayve had seemed as close to evil as anything could be.

But, standing within Sathe's heart, even Drayve's depravity seemed like a shade of gray—dark gray, yes, but nothing to this.

Drayve had been driven by base appetites and a selfishness born of overindulgent parents. That didn't redeem or excuse him, but compared to the hollow of Sathe's heart, it was at least comprehensible.

This realm, this inky darkness, was a temple to evil itself. The very air worshiped cruelty for cruelty's sake. Even Sathe's ambition, his hunger for power, came second to a deeper, darker motive: the love of evil. The worship of it. The hunger to feed it.

Power was merely a reward for devoting himself to a force greater, deeper, more horrible than himself.

That realization shook Mikoneh to his core.

He stood in a domain outside the bounds of Sirinhigha. This place was a shrine to pure devilry—and he was chained to it.

His heart throbbed. Worse, Reven was snared by it and had been for ages of time. The thought lent Mikoneh courage. He steeled himself and strode through the abyss, seeking the one thing that wasn't blackened. It couldn't be hard to find, not against the murky channels of zealous devotion.

He reached out with his senses. Seeking. Craving.

He couldn't abide to stay long.

'Here.'

He moved toward the weak, earnest voice that beckoned him. In the all-embracing darkness, he couldn't see where walls stood, and he slammed into one, then felt his way around a corner. It was like a labyrinth. Sathe's heart was too dark for Mikoneh to see his own hands, but he didn't dare summon flame to give himself away.

He paused. *Maybe I should. What would happen if I torched the Mage's heart?*

He hesitated, torn between caution and impulse.

Find what you're looking for before you make a ruckus.

He moved ahead, hands outstretched to cushion himself against the unseen walls. His progress was slow, but twice more the small voice called out, guiding him onward. Walls gave way to what felt like a wide-open space. He quickened his step—and tumbled from a ledge. His stomach flipped. Reflexively, his wings burst from his back and caught him. They carried him down into darkness.

No, not all darkness. Pulsing with the faintest silver light, an orb hovered in the depths of the hole. Mikoneh reached for it, lowering himself by degrees. Despite its feeble throbs, the palm-sized orb was stunning, like a strangely cut oval gem made of soul light. Warmth emanated from it.

Mikoneh cupped the orb. The warmth flooded him, and the orb disintegrated, pulsing through his frame.

Elatharin. The true name tolled through Mikoneh's body, carrying a vision of a great dragon with green and blue scales soaring over snowy mountain peaks, white mane bright in the sun.

He blinked and the vision receded. Wings beating in the blackness, he took a moment to collect himself—to feel human instead of sailing through the air with the dragon called Elatharin.

I did it. I stole the true name.

Fear seized his lungs. *If Sathe finds out, he can steal it back, as long as we're bonded.*

Mikoneh inhaled, mind racing too fast to clamp down on a solid idea.

Stop panicking, Mikoneh. Strategize.

If Sathe hadn't reacted already, he hadn't realized what was taken. Which meant Mikoneh simply had to avoid giving himself away. Where could he stow the name?

The answer dawned immediately: Sathe's heart was the farthest from his consciousness. Though he'd devoted himself to the worship of corruption, it was a seldom-used device just the same. The Mage leaned on logic above emotion and surface emotion above deep feeling.

He won't look in my heart.

Sathe might prod his thoughts, torment his body, and rack his soul—but he'd left the heart alone, apart from ugly words.

Hear that, Elatharin? Stow away in my core. He won't find you there.

Mikoneh's heart throbbed, and he found himself laughing. The dragon's true name had already lodged itself there, for where else would it dwell?

She was right.

He stilled. He didn't know who *she* was. Or how he knew to do what he did. Or where he'd found his answer. But he'd found it.

Shutting his spiritual eyes, he willed himself from Sathe's core. The darkness gave him up with reluctance, but he fell back into his body. The last tendrils of evil fell away. Mikoneh rolled onto his side, trying to keep from drawing Sathe's notice.

Sleep. Just sleep.

A heaviness filled him up. He succumbed, and gladly.

CHAPTER 45

BLOOD AND SCALES

- From Athonen d'Ereth's *The Fall of Mages in the Age of Dragons*

Ter appeared in the gloom of the cave on Oceana's east coast, with Hilker at his back. A grimness lined the little fae's jaw. Maya studied Ter with growing dread. Beside her, Penn and Akonn had fallen still, watching the Ephe'ahn with narrowed eyes.

Owenekiras alone looked no different—but then, he was always solemn.

Ter sighed and eased himself down at the campfire where the small group sat. Hilker joined him, disturbingly quiet, though the Wind Elementalist usually had *something* to say.

Only the Dragon King stood apart, almost one with the shadows of the snug cavern.

"He's good and stuck," Ter said.

"This we already knew," Owenekiras said.

"Yes, well." Ter's ears fluttered down. "Sathe's ultimatum is as you suspected as well. You must withdraw from the fight for sovereignty over Sirinhigha, else Mikoneh's mind will be broken."

Maya shoved her knuckles over her mouth to keep from making a noise. Pinning her attention on Owenekiras, she waited. For a long moment, he didn't move. The shadows curled in around him, and the air cooled by degrees.

"Now what?" asked Penn.

"Now," Owenekiras said in soft tones, "we make our move."

"What of Mikoneh's mind, my lord?" Penn said.

The Dragon King moved toward the campfire. Orange flames cast light in his silver eyes, turning them molten. "Believe me, Lord Penn—I will not let permanent harm come to him while I yet draw breath."

The firmness of that tone, the faint rumble in those words, inspired deeper stillness. Maya could sense Penn's unspoken question: *Why was Mikoneh so important?* She ached to ask it herself. But she didn't dare. Her every instinct was fine-tuned to acknowledge a fact that frightened her deeply: Owenekiras Rokahn was livid.

"There is one other, hm, issue..." Ter's youthful voice cut into the mounting tension.

Owenekiras's eyes flicked toward the Ephe'ahn.

"Sathe *told* him." One fae ear flicked down, then righted itself.

"How much?"

"Enough. Mikoneh understands—on some level—his value."

"Ah." Owenekiras's cool gaze fell on Maya. "Then perhaps they should both know."

"So I wondered," Ter said.

"Know what, my lords?" Penn had found his voice again.

Akonn shifted beside him. "Should I escort Master Penn outside for a moment?"

Penn's eyes widened. "Is this something that puts Maya in danger?"

"No." Ter's smile was tight but still warm. "At least, no more than she is already. This simply pertains to her—hm, birthright."

"My blood parents." Maya's voice sounded far away in her own ears.

"Very well." Penn stood.

"No, stay." Maya caught his hand and tugged. "Can't he stay?"

"If you wish." Owenekiras's voice was quiet. He stooped to sit at the fire, cape rippling, his dark hair tinted orange in the glow. "I don't expect you to embrace your heritage, but it's fair that you know it."

"Why not speak about it before now?" asked Penn, settling himself down beside Maya.

She set her hand on the viscount's arm. "Let's listen for now and ask questions afterward." Her chest was taut. Her nerves hummed. Her heartbeat had quickened—but she was more eager than afraid. She'd ached to learn about her birth parents since she'd accepted that they weren't Fa and Mama—but she hadn't dared to ask. Part of her had felt guilty for knowing a truth her twin didn't. Despite her resolve, another part of her had felt that it was a betrayal of her surrogate parents. But that was foolish. Knowledge of one didn't erase the existence of the other. Adding was never a subtraction. "Please proceed, Lord Rokahn."

He inhaled, then took the plunge. "You and your brother were placed in Jonatten and Seranni's care after your mother was murdered."

Maya blinked. Her chest tightened more. Somehow, though she'd suspected her blood parents were dead, she hadn't expected that. Most orphans in Oceana resulted from skirmishes or disease. Not murder. Penn caught her hand in his. He squeezed gently.

Owenekiras didn't break eye contact with her. "She had been in hiding with both of you, protected from those seeking to harm your father in his political position. Unfortunately, your parents were betrayed—somehow. Your mother died protecting you both. It became clear to your father that keeping his kin near, and associated with him, would only bring greater harm to both of you. Death, at the least. Enslavement—such as Mikoneh faces now—at the worst. Your father trusted none better than those who raised you as their own."

Maya inhaled a sharp breath. Realization unfurled within her. "You're saying..."

"Yes." Owenekiras dipped his head. "You are the children of House Rokahn. My offspring and heirs."

Penn's jaw fell open.

No one else stirred. They'd known. Even Hilker.

Maya studied the cold face, the silver eyes, then the hard lines of the Dragon King's obsidian armor. Tears collected in her eyes. She smiled. "I can see it now. I should've seen it sooner. It's so obvious, looking back." She stood, brushed her tunic straight over her breeches, and approached Owenekiras.

His face was impassive. Cold as stone. But his eyes remained trained on her, watchful. She knelt before him. He didn't move.

Trembling, Maya stretched her hand out and rested her fingers against his smooth face. His skin was cold. He didn't react. Something insisted she draw back, but she couldn't. This was her *father*. The man who gave her life. Who gave her up to spare her from her mother's fate. Whatever his outward mien, he'd proven his love.

"I'm glad you told me," she whispered. "I'm glad I know who you are." She pulled her hand back. Hesitated. Then flung her arms around his neck. His armor was cold and inflexible, just as he was. The steel angles dug into her, but she didn't care. She'd thought that after Fa's and Mama's deaths, she and Mikoneh were alone. That they had no kin at all in the world.

Yet that wasn't true. They had a father—and he was one of the greatest and most feared men in all the kingdoms of Sirinhigha.

That thought brought their situation crashing back into her mind. She drew back. Owenekiras hadn't moved; hadn't lifted his hands or drawn away. He'd merely held still while she'd embraced him.

He doesn't feel like he can reciprocate.

"I don't hate you," she blurted out. "Or blame you. You did what was best for us, to protect us, and you gave us a wonderful gift to be raised by your trusted generals. If you think all that makes you a bad father, you're wrong."

He searched her eyes, then inclined his head. "I thank you for your honesty."

Maya settled back on her heels. "Sathe told Mikoneh about this, right?"

"Some of it, at least," said Ter.

"And the Mage is using it as leverage to bind your hands."

"Yes," Owenekiras said.

She twisted a lock of hair around her finger. "What will you do?"

A hardness tightened Owenekiras's eyes. "Defy him. No Mage will dictate to me."

"That's dangerous for Mikoneh, my lord," Penn interjected.

Maya glanced at her friend, trying to read his face. What did he think of all this? All she could read was concern for his captive friend.

"Yes," the Dragon King said, "but so is leaving him to Sathe's whims."

"True, that," Hilker spoke up. "No Mage can long avoid damaging a dragon. They're too greedy. Power is their bread and butter. Sooner or later, Sathe'll push too far and leave the Dragon Prince a mere lump of blood and scales."

"That can't happen." Maya's heart jumped into her throat. "Please."

Owenekiras's gauntleted hand fell on her shoulder. "It won't. That I promise you. And your brother is strong. He's fighting well."

"Indeed, he is," Ter chimed in. "The flame is back in his core—and his eyes blaze with light. He's wounded, yes, but not feeble."

"Never feeble," Penn said firmly. "That man would survive a flooded island."

"Yes," said Hilker, eyes twinkling. "'Specially since he can fly."

Maya paused at that. "Right." She glanced at her father. "You'd mentioned before that he was flying when you found him."

"So I did," Owenekiras said.

Her mind clamped on that and wouldn't let go, though she tried to tell herself it wasn't the most important question now. If *she* could fly, that might make rescuing Mikoneh easier. In her training bouts with Hilker, she'd been learning to harness the wind element, using the spirits to lift her off the ground—but it was slow going, and she was impatient. The wind spirits thought dropping her was hilarious, and her tailbone was bruised from several attempts to walk on air.

"Is flying difficult to learn?" she asked.

"Not for a Rokahn," said Ter. "Especially not for one who has used their wings before. You and your brother were most proficient as toddlers, as I recall."

She blinked at him. "We were?"

"Oh, yes," he said. "You each took to your dragon nature very swiftly after your births. Alas, when you were taken east by Jonatten and Seranni, it was imperative that your abilities were made dormant. Young dragons must be supervised by their elders, or the little ones might accidentally set a village on fire or summon a tornado during a tantrum." His ear twitched. "The good news is once you've flown, your instincts never turn rusty."

Hope stirred in her chest, but she tried to push it down. "Would it be helpful if—if I learned how? Again, that is."

"Yes." Owenekiras held out his hand. On his open palm lay a pale fruit that resembled the exotic coconut Maya had once tasted at the Relvin Fair. "Eat this. It will stir your dormant blood gently."

He unsheathed long black claws, punctured the fruit's pale shell, and twisted the fruit, slicing it in two. He pried the two halves apart, revealing a soft center that was almost iridescent. "This is *korta*, commonly called dragonfang fruit. It's very good for hatchlings, offering the essential nutrients needed for proper growth and vitality. Grown dragons benefit from it as well."

Maya reached for it, already salivating. Her body ached for a bite like she'd been starving all her life. Accepting it, she inhaled a long breath. It was sweet yet tangy. Gingerly, she took her first bite. Flavor—somewhere between a ripe strawberry and a crumble tart—exploded on her tongue. Her bones hummed as though the nutrition of the fruit was sinking in even before she swallowed.

"It's toxic for non-dragons to eat, unless one is bonded," Ter added. "I suggest not sharing with Master Penn or Hilker."

She continued to munch, nodding vague acknowledgment. Usually, she'd be eager to share and disappointed by Ter's statement, but that driving hunger insisted she keep every morsel for herself. Only when she'd eaten every shred of *korta* and licked the juices from her fingers did she pause to center herself on the issues at hand.

Owenekiras dug into the folds of his cloak and withdrew a second dragonfang fruit. He handed it to her. Strangely, she didn't feel compelled to eat it. In fact, she felt more satisfied with the single fruit than she did after a meal. "Keep that for later," he said. "You'll need one a day—no more or less—for a long time."

She nodded, then tossed the *korta* to Penn. "Will you please put that in my satchel?"

He nodded and shifted to obey.

A half-formed question bobbed back into her thoughts. "Father?"

Owenekiras tensed, his eyes settling on her like iron anvils.

"If Sathe wanted to use Mikoneh as a hostage just to threaten you, why did it have to be him rather than me?"

"Two reasons. First, he couldn't bond with you. Only females can bond with female dragons, and the same applies to males. The only exception is a war bond, which is a separate matter, and rare. Even if he tried forcing a bond between you and a female Mage, the nature of a female bond is as different as your biology is from a male. He couldn't harness your will for his second goal—a goal that transcends his threats towards me.

Mikoneh will become one of the strongest dragons in the known universe. It is part of his calling as my heir. He is the eldest twin. Sathe wishes to weaponize Mikoneh in the coming war, once your brother is fully broken down."

"But you said he's too small—too young."

"As he is now, yes. But..." Owenekiras frowned. "There are ways to grow a dragon up faster. Ways that are damaging without tremendous care."

A tremor coursed through her. "We can't let that happen."

His eyes narrowed. "Indeed not. Sathe believes they're safe now that he has delivered his threat through Ter. He doubts we will act, especially right away. As a result, he will relax despite himself."

"What's the plan?" asked Penn.

A smile edged the Dragon King's mouth, and a cold light flashed across his silver eyes. "We attack Nauttia Castle." He turned toward the cave maw. Thunder rumbled in the heavens beyond. "By storm."

Chapter 46

Wing Toward the Storm

"The aftershock stripped all people, human and fae alike, of their magic for a time. It is that incident which made some kingdoms forsake magic altogether."

- From Athonen d'Ereth's *The Fall of Mages in the Age of Dragons*

The breakers crashed below the bluffs. The wind wailed.

Mikoneh strode onto the balcony overlooking the eastern ocean, ignoring the lashing threads of his hair and the fluttering of his borrowed shirt. Among humankind, Sathe seemed content to let Mikoneh remain dressed. Never had Mikoneh valued his privacy so much.

Earlier, servants had set up a bathtub with oils to clean himself and supplied finer clothes than he'd ever worn in his life, from cream top with billowing sleeves and burgundy surcoat to gray breeches, black boots, and a silk handkerchief.

He'd been relieved to scrub the tunnel dirt away and had slipped into the smooth clothing with a sigh of relief—but he wouldn't wear the surcoat. He refused to look like an Oceanean lord—especially now that they aimed for war.

Coerced or not, no one in the castle resisted Sathe. They cowered to protect their own necks.

Be fair. They have families to protect.

Yet he couldn't stifle his anger. It was all he had left to fight with, so he leaned into it, seething.

Sathe was nearby, though he'd stepped into the hall to converse with his fellows. The Mages Mikoneh had glimpsed past the door before it shut wore skin, much like Sathe. Higher ranks, then. They were settling into Nauttia, preparing for the long campaign against the world.

It's madness to send armies out a month before the snows.

The Mages evidently didn't care about that. What were mere human lives to them?

Resting his hands on the balustrade, Mikoneh considered the ships bobbing in the harbor. The storm grew stronger. Clouds thickened on the coastline. The gales ripped golden leaves from the courtyard trees below and scattered fallen foliage. The scent of brine and fish mingled with the crisp promise of rain.

He shut his eyes, basking in the fury of the coming squall.

A hand seized his arm and wrenched him around. "Come back inside," Sathe said between clenched teeth. His dark hair whipped around his face, and his eyes were glittering slits of wrath.

Mikoneh followed, too startled to resist. The Mage was livid about something, but it couldn't be aimed at him, or Sathe would have lashed out already. Still, Mikoneh braced for the tantrum that was certainly building beneath quiet ire.

"Sit." Sathe jerked Mikoneh toward the settee.

To avoid unnecessary pain, Mikoneh sat, though an impulse screamed at him to jump from the balcony and wing toward the storm.

"What's wrong?" he asked.

Sathe's glower was as frigid as the highest peaks of the Andyan range. "Nothing that regards you."

An image of Reven flashed over Mikoneh's mind, but nothing to detail why the specter made Sathe so upset. He dropped the issue at once. Beneath his compulsions, instinct told him to stay still and let the storm within the room pass, while the torrent outside grew wilder.

"I must step out for a moment," Sathe said. "I'll not be far, and I'll return soon. Don't go out onto the balcony. Do you understand?" His tones were almost parental, as though he spoke to a child.

Mikoneh nodded, stifling a scowl. He tracked the Mage's exit, then slumped against the straight back of the settee, exhaling a heavy sigh. Sathe had been brooding since dawn. At one point, he'd knocked Mikoneh's plate from its tray, spilling breakfast over the rug. Irritation had surged within Mikoneh, but he'd choked back his temper all morning. His gut assured him that was the only way to avoid serious soul damage.

How can someone so cold be so blasted bad-tempered?

His own temper was often difficult to control, though Fa had taught him how to let out his anger in a constructive way —mostly through sword training. That was more difficult in the wake of his parents' deaths, but he still tried to implement what that good-hearted man had taught him. Mama had understood Mikoneh better. She'd been the more temperamental of the married couple, often banging and clattering pans whenever she was cooking, while she mumbled under her breath about this or that frustration. Unfortunately, her cooking had often suffered for it, and she wasn't especially good in the kitchen to begin with.

In fact, none of them had been—Maya least of all. It was up to Mikoneh to learn how to bake bread, roast meat, and steam vegetables. Luckily, he'd taken to it easily. Probably a consequence of his element.

Mikoneh stared at the ceiling, surprised to find himself smiling. His muscles had relaxed, too. Thinking of those sunshine days had somehow eased his tension, despite the hopeless situation stretching before him.

Don't think. Just rest.

Thunder grumbled outside. The wind spattered raindrops inside the room, and the curtains framing the balcony doorway fluttered like streamers. Mikoneh sat forward and leaned his elbows against his knees. He tried to combat the climbing desire to fling himself into the storm.

No matter how far it carried you off, Sathe could just call you back.

His muscles tensed. A dull ache started in the crown of his head. He pressed his palms together, tight. His jaw throbbed beneath his clenched teeth.

Bide your time. Don't act rashly.

Something outside cracked. Light burst across the room. Thunder boomed in the heavens. Mikoneh lurched to his feet, and bolted onto the balcony. Rain drenched him in a curtain of water. He shoved back his plastered hair and leaned over the balustrade. The tree in the courtyard had fallen over, crisped by a bolt of lightning. It smoldered in the deluge.

The hair on the back of his neck bristled. He gripped the stone railing hard, abandoning the sight below to search the roiling heavens. His insides writhed. His mouth went dry. The sea level had grown, and the wind was shrieking at incredible speeds toward the mainland.

A hurricane.

Definitely a hurricane.

He started to laugh. Oceana was trying to conquer the world, but its capital was about to be ravaged by an act of nature.

His mirth faded. Could Mages hold back such a storm? Would Sathe and his skeletal army stand against the sea and rebuke their watery demise? Did a Water Elementalist have enough control to stop the ocean?

If this is how it must end, so be it.

He'd meant to destroy Sathe. This was one way to accomplish that. He just needed to make sure the Mage was standing in the hurricane's path, no matter what.

Mikoneh couldn't use himself as bait. He'd obey any direct command. Instead, he needed to find Sathe and—

He paused.

Sathe was probably seeking the Revenant. If so—if that had been the source of the Mage's anger—what did that signify?

Don't think about it.

He couldn't risk giving anything away.

Thunder rumbled again. His mind flitted back to the storm. He didn't know much about hurricanes. Tucked away from open water, Relvin didn't experience them like the coastal provinces—but he did remember what Mama had taught him in his childhood lessons. Usually, they weren't accompanied by thunder.

Is this an unnatural storm?

Hope surged, swelling in his chest. He curled his hands into fists and laughed into the wind. The castle trembled. Mikoneh shot his hands out to catch the balustrade, startled by a second vehement lurch beneath his feet.

Odd. The hurricane hadn't gained enough power to shake

the earth—yet it happened again, heaving Mikoneh off the flagstones. He clung to the balustrade tighter to avoid tumbling over its brink into the pounding gale wrenching the last leaves from the trees in the courtyard.

Another quake hit. Stones cracked. The castle rumbled.

His dragon instinct hummed.

A few more bucks and the entire castle would shatter. He righted himself and craned his neck to find the bedchamber doors within. No sign of Sathe.

Another quake rocked the world. The castle moaned. More stones cracked.

Well, I'm not going to die waiting around!

He pulled out his wings, ripping through his shirt. White tatters swirled away in the wind eddies. Mikoneh threw himself into the sky after them.

The gale caught him—jerked him away from the castle just as a ferocious roar and deafening crack split the air. He wrestled the storm to turn toward Nauttia Castle. It was collapsing in a fountain of stones and wooden beams. A shiver shook his bones. If the denizens of that castle screamed, he couldn't hear them over the torrent. Rain pounded his face, and his wings strained to hold him upright.

Pity stabbed his heart. Though he wasn't Oceanean by birth, Mikoneh had grown up under King Nilo's banner. Whatever flaws the man had, he'd not been a tyrant. And though Nilo had chosen war, what threats had led to that decision? Was justice served by the king's death beneath the bones of his own castle?

Maybe he got away. Surely, some courtiers and servants did.

The wind caught Mikoneh's wings and forced him away from the tumbling walls. He ceased to fight, letting it take him where it wanted.

Firebrand.

He grimaced. He was a mere speck in a swallowing torrent—but still a captive.

I'm here.

Are you injured?

No, I got away in time.

I am underground. Find me.

That's gonna have to wait. Mikoneh allowed his vision to trickle between their bond, to give Sathe a sense of his whirlwind plight.

Find shelter, and when the storm is finished—*seek me. No one else.* The command boomed through him.

Got it.

Unable to resist the hands of the hurricane, he shut his eyes. Instead, he let them toss him hither and thither—held in the throes of a desperate numbness—until the tossing slowed, and the rain grew steadier. He opened his eyes. Hints of sunlight pillared from the angry clouds. He'd been driven inland, westward, and he found himself above the dense forest outside the hurricane's path. Stray droplets fell from the silvery gold sky.

He righted himself, wings beating in place, keeping him several feet above the treetops. His senses settled slowly, and he turned east to eye the hurricane.

Sathe had ordered him to return—but the storm still raged on the coast. Mikoneh didn't have to obey yet. He felt no impulse to heed the Mage, which meant he had time. How could he best use it? How long did hurricanes last? How far could he get? Where could he find—

His mind exploded with pain.

Sathe had ordered him not to seek anyone else. He forsook his desire to find Ter and settled on aiming for the trees. He could hide there, and maybe...maybe something would—

"Mikoneh!"

That voice. He ripped his attention from the deciduous forest.

"Maya!" His voice broke on a sob. There she was, on the back of an enormous, majestic black dragon. A mane of aqua blue fluttered behind the dragon's head. Great wings beat the air. The wings' underside was a gradient of blues from deepest aqua, to palest electric blue, shot with veins of silver. The membrane almost appeared like lightning beneath a darkening sky.

His twin and the dragon were soaring toward him at full speed. He lifted his arm, waving it, feeling all of five years old and ready to weep. But he held his emotions in check, apart from the foolish grin on his face. Saved. Somehow, someway, they'd come to save him.

You're not free yet.

He tried to stifle his joy—to not bring Sathe's attention to it. And while he knew he'd already failed, for some reason the Mage didn't lash out. Perhaps the storm was too fierce, and the Mage couldn't do anything but hunker down to avoid being crushed.

Mikoneh didn't dare reach through their bond to find out.

The dragon shot past him, too large to stop all at once, but Maya jumped from the black scales and fell toward her twin with arms wide open. Mikoneh swept upward to meet her. He caught her with only a faint downward dip of his strong, midnight-blue wings, and held her close, burying his face in her neck. She did the same.

The twins wept and clung to each other. Mikoneh never wanted to let go—not ever again—but Maya pulled back and shoved something red into his mouth. Leaves, judging by the texture. Bitter, then revoltingly sweet. He grimaced at the contrasting tastes.

"Chew and swallow," she said in her firmest tones.

He obeyed, glad to choke down the herb—or whatever it was. He smacked his lips, trying to bring his reeling thoughts back into alignment. "You're here."

Maya laughed. "Really? I hadn't noticed." Her smile fell. "We don't have a lot of time. Fly there." She stabbed her finger toward a shadow among the trees farther west and slightly north.

Mikoneh obeyed, glad to put another league between Sathe and himself. He tried not to draw the Mage's notice, but how much longer he could escape it he didn't want to consider. His wings carried them well. Maya didn't feel heavy. Was it possible that when he drew on his dragon blood, his strength increased?

The enormous dragon surpassed them, then dropped into the shadowed area, disappearing. A few wingbeats later, the twins neared the shadow. It was a clearing. In the damp meadow below, Owenekiras Rokahn stood in human form among the glistening flowers. His armor shone in the stray droplets leaking from the dappled sky.

Mikoneh swooped lower, then angled his legs beneath him and dropped Maya a few feet above the grass. She landed lightly, then he folded his wings and touched down beside her. He turned toward the Dragon King, stomach knotting. His father. Was that the truth or had Sathe been lying to him?

You already know the answer, he told himself.

Owenekiras Rokahn lifted one hand.

A jolt ran through Mikoneh. Sathe's panicked voice filled his mind.

Return to me immediately!

The command seized him. He stretched his wings.

Owenekiras's gauntleted hand snapped into a fist. Aqua light rippled across the clearing, pulsing outward in a circle from the center of the meadow where the Dragon King stood.

A pulse tore under Mikoneh's bare feet and shot up his veins. The ground held him fast. Sathe's violet-colored command surged through him with renewed vigor, but he couldn't budge.

A second pulse followed—this one a flaming silver light.

Sathe's spiritual hands groped at Mikoneh's soul.

The two magics clashed. Mikoneh screamed. Pain roared through him, terrible like fire scorching his bones, yet cold as the rime of the northern mountains. He arched his back, wings trembling. His vision blurred. Colors collided before his mind's eye.

The taste of copper blazed on his tongue.

Sathe's screams filled his mind.

RETURN TO ME!

He couldn't. The Dragon King's silver magic paralyzed him—overwhelmed him—tore apart the violet chains on his soul. Sathe's presence—those deep roots—ripped from Mikoneh. He screamed louder. His vision turned white.

He fell backward, landing hard on his wings.

The silver light died.

Reality filled his senses. His harsh breaths. The questioning trill of a bird. The sweet scent of meadow flowers. The waxy feel of wild grass. The taste of his blood mingled with the tang of Hollow. Tears ran from his face, into his hair.

"May I touch him now?" asked Maya. Her gentle voice was nearby.

"Yes. It's safe," Owenekiras answered.

Grass crunched. Cloth rustled. Maya's hand brushed Mikoneh's shoulder, then caught his chin. She lifted his head, and he cracked his eyes open to find her smiling through tears of her own. He tried to say her name, but his voice broke. He shifted, then dropped his head onto her lap. His body shook as though he'd caught a fever. But the infection wasn't in his body; he already knew that. It was in his soul. Sathe's contagion—ripped out.

Am I free? He didn't dare believe it.

Heavy footsteps approached. "Your bond is severed, but Sathe still has a power over you." Owenekiras's voice was a gentle rumble.

The realization tore through him. "My...blood. He still... still has..."

"Yes," Owenekiras said. "He likely took more than a few precious drops while you were captured. It would make strategic sense, and while Sathe is many vile things, a fool isn't one of them."

"What do we do?" asked Maya in strained tones. Her fear twisted Mikoneh's heart, but he didn't have the strength to sit up and comfort her. His body was limp as a sodden rag.

"We hunt the Mage down and end him as we first planned." While Owenekiras's voice was level, there was an indisputable anger curling around those words.

Strength flooded Mikoneh. He lifted himself upright and twisted to eye the Dragon King. His father. Mikoneh pulled in a long breath. His limbs still trembled, and his vision wobbled. That didn't matter. "I'm coming with you. I want—no. I *must* destroy him. Please."

Owenekiras's face gave nothing away. It was harder than stone. At last, he nodded. "I think you must for your wellbeing above all else. You should witness his end."

"Thank you." Something loosened in his chest. "And thank you for freeing me. I didn't know if it was possible."

"Had we more time, I could have used a gentler method." Owenekiras's eyes narrowed marginally. "You will feel strangely for a while yet. The *tiassana*—the red leaves Maya gave you—

will help to heal the tear in your soul. She has more. Use them, along with a special fruit she has, daily."

Maya caught her twin's arm. "I'll take care of you. You'll recover soon."

A mist drifted across his eyes, and his throat closed, but he swallowed and fought back the rush of guilt. "I'm just sorry the cost was so high. King Nilo was under Sathe's orders, but through threats—not unlike me."

"He's not dead." Maya leaned forward. "Hilker promised."

The words didn't make sense. He just stared at her.

Maya's smile brightened. "He's my teacher. He's a Master Wind Elementalist. He and Father—" She broke off, eyes widening.

The word jolted Mikoneh, bringing new emotions, too strong and chaotic to understand. Though he'd accepted the truth of their connection to the House of Rokahn, hearing her confirm it was still a heavy weight. He read her fear well enough, and he tried a smile. "It's okay. I already knew."

"Right." Maya tried again. "Hilker and Father—they conjured that hurricane. And I used the wind to guide you through it. Hilker would've helped me, but he, Ter, Akonn, and Penn sneaked into the castle ahead of the storm to protect the denizens and distract Sathe. Hilker said he'd use wind to keep the stones from crushing anyone, while the other three fought any enemies along the way."

"Penn can't fight Mages."

"No, but Ter and Akonn can," Maya said. "And Penn wanted to be useful. He knows King Nilo. He might persuade the king to call back his army, he said, or dangle the risk of the hurricane destroying all of Oceana. But don't worry. Father wouldn't really do that. It's just a tactic." Maya took Mikoneh's face in her hands. "You look so gaunt. I won't ask if you're well—but you will be again. I'll make sure."

His smile deepened, though he still felt numb inside. "Thanks, Maya. I don't doubt it, and I'm—" Prickles started along his flesh, climbing up his arms. He twisted around at the same moment Owenekiras turned. A faint crimson glow wafted from the dense trees. A doe sprang from the foliage, her eyes wild. Birds took flight from the branches.

Maya darted to her feet and raced to stand between Mikoneh and the approaching Revenant. Mikoneh lurched upright and caught her arm, while Owenekiras stalked toward the specter. Silver lightning sparked on his fingertips.

"Wait, don't attack him!" Mikoneh's voice rang across the clearing, more desperate than he'd expected to sound. "He's not here to hurt me."

"Explain," Owenekiras said over Maya's scoff.

"I stole his true name." The words came out in a rush. Somehow, despite Sathe's absence, and the torn places in his soul, Mikoneh didn't quite believe the Mage wouldn't hear him and react.

Owenekiras twisted toward him, a hint of surprise breaking through his monolith façade. "You did?"

"Yes." Steeling himself, Mikoneh padded past the Dragon King, toward Reven, who'd halted at the forest's edge. "You can approach, Reven. They won't fight you."

The familiar cloak of sorrow spread across the grass. Flowers drooped. Vibrant colors dimmed. Mikoneh ignored all that, offering the Revenant a smile.

"I'm glad you came, Reven."

'I had to, Master.'

Mikoneh shrank back, shuddering to his core. "No—No. I'm not that. Never." He hesitated, then glanced over his shoulder. Maya's horror had changed to pity, while Owenekiras watched with his pristine stoicism. "How do I return the true name?"

"How did you steal it?" asked Owenekiras.

"I walked into Sathe's heart."

Owenekiras arched one brow. "Ah. This will not require anything so intimate. You have a rare gift, it seems. Your second element must be spirit of spirit. Cup your hands like you're lifting water from a stream." He demonstrated.

Mikoneh mimicked him.

"Remember the moment when you stole the true name—but do not speak it aloud. Never aloud. That silver light that infused you—the warmth, the steadiness. Tap it now. Clasp it between your hands."

It came at a thought. A pinprick of light flamed above Mikoneh's hands like a candle's glow. Its warmth flooded his insides, soothing the tear, softening the burns. He stared at it for a long moment, then cupped his hands around it, containing the tiny essence.

"Now," Owenekiras said, much nearer than expected. His steps had been soundless. "Place the Revenant's name within the spirit flame. Keep it there. Once you know it won't leak away, approach the Revenant, and place the true name in his heart."

Mikoneh hesitated. "What will happen to him then? Will... will he die?"

"He will be freed. A spirit, liberated from his captivity."

"I know where his body is. Or—I did. It's preserved."

"Ah." Owenekiras's heavy gaze lifted, perhaps moving to study the Revenant. Mikoneh didn't dare break his concentration on the flame to find out. "The Revenant won't be forced to move on. He will remain here in the principal plane. But we should secure his body before Sathe can damage it. Wait on returning the true name for now."

"I already have it inside the element."

"Then rest the flame against your chest. Will it to return to where it was."

Mikoneh obeyed. Warmth flared up, welcome, soothing. The true name settled in his heart again. He exhaled. "It's done."

"Good."

Mikoneh turned to the Dragon King, blinking in the strangely heightened daylight. "He's a dragon."

Surprise flitted across Owenekiras's face. Then a cloud settled on his brow, dark and brooding. "Mages never learn."

"He's been a captive for millennia. Since the Age of Dragons, I think."

That darkness deepened. Owenekiras turned toward the waiting Revenant. "We will restore you if we can. This much I vow: You'll not be subject to a Mage's will again."

The Revenant's cowl bobbed slowly in acknowledgment.

Maya inched closer. "So, he's safe. He won't…"

"He never wanted to hurt us," Mikoneh said. "He was under orders—and a dragon controlled by Mages can't fight. I…I learned that firsthand." His strength waned, as though his trauma had been lurking in wait for him to remember. He staggered sideways.

Owenekiras's strong hands caught his arm. "Steady. We must secure the Revenant's body while we still have time. I cannot control the hurricane much longer before nature will have her way."

Maya tucked her arm around Mikoneh's. "We've got you, Miikeh." The childhood nickname brought a flood of soothing memories with it.

"I know, Maya. I can't tell you how good it is to see you." Trembling, Mikoneh forced his head around until he found the Revenant still waiting near the forest border. "Reven, can you lead Owenekiras to your body? Is that possible?"

The cowled figure nodded.

"Thank you." Mikoneh's vision wavered again. He slumped harder between his two companions. "Sorry. I think... I need...to sleep."

Blackness claimed him.

CHAPTER 47

A SEA OF WORRIES

"Many Mages fell never to rise again."

- From Athonen d'Ereth's *The Fall of Mages in the Age of Dragons*

Maya stayed near her slumbering twin outside a dim underground chamber. Beyond the threshold, a man on an altar lay in eternal repose. The foul smell of the tunnel network taunted her senses. Owenekiras entered the chamber with the Revenant, and they stood at either end of the stone slab. The specter's crimson glow stained the rock walls, casting some of its light out into the earthen corridor.

Glancing at Mikoneh, Maya satisfied herself that he wasn't going to stir anytime soon. A single glance would tell anyone he needed rest desperately. His hollow cheeks and hunted expression had fractured her heart. Fury writhed within her. A desire to find Sathe and—and—and *eat* him. That must be her feral dragon heritage bleeding through.

You can't do anything right now. Stop seething. And don't eat people.

It couldn't be good for digestion.

To distract herself, she inched toward the door into the small, eerie chamber. The Dragon King—*Father*—was busy studying the runes carved around the altar. The Revenant stood in perfect stillness, like a statue meant to inspire terror and heartbreak in some strange blending.

She squirmed, then focused instead on the body lying across the altar. If that was indeed what the Revenant had been before his capture, he'd once been a beautiful, elegant man. His profile was flawless, his body long, lithe, and powerful. Though he slept a dreamless sleep, profound gentleness radiated from his benign features. He'd been a great man—that was apparent. But far more important, he'd been a *kind* one.

Can we return his soul to his body? She frowned. *Even if we do, will he be the same?*

A month spent in Sathe's company had left scars upon Mikoneh's soul and aged him by several years. Perhaps he would return to who he'd been before. But Maya wouldn't lie to herself. Mikoneh's fresh trauma would remain, just as the old did.

Life changes all people, and no one can escape from that.

She curled her hands into fists. That didn't matter. She loved her twin, no matter what. Even if he'd become a broken husk—even if he'd been found in the same state as the Revenant's body—or if he'd been warped into something less than human—she would love him.

But he's doing better than I'd feared. Thank the Nijaal for that.

In truth, she was concerned about that as well. Mikoneh always pushed his trauma away, not tackling it, pretending he was strong. She couldn't let him avoid healing to escape the pain.

Owenekiras rested a hand on the corner of the altar. His eyes narrowed. Aqua blue light flashed from his palm, engulfing the slab. The light vanished. The stone along the center of the altar cracked.

"Mayanaleh," the Dragon King said.

Hearing her full name startled her, though it shouldn't. Of course, he would know it. He'd probably given it to her.

"Yes?" she asked.

"Please wake your brother. Bring him here. We must go swiftly, and I cannot carry them both in this form."

She paced across the corridor, crouched beside Mikoneh, and shook him. "Wake up. Come on, sleepyhead."

Mikoneh groaned, then cracked one eye open. He stared at her for a long moment, then he stiffened and sat straight. "Maya? Maya!" He caught her. "It—it was real." He was trembling again.

"Yes. You're here, I'm here. We're both safe."

He looked suddenly ready to shatter. A veil fell over his face. "No. We're not safe. Not until Sathe is gone."

Her heart cracked more. "Soon," she whispered. "Can you stand?"

"Yeah." He struggled to his feet, limbs quaking more. Arms wrapped around each other, they entered the chamber and approached the sundered altar. Owenekiras had gathered the slumbering dragon lord into his arms. The figure dangled there, limp as a corpse. The Revenant had drawn closer to the Dragon King. They waited, neither hinting at their hidden emotions.

The twins crossed the room one shuffling step at a time. The thunder of running feet and the rattle of bones filled the corridor beyond. Mages. Still far off but coming fast.

Maya quickened their pace. Just a few steps more. Mikoneh stumbled but righted himself at once. They reached Owenekiras.

"Touch me," he ordered.

They each caught his cape. Aqua light filled Maya's vision. The world tipped, then righted itself.

They stood in broad daylight within a forest at the roots of snow-capped mountains. For a moment, Maya was too dazzled to register where they were, then she recognized the peaks from her ride across Sirinhigha on the back of Owenekiras in his enormous dragon form.

They were in the north, at the very foot of the Andyan Mountains. Every hearth story Maya had grown up on claimed that beyond those mighty peaks lay the realm of the fae and fantastical. Even Fa and Mama hadn't disputed the claim. They'd only smiled when she'd asked if it was true.

Because they knew.

Gripping Maya, Mikoneh studied the same view. In the sun's glow through the wide-spread boughs his golden eyes were vivid. His hair, tangled and loose from the hurricane, framed his face and softened the gauntness of his cheeks. He looked almost childlike in his quiet wonder. A tear rolled down his cheek.

Through the pang in her chest, Maya smiled. She hadn't lost him. Then she tensed. "What about Penn? And the others?"

Owenekiras had moved out of view. She turned with Mikoneh to seek the man among the trees—and faltered.

An Ephe'ahn village spread before her at the end of a wide

path. Rooms hung from trees where decks ran in rings around the enormous trunks. Houses hunkered among the massive roots. A song started among the trees, welcoming, though she didn't understand the strange words. Her smile widened. These fae villages felt like home away from home—or perhaps more of a home than she'd known since her family's cottage had been devoured in violet flames.

Owenekiras was striding toward the village at the end of the well-tended path lined with white stones. He still carried the Revenant's body, his posture straight as though it weighed nothing. The specter drifted along at his side.

"Let's keep up," Mikoneh murmured.

She shook herself and moved after them, though her pace was hampered by Mikoneh's ginger steps. She tightened her hold around his waist.

"Almost there," she whispered.

He nodded through a grimace.

Nearing the village, Maya glimpsed several childlike faces peeking fearfully out from the roots and carved shutters, and one or two youthful fae looked down from the upper tree decks. Like in Kenooshin, this village showcased a range of skin tones from palest peach to deep brown, and the hair varied from pale blond to darkest raven—but every set of eyes was the same sky-blue color. The age range stretched from toddler to adolescent. Yet Maya suspected that, like Ter, many were older than they looked.

One Ephe'ahn moved toward them, a smile on her twelve-year-old face despite the Revenant's presence. "Welcome, Your Majesty." She offered a courteous bow without letting the arrows dump from the quiver at her hip. Her woodland garb was a blend of browns and grays, perhaps meant for stealth along the mountain passes with the snows coming on.

"Thank you, Hess," Owenekiras said. "I require several of your guest beds."

"Please." Hess motioned to the largest tree. "Be at home in our peace."

He moved past the Ephe'ahn, drawing the Revenant with him. As the cowled figure passed, the Ephe'ahn leader flinched. Maya caught Hess's eye and offered the biggest smile she could. The fae returned it with a dip of her head, then her gaze flitted to Mikoneh, and her blue eyes widened.

Maya's chest twinged. *He does look terrible.*

They climbed the tree stairs at an arduous pace, but at last Maya settled Mikoneh onto a bed under the glow of several giant mushrooms. A butterfly the size of her foot swooped from the ivy-woven ceiling and settled itself near Mikoneh. He fell into a deep slumber at once, oblivious to his surroundings.

"I'll return shortly," the Dragon King said.

Maya whirled toward Owenekiras, who stood in the enclosure's doorway. He'd deposited the Revenant's body in the next hanging chamber.

"You're going back for the others?" she asked.

"Yes."

She took a step toward him. "Be careful."

He inclined his head, then turned and strode down the ramp onto the deck. Maya drifted across the little room and peered out to watch her father descend the stairs. Hess waited for him at the tree roots where they conversed a moment before he moved on.

Maya blinked. *Is the Revenant staying here?* She twisted around and found her answer. The nearby hanging chamber glowed with eerie crimson light from every crack and crevice.

Her mind settled into a sea of worries. How could they return the poor soul to his body? How could they track down

Sathe and destroy him—especially with Mikoneh in his current condition? It all felt so overwhelming, so impossible.

She scowled. *Stop that. Stop it, Maya. Rescuing Mikoneh seemed impossible, too, but Owenekiras managed it.*

She hurried down the short ramp and moved along the deck to spot the Dragon King before he vanished beyond the trees. Owenekiras wasn't a reckless man. He was meticulous. Careful. Powerful.

We have a better chance against the darkness of the world than we ever knew.

A smile spread over her face. She could cradle hope like she hadn't dared in the past year. She could feel safe like she hadn't since the night Fa and Mama died. And she had more kin than she'd dreamed.

Whatever happens tomorrow, today is a victory.

Owenekiras returned at dusk, with Penn, Ter, Akonn, and Hilker in tow. All were grimy and tousled, but whole and hale. Maya raced from the hostel where she'd been conversing with several Ephe'ahn at a tiny table—and flung herself into Penn's arms. He stumbled backward laughing.

"Glad to see you, too," he said, drawing her back to look her over. "Are you well?"

"We have him. He's back." Her words were a slur in her haste to extend the news.

"So Lord Rokahn told me." Penn's eyes shone. "He also said Mikoneh seemed surprisingly well."

"He is. I mean—considering. You know how he is." Maya caught Penn's wrist. "Come, I'll show you. He's still asleep—he's so tired—but he's going to be fine."

Penn chuckled, allowing himself to be dragged after her. She was grateful. Surely, he needed a bath and a hearty meal after the day's battle—but Maya needed him to come. To confirm Mikoneh was still there. That she wasn't dreaming. She'd gone up into the tree to check on her twin half a dozen times since Owenekiras had left, and though the Ephe'ahn folk hadn't commented on it, their glances had sported pity and amusement in turns. She'd stopped climbing the stairs after that.

As they ascended to Mikoneh's chamber, Penn relayed the day's events in good-natured tones. He assured her that King Nilo was well, along with most of his family, courtiers, and servants. Many of the guards and knights had likewise been spared from the crumbling walls and even the skirmishes against the Mages.

"Hilker was amazing," Penn said, shaking his head. "I'd never have believed the wonders wind can perform under a master's hand. But he was nothing next to Ter."

Her step faltered. "Really?"

"Oh, yes." Penn's eyes were bright with the memory. "He was a wild thing. His speed—his agility—and that style of fighting. I know he didn't seem it at the time, but he was holding out on you during your quarterstaff bout."

Maya laughed. "I wondered. After all, he's much, much older."

Penn shrugged. "But he's such a little fellow. That didn't stop him at all, believe me. He had those Mages retreating—" His voice cut off. "Once, I thought I saw... It seemed like his eyes were glowing red, Maya. It must have been a trick in the stormlight, but by all the Nijaal, it gave me a fright."

They'd reached the ramp leading to Mikoneh's room. She stopped and turned toward Penn. "Did all the Mages leave? Did the king agree to recall his armies?"

Penn frowned. "For now. It's all very tentative. I did what I could, but my father's been an advocate for war. Nilo was confused by my intervention until I explained what's been going on in Relvin. He appeared genuinely upset that the Mages were infiltrating his provinces under his nose. That wasn't part of their agreement, it seems. Even so, it's obvious the king couldn't do much to stop what was going on—and didn't try. He's a coward."

Maya squeezed his wrist. "Well, it's in other hands now. We've done what we can."

The viscount smiled faintly. "For the moment that's true." He bobbed the wrist Maya was holding. "Lead on. I'm eager to see your wayward twin."

They entered quietly—and she blinked. Mikoneh was sitting up, a *korta* cut in half and mostly eaten. He looked up, chewing. Despite his hollow cheeks, his eyes were clear. That stubborn set of his jaw was back. He offered them a grim, determined smile. He'd even changed into the blue jerkin and gray breeches the Ephe'ahn had laid out for him. The clothes hung loose on his frame.

"Welcome back, Penn. What kept you?"

Perhaps it was his tone, or the strong set of his shoulders. Or maybe reality struck her at last. Whatever it was, Maya burst into tears and couldn't gain control of herself. Both men waited patiently, offering soothing words. She'd come so close to losing her whole world—but instead, it had grown. Finally, dabbing at her eyes, she scooted onto the bed beside her brother and rested her head on his shoulder.

Mikoneh ate and listened to Penn recap what he'd already told Maya, modestly underplaying his own part, judging by the words he chose. Once the viscount was finished, Mikoneh pushed his fruit shell aside and wiped his mouth with his sleeve.

"Glad that's settled for now," he said quietly. "We have other goals to aim for."

"You mean Sathe." Penn nodded. "Lord Rokahn mentioned retrieving the blood. Back where we started. But how can we defeat a Mage? They're nearly immortal."

"About that." Mikoneh folded his hands on his lap. "I have an idea. It's reckless and stupid—but I think it's our best chance."

CHAPTER 48

THE CRIMSON LIGHT

"Most believed the Mage Queen had been destroyed."

- From Athonen d'Ereth's *The Fall of Mages in the Age of Dragons*

"How do we track down Sathe?" asked Penn.

Mikoneh paused between mouthfuls of acorn soup and slabs of fluffy bread. The viscount's question was fair.

Despite eating that odd *korta* fruit recently, which had eased something in the rips of his soul, it hadn't touched Mikoneh's hunger. Luckily, Maya was a perceptive healer, and she'd insisted Mikoneh join them in the hostel below for a proper meal and a needful discussion. They'd arrived to find their other companions already gathered and deep in conversation. None had taken time to wash, but all—except Owenekiras—were shoveling down food.

Maya had led Mikoneh toward a human-sized table close to those already seated, then she'd ordered him to sit while she fetched their dinners. Waiting, he'd tuned into the debate between a white-haired fae and a middle-aged human about who should attend the Dragon King on the hunt for Sathe.

Maya had returned with soup, bread, and fruit, and she'd whispered the names Mikoneh didn't know. Captain Akonn of the Sword was the fae. Hilker was the older man—the Wind Master, apparently. No one had asked the obvious question—until Penn couldn't seem to abide it anymore.

How do we track down Sathe?

Silence fell. The few Ephe'ahn seated in the corners of the cozy, fire-lit room tipped their long ears toward the group of taller folk seated at the center of the hostel.

Penn persisted. "We tracked them to Oceana using Lord Owenekiras's connection to Mikoneh, right? But that's not going to help us now. Or do you already know where he's going?" His tones were courteous. It was obvious he respected these men.

"We don't," Akonn said. "Though we can make guesses. The issue is that Sathe has several holes he could've crawled into, and he won't stay still. We need to run him to ground."

"Difficult," Hilker grunted.

Mikoneh set down his spoon. "Not impossible though."

Every set of eyes fell on him. Maya's palpable worry needled his senses, but he chose to ignore that. He couldn't stay hidden forever inside Ephe'ahn villages while Sathe tormented him with his stolen blood. Sooner or later, he'd crack under that pressure. This must end—now. After *that*, Mikoneh could work through what the Dark Mage had done to him.

First, Sathe needed to be destroyed.

"You have an idea?" asked Owenekiras. Up until now, the Dragon King had been silent, evidently content to listen.

Mikoneh lost the thread of his thoughts. He studied the stoic face, and the unreadable eyes as cold as Sathe's.

They're not the same.

"Mikoneh?" Maya rested her hand over his. Her golden eyes—whose pupils were now slits, he realized—shimmered with worry.

That's what my eyes must look like now, too.

"Mikoneh?" Maya gently pressed.

He shook himself. "Sorry. I'm still tired."

"No one here will judge, lad," Hilker said.

"Where's the Revenant?" Mikoneh asked.

"Above," Ter answered from a small table he had all to himself. "He's standing near his body."

"I think he can help us," Mikoneh said.

The gazes shifted to Owenekiras. The Dragon King nodded. "You're right, if you're willing to command him."

Mikoneh's chest tightened. "Is that the only way he can track down Sathe? By command?"

"A Revenant's power is only as great as the order he's given. On his own, he can tap nothing."

Exhaling, Mikoneh tried to unravel the knots in his stomach. He didn't want to control Reven even once—but he also couldn't remain under Sathe's influence.

I can ask Reven. I can give him the choice whether to let me command him or not.

"If I did that," he said aloud, "it would be enough, right? Sathe used the Revenant to hunt me down. I figured it could work in reverse."

"Yes," Owenekiras said. "It's a good move."

"Indeed," agreed Ter.

"But what then?" asked Penn. "Maya said you intend to go along, Mikoneh, but isn't that walking right back into the viper's nest?"

"No." Mikoneh shook his head. "I think I have a plan for that, too." He glanced toward the Dragon King. "Unless you already have one."

"I have several," Owenekiras answered. "Perhaps one will gain us the victory. We'll not know until we employ them one by one."

Maya tightened her hold on Mikoneh. "Am I allowed to come?"

"You, Hilker, Penn, and Akonn will remain here," Owenekiras said before Mikoneh could speak. "None of you can contend against Mages in such numbers as we may face—and you will be needed in other conflicts should we fail."

"But—" Maya cut herself off, then sighed. "I won't argue because you're right. This is beyond me. But please promise me Mikoneh will be kept safe."

"Maya." Mikoneh snared her fingers in his hand. "That's not a promise anyone can make. I'm putting myself in danger, but it's my only recourse. If I don't, Sathe will claim me again one day. And frankly, I'd rather die than face that."

She searched his face, then bowed her head. She tried to speak but couldn't seem to find the words. He squeezed her hand tighter, unable to offer her comfort. Not yet. Not when he knew he was headed for what might be his death or far, far worse.

"I need to speak with the Revenant." Mikoneh stood, scooting his chair backward with a loud screech. Moving toward the stairs at the back of the hostel, he felt every gaze at his back. He shut the door with a low sigh, then straightened up and ascended to find Reven. His body was still over-wrought, but not as much as before. The dragonfang fruit had helped more than he could've hoped.

The hanging enclosure he sought was easy to spot. He

approached the crimson light with growing apprehension but deepening resolve. This was their one hope. Mikoneh couldn't return Reven's name until Sathe was destroyed. If either wanted the chance of freedom, they must seek it together. He conquered the ramp and slipped into the chamber where Reven's body lay. The hovering Revenant was an eerie shape in the red light.

"Can we speak?" Mikoneh asked.

Reven turned toward him and nodded from inside his deep cowl.

"I need your help to find Sathe, but..." The words caught in his throat.

'*Tell me what you need.*'

"I don't want to use you, Reven."

'*If you must command me, do so. I wish to aid you, Mikoneh Rokahn.*'

He stiffened. The use of that surname jarred him, but it wasn't as unwelcome as he'd thought it might be. It was simply another bizarre fact among those he'd recently discovered. It was also one that didn't bear absorbing until his life was his own again.

He took a step toward the specter. "Will it hurt you if I give a command?"

'*Not greatly.*'

"So it does hurt?"

The Revenant twisted away. '*It always hurt when Sathe commanded me, but that may be because I resisted. Perhaps yours would be different.*'

"Do I just...order you?"

'*Yes.*'

"Will it work?"

'*Yes.*'

Mikoneh inhaled, then nodded. "Tonight or tomorrow?"

'*Command me at once and I shall find him for you. There is no reason to delay.*'

He stepped closer to Reven. "I could free you instead, but I don't want to do that until I know whether you can return to your body. I think I know how to find out...but that's part of why I need to locate Sathe."

The cowl angled toward him. The crimson light flickered brighter. '*I trust you.*'

Those words—so simple—moved Mikoneh. He'd somehow been afraid that his time under Sathe's power had broken him beyond repair. That no one would dare rely on him or trust him again. Yet, they all seemed to. Reven's declaration was verbal proof of that.

"Thank you, Reven. I command you to find Sathe and report to me his present hideout."

Did the Revenant shudder under the force of that order?

Reven dipped his cowl. '*As you wish.*'

The specter vanished.

A wash of weariness forced Mikoneh to sit on the edge of the bed. He twisted to study the slumbering man lying under the leaf-woven coverlet. In the absence of the crimson glow, the soft luminescence of the mushrooms was soothing.

Mikoneh shivered, though he didn't feel cold. It wasn't that, and he knew it. He was afraid. Terrified. He never wanted to face Sathe again. But he must. He knew, beyond everything else, Owenekiras was right. If Mikoneh didn't witness the Mage's demise, would he ever believe himself free? Would he ever escape from the torture that evil man had inflicted on him?

He knew the answer. And he knew he must resist his fear with every fiber of strength he had left. If Reven succeeded, soon Sathe and Mikoneh would face off one last time.

Mikoneh had a plan—a good one. If it worked, he would rid Sirinhigha of a terrible monster. If he failed…

I won't because I can't afford to. It's that simple.

Soon. Soon it would be over.

CHAPTER 49

GUARDING TRUTH

"An extensive search offered no proof of her demise, and there were signs of retreat into the underground warrens."

\- From Athonen d'Ereth's *The Fall of Mages in the Age of Dragons*

Dawn glowed red over the large eastern peaks where the snow hadn't stuck yet. Mikoneh had dozed, but never deeply slept. Nightmares plagued him. He'd suspected that might happen when he'd retired to his guest chamber, and he'd risen earlier than anyone else to watch the sun rise. He took a seat at the deck's ledge, letting his legs hang free. The morning breeze teased his hair, doing its best to assure him that he was here, that this was real.

It didn't feel real. Maybe someday it would.

A child's steps approached along the deck behind him. "They say," said Ter, "that when darkness hunts the dawn, the sun learns to fly."

Mikoneh glanced up at him. "What's that supposed to mean?"

The Ephe'ahn shrugged. "Night enters our lives—blotting out light and hope, hunting it like a starving predator. It will do all it can to keep us from reigniting. But rise we can if we try. And then we will soar—just as you have done despite what Sathe tried to do to you."

Mikoneh lowered his gaze, shuddering. "He didn't *try*. He succeeded."

"Are you broken, Mikoneh?"

"I'm...cracked. I tried not to be, but...I failed. Ter, I failed. Just like in Relvin. Just like I'll probably fail when I meet Sathe again."

"Hmm. What is failure to you, I wonder."

"Failure is losing," Mikoneh mumbled.

"Ah. Losing what?"

"Everything. Loved ones, companions, myself."

"But that is inevitable, my friend." Ter sat down beside Mikoneh at the deck's edge and swung his legs. "Death claims us all, does he not?"

"You know what I mean."

"No. I'm afraid I don't." Ter's ear flicked. "You say you failed, but you still have what you had *before* Sathe captured and wounded you. You have your beloved sister, your good friend, and yourself."

"But I'm...not the same." Mikoneh's voice was a hoarse whisper. "I know that much. It doesn't feel real yet, but when it does..." He couldn't finish.

"But you aren't gone."

"I'm lost."

"Ah, there it is." Ter nodded. "Very well, you have failed to keep yourself found. Now what shall you do? The failure has set in. You have lost yourself. Does that mean the battle is over?"

Mikoneh grimaced. "I can't surrender."

"Why ever not?"

"Because...I won't surrender."

"Why?"

Flames licked at Mikoneh's insides. "I refuse to lose—okay?"

"But aren't you lost already? Didn't you *fail*?"

Mikoneh stared at him. His fists shook. "I—I don't know."

Ter hummed a few cheery notes, swinging his legs. "Most people favor sunsets. Not me. I like the promise of morning and a fresh day. What about you?"

"I suppose I like both," Mikoneh sighed. "But I prefer the high sun most."

"Why is that?" Ter stared at the nearby peak.

"I guess because it's bright and full. It's...warm."

"Spoken like a proper Fire Elementalist. I couldn't help but notice you've embraced the fire spirits."

Mikoneh frowned. "They helped me."

"Loyal little things," Ter nodded. "Each type of the Spirits Elemental are, of course. None more so than earth—except perhaps spirit of spirit, but that one is elusive."

"Owenekiras told you, did he?"

"That you have manifested spirit of spirit? No. He didn't. I guessed. Your, hmm, *presence* has shifted. Just as your eyes catch flame now and then, so too, spirit has marked you."

"I need to harness it, to fight Sathe, but I haven't seen any spirits of—of spirit. Just the silver light." He turned to face Ter. "What can I do to embrace the element?"

Ter slanted his head, smiling. "Dear friend, you already have. It is part of you."

"But fire—"

"Fire is temperamental, and you had a mental block. Not so with spirit. It comes when *you* are ready, never prematurely."

"But I didn't..." He grimaced, trying to find the words. "I didn't do anything special."

"You sought out the Revenant's true name for *his* sake, not yours. Spirit answers selflessness, Mikoneh." Ter rested a hand on his forearm. "Do not discount your sacrifice, and do not call it failure. Few would be expected to aid another under the circumstances you faced. Your boldness and your courage are to be commended."

Warmth bloomed across Mikoneh's cheeks. "It's just how I was raised."

"And your parents' part in your actions bears equal commendation."

Mikoneh's lungs constricted. "They're not my parents, though. I mean—I love them. I miss them. I'm not saying..."

"Gain isn't loss, Mikoneh." Ter patted his arm. "You are luckier than most to claim two sets of parents. There are some in this world who never knew so much as one. Tell me, do you do your surrogate parents an injustice by accepting the facts of your blood?"

"No."

"Then accept it and learn of it. And so long as you do not erase their part to play in your life, you are not worse off. Indeed, you can only be better for guarding truth against emotion. While feelings are necessary, they can do us an evil if we use them to lie to ourselves and others. The facts remain no matter how we feel. So, what will you do with your newfound knowledge? Will you walk the new path your life has revealed and find yourself anew?" His ear twitched idly.

"I'll try."

"And that is the difference, Mikoneh, between failure and victory." Ter patted his arm again, then hopped backward. "I'd best head down. I think it will not be long before we are on our way, and breakfast should be gotten first." His smile was a bright beam of light.

Mikoneh tracked the Ephe'ahn's retreat, trying to wade through his churning emotions. Ter was right. Lying to himself was never an answer. Nothing was the same. But Mikoneh had survived another battle, scarred yet alive. He still drew breath. A new life lay before him and Maya. They should explore their relationship with their birth father. What it was, and what it could be. After all, the Dragon King had known Jonatten and Seranni. He carried a piece of them, just like the twins did. They shared the same loss. That was common ground enough to plant something in.

More than that, Mikoneh still lived. He hadn't become like Reven or been crushed into a mindless servant of darkness. He'd escaped—and if he told himself that long enough, he would believe it.

I'm alive. I'm trying. That's the difference between failure and victory.

A chill raced up his spine.

Firebrand, I know you're out there. You'll not hide for long.

The voice nearly pitched him over, but Mikoneh willed himself to smile. Hide? No, not him. Not anymore.

I'm coming for you, Sathe. Just wait.

Time for the dawn to hunt darkness.

CHAPTER 50

GREED AND RUIN

The Revenant appeared at breakfast.

Mikoneh nearly choked on his bite of nut bread, then shoved his half-eaten plate aside and stood. "You found him?"

The Revenant nodded.

A stillness fell across the hostel. Maya went pale. She remained seated beside Mikoneh, but Penn stood, his hand going to the sword at his side. His eyes were grim, as though he considered arguing again to join the hunt.

Mikoneh shot him a warning glance. They'd been over the facts twice that morning. Nothing would change. Maya and Penn *wouldn't* come. Last night Penn had been calm about the plan, but evidently the reality of what Mikoneh needed to do had hammered through the viscount overnight. Still, his glance silenced Penn. Mikoneh softened his expression, offering what he hoped was a reassuring smile. Penn returned his smile, though it was half a grimace.

"Where is the vile maggot?" Ter asked, striding across the room. He'd been seated at a large corner table along with Owenekiras, though both had been quiet. Hilker and Akonn were likewise subdued. It was a familiar grimness. Mikoneh had seen that same quiet rallying of souls among his seasoned rebels before each new skirmish.

They knew—they *all* knew—this was no basic hunt. The odds weren't in their favor. But it had to be done all the same.

So many are risking their lives for me.

Mikoneh checked himself. It wasn't just for him or for Reven that they endangered life and limb. The cause was greater than Mikoneh had known while fighting his own losing battle in the forests of Relvin Province. It was bigger than the encroaching threat of Cimin's kin-slaying emperor, or the greedy merchant wars of Lintha.

What Mikoneh had personally seen below ground was merely the sheath of a deadly weapon. Though Penn and Maya had detailed how Owenekiras was driving Mages from their warrens, Mikoneh had glimpsed into Sathe's mind often enough to know those efforts had hardly dented the forces lurking beneath the world's surface. Sathe hadn't awakened a tenth of the legions slumbering in the deeper catacombs.

And—though Mikoneh hadn't seen it—he'd *felt* a darker cloud looming, brewing on the northern horizon, wherever the Mage Queen hid. Destroying Sathe wouldn't end the conflict, but it would eliminate a general in the enemy's army and keep Owenekiras on the field without fear of Sathe recapturing his heir.

There will still be other Dark Mages.

Mikoneh curled his hands into fists. That just meant he had to explore his true nature—the blood of a dragon—and become too powerful to be a hostage or a tool. Which meant he had to survive this hunt and become the victor.

Reven was watching him. Waiting.

Mikoneh shook himself. "Will you answer Ter's question?"

'*Sathe is in TeshRelle.*'

That scorched realm, where even scavenger birds wouldn't nest.

"Thank you, Reven." Mikoneh caught Ter's eye. "How do we get there?"

"There is a Void anchor near TeshRelle. It has not been used since the Age of Dragons." Ter's ears twitched down. "Still, it is functional."

The faint scuff of a scooting chair brought Mikoneh's attention to the Dragon King. The man stepped from his table to join them at the center of the room.

"Are you certain you won't let me come, my lord?" asked Akonn, rising from his chair.

Penn wasn't the only one trying to change their plan.

"Remain here, Captain," Owenekiras said. "Protect Mayanaleh. Please."

Akonn's hesitation was a mere heartbeat, then he dipped his head. "As you wish, my lord."

"Well." Ter pivoted slowly on one heel to take in the room. "If we are ready, we had best not delay."

"Agreed," Owenekiras said.

Maya launched from her chair and flung herself into Mikoneh's arms.

"Be careful." Her voice caught on a sob.

He drew her close, embracing her as tightly as he dared.

Her frame—always so frail since she'd broken—felt strangely sturdy.

"Promise," he whispered. "You, too."

"Promise." She drew back, golden eyes shimmering with tears. "I have Fa's sword. I'll fetch it."

Her words warmed something in Mikoneh's chest. He thought he'd lost his blade forever. "Keep it." He pulled back. "It won't serve me in this fight. Keep it until I return." He wasn't willing to consider whether he'd ever see her again. The answer *must* be yes. He wouldn't leave his twin alone in a world set to burn in violet flames.

Trying is the difference between failure and victory.

He and Penn clasped each other's arms, then Mikoneh moved toward the hostel's front door after Owenekiras. Ter trailed them, and the three stepped outside. The Revenant followed a moment later. It was a crisp morning, but the day promised to be pleasant. Here autumn was still tame, though it was so far north. This area of forest was untouched by Mage influence—for now.

Owenekiras led them toward the northward path Mikoneh had trod yesterday.

"Why did we come to this village?" asked Mikoneh, taking in the beautifully carved homes tucked among the ancient roots.

It was Ter who answered. "Just as in Kenooshin, this village wields a protective barrier that shields you from Sathe's long reach. Also, Lord Rokahn suspected Sathe would flee north. TeshRelle was a good gamble. This brought us closer."

"Does physical distance matter when you activate Void travel?" Mikoneh smiled faintly at a toddling Ephe'ahn peeking around a sapling at the edge of the village green. The child smiled back and waved chubby fingers.

"Yes," said Ter, "in terms of energy output. It can be tiring to transport multiple people across a wider stretch—but it has little to do with the physical plane. You remember that magical network I mentioned—the corridors and doorways one can access via the Void?"

"Yeah. I remember."

"Well, the location of the doorways within *that* realm decides the energy output. Kagon—ah, that is the name of this village. Anyway, Kagon is closer to Oceana than any other village this far north. And with TeshRelle being a good guess, it made strategic sense to come here."

"That," Owenekiras said, "and it is one of only two remaining access points into the Nijaalin lands."

Ter's ear twitched. "Were you planning to visit Lady Katanni?"

Owenekiras glanced toward Mikoneh. "It may be necessary yet."

"Ah. That is true." Ter considered Mikoneh. "You are in pain."

Mikoneh's stomach twisted. "I'll recover."

"Yes," Ter agreed, "but a treated wound heals better. Once this Sathe matter is settled, it may indeed be wise to seek the Lady of the First Kin."

Mikoneh's stomach flipped. He nearly stumbled, though he couldn't say why the title shook him to his core. "First Kin?"

"They are the five original beings of Sirinhigha—which is where magic was born."

Mikoneh arched a brow. "Where else would it be born?"

"There are many worlds in this wide universe," Ter said, taking on a tone Mikoneh had often heard adults use when they were about to issue a lecture. "Many are inhabited with folk like you and me."

"You mean rabbit-people and two-legged dragons?"

Ter's chuckle was patient. "You're the literal type, I see."

"Yes."

"Even so, I shall continue. It all began here, where magic was first born. The Celes—which are beings born in a realm between Heaven and Hell to keep order—anyway, they helped to oversee Sirinhigha's birth. It is said that Life and Nature wept tears of happiness from whence the First Kin sprang up like flowers."

The story wasn't grounded in anything Mikoneh understood—yet something within him reacted to the term *Celes*. He almost...almost *knew* that word. Somehow it made him angry.

"Lady Katanni of the Nijaal was among them," Ter went on. "She is the First Kin who oversees—hm, what you might call mortal-kind."

"So, she's a goddess?"

"Ah, no. Not that. She works hand-in-hand with the Celes —and they are certainly not deities."

"What about the other First Kin?"

"They were given charge over other aspects of this realm. One was placed over justice and order. Another over nature, such as the Spirits Elemental. Another over magic. The last was the *Complété* itself. But perhaps this is not the right time for that subject."

"Maybe not." Mikoneh's head was throbbing, though he found himself intrigued.

They reached the edge of the forest. The sun had heaved itself over the eastern peaks and set the snow on the Andyan Mountains on fire. Mikoneh stared at the sight, dazzled. After an ageless month beneath the ground—stuck in the dank darkness and filth of Mage company, with only a few glimpses of the surface—he was overcome by the beauty he'd always taken for granted.

Ter brushed his fingers against Mikoneh's arm. "Ready?"

He tore his eyes from the peaks and nodded. "Yeah. Let's go."

At Ter's instruction, Mikoneh rested his hand on the Ephe'ahn's shoulder. Ter snagged a portion of Owenekiras's cloak. Then the world tipped and righted itself. They stood in a blackened land.

Once Mikoneh's equilibrium settled, he took in the decay of the dark, brittle cliffs, charred and flaking like burnt paper. The ground was cracked and scorched, as though dragons had breathed flame across it and destroyed all life in the soil. That was probably the case.

Somehow, Mikoneh could imagine those last moments before the Mage stronghold fell. The cries of terror. The last desperate surge of tainted magic against the overwhelming draconic forces in the sky. A sun that blazed with violet light. It had been a turning point in the war—a victory needed desperately by the forces of light after so much loss.

The taste of fire teased his tongue. He could almost *feel* himself in the fray, slipping among the dark forces, swinging a sword that blazed with silver light. They didn't see him coming. He was intangible—invisible—cutting his way toward the stronghold and the enemy that awaited him.

The stench of charred remains filled his nostrils.

You've returned, Firebrand.

Sathe's voice jarred him from a reverie he didn't understand. Owenekiras and Ter were watching him, their faces masks. Reven stood nearby, still as stone.

Did you wish to play again? The Mage's laughter rang through Mikoneh's head.

He set his teeth, fighting the churning of his gut. He didn't have time for fear.

Come to me. Come, let us settle this once and for all.

"He's close," Mikoneh choked out. "And he's using my blood."

Owenekiras nodded. "I can *smell* him."

How the Dragon King managed that through the charcoal and rot, Mikoneh couldn't guess. *Maybe he doesn't smell the past.* But why not?

Ahead, the ruins of the stronghold rose like a broken spear trying to pierce the sky, even in death. An image of what that fortress had once been flickered across Mikoneh's mind: a tall, spiraling tower, climbing heavenward. Dark as death. Evil as murder. A grand pillar of greed and ruin.

We had to destroy it.

He hesitated. *We?*

Violet lightning crackled across the sky. Owenekiras lifted his hand, and aqua streams of light blasted from his palm, meeting the tendrils of violet. They sparked and flashed, lifting the fine hairs on Mikoneh's neck.

He stepped to one side of the Dragon King, searching the blackened land.

There. Across the wide field, Sathe stood halfway up the broken tower along a jutting arched bridge. He was highlighted by the stream of lightning pouring from his hands.

"Go, while I have his attention." Owenekiras never took his eyes from the lightning bolts he fended off. "Execute your plan, Mikoneh. Ter, keep him safe."

Ter nodded, and the two sprinted from the Dragon King's side. Mikoneh didn't glance back to check if Reven was close. He knew the specter would follow to help when the time was right.

Mikoneh's heart slammed against his ribs. He had a plan— and Ter and Owenekiras had agreed to trust him, though they had backup plans ready just in case.

That's for the best. This could end very badly for me.

Yet if he succeeded...

They raced across the charred earth, arcing wide to come at the tower from the right side. Every step kicked up puffs of black dust that still tasted of fire and fear. In his mind's eye, Mikoneh glimpsed bodies strewn across the earth. The memory of screams filled his ears.

"Sathe's brother was once sealed here, wasn't he?" Mikoneh gasped out.

"Yes, near here," Ter answered. "Suld was bound by the Nijaal."

"How did he get out?"

"That I do not know."

Sathe can't be bound, then. If that's one of the backup plans, it's not enough. I must succeed.

He curled one hand into a fist and let the warmth of spirit touch his fingers, soothing his nerves. A blast and flash of lightning stole his focus, and he nearly tripped over his feet before he corrected himself. A bolt shrieked toward him.

I see you, Firebrand.

Ter darted ahead and caught the bolt with his bare hands, teeth ground together. He grunted, taking the force—though how, Mikoneh couldn't guess. The Ephe'ahn tipped his head toward the tower.

"Go on. I will catch up."

Mikoneh sprinted on, gooseflesh rising as Reven's presence drew nearer.

'*Tell me to protect you, and I will.*' The Revenant's voice slithered through his mind.

Mikoneh nearly refused. The very idea was revolting—controlling another life was utterly wrong—but he nodded. For both their sakes. "Protect me!"

A score of lightning raced toward them, and Reven

appeared, taking the strike full on. It absorbed inside him, not affecting the specter at all.

I knew it! I knew you'd stolen him somehow. Fool!— and hypocrite! You enslave your own kind, do you?

Mikoneh rolled his eyes. Sathe was desperate if his verbal assaults were so wide flung. Good. Perhaps Mikoneh could win this after all.

Stop doubting. Just run!

As they neared the tower's base, the ground sloped upward. Huge broken stones, once part of the mighty tower, littered the ground. Mikoneh ducked behind one and crouched down to catch his breath. Reven flickered out of sight, to keep from giving away their position. But that would do little. Sathe could sense Mikoneh, as surely as Mikoneh could scent him out. This wasn't a stealth mission. It was an inescapable conflict. A duel to the death, one way or another—because Mikoneh wouldn't be taken alive again.

He rested his head against the cold stone. Each breath rattled through his lungs. The world flashed aqua and violet above him. Dark clouds reflected the lights where they swirled in the firmament, hiding daylight. Shrouding any hint of life beyond this dead realm.

Even so...

Mikoneh drank in a long breath, then shifted his boots against the gritty ground. He bolted from the protection of the boulder. Lightning struck near his left foot. He dodged it. Reven took the next hit.

Even so, life exists. Hope exists. And I won't let Sathe destroy it.

He hunched down behind another boulder and risked a glance at the tower. Sathe remained on the broken bridge, sending out lightning in three directions to stall the others. To keep them back.

I need to get closer.

That would prove difficult. The boulders weren't much protection the closer Mikoneh drew to the tower. Sathe's vantage point was almost perfect.

I have to try.

Owenekiras had promised to buy him time. Mikoneh had to trust the man to deliver.

If anyone can, it's him.

The ground rumbled. Pebbles rattled free of the boulder, raining down on Mikoneh. He shifted and glanced toward his companions. Relief surged through him.

Owenekiras had transformed. The great black dragon, with blue lightning wings and mane, stood upon the field: a thing of majesty and cold fury. Its great maw opened wide. Aqua light —the essence of Void—poured forth in a storm.

Sathe's scream rent the sky, then Hollow flowed from the Mage's palms, not as lightning but as a beam of tainted light. The opposing forces met and exploded across the open sky.

Now, Mikoneh. Move.

He threw himself into the open and tore across the powdery ground toward the tower proper. The hard-packed earth jolted his bones with every heavy step. He yanked off his jerkin and threw it aside, then pinned his gaze on Sathe above. Wings sprouted from Mikoneh's back, and the wind caught him, lifting him higher.

Toward his enemy. His captor.

Flames bloomed at his fingertips. A fury like magma flooded his blood, painting his vision red. His wings thrust him toward the Mage perched at the edge of the broken bridge protruding from the tower.

Silent, Mikoneh aimed for Sathe, praying the Mage wouldn't see him swooping closer—closer—

Sathe turned. His eyes widened—no longer gold and slitted, with their bond broken. The dark irises caught the flash of approaching lightning. A

grin stretched over his pallid face. "Firebrand!" He shot out Hollow lightning to fend off Owenekiras's attack, then whipped around to face Mikoneh. Violet light enveloped his frame, and he lifted his arms as though to embrace the approaching dragon.

Mikoneh winged to a halt, unleashing fire. It poured over the tainted air, engulfing Sathe in tendrils of flame.

CHAPTER 51

THE ESSENCE OF SPIRIT

"The Dragon King severed every corrupted dragon bond he could. Alas, many dragons were wounded past all healing—and the Mage Queen had long ago murdered every Dragon Healer she could discover."

- From Athonen d'Ereth's *The Fall of Mages in the Age of Dragons*

The Mage's laughter filled the air. The fire couldn't burn him.

As expected. Mikoneh lowered his arms, chest tight, nerves thrumming. Sweat trickled down the sides of his face.

Sathe batted off the last wisps of flame, still chuckling. "Did you think an infant dragon could *touch* me? Was this your grand plan?"

"No." Mikoneh narrowed his eyes. "It was just hello. Reven!"

The Revenant materialized behind Sathe. The specter snatched the voluminous sleeves and jerked the Mage's arms behind his back.

Sathe's eyes narrowed, but his grin remained in place. "Using my own weapon against me. That's better. But still ineffective. He hasn't the power to kill me, Firebrand. None of you does—not even your precious *father*."

"He doesn't plan to," Mikoneh growled. "I handle my own fights."

"Oh? Like you did in Oceana against *Lord Drayve*? Is that why you nearly died at the stake?"

Mikoneh scoffed. "I escaped, or did you forget that fact?"

"I *let* you escape, and you know it well." Sathe's eyes gleamed. "What you are now—what you've become—that's thanks to me. You'd have remained a helpless human without me."

"Do all Mages skew the truth to suit their egos, or is that just you?" Mikoneh shook his head. "I didn't come here to banter, Sathe. I came here to destroy you."

Sathe threw his head back and cackled. The noise was unbalanced. Maddened. "You can't touch me! None of you can!" His eyes flashed violet.

Instinct screamed at Mikoneh.

He winged backward.

The tower exploded. Boulders flew through the air. Rocks battered Mikoneh's wings. The bridge crumbled beneath Sathe's feet, and he slipped from Reven's grasp. As he tumbled toward the ground, the Mage's eyes remained riveted on Mikoneh.

The ground.

Hundreds of Mages poured from tunnels in the cracked tower foundation. Scampering up like skeletal spiders. Shooting lightning toward Owenekiras in dragon form.

Mikoneh scanned the black field. No sign of Ter.

"Reven, secure Sathe!"

They couldn't lose him among the undead forces. If he got away...

It will never end.

Gritting his teeth, Mikoneh swooped low. Reven shot past him, trailing Sathe among the cowled forms. Violet lightning aimed at Mikoneh. He dodged, left, right, up—and soon he lost sight of the Mage general among the writhing masses.

Run, run. Catch me, Firebrand. Find me if you can!

Mikoneh ignored the man's childish taunts. He'd been so close.

Hollow lightning struck his wing. He cried out and tumbled backward, plummeting toward the field. Reven caught and cradled him like an infant. Mikoneh hissed under the growing pain, anger blazing in his chest.

"Put me down and find him, Reven." His voice was a low growl.

The Revenant touched down on a hill near the field and gently set Mikoneh on his feet. Then he shot off, a mere streak of crimson light. Mikoneh stretched his wounded wing forward to examine it. The membrane was blackened where the Hollow had struck. Pain pulsed from the spidering lines of violet bleeding along the fiery veins. Was it spreading?

What will the taint do?

"Mikoneh!" Ter's voice.

He jerked toward the field. Running at him, a flock of Mages on his heels, Ter was waving both arms.

"Behind you!" Ter shouted.

Mikoneh tensed, whirling. He expected a cluster of Mages —or perhaps Sathe—but instead the toadish monster from the tunnels loomed over him. Beady black eyes met his gaze. The creature spread its enormous lips in a smile that was neither human nor benign.

Chills surged up Mikoneh's flesh. Flames sparked in his palms. He flung his hands before him and summoned the fire spirits. They rushed at the monster—and the thing swallowed them in a giant gulp.

Mikoneh stumbled backward.

"*Dodge!*" Ter yelled.

Mikoneh leapt aside. An arrow whistled past his head, a mere inch from his pointed ear. It lodged in the monster's eye. The creature lurched backward, issuing a deafening roar. Ter reached Mikoneh's side in the next heartbeat.

"Leave the Undrik to me." The Ephe'ahn nocked another arrow, then unleashed it, taking out the monster's other eye. "Find Sathe."

Mikoneh spun away with a grunt and stared at the field where the Mages had been chasing Ter. They'd all been wrapped in ice from heel to skull. Beyond them loomed the Dragon King, scales glistening as though ice was etched between each one.

"Your ride is there," Ter said, not sparing him a glance. "Take it."

Mikoneh raced down the hill. His damaged wing still burned with taint. He folded it against his back, along with the other wing. Black powder puffed up around him, agitating his lungs. Adrenaline surged through his limbs, urging him on.

Owenekiras spread his wing across the ground to give Mikoneh a path to his spined back. Doubling his pace, Mikoneh conquered the wing and caught up threads of blue mane.

"Ready!" he shouted.

The great dragon spread his wings and launched into the sky. Wind tugged at Mikoneh's hair. His wings quivered, anxious to take flight—but he resisted the call. Leaning out as far as he could, he searched the swarm of Mages congregated around the tower. Many were frozen. The rest aimed Hollow at their brethren to free them from the rime.

"How long until they break free?" he yelled into the wind.

Owenekiras's answer thundered through his mind. *'Mere moments.'*

They had no time. *Sathe will stay in hiding unless I can trick him.*

"This isn't working," he said aloud. "We can't capture him unless I'm the bait."

The dragon wheeled over the field, silent for a moment. *'What did you have in mind?'*

"He needs to capture me."

'Out of the question.'

"If he bonds with me again—"

'No.'

"We have to draw him out somehow!"

'I will draw him out.'

"You know you can't—but I can. It may not need to be a completed bond. He just has to believe I'm his."

'You're taking a great risk.'

He leaned against the dragon's long neck. The scales felt cool beneath his hand and seeped beneath his clothing. "Trust me, please."

Violet lightning scored the sky. More Mages were free and aiming their magic at the dragon. Owenekiras craned his neck, opened his maw, and blasted ice at the field. The Mages who didn't shield themselves swiftly enough were encased once more.

'I will trust you, Mikoneh.'

The Revenant appeared at Mikoneh's side, cloak unaffected by the streaming wind. Hiding his startlement, Mikoneh twisted to face the specter.

"Find him?"

Reven nodded.

"Is he still in TeshRelle?"

Another nod.

Mikoneh let himself grin. "I need to get knocked toward the ground—and I need it to look authentic. When the next bolt of Hollow comes close—"

Violet light exploded across the air, narrowly missing Owenekiras. Reven shot out his elongated hand, using the force of his aura to throw Mikoneh backward. The latter lost his grip and tumbled from Owenekiras's back with a genuine yelp.

That works, he thought to himself, torn between terror and wild amusement.

His wings caught him, the injured one throbbing. He glided toward the ground, his motion erratic, as one wing compensated for the hobble of the other. He touched ground at the edge of the field, near a craggy stand of rocks at the base of a mountain. It was blackened like the rest of the realm.

He wasn't connected to Sathe any longer, yet every instinct honed over the past month screamed at him that the Mage was near. This was the moment. Their last stand.

It must be.

He reached for the essence of spirit. He still barely knew how to harness it. He wasn't certain his plan would work— and yet...

"It's just you and me now," came Sathe's wintry tones.

Mikoneh whirled toward the shadows beneath the craggy rocks. "You're a coward, Sathe."

"Am I?"

"You claimed we couldn't defeat you, yet you ran—ran

from *three* people. You even had to summon your minions to thwart us."

"Taunt me," Sathe said. "But remember what pain I can deliver when you're disrespectful."

The memories of his captivity swelled as though the Mage's words had triggered a spell. Mikoneh swayed on his feet, unable to shield against the humiliation, the violation, the terror, and the spite. It was enough to choke him.

'*Mikoneh, be strong.*' Owenekiras's voice was like a clarion note against the trauma.

Drawing his shoulders erect, Mikoneh eyed Sathe with forced calm. "You'll never hurt me again."

Sathe chuckled, drawing closer. He was a looming presence set against the obsidian backdrop of the cliffs. His robes slithered across the parched ground behind him. "Lying to yourself will only make the punishment worse."

"I mean what I say." The fingers of his right hand prickled with silver light.

Sathe began a chant. He clutched a parchment inked with runes in a complex circle.

Mikoneh hesitated. Did the Mage need an altar to force the bond—or did that only make the magic easier to harness?

He drew back a step, nerves thrumming.

Sathe's eyes glittered.

Far away, the snap and crackle of Hollow and Void flashed in the sky. A dragon roared. Shouts filled the air. None of that could matter. It was just him and Sathe. Just the two of them. And soon, only one.

Mikoneh drew a dagger from his belt and set it against his own throat. "Stop chanting, Mage."

Sathe froze. His lips curved up. "You wouldn't."

"Care to test that?" Mikoneh held those cold eyes. "I'll not be bound to you again, no matter what price I have to pay."

The cruel smile tightened. "What about your twin? Would you truly break her heart again? I know how fragile she is—I *saw* it in your mind."

Mikoneh's hand trembled. He tightened his hold on the dagger. "She's stronger than you think. Stronger than *I* thought."

"You'll test that strength just to spare yourself?" Sathe sneered. His eyes gleamed with frostlight.

"Yes. Along with sparing my family the heartache of watching me help you."

"So noble." Sathe scoffed. "So like a dragon." His eyes narrowed into slits. "Put the weapon down, Firebrand. Return to me. Our game of Fang and Claw has ended."

"You're right, Sathe. Our game ends today—but not because you own me. You never did."

"I owned you, body, mind, and soul. You were mine, and you will be again." He lunged forward, one clawed hand outstretched. Violet light swirled around the rune-filled parchment. He shouted his chant.

"Reven!" Mikoneh stumbled back. Before him, the Revenant materialized, absorbing the Hollow taint. Blocking the parchment's power.

Sathe staggered to a halt. "Who's the coward?" he laughed.

"Reven, hold him."

The specter vanished, then winked into sight behind Sathe. The Mage tried to run, but Reven was faster. Tendrils of red wrapped around the robed man's body like slithering serpents. While Mikoneh couldn't read the specter's expression, Reven's emotions ribboned over the air, almost tangible: hatred, fury, hurt, and a prevailing sense of justice.

My turn. Mikoneh strode forward. He held himself tall, gathering his resolve and steeling his nerves. Too often Sathe had made him feel like a child, but he wasn't. He was a grown man. And this Mage—this *monster*—would never diminish him again.

The tendrils of crimson heaved, dragging Sathe to his knees. He hissed, then jutted out his chin. "What can you do to me? *Nothing.*"

Mikoneh halted before him, staring down into those eyes. He let himself smile. "Then, why do you look so afraid?"

Sathe scowled. "I'm not—"

"You should be!" Mikoneh's voice cracked. Fire spirits appeared at his shoulders, drawn by his raw fury. "You robbed and tormented me. Every moment with you was a private hell. But that ends now, Sathe—and not just for me. I'll never let you wound another soul—living or dead. Not ever."

"Even if you could, do you think you'd be safe?" Sathe chuckled. "How do you think I found you, Firebrand? Do you believe I was in Relvin—in Drayve's pathetic company—by chance? Do you believe I'm the only one interested in you?"

Mikoneh crouched to come level with Sathe. "You think I care?"

"You should."

"You're probably right." Mikoneh tipped his head to one side. "Tomorrow, I'll focus on that. For now, it's all about you."

Sathe started to grin. Mikoneh slammed his fist into the Mage's jaw. Sathe's head lurched back, then he started to laugh. "You're going to *bruise* me? That's your master plan?" Sathe straightened his head, his sneer deepening.

Silver light sparked in Mikoneh's clenched fist. He uncurled his fingers, revealing the glowing hue. The Mage's mockery died. His eyes widened. Had he any blood in his face, he'd have grown even paler.

"Wait—stop."

"Know what this is, Sathe?" Mikoneh flipped his palm back and forth. The silver glow heightened.

"But you're fire..."

"I have two elements, as it turns out." Mikoneh brought the glow closer to Sathe's face. The light shaped into a flame. "And I found out something interesting when I was held by you."

Sathe swallowed. Perspiration beaded his brow. "Don't be a fool."

"Oh, I won't. Promise." He lowered the silver flame to Sathe's chest. Drawing a quick breath, he plunged it into the Mage's heart with a silent command: *Steal his true name.*

The Mage spasmed, eyes bulging. His mouth fell open, though he remained alive and whole. Every muscle in his body tightened. "Take it out! Take it out!" His scream throbbed through Mikoneh's sensitive ears.

He leaned close. "*No.*"

Sathe screamed before the silver flame emerged. Shaped like a palm-sized dragon, the spirit winged into Mikoneh's open hand and slipped beneath his skin, sending a warm tingle through his body. Knowledge flooded his mind. Sathe's true name settled into his core.

Mikoneh rose to his feet and stared down Sathe. The Mage trembled. He seemed small and vulnerable.

Dilliandaran, you are mine.

CHAPTER 52

LIKE ICE

"Dragon clans slipped into obscurity after that, most taking human shape to heal from their wounds. After 20,000 years, few humans believe they exist anymore. Most dragons have forgotten what they really are as well."

- From Athonen d'Ereth's *The Fall of Mages in the Age of Dragons*

Reven's tendrils vanished. The Mage slumped forward onto his palms, a sob escaping his lips.

"Thief. Monster," Sathe whispered.

"No," Mikoneh said. "This is justice, poetic and right. You've stolen more than I can weigh upon a scale."

The Mage shook harder, then lifted his head. "Spare me. That's all I ask. I'll tell you anything. Everything!"

"You'll tell me—and then I will end you. There's no room for mercy here. If I let you live, you'll eventually escape. Nor do

I have any desire to enslave a fellow life, no matter how depraved it is."

Sathe scoffed. "Yet you've taken the Revenant."

"I'll free him as soon as I can. *That* is my first question for you: Can I return him to his body and restore his life? *Tell me.*"

The Mage quaked, but he couldn't resist the command of his master. "Y-yes. It is possible."

"Could you accomplish it?"

"I? No. Another could."

"Who?"

"Lady Katanni knows how." He ground out the words like they burned him.

Relief soared through Mikoneh. "Next question. What can you tell me about the Mage Queen's plot?"

"Very little," Sathe said. "I...I've fallen out of favor. That's why I infiltrated Oceana. To raise an army. To prove my worth and loyalty. It was working...but my brother was killed by a—a True Seer. That angered her all over again. My efforts to control you were my last hope."

"So," Mikoneh said, "even among your own kind, you're detestable. That figures."

Sathe caught the fabric of Mikoneh's trousers. "Spare me. I wasn't only cruel to you."

A harsh laugh ripped from Mikoneh's throat. "I didn't know you were delusional."

"Surely—"

"*Don't.*" The command pulsed over the air. Sathe shrank under it, while Mikoneh trembled under the weight of his own wrath. *Be calm. Stay calm.* "What *can* you tell me about the Mage Queen's movements?"

The Mage straightened up. "She sets her sights on Simynshin and Cimin. Everywhere else we have many footholds. But in those two kingdoms, only a few. She targets King Prettem most. Simynshin's son and heir—Prince Atlanse—he resists. His weakness is his daughter. But the Mage Queen must move with great care."

"Do you know anything else about the strikes on Simynshin and Cimin?"

"No—but I can learn more. I have allies—"

"What can you tell me about any other Mage plots?"

"I know things…"

"No guesses, Sathe."

"I—I can learn."

"So, you know nothing else."

Sathe's shoulders drooped. "But of you, I know a little more."

"Tell me."

"You have an enemy. You, yourself. A great one. I don't know its origin or shape—only that it came to me. He. I believe it is a man, or something like one."

"What else?"

"He hates you—but he doesn't want you to die. He revealed your whereabouts in Oceana, yours and your family's, for a single price."

"What price?"

Violet light shone in Sathe's eyes. "*Pain.* Yours. He asked that you suffer tremendously."

Mikoneh flinched despite his efforts not to react. "Do you know why?"

"No. I only read his hatred. It was deep, dark, and…almost sweet."

"Can you describe him?" Mikoneh's insides crawled like spiders had gotten under his flesh. He couldn't think of an enemy beyond Sathe or Drayve—not anyone he'd personally injured to such a point. Yet the enmity...it was strangely familiar...

"I never saw his face," the Mage said. "I never learned his name. I was skeptical but desperate enough to agree. After all, the price was negligible. If you weren't what he claimed, I could make you suffer to fulfill my end, then leave you to whatever fate. But you *were* the dragon heir of Rokahn. He knew that. Somehow, he knew. When no one else could find you."

"Enough." Mikoneh nearly kicked Sathe. Fear and fury warred within him. He drew several breaths to clear his swirling head. "What happened to the man after he revealed my location?"

"He vanished. I've not seen him since." Sathe's lips curled up. "But he was right. He told me—told me you were cleverer than even you knew. More skilled. A worthy asset for my goals."

"Anything else?"

Sathe's eyes darted around, as though he sought a hasty answer.

"Anything you know that is vital to Owenekiras's cause?"

"His sister—" Sathe hissed. "But I cannot say more. I'm bound to silence. Perhaps...perhaps if you spare me."

"He can tell you no more," Ter said from behind Mikoneh.

Turning, Mikoneh tensed. The Ephe'ahn was taller than before—the height of a twelve-year-old—and his irises glowed crimson. He clutched his bow and a quarterstaff. His quiver was empty of arrows.

Sathe scoffed. "Don't trust the human-slayer. He's crueler than any Mage."

Ter placed himself at Mikoneh's side. "Are you a judge now, Sathe?" His voice was cold and low.

The Mage tugged on Mikoneh's pants again. "Please. Spare

me. I can tell you things—about the Age of Dragons. About what your father and his"—Sathe's eyes cut to Ter—"colleagues did. The atrocities."

"War is nothing but atrocities," Ter said. He whipped out his staff and knocked Sathe's hand loose. "There. That is better. You might have caught a disease with further contact, Mikoneh." His voice was still tight, but some of the old warmth framed those tones.

Mikoneh took a step back from Sathe. "Ter's right. I think this conversation is over. I only need one more thing. How many vials of my blood did you take?"

Sathe flinched. "Three."

"Where are they?"

"I have them."

"No other Mage has my blood?"

"None," Sathe spat out. "Spare me—"

"Discard them. *Now*."

The Mage's hands shook, but he reached inside his robes and produced three glass vials full of blood. He dropped them to the ground.

"Good. I believe that concludes our conversation. So ends our game, Sathe. I win."

The Mage's eyes bulged again. "No. Please. I can't die. Spare me, I beg—"

"*Dilliandaran*, die." The words fell from Mikoneh's lips, but they sounded far away. Unattached. The moment was surreal, though his sense of justice was tightly wound around his resolve. He hated to kill, but he acted when it felt right. This was such a moment.

Sathe's soul was a cankered husk of want and evil. He had no light, no truth, no redemption within him. He couldn't be held captive forever. He couldn't be bound. To let him live was to risk further damage to innocent souls, and Mikoneh didn't want to keep Sathe's true name within himself.

This was the only answer Mikoneh could find.

Sathe cracked like ice. His skin lost its luster and mummified. His eyes were wide and afraid, then they rolled backward into his skull. He fell forward in pieces that crumbled to dust. He'd cheated death for centuries, but at last, it had claimed him.

Mikoneh stood above the powdered remnants of his captor. Too numb to cry. Too numb to rejoice. He turned toward Ter.

"Now what?"

"Now," Ter said solemnly, "we leave this fell place."

"Good." Mikoneh's gaze drifted back to the Mage's remains. "I never want to come back here."

He stooped to claim the vials, then rose and turned toward the field, expecting to find the black dragon still fighting the Mages. Instead, he found Owenekiras in human form standing among the rocks and boulders riddling the base of the craggy mountain. Beyond him, the field stood empty.

"They fled," the Dragon King explained. "In the moment you stole Sathe's true name, they lost their general. In their current state, lesser Mages cannot remain conscious for long without a leader to fuel them. They will return to the tunnels and await a new master in slumber."

"Best to collapse these tunnels, then, now that the two brothers are dead." Ter spoke in lighter tones than before, though they were still grim. His irises remained red.

"Agreed." Owenekiras studied Mikoneh. "Are you well?"

A weak smile spread over his face. "No. But I will be."

The Dragon King nodded. "Ter, guide Mikoneh toward the anchor. I will join you momentarily."

"Of course." Ter took Mikoneh's arm. They strode toward

the green meadow beyond the boundaries of TeshRelle. Reven followed close behind. Mikoneh didn't look back, even when he heard the thunder and felt the resounding quake that followed.

Let that be the end of Sathe and TeshRelle alike.
Even if the war is just beginning.

CHAPTER 53

SERIELIAS

"The war was finally over. But the Lady of the North suspected the Mages weren't gone forever. She claimed they would rise again. I'm inclined to believe her."

- From Athonen d'Ereth's *The Fall of Mages in the Age of Dragons*

The three companions returned to the village at dusk, while Reven stayed at the borders. The glow of sundown set fire to the golden leaves, and the flickering, blue lanterns were a welcome sight after the gloom of Tesh-Relle. Ephe'ahn stood to either side of the path, singing a quiet song, perhaps in welcome, or perhaps to bid farewell to the waning daylight.

Mikoneh allowed Ter to guide him through the hostel and up the spiraling stairs. Owenekiras remained below, presumably to speak with the village leaders.

Maya met Mikoneh halfway to the deck and flung her arms

around him. Only Ter's steady hand kept the twins from tumbling over the edge. Holding his sister tightly, Mikoneh whispered reassurances. His eyes locked with Penn's. The nobleman smiled with relief from several stairs above.

At last, Maya drew back. She searched her brother's eyes, brushing hair back from his face. "You're well now, right? He can't claim you again?"

"Sathe is dead." The words unlocked something in him. He sank to his knees, dragging his twin down with him. Caught in the throes of relief, Mikoneh didn't know if he wept or laughed. Maybe both. His cheeks were wet.

It was a long time before Penn and Maya guided him to his room. Ter stayed close, now reverted to his eight-year-old form, with blue eyes that shone with worry. When the Ephe'ahn had changed back, Mikoneh couldn't say.

He frankly didn't care.

He was too weary, and too overwrought.

Tomorrow. He could care about things tomorrow.

DEWDROPS SPARKLED on the colorful leaves. The morning was warm, like the last kiss from summer before the cold settled in.

Mikoneh sat on the ledge of the tree's high deck in fresh clothes, taking in the quiet. Though the Ephe'ahn villagers were awake, they made little noise while going about their first duties. Even the children—if children they were—moved with soft efficiency. He was grateful.

He'd woken early to find Maya sleeping nearby. Knowing her, she'd likely meant to stay up all night to watch over him. But she'd never been able to outlast the night—her one failing as a healer.

That didn't matter though. He was thankful for her care. It would go a long way toward believing himself truly free of Sathe's clutches. He didn't know how to tackle what the Dark Mage had done to him. Didn't know how to touch the horrors and humiliations—like the village he'd massacred—but he knew, in time, he must. Just like when Fa and Mama died, eventually he'd succumb to grief and wrestle against destruction.

For now, he was grateful to be numb.

Motion below caught Mikoneh's eye. He leaned out and tensed.

Minno. The sniveling coward who'd betrayed Mikoneh to the Mages dared to come here?

Owenekiras Rokahn stepped from the hostel to meet the gray boy midway across the village green. They halted several feet apart. From his vantage point, Mikoneh could tell little about their conversation. Neither gestured, and their voices were far too low to detect.

On impulse, Mikoneh climbed to his feet and drew out his wings. He winced as pain flared across the damaged appendage. Ignoring that, he jumped from the deck and glided toward the man and boy.

Owenekiras looked up, silver eyes bright in the dawn light. His expression remained closed, though he said something that brought Minno's head around. The boy's eyes widened before Mikoneh landed nearby.

"It's true, then," Minno said. "You got away."

"Yeah." Mikoneh clenched his fists. "What are you doing here?"

"I came about a separate matter," Minno said. "One that does not concern you."

"As my heir," Owenekiras said, "anything that concerns me concerns Mikoneh."

The gray boy paused. "I see. Then he is aware. Well." He turned away. "I've delivered my message. Do with it what you will."

"Not so fast." Mikoneh marched toward him. Minno turned back, emotionless even when Mikoneh snatched his collar. "You owe me an apology, brat."

Minno gave his slow blink. "Why? You escaped, Sathe is dead, you're a long-lost prince of Rokahn. It appears everything worked out rather well. Perhaps you should thank me."

Mikoneh ground his teeth, then shoved Minno away. Tightening his fist, he slammed it against the boy's jaw. Minno stumbled back and fell to the ground. Pain blossomed across Mikoneh's knuckles. He didn't care. "That's just for starters," he growled.

Minno sat upright, his hand resting on his jaw. "That's a good right hook."

Owenekiras stepped forward. "I'll not stop you from punishing him, for it would be just. He betrayed us both. But perhaps that should wait."

Mikoneh glanced toward Owenekiras. "Is something wrong?"

"If we're to free the Revenant, it's best we set out to do so now. A matter of urgency takes me to Simynshin almost at once."

"You're going to free the Revenant?" asked Minno.

Both men ignored him. Mikoneh frowned. "Isn't Lady Katanni hard to reach?"

Owenekiras's eyes flicked to Minno, then away. "I've tried to reach her directly, and it hasn't worked. We cannot use the Void."

Minno stumbled to his feet. "I'm coming."

"No," Owenekiras said. "You aren't allowed."

"You can't stop me," Minno said in his flat tones.

"Shut up," Mikoneh said. "What's happened in Simyn-shin?" Sathe's words concerning the Mage Queen's focus on that kingdom came back to him.

"I will explain later." The Dragon King glanced at the hostel. "Best we leave now. Wake your sister and your friend if you wish them to come."

"What about Reven's body?"

"I have already seen to that."

Mikoneh nodded and took off. Within a quarter turn, they met again on the sward. Ter was coming as well, but Hilker and Akonn had agreed to stay behind. Probably to keep an eye on Minno, who stood to one side as they assembled outside the hostel. Judging by his sullen expression, he'd been soundly told off.

Will that stop him? Mikoneh wondered.

Smiling, Maya presented Mikoneh with Fa's sword. It was cradled in an ornate leather sheath gifted by the Ephe'ahn village. With reverence, Mikoneh stroked the well-crafted leather, then strapped the sheath to his belt. The blade hung there, its weight reassuring. Somehow, he felt more himself with the battered weapon close at hand.

They left Kagon to a cheery farewell song from the villagers. Reven joined them along the path. Outside the forest walls, Owenekiras transformed into his dragon shape, and the company climbed onto his back. Mikoneh asked Ter where Larkynven was, and the Ephe'ahn explained that the black and red dragon was seeing to a matter elsewhere.

Owenekiras rose high into the sky. Despite his numbness, Mikoneh settled into the flight, soaking in the penetrating joy. The Dragon King carried them over the snowy peaks, and through a shimmering wall of light Mikoneh didn't see until they reached it. His body tingled as he slipped through the filmy substance and entered the fae lands.

A great lake stretched before an ancient forest. Did the forest emanate a blue glow like in his half-remembered dreams?

Owenekiras landed on the lake, more graceful than a swan, sending waves against the ancient trunks. These trees were taller and older by far than anything south of the mountains.

Mikoneh took Maya's wrist, and they walked down the glittering black wing together. Reven and Ter hovered close, as though to shield the twins, yet Mikoneh felt no concern in this place. It was peaceful, entrancing. Somehow, it soothed the cracks in his soul a little.

Ter stepped onto the water first, and Mikoneh wasn't surprised that the Ephe'ahn stood as though on solid ground. Maya gasped, then pulled free to step onto the watery surface. She laughed and spun in a circle.

Mikoneh grinned and strode from the dragon's wing to join her. Penn came last. Free of his passengers, Owenekiras shrank into human form at the center of the lake. He walked toward them with a confident stride. When he arrived, Ter led the way toward a watery pathway between the majestic trees. A hush blanketed the forest.

"Is this where the Nijaal live?" asked Maya.

"Yes," Ter answered. "It is the oldest spot in Sirinhigha."

Her eyes widened.

Despite the size of the trees, they were widely spread, and water surrounded the bases. Tiny, flickering shapes darted among the trunks.

"Fairies?" asked Maya.

"Of a sort," Ter answered.

Eventually, the path gave way to a wide pond in the center of the trees, making up a kind of watery clearing. Two rows of tall, slender, graceful people—Nijaal, presumably—stood in columns before them. At the head of those flanks—

Mikoneh's heart missed a beat.

Lady Katanni. He knew her. How, he couldn't say. But he did.

Almost like I've dreamed of her...

She was gowned in white and green, with long wheat-blonde hair that hung straight and trailed down to her calves. Her emerald-green eyes were pinned on him. She wore a kind, inviting smile.

"Welcome to *Serielias*, First Sanctuary of Magic," she said.

Mikoneh sank to one knee, overcome with emotions he didn't understand. Perhaps it was the sacredness of the place or the familiarity of the stranger before him. He couldn't define the nebulous feeling.

"Please, my lady," he found himself saying. "I'm told you can return my friend—the Revenant—to his body. Will you?"

Owenekiras moved next to Mikoneh and waved his hand before him. The Revenant's body appeared on the water at the Dragon King's feet. In the subdued light, he looked dead. Mikoneh turned his attention back to the Lady. She glided closer, her eyes fastened on the slumbering face.

"Yes, he has been perfectly preserved. I will help you." Her emerald gaze moved back to Mikoneh. "I will need your assistance."

He stood. "Because I hold his name?"

"Yes." She glanced at the other Nijaal. "Bring him to the altar."

Mikoneh tensed, but surely it was an altar of light. *I trust her. Above all others, I trust her.*

Two Nijaal glided over and lifted the body between them. Their motions were graceful. Their treatment, respectful. They glided off, heading north. Katanni beckoned to Mikoneh, and he followed close behind her trailing hem. The rest remained behind at a soft word from Ter.

Mikoneh strode past the surrounding trees, along another

path, and finally into a second clearing. This one was smaller but no less beautiful. At the center of the pond, an altar of clear crystal jutted from the water. The two Nijaal reverently placed the body across the smooth surface, then backed away and departed with a bow.

Katanni positioned herself at the head of the altar. She searched Mikoneh's face, her smile deepening. "Call your friend, Mikoneh Rokahn."

He turned back the way he'd come. "Reven."

The crimson specter appeared before him, then fell to one knee.

"That isn't necessary," Katanni said. "Rise, Lord Dragon. Position yourself at the foot of the altar."

Reven drifted forward and obeyed. The play of blue light, rippling water, and the crimson glow cast strange shadows across the slumbering lord's features.

"Come." Katanni held out her hand to Mikoneh.

He approached, his heart hammering. Warmth enveloped him as he slipped his hand into hers. He stared into her stunning, calm, ageless eyes. She was a tall woman, nearly his height. Her complexion was fair and flawless. High cheekbones and full lips accented a beauty deeper and far more abiding than any physical trait.

"Prepare to return the true name only when I direct you," she instructed as she gently guided him to one side of the altar. Releasing Mikoneh's hand, she turned her attention to the body. Her chant was low and soft. Nothing in the words was menacing. It was like gentle rain on a pond. The altar began to glow with aqua light, highlighting runes wrapped around its base. Instead of the cold terror that Hollow taint had invoked, this was soothing and warm.

The crimson light around Reven flickered, then failed. The cloak curled away from the specter's shoulders, and the cowl vanished. As Katanni continued to chant, the mistiness around Reven's features wisped away, until the spirit wore the same features as the body. Reven stared at Katanni, amazement written across his transparent face.

The Nijaal ceased her chant. "The taint is removed. Mikoneh, prepare his true name."

Mikoneh summoned spirit of spirit on his fingertips, then pressed his hand to his heart. The true name answered his summons. "Ready."

"Thank you." Her eyes moved back to Reven. "Step into your body."

She took up the chant anew. The runes blazed brighter.

Reven slid through the altar to stand at its center. His gaze darted toward Mikoneh, a faint smile on his lips. The chant lifted toward a higher note, and something moved within Mikoneh's chest in answer. Light gathered around Reven's spirit, pulling him into his body.

Katanni motioned, catching Mikoneh's eye. She nodded.

He reached into the glowing light and rested his fingertips over the body's heart. Silver light flared, twining upward to join the aqua magic in a spiral. Reven gasped, then vanished in the magnifying brilliance. A last flash momentarily blinded Mikoneh, and he turned away.

Silence fell over the forest. He twisted back around, heart humming. Upon the altar, the dragon lord's chest rose and fell. Mikoneh's vision shimmered, but he blinked back the tears.

"He must remain here for now," Katanni said. "He will not wake soon. His ordeal has been long and horrendous." She glided close and set her slender hand on Mikoneh's shoulder. "But you've done for him what few could accomplish. You've given him new life. He'll be indebted to you."

Mikoneh shook his head. "He was what kept me fighting during—" He cut off. "I owed *him*."

"A debate I think you and Lord Jensirin will have for many long years." She laughed: a beautiful, soothing sound. "Yes, that is his given name. Jensirin. You will find you have quite forgotten the name of his soul now that you've given it up."

Mikoneh grinned. "You're right. I can't recall it. Which means it's safe now."

"So it is. Now, let us return to your companions. Your twin looked anxious."

With some reluctance, Mikoneh followed her. He didn't want to leave Reven—Jensirin—alone. He didn't want to leave the forest at all. But urgent matters awaited in Simynshin, and Mikoneh wanted to help if he could. He wanted to fight Mages wherever they sprang up, to keep them from their fell purpose. His step quickened.

Midway along the path, Katanni paused and turned to him. Her eyes were vivid even in the gloom beneath the looming trees. "Your wounds—they're many and deep. But you're strong, Mikoneh. You fought well and hard against Sathe."

"How do you know?" he asked, strangely breathless.

She smiled. "I know what lies within my province. You are part of that." She turned to go on.

He reached for her but let his hand drop. "Do I know you, my lady?"

She paused and didn't look back. "Of course, have we not met?"

He held his ground. "I mean before today."

"Perhaps," she said, gliding on. "In another time."

He opened his mouth to ask more, but she turned back toward him. Stepping close, she set her hand against his shoulder. "That taint will slow your healing."

A shiver ran up his spine, and cold claws ripped through his hidden wings—then warm relief, like sunlight after a storm.

Katanni stepped back, holding an orb of violet light. He stared at it, shuddering.

"Thank you."

"You're most welcome, Mikoneh Rokahn." She set off down the path, and with the flick of her hand, the orb of taint vanished into thin air.

When they reached the larger clearing, Mikoneh offered Maya a reassuring smile. "He's free and alive."

"Thank you, Lady Katanni," Owenekiras said. "Had I known of Lord Jensirin's predicament—"

"You could do little," Katanni said, smiling. "And you well know it."

The Dragon King inclined his head. He paused, then looked up. "Minno seeks you."

Her smile faded. "Ah. I had hoped…" She shook that off. "Go now with haste to Simynshin and give Prince Atlanse my salutations."

"As my lady wishes." Owenekiras bowed at the waist. "Be well."

She brushed her fingers against his hair before he straightened. "Be well, my black knight."

He rose and glanced at the twins. "Come."

The company moved toward the path they'd first traveled. Mikoneh lingered. Eyeing Katanni, he tried to drink in every detail, reaching for something he should recall…

She turned toward him. "Seek answers, Mikoneh. But don't lose your current path in their pursuit. Your ride is leaving without you." Her eyes caught the light, and her smile grew teasing.

He grinned, unembarrassed. She felt…like a friend.

"I'll see you again, won't I?" he asked.

"Yes. Very soon. Farewell for now." She offered him a gentle smile, then turned away.

Mikoneh moved along the watery path. The sun gleamed at the end of the dim forest. His steps were slow, but he quickened them, setting his sights ahead. The future was uncertain, and war hovered like a storm, but he had his kin, his birthright, and his freedom.

That was enough to arm himself against any foe. It was enough to know where he was.

Squaring his shoulders, he stepped into the dawn light.

Continued in
BOOK TWO: A SILENT SONG IN WINTER

DEAR READER

I can't express how honored I am that you've picked up this book. From my heart, thank you!

While the tale is fictitious, and the characters herein are *not* self-inserts, I did delve into my personal life experiences to grasp the emotions and trauma of the characters. As writers, it's what we must do if we hope to feel genuine.

Of course, I've never been held captive by a monstrous Mage or fought with a sword or quarterstaff—but I *have* experienced firsthand the painful betrayal by people I loved and trusted. I've also watched my house go up in smoke—and while, thankfully, I didn't lose my parents or siblings, I did lose several dear pets. My heart still hurts when I contemplate that.

I have also experienced a severe miscarriage of justice upheld by corrupt officials. It nearly shattered my family. We still bear the scars, and always will. The details of that I will keep to myself.

I say all this, not to garner pity, but to express how cathartic this book was to write. The twins' struggles, not just against ugly outside forces, but with their own anger, powerlessness, and trauma helped to heal those emotions in myself a little more. Each experience and each feeling that I endeavored to paint was an opportunity to examine festering wounds and lance them.

I'm not finished. These twins, bless them, will continue to wrestle against darkness and despair, digging their way to a better place, bit by bit. And with their help, so will I.

That's why we create—we humans. To overcome, to express, to explore. To understand our hearts and souls and shout the answers we find into the void, hoping someone will see, understand, and maybe heal with us. If that's you, dear reader, be welcome. There is no judgment here. Only love and compassion. Because—while I don't pretend to be worse off than anyone else—I know all too well the harrowing pathways in hell. Through the words in this book, my friend, I hope you feel that you don't walk your path through that fiery scape alone.

If the story touched or impacted you, please consider leaving a review. It would mean so much to me.

Be well, dear reader.

—M. H. W.

REGARDING SULD

Some events mentioned in this book, such as the firedrakes and the fight against Sathe's brother Suld, are chronicled in my science-fantasy series: *Record of the Sentinel Seer*. If you're interested in exploring that side of events, check out Lekore's story, particularly Book 4: *Paths of the Broken*. *

I do my best to make certain each of my series can be read independently of the others, but your experience may be enriched—and certainly you'll catch a *lot* of Easter eggs—by reading each story in my connected Mithrinn Universe.

Stay magical!

—M. H. W.

---

* It should be noted that *Paths of the Broken*, where Suld appears, doesn't stand well on its own, as it's part of a larger plot. I recommend starting with Book 1: *Prince of the Fallen*.

Glossary

People

Akonn – Captain of the Sword.
Athonen d'Ereth – A Scholar of the Spire.
Atlanse Chenta – Crown prince of Simynshin.
Cal – A dragon.
Cisharri - A fairy of the Moon Veil.
Crind – An Oceanean rebel.
Denroch – A fairy of the Moon Veil.
Drayve – Earl of Relvin Province in Oceana.
Hess – An Ephe'ahn of Kagon Village.
Hilker – A Master Wind Elementalist.
Jensirin – A dragon.
Jonatten – The twins' father. Deceased.
Katanni – A Nijaal. Also called the Lady of the Wood.
Kevva – An Oceanean woman and former friend. She betrayed the twins.
Latta Chanta – A Simynshinian princess; daughter of Atlanse Chenta.
Larkynven – A dragon.
Larta – One of Owenekiras Rokahn's officers.
Ligg – A Mage working under Sathe.
Mage Queen – A legendary figure from the Age of Dragons.
Maya – Mikoneh's twin sister. A healer.
Mikoneh – Maya's twin brother. Former leader of the Oceanean rebellion.
Minno – A mysterious boy clad in gray.
Mivena – An elven ally of the fairies.
Nilo – King of Oceana.
Owenekiras Rokahn – The Dragon King. Also a banished prince of Rokahn.
Penn – Viscount of Relvin Province in Oceana. The twins' friend.
Reteris – A firedrake in the North.
Reven – The Revenant.

Sathe – A Mage General serving under the Mage Queen.

Seranni – The twins' mother. Deceased.

Suld – A Mage General serving under the Mage Queen. Sathe's brother.

Tem – An Ephe'ahn of Kenooshin Village.

Ter N'Avea – The Ever Present. An Ephe'ahn.

Torel – A Mage Captain serving under Sathe.

Trinn – Lieutenant of the Sword.

Vlest – A fairy of the Moon Veil.

PLACES

Andyan Mountains – The mountain range separating the Fae Lands of the north and the human kingdoms of the south.

Blighted Lands – A barren scape in the west of Cimin.

Cimin – An empire in the northeast of the main continent.

Crestfel – Capital of Cimin.

Elemeer Plains – A place lost to history.

Elenth – Capital of Simynshin.

Holore – Capital of Lintha.

Hyanython, Citadel of – A ruinous fortress in the heart of the Simynshin Forest.

Kagon – An Ephe'ahn village at the foot of the Andyan Mountains near Cimin.

Kenooshin – A Ephe'ahn village in the Simynshin Forest.

Kwilaj – A cluster of islands to the east of Cimin.

Lintha – A kingdom in the southeast of the main continent.

Mithrinn – The universe.

Molten Gold, Isles of – A cluster of islands to the south of the main continent. Pirates make their home here.

Moon Veil – A fairy ring on the main continent.

Nauttia – Capital of Oceana.

Oceana – A kingdom in the east sandwiched between Cimin and Lintha.

Pae'Tal – An island in the high northwest.

Principle Plain – The living realm where mortals dwell.

Relvin – A province in Oceana ruled by Earl Drayve.

Rokahn – An island kingdom in the southwest. Ruled by the Rokahns.

Serielias – The realm of Lady Katanni in the Fae Lands.

Simynshin – A large kingdom spanning most of the western half of the main continent.

Sirinhigha – The name of the main continent and the world.

Spire, The – A natural mountain fortress in Cimin where a clan of scholars dwell.

TeshRelle – A blackened land in the northeast above the Andyan Mountains.
Vorsah – Capital of Rokahn.

TERMS

Age of Dragons – An era 20,000 years ago that broke the fabric of space and time. A faulty substitute was erected in its place. Dark Mages rose to conquer all and were defeated at a high price.

Complété – The fabric that once held the universe together. It was shattered in the Age of Dragons.

Dayonryse – [translation: Dawn Rise] — A spell cast by Ter to slow time in a specific location.

Dragon Healers – A rare type of magic user (human or fae in origin) who could heal dragons of various types of ailments. Their gifts varied. No known dragon healers exist on Sirinhigha.

Elementalist – A person who can consciously control an element (or more) and can see the Spirits Elemental.

Firia Leaves – A pain-relieving herb.

Hollow – A type of tainted magic. Half of the fabric holding the universe in balance.

Korta – A fruit strong in nutrients for young dragons. It is poisonous for humans to eat.

Sword, The – A league of elite swordsmen serving under the Dragon King's banner.

Tiassana – A kind of leaf that keeps dragon bonds healthy. It can also be used to sooth broken bond wounds.

Void – A type of light magic. Half of the fabric holding the universe in balance.

RACES

Celes – Guardians dwellings between Heaven and Hell.

Dark Mages – Once called Mages (or Light Mages) before they succumbed to corrupt magic. Mages were once all human, but their magic has been tapped by fae races upon rare occasions as well.

Ephe'ahn – A type of woodelf.

Fae – A broad term for the magical races of Sirinhigha. These include the many kinds of elves, as well as dragons, fairies, gryphons, Pegasi, Nijaal, and many more.

First Kin – The first five beings born on Sirinhigha, tasked with protecting order, mortality, nature, magic, and balance.

Humans – A broad term for the different races of humankind regardless of origin. The non-fae. These include the Rokahnians (though this point is debated among scholars of Simynshin and Lintha due to their rumored fae origin*), the Cortharans (most Simynshinians, Linthians, Oceaneans, and Ciminians are of this race), the Jemarri nomads, and the Kwilaj Islers.

Nijaal – The oldest race of fae. Elder elves.

Spirits Elemental – Guardian spirits over the living realm (also called the Principle Plain). The five main types are: Fire, Wind, Water, Earth, and Spirit. Sub-types include Lightning, Ice, and Metal.

Undrik – A nightmarish toad-like monster capable of controlling dreams under certain conditions. Favored pets of Dark Mages. They can absorb magic and store it as energy.

---

*   The scholars of the Spire hold that Rokahnians must be excluded from the human list altogether, but there is no concrete proof to support the Spire's claims that Rokahnians are of fae descent per Simynshin's scholars.

ACKNOWLEDGMENTS

Foremost, I thank my Savior without whom I would be broken beyond repair. Also, my parents, who gave me common sense, humor, and a thirst to learn all I can. Especially through books!

I must also thank my sisters, Heidi and Tawnee, for reading everything I write without fail. You're both the best!

Special extra thanks to Heidi for lending me the world of Sirinhigha, which she crafted ages ago, and letting me go crazy with it. This place has been part of my life since I was very small, and it feels amazing to bring it to full color on behalf of its creator. I'll try my best to do justice to your lush world, sister mine!

Thank you to my alpha readers, Cathryn deVries and Heidi Wadsworth, for tackling this book in its early stages and pointing out the big, big problems. And to my beta team, Beba Andric, Laura A. Barton, R. K. Goff, and Mandi Oyster—for helping to smooth the rough edges and pinpoint the stealthy issues. You're all amazing!

To my editor, Sarah B., who encouraged and elevated me while homing in on what would make the story the best it can be. Your devious mind terrifies me!

And to my characters, especially Mikoneh. He's been (not so patiently) hanging out in my head for 20+ years waiting for his turn to make his entrance center stage. I've written and scrapped his story three times—and finally I've got it right. Sorry I'm so mean to you, Mikoneh! (I'd say I won't do that anymore, but my mama taught me not to lie.)

Just as importantly: my thanks to you, dear reader, for taking a chance on this book. I hope it didn't let you down.

— M. H. W.

About the Author

Writer of fantasy, magic weaver, dragon rider! Having spent the past two decades devotedly writing fantasy, it's safe to say M. H. Woodscourt is now more fae than human.

All of her fantasy worlds connect with each other in the Mithrinn Universe, forged with great love and no small measure of blood, sweat, and tears. When she's not writing, she's napping or reading a book with a mug of hot cocoa close at hand, while her quirky cat Wynter nibbles her nose.

Learn more at www.mhwoodscourt.com

Also by M. H. Woodscourt

The Ember Lily
High Fantasy/Young Adult

The Crane Maiden

Dragons of Rokahn
Epic Fantasy/Adult

When Darkness Hunts the Dawn

A Silent Song in Winter

The Burden of a Broken Crown

Where Souls Dwell in Shadow

Mark of Valliath
High Fantasy/Young Adult

The Storyteller True

The Shattered Arch

The Marked Prince

The Blood Fountain

Record of the Sentinel Seer

www.ingramcontent.com/pod-product-compliance
Lightning Source LLC
Chambersburg PA
CBHW022249310726
48973CB00001B/18